Here's what *Romantic Times BOOKreviews*
has to say about

RHYANNON BYRD's

BLOODRUNNERS series from
Silhouette Nocturne

Last Wolf Standing
"4-1/2 stars...Fast paced and exciting, Rhyannon Byrd's
Last Wolf Standing is hard to put down."

Last Wolf Hunting
"Top Pick. 4-1/2 stars."

Last Wolf Watching
"Top Pick. 4-1/2 stars...Rhyannon Byrd's
compelling, sexy characters and exciting story make
Last Wolf Watching a must read."

RHYANNON BYRD

EDGE *of* HUNGER

HQN™

Recycling programs
for this product may
not exist in your area.

ISBN-13: 978-0-373-77367-1
ISBN-10:   0-373-77367-6

EDGE OF HUNGER

www.HQNBooks.com

Printed in U.S.A.

Dear Reader,

I'm so excited to present *Edge of Hunger*, the first book in my new PRIMAL INSTINCT series with HQN Books. Set within a world where paranormal creatures live hidden among an unknowing humanity, the opening trilogy of this dark, provocative series tells the story of the Buchanan siblings, beginning with the rugged, deliciously sexy Ian Buchanan.

Ian is the ultimate bad boy, who finds himself fighting a dangerous, uncontrollable temptation when psychic Molly Stratton comes to town, claiming to bear messages from his mother's ghost...and a warning that his life is about to change forever. Suddenly Ian must embrace his violent, visceral hungers if he's to protect Molly from an ancient evil that has mysteriously returned to our world, causing the darkness that dwells within him to awaken. A primal darkness that will test the very bounds of Ian's control, while proving humanity's only hope for the future.

I'm thrilled to be sharing Ian and Molly's story with you, and hope you'll come to love their wickedly seductive romance as much as I do.

All the best,

Rhyannon

To Erotic Romance author Madison Hayes,
who is not only a genius of words,
but a treasured friend I simply could not do without.

Thanks for all the endless support, and for always
being there when I need it most!

You're the best!

Lots of love.

Rhy

EDGE *of* HUNGER

The hunger is coming…

CHAPTER ONE

There will be time, there will be time
To prepare a face to meet the faces that you meet…
—*T. S. Eliot*

Henning, Colorado, Friday Afternoon

THE WOMAN WAS TROUBLE.

Ian Buchanan knew it the second he set eyes on her as she climbed out of a banged-up, dust-covered, dark blue rental. Knew it as he set down his hammer, watching her walk toward him, her small frame backlit by the burning orange glow of the sweltering afternoon sun while she carefully made her way through the rugged terrain of the building site.

And the first words out of that soft, pink mouth—her lips glossy and sweet looking, voice mellow with a sexy, husky little rasp to it—confirmed his suspicions.

"Mr. Buchanan, my name is Molly Stratton and I'm here because…well, I know this sounds crazy, but your mother, Elaina, asked me to come and find you."

She didn't laugh. Didn't smile. She just stared up at him with the biggest pair of brown eyes he'd ever seen. Waiting.

"Is that right?" He ignored her small outstretched hand while he pushed his sunglasses up on top of his head, picked up his Coors, and took a long swallow of the beer. The glass rim of the longneck was cool against his sweat-salted lips, the beer even cooler as it went down his dry throat in a long, icy glide. She watched him while he drank, her dark gaze snagging on the column of his throat as it worked. A soft wash of pink warmed the delicate crest of her pale, freckle-dusted cheekbones as she stared, those full lips parted the barest fraction. Something down low in Ian's belly cramped in reaction. His blood went thick.

Oh, yeah, she was trouble, all right.

Ticked at himself for reacting so easily to her, he set the bottle back down on top of his battered cooler with a distinct thud, noting from the corner of his eye the way she flinched at the harshness of the sound.

She was nervous—and obviously crazy as hell. Either that, or a pathetic little con, looking for an easy score.

"So tell me, sunshine," he drawled, injecting just the right amount of ridicule into his deep voice. "You talk to the dead often, or is today just my lucky day?"

Reaching up to hook her windblown hair behind her left ear, she held his hard gaze without so much as a flicker of those long, thick lashes rimming the deep cinnamon brown of her eyes. "As a matter of fact, I do. How often depends on them…not me."

Ian stared at her while those strange words played through his mind. She'd stopped just a few feet away from where he stood, her gaze both shy and direct in that way that always captured a man's attention. The bristling Colorado mountain breeze played havoc with her shoulder-length, honey-blond curls, carrying a scent to his nose lost somewhere between want and need—and something hot caught fire in his blood, like a burning glow heating him from within. Even down deep, in those forgotten places where things always stayed cool and calm…and lifeless—where nothing and no one could touch him—he sensed an uncomfortable spark of awareness.

Dropping his sunglasses back down to shield his eyes, Ian picked up his hammer and went back to work, bracing the wall he'd just raised. He no longer held her gaze, but he still *felt* her, like a fine tension that vibrated from her body to his own, its rhythm rapid and quivering.

What the hell?

"I know it sounds…impossible," she added, "but it's true."

Yeah, sure it was.

"Don't they have medication for people like you, Miss Stratton?" he asked with a heavy dose of sarcasm, determined to ignore her…the heat…the irritating beads of sweat snaking down his spine beneath the damp cotton of his T-shirt. Not to mention the unwanted sexual hunger twisting belligerently in his gut. "What'd you do, miss a dose?"

"I'm not psychotic or delusional." She sighed, sounding tired. Weary even. "And I'm not after your money or—"

"Good," he grunted with a low laugh, his grin crooked as he glanced up at her through the dark shield of his glasses, "because I ain't got any. Would you believe I blew every cent I own on the Psychic Friends Network?"

She frowned, but determination etched the delicate angles of her face, giving her the illusion of being tough, when he knew instinctively that she was anything but. Crazy? Obviously. But there was something vulnerable and soft in her that fascinated the hell out of him.

God, he was so fucked.

"Look, I realize this seems like some kind of joke to you, but I'm not trying to scam you," she murmured, her left hand fidgeting with the bottom button of her shirt, just above the waistband of her jeans. "I really don't want your money or anything else. The only thing I'm asking is that you pay attention to what I have to tell you."

"Now see," he replied in a slow slide of words worthy of any natural-born Southerner, "the problem is that I'm too much of a bastard to *pay* you even that." He pointed the hammer in the direction of her car, needing her gone. Now. Before he gave in and forgot why bedding her would be such a bad idea. "So why don't you just hightail your crazy little ass out of Henning and back to wherever it is you came from."

A soft sound of irritation rumbled in her chest, making him grin despite himself. It was refreshing to know that *little miss innocent looking* had a temper, and he found himself wondering what she looked like when that passionate temper was truly riled.

Sweat popped out on his forehead that had nothing to do with the heat rolling up at them in waves from the sweltering ground—and everything to do with the feminine package standing before him. It was his own fault, but he'd been too long without a woman. Now he was in a bad way, and Ian knew he should've ignored his waning interest and dropped by Kendra Wilcox's earlier in the week. If he'd gone ahead and gotten laid, then maybe he wouldn't be getting geared up over the strange little female standing in front of him, talking about conversations with his mother's ghost.

"Look, Mr. Buchanan. If forgetting about this whole thing was an option, then believe me, I would. Unfortunately, it isn't. I've no other choice than to follow through with this, whether you act like an arrogant jerk or a gentleman."

Mumbling around the nail he'd just placed between his lips, Ian arched one brow. "Much to my mother's heartache, I never did take to the whole Southern gentleman way of life. It all started the fateful afternoon I put a frog down Sally Simpson's pants in kindergarten," he informed her, setting the nail in place. He flashed her an unrepentant smile, getting a perverse pleasure out of pushing her buttons. "And I've never changed."

"And you sound remarkably proud of that fact." Her voice held a hint of challenge that twisted the irritating hunger in his gut a notch tighter, and he nearly smashed his thumb as he swung down on the nail head. "A rebel through and through."

"Which really shouldn't come as a surprise," he rumbled softly. "If you're so chatty with my mother, then I'm sure she's already warned you that I'm a stubborn son of a bitch. You're wasting your time here, Molly."

The use of her first name had her blinking with an odd look of surprise. And damn, but if he didn't feel that strange little jolt between them again, like something electric and tangible skittering on the air. Something too intimate for comfort. He didn't know why he'd used her first name, but he couldn't deny that he liked the way it felt on his lips.

"She's told me enough for me to know that you'd be less than cooperative," she answered after a moment, while the wind picked up, molding the soft cotton of her plain white shirt to a petite pair of high, rounded breasts. "She also warned me that you'd react this way."

Ian cut her a sharp look from behind his dark lenses, but bit back an even sharper retort. It was twisted, but the harder she pushed him, the more he wanted her.

"So, we can either go ahead and have this conversation here," she pressed on with firm conviction, taking advantage of his silence, "or I can follow you around night and day until you give in and listen to what I have to say. Your mother isn't going to leave me alone until you do."

Bent over, his weight resting on one arm while he held the hammer in the other hand, Ian studied her. Studied her in the way a fighter sizes up his next opponent. She sounded so confident, but her body language told a different story. The little details he picked up on, like the way she kept licking at her lower lip, her left hand now clenching and unclenching at her side while her right held on to the leather strap of her purse as if it was a lifeline, told a story of their own. White knuckles. Rigid spine. In the base of her pale throat, her pulse fluttered with a telltale sign of nerves. Or was it fear? Arousal?

Whatever it was, Ian suddenly found himself captivated by the intimate sight of the pulsing vein beneath that smooth, flawless skin. It looked too delicate, too fragile, like something he could so easily sink his teeth into and mark. Taste. Something that was too much like the dreams he'd been having, and it scared the shit out of him.

"Even if what you're saying is true, which I don't believe for one second, what could my mother want with me?" he asked in a low, rough blast of words that felt ripped out of his chest, all traces of sarcasm and humor gone. "We didn't talk for the last sixteen years of her life and she's been gone for five months. Seems a little late to start mending fences now."

"Elaina regrets that all those years were wasted," she said with such an earnest expression, he honestly believed that she was buying her own bullshit. God, she really was a whack job. "Still, she contacted me because there are things she wants you to know. Important things she wishes she had explained while she still had the time. But first…" She paused, and the look in those big brown eyes made him want to reach out to her and— hell, Ian didn't have a clue what he would have done. He was saved from finding out when she cleared her throat, wet her bottom lip with a nervous flick of her tongue, then quietly said, "I'm sorry to have to tell you that someone close to you is in danger."

Aw, shit. What kind of sick game was this woman playing? Whatever it was, his patience was at an end.

"In case you've missed the clues, Miss Stratton, I'm going to spell it out for you all nice and slow like. I do *not* think this kind of crap is funny." Each word came from his lips with biting precision, his voice low, hard, expression even harder as he pulled off his glasses and glared at her through narrowed eyes. "Never have, even when my mother was parading her psycho friends in and out of our lives and putting my little brother and sister through an emotional wringer. I'm warning you now, get back in your dingy little rental and just get the hell away from me."

She crossed her arms over her chest, as if she could shield herself from the blast of his anger, but she didn't budge. "Trust me, Mr. Buchanan. *Ian.* I'm not enjoying this any more than you are, but I made a promise to your mother and I'm keeping it. I know she made mistakes, but she's trying to set things right. And if you don't listen to her—to me—*to us*…then someone *is* going to end up hurt. I can feel it."

Why in God's name do I always have to go for the psychotic ones? he silently cursed, running one hand through his hair so hard that his scalp stung. *Must be in my goddamn genes.*

That was one of the reasons he'd kept things going with Kendra—the simple fact that she *was* so different from the women he usually hooked up with. The hard-nosed CPA didn't take to bullshit any more than Ian did, and they both got what they wanted from each other, even if their encounters left him with that gnawing edge in his gut. Left him cold inside. Left him… wanting.

It sucked, sure—but he'd learned to live with it.

"Like I said before, my mother died five months ago. Now get off my property. This is private land and you're trespassing."

He watched her mouth firm. Then those delicate, narrow shoulders pulled back, determination showing in every rigid line of her soft, womanly body. "No."

Ian laid down his hammer and rose to his full height,

expecting her to turn and hightail it away. At six-four, he was tall and broad, with enough muscles to make most people back down when he wanted them to. Wearing his meanest scowl, he held her stare, the look in his eyes purposefully hostile and fury-darkened. When he finally spoke, his words came in a low, silken rasp that he expected to buy results. Immediate ones.

"What do you mean, no?"

WHAT DID SHE MEAN? She had no idea.

You are insane, Molly. Freaking certifiable.

How did you explain death and ghosts and pure, bone-chilling evil?

How did you explain the existence of hell on earth…or the fact that monsters really did hide in the shadows?

That something was watching you over your shoulder?

That we, humanity, were no longer alone?

How did you explain to someone that their entire world was about to change, never to be the same again?

Molly didn't know—didn't have the answers. She was only the bearer of bad news, not its source, and she thought of the old saying: Don't shoot the messenger.

Somehow, she didn't think Ian Buchanan was going to be so understanding. Her mind felt dazed, and she knew why. It was pathetic, but the man's physical presence had short-circuited her mental faculties. He was…she faltered for a word that would do all that beautiful, hard-edged male power and arrogance justice, but failed. Elaina had warned her that he'd be distrustful, but she hadn't mentioned how bitter he'd become.

Or how gorgeous. Despite his crass rudeness, the man was a walking, talking poster boy for every woman's hidden bad-boy fantasy.

Beautiful and dark and delicious, he was everything Molly had always thought a man should be, but had never encountered. Hard, rugged lines. Ink-black hair, thick and healthy and windblown. And those eyes, the deep fathomless color of a clear blue sea. They were so much more than attractive. They held a fire. A dark, dangerous intensity that made her insides tremble. Made her breath catch. Made the air around her feel alive, as if it were crackling with electricity.

Not good, Molly. Stay focused.

"I can't give you any proof, Ian," she said, and there was no missing the hard edge of desperation in her words. "But if you don't listen to me, if you won't work with me, someone is going to die. Someone you care about."

"I don't know what you're trying to pull, but it isn't going to work, because anyone who knows me can tell you that I don't give a shit about anybody but myself."

"I don't believe you," she argued. "Not after the things that Elaina has told me about you."

He smiled coldly, clearly disbelieving every word she'd said. "You wanna lead some guy on a wild-goose chase, try some other sucker, but leave me out of it. In fact, why don't you give the local sheriff a call? I can guarantee he'll get a kick outta you, sweetheart. You're just Saint Riley's type. He'll be more than happy to help you try and save the world."

"Dammit, this isn't—"

She'd reached out to grab his arm as he moved past her, recognizing it as a mistake the second he looked down, the deep, raging blue of his gaze driving straight into her, all hostile and violent and strangely arousing.

The words tumbled past her lips without any direction from her brain. "She said that when the darkness calls—"

He tensed so quickly that her voice faltered, and she knew she'd struck a nerve. There was no give in the burning, powerful muscles beneath her hand—the bulging bicep rigid with fury…and something that she couldn't put a name to. Taking a deep breath, Molly repeated the words Elaina had told her to say. "When the darkness calls, your mother said that you'll know. That you'll find—"

"No." His lips barely moved as he ground out the word. "No fucking way."

Trying not to get lost in those feverishly blue eyes, Molly stared up at him, imploring him to believe her. "She wants me to explain, Ian. Explain the things that she should have told you before. Warnings that she should have given you before you left home. Please, just listen to me!"

"You can find your own way back down the mountain," he growled, yanking his arm from her hold with ridiculous ease. "Just stay the hell away from me."

A moment later, he was slamming the door to his truck while he cranked the engine, leaving her standing in the cloud of dust kicked up by his tires.

When he cast one last look in his rearview mirror, she was still standing in the same spot, alone…watching him run from something that Molly knew he had no chance of evading.

It was one of the elemental truths of the universe.

Night would always follow day. Summer would always follow spring. Death would always follow life. And try as you might, you could never outrun something that was already a part of you. She'd learned that lesson the hard way—and still carried the guilt to prove it.

Whether he believed her or not…listened to her or not…gave in or forever told her to go to hell, Molly knew one thing with absolute, undying certainty:

Ian Buchanan's past had finally caught up with him.

CHAPTER TWO

The Midnight Hour

KENDRA WILCOX'S MOTHER had always warned her about picking up strange men. Especially beautiful ones. Ones who were too good to be true. But the stranger she'd met back at the bar was her best chance at getting over Ian Buchanan once and for all. No way in hell was she going to turn him down.

She'd waited for hours, but Ian hadn't shown for their weekly Friday night bump and grind. Now she was pissed enough to do something reckless. Not that she cared about Ian Buchanan, she silently vowed, knowing very well it was a lie. Damn pain in the ass had wormed his way under her defenses, and she knew she was going to end up hurt. Hell, she was hurting already.

She needed this. Needed tonight. Needed to bang him out of her system, which was why she was now speeding down the road with the windows down, the midnight wind whipping through her hair…in another man's ride.

Mr. Tall Blond and Deadly Handsome was going to be the perfect medicine for what ailed her. And if Ian found out about it later, all the better. His outrageous ego could use a good dent or two.

Kendra turned her head and smiled at the stranger beside her, remembering how he'd asked her, back at the bar, if she liked to be taken in the moonlight, under the skies, where she could scream as loud as she liked when she came—and he'd promised she'd come, harder and heavier than she ever had before. Thinking it would serve Ian right if she found someone new to scratch her sexual itches, she only hoped he proved to be as good as he claimed.

They pulled into a grassy meadow a few miles outside of town, and he came around to her door, taking her hand to lead her out into the verdant open field. She felt wild and reckless, like the night, the shots of tequila she'd downed with him before leaving the bar making her head feel fuzzy. Her mouth was dry.

The tall, blond Adonis smiled down at her, his ice-blue eyes shining bright and deliciously wicked in the silvery rays of moonlight bathing their bodies. Her head filled with the fertile scents of the forest, the damp ground beneath her feet, and his masculine warmth. He was so hot, he felt as if he had a fever, the skin of his palms burning as he curved them over her shoulders.

"Do you like it hard, Kendra?"

"Oh, yeah," she slurred, pushing out her chest so that he could see her braless nipples pressed clearly against the thin cotton of her tank top. "The harder, the better."

A low laugh rumbled up from his chest. He grabbed the thin cotton, ripping her shirt in half, making her gasp, then bent forward and captured one naked nipple in the dark, electric heat of his mouth. Between her legs, she grew warm and wet and swollen. Oh, yeah, this beauty was going to be sweet payback against Buchanan. She hoped he told everyone in Henning about tonight. Hoped Ian would hear all about how wildly she'd ridden this gorgeous stranger beneath the hazy light of the moon.

His teeth grazed her flesh, making her shiver and she started to call out his name…only to draw a blank.

Holy shit! She couldn't remember it! The thought struck Kendra as hilariously funny and she gave an uncharacteristic giggle, making him grin against the underside of her breast. Oh…wouldn't her mother love to know that a man she couldn't even name was pressing his mouth against her naked skin, kissing his way up to the hollow of her throat.

"Tell me how bad you want it," he whispered, nipping at her shoulder in a way that had her blood surging.

She grabbed at his denim-covered cock, and he laughed softly under his breath.

"Beg me, honey. I love to hear a woman begging for it." His breath washed over her throat as he rasped the words against her sensitive flesh, his hands sliding across her ass, fingers kneading her through the denim of her jeans. "Beg me to make you scream."

"Please," she gasped, tilting her head to give him better access, ignoring the sudden warning note in her head that signaled something wasn't…quite right.

Just go with it, Kendra. He can make you forget. Forget…everything. Forget…Ian.

Almost as if the stranger had read her mind, he pressed his forehead to hers, whispering, "Don't worry, Kendra. After I'm done with you tonight, there won't be anything left for Buchanan."

She pulled back to look up at him, and her breath caught. Something about his face seemed…she didn't know. Different somehow. She blinked her heavy lids, trying to bring him back into focus through her blurry vision, but her eyes refused to cooperate. Then one hand lifted, cupping her cheek, his thumb stroking gently…so gently against the corner of her mouth. In the moment, she forgot everything but his touch. It was reverent. Like a lover's—and she realized that in all the time she'd known him, Ian had never touched her like this. Like she was special to him. Her lower lip trembled. She sighed, floating, somehow lost in the searing heat of this stranger's gaze.

Then he smiled.

The curve of his lips was so beautiful, it took her tequila-soaked mind a moment to realize what he'd just said.

Buchanan! What the…? How did this man—this newcomer to the mountains—know about her and Ian?

"How—"

"Shh…" he whispered, pressing his hand over her mouth. "No more time for questions."

He gave a low, rough laugh, and Kendra watched in shock as his face seemed to rearrange itself within his skin. She heard something pop, then crack, followed by the chilling sound of bone snapping into place.

Panicking, she turned to run but stumbled. He had her down before she'd gone more than a few yards, his muscled weight crushing her into the damp ground.

"That's my girl," he murmured, flipping her to her back and pinning her arms above her head with an effortless strength that awed as much as it terrified. She watched through wide, burning eyes as his intent spread across the distorted features of his face like a stain, and a choked sound broke from her throat. A dry cry lost somewhere between a sob and a whimper. "No more time to play, Kendra," he whispered. "Only time enough to die."

And he wasn't lying.

Everything that happened after that came to her in nothing but broken fragments—consciousness shattered by terror and disbelief and indescribable pain. She wanted to cry, but her mind was too numb. She wanted to fight back, but her body lay there upon the blood-soaked ground, too broken and weak.

She wanted to tear the son of a bitch to pieces, the same way he was tearing her apart—but in that, she failed, as well.

He'd cut her; deep slices in her stomach…her chest? She couldn't tell; she hurt everywhere. Even deep inside, where he'd ripped her open with the vicious pounding of his body into hers. Everything faded—the sapphire stars in the sky, the chirping of the grasshoppers, the rich pine scent of the towering trees—until there was nothing. Nothing but the great rolling waves of pain that made everything black and ugly and raw.

She thought of Ian, and realized how stupid she'd been.

But her last thought, as his teeth sank into her throat, was that mother had been right after all.

And wasn't life such a bitch of a waste.

Then Kendra Wilcox thought no more.

CHAPTER THREE

Saturday Morning, 3 a.m.

IAN WAS DREAMING OF HOME. Dreaming of the Deep South in the late fall, when he was young. It was the same strange dream he'd been having since he'd run away at sixteen. He sat huddled around a crackling fireplace with his small family. Dinner simmered on the stove, filling the weathered house with the rich scent of beans and corn bread, while young Riley sprawled on the threadbare rug and little Saige cuddled on his mother's lap, begging for another story about their ancestors.

"Many years ago," his mother murmured, "before this country was even discovered, our ancestors walked the earth, but they weren't like us—"

"They were Merricks, weren't they?" Saige interrupted, all but bouncing with excitement.

"Yes, sweetheart," his mother answered with a smile, "they most certainly were."

"And they kicked butt, didn't they?" his brother added, grinning a little.

His mother winked at Riley. "That they did."

"Until the Casus massacred them," Ian inserted drily,

sitting on the floor by the fire. He wrapped his thin arms around his scuffed knees; his lip curled in a snide expression his mother had always said was too scornful to belong to a twelve-year-old.

"That's not true!" Saige protested, sticking her tongue out at him.

"Oh, yeah? Why do you think they're all dead?"

"But they're not all dead," his mother said softly, and all three heads turned sharply toward her, big eyes curious and uncertain. This was a strange twist, for the stories had never taken this direction before. Not once, in all the countless tellings.

"What do you mean they're not dead?" he asked quietly, though his words sounded belligerent and hard against the heavy silence of the house. He fought the urge to flinch as a log cracked sharply in the fireplace, the wet wood popping, then splitting.

Their mother's slim brows arched high on the worry-wrinkled span of her brow. "Did I ever say they were dead?"

"If they're not dead—" his eyes narrowed in suspicion "—then where are they?"

"Right under your nose," she explained with a small smile that made him feel a little sick inside. She held his stare, the corners of her mouth curving just the tiniest bit—a strange glow warming the deep, dark blue of her eyes. "And one day, when the darkness calls to you," she whispered, her voice so low he could barely hear the words, "when you can feel it in your bones, feel it roaring through your veins, in the beat of your heart— when your dreams are no longer your own, Ian—you're going to meet him."

Trapped within the oppressive layers of sleep, Ian stared at his smiling mother until his vision became cloudy, the silhouette of her body hazy against the thickening darkness. He knew what would happen next—but he couldn't stop the recurring dream from bleeding into a nightmare. His throat hurt as the beginning vibrations of a feral growl shivered in his chest, his body aching as every muscle went rigid with a painful, gripping tension.

He tossed beneath his sweat-soaked covers, struggling to throw off the thick curtain of sleep, but he couldn't shake it, as if the dream had lain itself out over his body in a wash of warm, wet cement, binding him in place as it hardened. His teeth gnashed, grinding and angry, but the dream kept going, like a film clip set on continuous replay.

The dream was changing…sucking him deeper… pulling him into darker, treacherous waters, where danger lurked in the thick, murky depths beneath his feet. Gone was his childhood home, his mother, his freckle-faced sister, Saige, and scrawny, pain-in-the-ass little brother, Riley. Now the ripe scent of the forest filled his head, humid night crowding around him like a falling sky, smothering and dark and too close for comfort. The heavy weight of midnight black surrounded him while the tension in his gut wound tighter, knotting and coiling…and then he saw it. The small, flickering glow of a campfire in the distance, its shivering light just visible through the stygian darkness. The wind surged, bringing with it the rich, provocative scent of sex, while a deep, rhythmic pulse of music suddenly began to fill the unnatural quiet of the woods.

He stood silent and still, aware of the slow, heavy thudding of his heart, of the intense surge of blood swirling through his rigid body. His hands flexed at his sides, the tips of his fingers burning with sharp, piercing sensations, while the thick wave of hunger rolling through him settled heavily in his cock. He breathed in, and broke open in some weird metaphysical way, aware of something unfurling from deep within him, stretching to existence within his fevered skin. Something that felt at home there in the clinging web of darkness. His senses sharpened, acute and predatory, while his body swelled, growing stronger, the muscles buried beneath his burning skin bulging with a primitive, animal craving that demanded freedom.

That wanted to answer the provocative call of the darkness.

Suddenly he was aware of the warm wind against his now-naked flesh. Of the damp air in his lungs, the fertile ground beneath his feet, too many smells assailing him with a chaotic swarm of information. The details consumed him, crowding his mind, battling for supremacy, until one need conquered, dominating all others.

The urge to hunt.

Lifting his nose to the wind, he searched for the thing he craved, just so that he could chase it and take it down. His nostrils flared and he sniffed, sorting through the sensitive data intake rushing into his head, and then he found it.

Yes, the creature within him hissed with thick satisfaction. *Right there.*

The change was almost complete. Some inherent part of him struggled against it, but the hunger was too strong. He exploded into action and felt himself running, charging, lungs heaving, thighs and calves working with preternatural force as he raced through the thick tangle of foliage and trees, their leaves and branches whipping against his face and arms and legs, leaving bloody scratches on his skin…and he knew what would happen next.

He'd been having this nightmare for weeks now. And each time it ripped something inside of him open a little more. Cut him just that little bit deeper.

No! Ian roared from the darkest depths of his unconscious psyche, while the dream kept going, each moment pissing him off more than the last. *Goddamn it! No! Wake up, you idiot! Wake up!*

But he couldn't shake it. No, something dark and hungry in his gut wanted this too much—needed it—and an ugly, twisted feeling cut through him. Shame. Bitter and foul and consuming. But the craving was too huge to ignore—to overcome.

He *needed* what was out there.

Ian thrashed in the tangle of his damp sheets, drenched and aching as he struggled to throw off the infuriating bonds of the nightmare. But its claws were sunk too deeply into his flesh, trapping him in place. It was the same as it had been in all the other dreams. He saw himself breaking through the edge of the forest, rushing into the middle of a gypsy campfire. He saw the rapid, sensual swirl of the dancers as they spun around the rioting flames, the rich colors of their skirts flapping rapidly in the breeze, long hair flowing behind them in a wild explosion of curls. Along the shadowy edges of the campsite, couples writhed in ecstasy, the ripe, musky scent of sex filling the air while the pulsing music grew louder. Around the fire, the dancers moved with increasing urgency, clapping and stamping their feet, singing and laughing in their decadent revelry.

And a low, eerie chant began to hum beneath the music. Something thick and husky that sounded like *Merrick...Merrick...Merrick.*

They knew he was there. Dark sloe eyes caressed him, ruby-red lips curling in feline smiles of invitation he couldn't deny. He reached for the one who first dared to dance too close to him, taking her down to the ground right there, aware of the sizzling, searing looks as the others watched.

Clothes were shredded in seconds. Then he took her the same way he did in each dream, spreading her long legs, thrusting into the slippery entrance nestled there within her crimson folds, the ebony curls above glistening with her juices, and he hammered her into the hard, damp floor of the forest.

Ian fisted his hands in his sheets until the fabric ripped, his body taut upon the mattress, his weight resting solely on his head and heels—and in the dream, his hands clawed at the rich soil, eyes narrowed and hot as he ground himself into the panting, dark-eyed girl. He slammed into her harder, with a viciousness that shocked him, but he couldn't get deep enough, as if he were trying to reach something that she couldn't give him. The need raged through him, savage growls crawling from his throat, like something wild and predaceous, but she wasn't afraid of him. Sharp nails clawed his flesh, her voluptuous body arching and writhing beneath him, low, moaning pleas for more flowing from her lips while the others cheered them on. The music grew louder…swelling with each pulsing beat, until his head roared with it.

He thrust himself into her giving flesh, searching… aware of the pain his size brought her, but he couldn't find what he needed. He snarled, throwing back his head, an animal roar ripping from his chest, the desperate sound slicing through the music and raucous laughter. His eyes screwed tight, the tendons in his neck bulging while his temples throbbed. His heart thundered, threatening to explode…building and building and building. And then he felt it.

Something…different. Something that had never happened before within the terrifying landscape of his nightmares.

It was the small, shy touch of a hand against his chest, pressed right over the painful thudding of his heart. Ian froze on a hard downstroke, sublimely aware of the delicious change in the body beneath his own, his rigid cock buried thick and deep within an impossibly snug, cushiony feminine channel that gripped him so tight it actually hurt.

He swallowed, his eyes burning from the sting of sweat as he lowered his head and stared down at the woman now lying beneath him. The gypsy was gone, and in her place was a shy, petite honey-blond gazing up at him with big brown eyes.

Oh, hell. It was her. *Molly.* Something in Ian's chest snapped, making him jerk on top of her. He didn't dare breathe or blink or speak, terrified of breaking the spell and losing her. He couldn't let that happen. No, suddenly the most important thing in his world was holding on to the dream with everything that he had.

Holding on to the woman.

With the sound of his blood roaring in his ears, Ian shifted, grinding against her, making sure she had every inch of him buried inside of her, the base of his shaft rubbing against the pulsing heat of her clit. Her eyes went wide, full of shock and surprise and the hazy kind of pain that could only be seen in a woman's gaze when she was being thoroughly taken. A strange, voluptuous kind of pain sharpened by the biting edge of pleasure. Her lips parted, and he read the word that slipped silently from her mouth.

"*Ian.*"

She knew. Knew who he was. Knew he was the one penetrating her, staking her to the ground.

He wanted to smile at her, wanted to run his dirt-covered hands over her face, along the trembling pulse at the base of her throat and tell her it was okay, that he wouldn't harm her, but he couldn't say the words. His blood was raging, his body hot, streaming with sweat, and he knew his eyes looked wild. Savage. The intensity riding him was too violent to disguise—too ripped open and raw, stripping away whatever thin veneer of civilization he normally managed to pull around himself.

She stared up at him, panting and soft and rosy, pale skin gleaming and flushed. He knew, without any doubt, that she was as innocent as she looked. Not virgin, but…close. Whatever experience she'd had with men was limited, brief, fleeting.

That was about to change.

Watching her closely, he pulled back, then sank back in. He could have come just from thrusting into her—

but no way in hell was he going to let it happen. He had to savor it…savor *her*. Make it last and wring from her everything she could give. Had to demand it, make her crazy. He wanted her screaming and clawing and crying with pleasure by the time he was finished with her. Wanted to break her apart, scattering the pieces until she had to have him put her back together again.

Shifting to his knees, Ian pushed up on his hands, muscles bulging and hard in his arms, and stared down at the tender place where his body joined hers.

"Watch me," he growled.

She shivered and lowered her gaze, her shock at seeing his possession unmistakable in the thick look of lust that clouded her warm brown eyes. It rushed through him, the destructive power of that look, trashing his control, tearing some kind of violent, primitive sound from his throat. She was tight and he was big, too big to just slide in, no matter how slick she was. He had to put his strength behind it and drive at her, slamming her into the ground, the keening sound of her pleasure making him see red.

With a hoarse groan, Ian lowered himself over her, needing the tight tips of her velvety nipples against his skin, needing to cover her, to own her…and he suddenly realized that they were alone in the forest. The music was gone, the gypsies, the wild celebration—the churning noise replaced by her husky cries and the wet, slapping sounds of his body thrusting into hers. He drove her across the ground with his hips, taking and claiming and letting loose every hard, tight emotion that he'd always kept locked up, hidden away—and then she undid him.

He watched, dazed, as the damp, silken beauty of her mouth curled, lips lifting to form an incandescent smile that lit her up, made her glow, and something powerful and terrifying ripped through him. His control snapped, and he went over the edge, digging one hand around her thigh, lifting her leg up high as he shoved deep…then deeper still, his other hand fisting in her hair, pulling her head to the side. She sobbed, a sound more pleasure and anticipation than pain, and he lost it. His gums burned as he felt the terrifying length of his fangs slip free.

She cried out, stiffening beneath him, but he couldn't stop. He buried his face in the crook of her neck, breathed a damp patch of lust against her throat, and greedily sank his teeth into her. Molly screamed, jerking beneath him, and he bit deeper, the ecstasy and bliss instantaneous, hot and thick and sinful.

The warm, rich spill of her blood filled his mouth in a smooth rush, flowing down his throat, and he swallowed hungrily, growling as he pulled against the wound in her neck, dizzy with pleasure at the lusty taste of her. *More.* He needed *more.* Working his jaws, he pulled tighter against her, feeding from the small punctures, every inch of his body aware of her flying apart around him in a shattering climax that squeezed his shaft like a clenching, silken fist.

With a snarling cry, he ripped his fangs from her, drugged by her taste, by the evocative sight of her crimson blood dripping down the pale skin of her throat. She gasped breathlessly as he leaned down, dragging his tongue over her flesh, taking the meandering trails of blood for his own, trapping them in his mouth. He lifted his head, staring into her dazed eyes, and for the first time in his life he was completely focused on every mind-shattering detail of the woman beneath him. The rapid quivering of her heart against his. The panting of her sweet breath and the delicate shiver of her hands across his back. She was too small for him. But it was too good, the feeling one he wanted over and over and over.

He was painfully aware that nothing had ever felt so perfect…so right. That no one had ever felt like this. Like *his.*

Ian shuddered from the dangerous, unsettling thought, already closing himself off even as she blinked up at him, dewy cheeks flushed and so beautiful that it took his breath away. He watched in horror as those bee-stung lips curled up the slightest fraction, her eyes shining as she gifted him with another sweet, shy smile—even after he'd fed from her like a bloody monster—and fear, sick and meaty and rank, sliced through him.

Danger! Red alert! Get the hell out of here, you dumb-ass son of a bitch!

Her mouth opened, small hands clutching at him, and he thought he heard her scream his name in panic as she lost her hold—but in the next instant, he jerked awake, his body drenched in sweat, heart hammering like a staccato drum in his chest, painful and piercingly sharp.

Rolling to his side on the damp sheets of his wrecked bed, he felt his lips pull back over his teeth as he fought to get control of his ragged breathing, to find a slower intake of air that didn't make his lungs burn, his vision swim. Squinting through his narrowed eyes, he focused on the digital glow of the clock sitting on his dresser, the blinking of the numbers making him think of a bomb slowly ticking its way to detonation.

When the darkness calls, Ian…

Like hell! He had enough to deal with right now! He didn't need his mother's words whispering through his brain. Not when he was on the edge and a breath away from losing what little control he could claw on to.

He drew in a deep, desperate breath through his nose, eager for the scent of something clean and fresh, something that could pull him out of the ugliness in his head. But the smell of the room reminded him too much of the acrid taste of fear. And there was no denying that he was afraid—that terror beat through his body like a deafening, rolling wave of thunder.

Visions of blood and lust, of violent sex and ungodly, animalistic hunger, still burned through his mind, but he fought against the waves of memory, focusing on regaining control, slowing his heart…his breathing. Struggling to keep from coming all over his sheets like some green-eared teenage boy in the throes of a wet dream.

Goddamn it! It was her! She'd planted this in his head with her little mind games today. And he refused to think about how he'd felt with her—*in* her. No way. That was emotional no-man's-land.

Seconds ticked by that flowed slowly into minutes, while he lay there, struggling for control of his body— fighting the urge to replay the dream in his head, knowing it would destroy him. Send him out on a shaky, treacherous ledge that only she could rescue him from. He sucked in air through his gritted teeth, heavy and hard, welcoming the dull throb beginning to pound through his head, until he suddenly became aware of someone knocking on his door. Loud and rattling, it shook the thin wood within its weathered frame like a lone reed caught in a gale-force wind.

Rolling onto his back, Ian took quick stock of his condition. He was drenched in sweat, his body hot, muscles aching, and a wry look downward showed he was in some deep shit, and it was getting deeper by the minute.

The knocking rattled his door again, sharp and insistent. He threw his legs over the side of his bed, running one shaky hand through his damp hair, trying to throw off the jittery feeling the dream had left in his gut. It was probably Riley, asking for help. Again. Why his brother thought he would want to run off and play Galahad with him, he had no idea. Probably Riley's attempt to keep an eye on him, making sure he still walked the straight and narrow.

Huh. As if he wanted to go back to the way he'd been before coming to the mountains. Thanks, but no thanks. He was done with living on the edge. Done watching his back 24-7. The constant strain of fighting his way through each day had worn him down and he had no desire to ever return.

Grabbing his jeans from the floor, Ian navigated through the dark rooms of his apartment, hoping it wasn't his brother…or Kendra. He'd left her a message earlier, just wanting to check on her, after the whacked-out stuff Molly Stratton had said that afternoon.

"Jesus, give me a goddamn minute!" he called out when the knocking grew louder, impatient and strong.

Hitching his jeans up over his hips, he closed a few buttons as he reached for the door, pulling it open.

And there she was. *Little Miss Molly.*

Holy shit. What had been a serious hard-on turned into a burning lead pipe in his jeans, curving high to his left, so that the partly closed denim only just managed to keep him from flashing her his goods.

She still wore her jeans, but the white shirt had been replaced with a soft sage-colored T-shirt. Her braless nipples pressed against the thin cotton, thick and tempting, like hard little berries that he wanted to roll around on his tongue. Ian stared, unable to believe his eyes, wondering for a moment if he was still somehow trapped within the dream.

The silence stretched out, punctuated only by their soughing breaths, until he finally took a step forward. His brain justified moving closer to her as an intimidation tactic, but his cock knew better. He just wanted to be near her. Wanted to watch the soft flush bloom across her fair complexion. Wanted that warm honey scent of her skin in his head. She blinked up at him, pulling that full lower lip through her small white teeth, and his patience snapped. "How the hell did you find me?"

"I asked around." He struggled to focus on her words and not the husky sound of her voice that seemed to roll down his spine, or the sleep-rumpled look on her freshly washed face—but it was impossible. "A teenager down at the gas station told me you were staying here while you finish your house."

He ripped his gaze away from the curve of her mouth to glare into those big brown eyes, hazy and soft beneath the glowing moonlight. "Parker needs to learn to keep his mouth shut," he muttered in a quiet rasp.

Her mouth twisted. "I think he thought I was in trouble, so please don't be angry with him."

His eyes narrowed. "Why?"

She blinked, startled by his tone. "What?"

"Why did he think you were in trouble?"

"Oh." Her gaze slid away from his, focusing on his chest, which was bare. He watched, seeing the moment when she realized where she was staring…and the heat crept back up across that flawless skin. But she didn't look away, and the heat spread into her eyes, the smoldering burn there slamming down into his already aching erection, making him wince. He wanted to rearrange himself, but didn't want to draw that luminous gaze any lower. That'd be too much.

"Molly!" he snapped, the harshness of his tone making her jump. He snagged that startled gaze as it flew up and growled, "Why did Parker think you were in trouble?"

"Oh, sorry," she mumbled. This time she didn't look away from his face, keeping her eyes above his broad shoulders, and he almost grinned. "I was…um, upset, when I talked to him a little while ago. But I'm okay now."

"Upset how?" he demanded, grabbing her chin. He tilted her face into the soft stream of light barely reaching them from the streetlight down on the corner, and could see the sticky trail of tears that had dried on her skin. "You were crying," he said in an odd monotone. "Did someone hurt you?"

"No," she whispered, shaking her head, the soft,

silken ends of her hair brushing against his wrist. "I was just…emotional. But I'm not hurt."

He curved his hand around the back of her skull, and made a fist in her hair, pulling her head back so that he could stare down into those deep brown eyes. Her hair was soft, so damn soft. He just wanted to rub his face in it. Feel it on his skin, on his body. Wanted it wrapped around his fist as he made her do things good girls like her never did; which was why he always steered clear of them. He'd realized long ago that he couldn't do the pretty when it came to sex. His urges ran too dark, too raw, too primitive for the likes of soft women. Hell, just look at the sick stuff he'd been fantasizing about in his sleep!

She claimed she wasn't hurt, but he refused to think about how he'd been…*hurting* her in his dream. Fucking her to within an inch of her life on the hard forest floor, sinking his goddamn teeth into the fragile column of her throat.

Drinking her blood.

Hunger clawed at his insides with vicious insistence while he slowly looked her over, feature by feature, and he knew the time for retreat when it came. "If nothing's wrong, then why the hell are you here?" he grated.

She trembled, and he didn't know if it was from his look or the harsh sound of his voice. "I'm sorry for barging in on you, but I wanted to…to check on you. I was…worried."

She'd been worried about him? Something scary and soft shivered through his insides at her strange words, and he let go of her, refusing to acknowledge the pleasure he got out of just touching her, feeling her warm curls sift through his fingers as he pulled away. "Why would you be worried about me?"

She rolled her lips inward, brown gaze zinging from his face, to the hard bulge of his biceps, and back to his chest again, the smooth curve of her cheeks turning red. Her arms wrapped around her middle, as though she was holding herself together. "Because I felt it."

Leaning against the doorjamb, Ian crossed his own arms and glared at her. "Felt what?"

Her lids lowered, shielding her gaze from him. "Your dream," she said thickly.

Something inside his gut clenched so hard, he felt the tremor slam through his body like a physical blow. "What the hell are you talking about?"

Her gaze flicked up to his. "You…you did something to me."

Shock gripped him and he uncrossed his arms, his hands fisting at his sides. For a long, tense moment, he stared her down. The energy in him was pumping, making him feel wired, on edge, crawling up his spine, curling around the backs of his ears. He tried to keep it together, but hell, he was creeping himself out. No wonder she was looking at him as if he was some sort of monster from the deep, dark lagoon.

Hell, for all he knew, he was.

Ian worked his jaw, aware that he had to scrape the words out of his throat. "What did you say?"

"You did something to me. In…the dream." She wet her lips, her blush visible even in the hazy moonlight coming from above, shining around the pale wash of her hair like a halo, making her glow. She looked…soft, like something warm and sweet that you just wanted to wrap yourself around; that you wanted to feel melt over you like a warm summer rain. A sweet piece of candy that you left on your tongue to savor, to enjoy as its flavor trickled down your throat. All sunshine and smiles. Things he didn't want—things he sure as hell didn't deserve.

She looked ethereal, surreal…something too good for him to touch, even if she was out of her goddamn mind.

Yeah, and you're so together, Buchanan. A rock. Just a grounded kind of guy.

He ignored the sarcastic asshole living in his head, and tried to get his mind around what she was saying. Another scam? That had to be it. She was messing with his mind, though God only knew why. What could she want from him? He had nothing to give. Nothing but a screwed-up past and a questionable future. If it was a con, he couldn't imagine what she hoped to get from it.

As if reading his thoughts, she whispered, "I'm not making this up. And this time, I can prove it to you, Ian."

He knew he was trying to intimidate her, knew it made him an ass, but he did it anyway. "And what was I doing in your dream, baby? Did I have you tied to my bed, making you beg for it?" He gave a gruff laugh, lifting his brows. "Come on, Molly. Tell me. If anything else, this should prove to be some pretty entertaining bullshit."

Her mouth trembled, cheeks fiery and warm, eyes glassy and wild with a sheen of moisture, but he knew she wasn't going to cry. No, she was…turned on, he thought with a sharp, cracking jolt of realization that slammed through him. His words had aroused her as much as they had him.

He watched her head shake from side to side, heard a low, trembling "no" whisper past her pink mouth. His eyes narrowed as he studied her, and it hit him that she looked like a woman who'd just rolled out of bed with a lover. Something aggressive and violent twisted in his stomach. Had she gone out and found some jerk-off to nail tonight, while he'd been alone in his bed, dreaming about her?

"It didn't happen like that." Her words came in a rush, and she slumped against the door frame, her body melting against the weathered wood as if she needed it to keep her upright. But her eyes changed, filling with an inner strength that aroused him even more than her shivering innocence, if that was possible.

He wanted to demand who she'd been with but heard himself say, "Yeah? Then just what did I do to you in this dream, Miss Stratton?" He wanted to shake her up, throw her off balance, the same way she'd done to him. "There's no way in hell I'd get you beneath me and not fuck you. *Not-a-chance-in-hell,*" he ground out.

"You did," she breathed softly, the wild look taking her eyes again. "You…we had sex," she said in a whispery little rush. "But…"

"Yeah? Spit it out, honey." He grinned and gave her a crude look, letting his inner asshole free. "I'm dying of curiosity here."

She trembled, hugging herself tighter, her mouth quivering, eyes bright and wide as she stared up at him. She blinked. Then swallowed. "You bit me, Ian."

He froze, locked into place, while the floor fell out from beneath him. "What did you just say?"

She swallowed again, trembling like a leaf, lifting

one hand to press her fingers against the left side of her neck, beneath the fall of her hair. "You bit me…and I can…I can still feel the marks."

Ian watched, trapped within a thick, oppressive daze, as she slowly pulled her hand away, turning her fingers for him to see. And there, glistening on Molly Stratton's pale little fingertips was a dark, crimson smear of blood.

CHAPTER FOUR

MOLLY'S HEART POUNDED to a painful beat as she watched Ian come closer, the movement of his body predatory and primal, like an animal's. He moved in a way that was too natural for a human male, too elemental, all that power and shocking intensity pulsing from him in slow, heated waves that made her want to shiver and melt all at once. She saw his muscles shift beneath the burnished silk of his skin, almost too gracefully for such a big man, as if strength came to him too easily, without effort and dangerously smooth. It reminded her of the way he'd moved over her in the dream.

He reached toward her with one large hand, the callused tips of his fingers scraping her skin, and moved the fall of her hair back from the side of her throat. The second he found the bite marks he'd made, his eyes flared into a hot, wicked blue, then narrowed, staring…unblinking. His breath surged between his slightly parted lips with a rough, uneven cadence.

She wet her bottom lip with the tip of her tongue, a wave of chill bumps spreading over the sensitized surface of her body, while inside, chaos reigned. Her heart fluttered wildly like a trapped bird that might burst from her chest with her next breath, the sound of her pulse roaring in her ears like the midnight break of surf against craggy, weatherworn cliffs. The subconscious landscape of her emotions was a dark, gothic setting, complete with smoke-gray skies and thunderous cracks of lightning rumbling like ominous bellows in the distance.

All you need is Shelley's Frankenstein *lurking in the shadows to make you feel right at home.*

She shook off the whimsical thought, wishing he'd just say something.

"Unbelievable," he finally breathed out in a low, stifled rasp. Molly watched the word as it formed on his lips, mesmerized by the shape of his mouth, the texture and hue, something inside of her coming a little undone by the salty, sweet scent of his breath. It sat on her palate like the promise of something forbidden and sweet, like a sin. Pure, perfect temptation. His fingers slid farther beneath her hair, curving around the back of her head, and she stole another quick look up at his eyes to find him watching her, his stare as hot as it was intensely blue.

Oh, God, she silently moaned, while her voice remained frozen, locked inside the prison of her throat.

His gaze moved over her face as if she was something he'd never seen before. Like Adam discovering Eve, he stared at her as though she were some foreign creature. A revelation. A curse. Something he should fear. Something that could destroy him.

"What do you want from me?" he ground out through teeth that were clenched in confusion and some indefinable emotion, his fingers tightening the slightest fraction in her hair. "How the fuck did this happen?"

"I…I don't know." Scraping the confession out of a

dry throat, Molly became aware of tiny pinpricks of sensation swirling through her system. She could feel its rush through her blood, behind her eyes, pulsing like tender heat in her lobes, against the backs of her knees. Desire, unfathomable and unwanted, and completely inexplicable, considering the circumstances. But there all the same. She couldn't deny, or ignore, its existence, no matter how badly she wanted to. She felt betrayed by the sheer depth of her reaction, as if lust had mounted a revolt against her common sense.

The sultry summer breeze blew harder, and his scent surrounded her, engulfed her, making her dizzy… making her want. His hand shifted again, slipping lower, curving around the back of her neck, and his skin was too hot, burning her flesh. So alive and warm and impossibly male. She blinked, and suddenly his body was even closer. So close now that his forehead nearly touched hers, their breath soughing together in a hectic, frenzied rush. "No more games. I want an answer, and I want it now. How did this happen?"

"I…I have no idea." She could tell from his grim expression that he didn't believe her, and the words rushed up from inside of her like a gasping, swelling burst of frustration and fear. "I swear, Ian. I have no idea how it happened. That's why I came here. I was worried. I needed to see that you were okay."

"To see that *I'm* okay?" he growled, lashes so long and thick they cast shadows against his skin. "Christ, woman. I'm not the one who almost had their fucking throat ripped out."

A police car came roaring around the corner in the next instant, siren blaring as it sped past the weathered apartment building and into the night. They both jumped, flinching from the jarring screech of the siren's wail.

Pulling away from her, Ian pushed one rugged hand back through his damp hair, the muscles in his arm and chest coiling and flexing with the action, drawing her eye. "I need a cigarette," he muttered, turning and disappearing into the darkness behind him. He didn't slam the door in her face, so Molly assumed she wasn't being told to leave. He moved deeper into the shadows of the apartment and she followed, pulling the door shut behind her.

Without the light from the street, darkness blanketed the room. The loss of sight made her other senses sharper, the panting sound of her breath filling her ears, the surface of her body so sensitive, it was as if she could feel the shadows against her skin. They slipped over her flesh like tiny, featherlight touches of a fingertip, stroking her cheekbones, her chin, the line of her throat.

Just stay calm. Don't freak. And for God's sake, don't start crying again. He'll think you're out of your mind. Not that he doesn't think that already.

Taking a deep, trembling breath, Molly squinted against the darkness, unsure of where to walk, until a low glow of light spilled into the murky gloom from a doorway on the far side of the room. Following the light, she found him facing her, one powerful shoulder braced against the far wall beside a window in the small kitchen, head lowered as he lifted his arms to light the cigarette perched between his lips. He'd switched on a small light that shone over the sink, the muted glow too weak to reach the shadowed corners, casting him in a hazy glow of gold.

Slanting a curious look in her direction, he spoke in a graveled, hesitant rumble. "Why did you scream my name at the end? Did I hurt you?"

She moved cautiously into the kitchen and collapsed into one of the pine chairs beside a small table, wishing she'd pulled on something heavier. The chill of the air conditioner seeped through her thin shirt, freezing her to the bone, while Ian stood there half-dressed, his body vital and big, covered with a light sheen of sweat, as if impervious to the cold. "No."

"Then why the scream?" he demanded, taking a long draw off the gleaming cigarette, the details of the room lost beneath the force of his presence. She had the feeling she could have been surrounded by ravenous predators and still have remained oblivious to the danger, her entire focus centered on the hard, beautiful bulk of Ian Buchanan.

"Answer me." The harshness of his gritty tone made her flinch. The soft glow of light glinted off the broad width of his shoulders, his skin gleaming like bunched satin, and yet, he was completely untouchable. Like a wild, caged animal. Beautiful, but deadly.

Molly looked away and drew an unsteady breath. "I didn't want…"

"What?" he snapped, the word lashing with whipcord strength.

A self-conscious shrug rolled across her shoulders, her eyes still focused on a distant patch of his kitchen floor. "I didn't want you to…leave me there alone." The confession slipped from her lips without any direction from her brain, startling and unintended. She wanted to snatch back the telling, vulnerable words, but it was too late. He was already absorbing them, working them over in his mind, that dark blue gaze zeroed in on her with ruthless, uncompromising intensity when she sneaked a quick peek at him from beneath her lashes.

"Tell me what you remember."

She flushed, keenly aware of the heat suddenly rising up beneath her skin, burning in her cheeks. Her tongue felt thick in her mouth, every part of her oversensitized, as if she were experiencing everything too keenly. The coolness of the air. The stuttering speed of her pulse. The press of that beautiful blue gaze, the mesmerizing color probably the envy of every woman he'd ever known.

"Molly!" he snapped again.

The words jerked from her lips in rapid succession, beyond her control. "We were in a forest. It was night. You were…different."

A rough, humorless laugh rumbled up from his throat, and he took another deep pull on the cigarette, his silence making her ramble with the need to fill the uncomfortable space. "We had sex, but you…you didn't…"

Her voice faltered, and in a graveled tone, he said, "Come?"

"Yes." She shivered, her body clenching with remembered sensation. It had been unlike anything she'd ever known, being under him, consumed by him.

"Believe me," he grimaced, the barest hint of a wry edge to his words, "I know."

Her gaze flickered briefly to the immodest bulge in

his jeans, and she wanted to ask why—why he hadn't allowed himself release when inside of her—but couldn't, suddenly afraid of what he might say. He'd seemed to enjoy what had happened between them, but she knew men were fickle creatures, not to be trusted with emotional issues. His words, if delivered cruelly, could cut her to the quick, and she was already feeling too raw, the defenses she'd spent so many years building suddenly seeming frail and unstable. She didn't know him well enough to trust him. Hell, she didn't know him at all.

And yet, for some inexplicable reason, she felt perfectly safe, alone there with him in the middle of the night, with nothing but the quiet stillness for company. Those storm-dark eyes moved over her face, lingering over her individual features. Then he lowered his head, reaching out toward the ashtray perched on the edge of the kitchen counter. She knew if she hadn't been watching him so closely, she would have missed it, that bleak shadow of fear that crept over the rugged angles of his profile. He slanted a sharp look in her direction when her breath sucked in on a gasp, and for a single instant, she could have sworn she heard his raspy voice in her head. Heard the unspoken question he was too afraid to ask.

"No," she whispered, her body trembling with a low vibration.

He ground out the cigarette in the stainless steel ashtray and turned toward her, feet braced apart in an aggressive stance, powerful arms crossed over his broad chest. "No what?"

She rolled her lips together. "You're not evil."

He grunted in response, distracted, and began pacing the width of the room. She watched his bare feet against the faded linoleum, long and dark, but as perfectly pro-portioned as the rest of him. Her gaze traveled up the length of his body, over the hardness of his thighs, the corrugated stretch of his abdomen, and he raised his arms, shoving his fingers back through the rumpled mass of his hair. She could do nothing but stare at the bulging power of his biceps with wide-eyed fascination. He was so perfectly sculpted, it was as if a master artisan had cut him from marble like *David,* and the gods had breathed life into him.

But he was no angel.

And yet…he wasn't a devil, either.

"I mean it, Ian. You're not evil, no matter how… physical your dreams might be."

"Yeah, and how can you be so sure? You don't know me. Don't know what I'm capable of. Don't know what I dream about doing to the women in my bed." He stopped pacing, turning his head to look at her, eyes sharp and dark, so blue they looked black. "Or maybe you do."

She struggled to ignore the surge of lust that poured through her, thick and warm in her veins, but it wasn't easy. Not with him prowling around, wearing nothing more than those barely buttoned faded Levi's. She could see the dark silky trail of hair slipping down into the shadowed V of his open fly, and a wave of hunger rolled through her so sharp and sweet and strong that she went light-headed, forced to lean her upper body against the table for support.

The corner of his mouth twitched—such a slight

fraction of movement, she knew she would have missed it if she hadn't been staring so intently.

Crap. He knew.

This was bad. She was already in over her head, and getting deeper with every moment she spent up on this damn mountain. But she owed it to Elaina. Dammit, she owed it to herself. She wasn't going to screw up. Not this time around. She had a chance for redemption, to make a difference, and she was going to grab hold of it, even if it killed her.

Which seems a likely possibility, her conscience muttered.

He moved toward her, stalking closer until he stood in front of her knees, his feet braced outside of her own, staring down at her. Leaning forward, he braced his right hand on the table at her side, caging her in. "I can still taste your blood in my mouth," he rasped, his gaze flicking over her face, lingering on the swell of her lower lip. "This kind of shit isn't normal."

"Not for most people, no. But you're not like others, Ian. That's what I've been trying to tell you. It's why I used up my entire savings to buy a plane ticket and come here."

"I'm a contractor, for God's sake. Not a fucking vampire." Impatience cut itself into his features, the shadow of bristle on his cheeks accentuating the hollows of his expression.

She shook her head, craning her neck as she stared up at him. "I never said you were a vampire."

"Then why did I…" He jerked his chin toward her throat.

"I only know what I've been told. According to Elaina—"

"Christ," he grunted, lifting away from her. "I don't want to hear any more bullshit about what my dead mother has told you."

Breathlessly, she said, "I'm telling you the truth. I swear it."

"Yeah, then explain—"

"I don't—"

"—how I'm able to wake up in my bed with the taste of your goddamn blood in my mouth!" he roared.

"But I—"

"And this time, don't lie about it! I want to know how it happened, Molly!"

She slammed her left hand down on the table, tired of him yelling at her…of not knowing how to make him listen. "I don't know how it happened! I swear. I've never dreamed about you before. I've never had anything like this happen to me before—sharing a dream with someone that is somehow, in some way, actually happening. All I know is what Elaina has told me, and I've been trying to tell you, but you won't listen! She led me to you, told me where to find you. Wanted me to warn you that you're in danger—that you're being hunted."

"It's the nightmares," he growled, his gorgeous, arrogant face set in a hard, obstinate expression that made her want to scream with frustration. "You've done something to me."

"No, that's not true. Think, Ian. You've been having nightmares for weeks now, and we only just met. I swear, I have nothing to do with them. The darkness… this all has to do with what's hiding within you. You know that. I know you do. Elaina's been telling you stories about the Merrick since you were a little boy."

He stumbled back another step, eyes bleeding to black, and shoved his hands into his hair. Locking his fingers behind his head, he glared up at the ceiling with his jaw clenched so hard it looked painful. Molly stared at the dark tufts of hair under his arms, the stark lines of his throat, wanting so badly to reach out and touch him. To place her hand over the center of his chest and feel his heart pounding against her palm, vital and urgent and strong.

"Ian, I know you don't want to believe me, but after what's happened, how can you still think I'm here to con you? This thing is real. I have the bite marks on my neck to prove it. We need to help each other figure it out, because I can guarantee you this is more than I signed up for. Elaina told me how to find you, wanted me to talk to you. To tell you things that she's afraid no one else will. But she didn't say a damn thing about…about whatever the hell it was that happened tonight. She told me this thing inside of you needs to feed for power, but she didn't say…"

Her voice trailed off, and he lowered his gaze back to her, muttering, "That it would feed off you? That it would take your blood?"

"Yes." She swallowed nervously, folding her arms across her chest, resisting the urge to lift her fingertips and touch the tingling warmth of the bite on her throat, the tender flesh slowly throbbing with residual pulses of pleasure.

His eyes narrowed, studying her with fierce intensity, and then he rasped, "Son of a bitch. You actually liked it, didn't you?"

"What?" She blinked, floundering for the right thing to say.

"Face it, Molly. Any other woman would have run screaming in the other direction by now. Would have hauled her ass out of Henning the second she woke up and found her throat bleeding. But look at you, coming here, wanting to talk. To help me. What is it with you?" He stalked toward her again, his body closing off any escape route. "You got a death wish? Or do you just get off on the hard stuff?"

Towering over her, his callused hand slipped under the fall of her hair again, his rough fingertip smoothing over one of the two puncture wounds, and she gasped at the insane rush of sensation that curled through her center, settling heavily between her thighs. Her sex heated…swelled, feeling heavy and empty all at once, and his nostrils flared, those dark eyes cutting to her own confused stare, and she knew he could smell the need. That dark, uncontrollable ache twisting deep inside, clawing at her, making her crave. Making her need things that she didn't even understand. That she feared.

"What's your answer, Molly?"

Shakily, she said, "Be crude if it helps you deal. I have a thick enough skin by now to take it. You may piss me off, but it's not going to scare me away. I'm not going to run."

"And you're not going to give me any answers, either, are you?"

Her eyes slid closed, tears threatening to spill from the excess emotion crashing through her system. "I wish I could explain how the dream happened, Ian. But I can't."

He sighed, the heat of his body covering her like a glittering ray of sunshine. "Okay, I'll bite," he drawled in a deep, graveled voice, and she could feel the press of his eyes on her face, watching her. "It's not like your story won't be entertaining as hell. So let's hear it. What *can* you tell me?"

With a deep breath, Molly lifted her lashes. "I can tell you about Elaina. I can tell you what she's told me."

"In your dreams, right?" he murmured, his gaze settling heavily on her mouth, making her lips tingle.

"That's how she talks to me, yes. Don't ask me why, because I don't know. It's just the way that it's been since I was a teenager."

He latched on to that like a pit bull with a bone, suddenly holding her stare. "What happened when you were a teenager?"

Flustered, she tore her gaze away from his and focused it on the table. In the center sat one of those store-bought scented candles that freshened the air, its name no doubt flowery and feminine. And that easily, something inside of her softened, shifted into a calmer focus, her body relaxing in the chair, tension releasing like the gentle escape of air from a balloon. She silently laughed at her screwed-up logic, ridiculously reassured, comforted even, by a freaking candle, as if it made him seem less dangerous. God, maybe she *was* crazy. The fact that he owned a scented candle didn't make him any less of a threat to her stability. Didn't make him domesticated or tame. He probably just didn't like his kitchen smelling like cigarette smoke.

Pressing one hand to her stomach, holding in the

wild spiral of emotions, she said, "What happened to me isn't important. It's what's happening to *you* that we need to focus on. There's something…inside of you, Ian. Something that you need to learn to control. Something that will cause you to be hunted. That's going to put the people you care about in danger."

"I told you before, there's no one I care about."

"I don't believe that," she argued. "I bet there's someone that you're worried about tonight. Elaina told me there is. And she's in danger from this…this evil that's going to try and hurt you both."

He moved closer, hands braced on the back of the chair, his warm, earthy scent surrounding her, the heavy look in his eyes as sexual as it was angry. "And what makes you think I care about her, or even like her?" A hard, gritty laugh slid past his lips, low and sexy as hell. "Trust me, little Molly-Do-Right, people like Kendra and me don't need to *like* the people we have sex with."

"Then why?"

His head tilted to the side. "Why what?"

"If you disliked her so much, why sleep with her?"

For a moment she didn't think he was going to answer as he pushed away from her again, as if she were something not to be trusted that could turn on him at any moment. He grabbed the black T-shirt hanging over the back of a nearby chair, then pulled it over his head, turned and stalked to the cupboard to the right of the sink. Pulling down a short, thick glass and a half-empty bottle of scotch, he splashed the liquor into the bottom of the glass. "You wanna know why I slept with her? Because I liked her body. Liked the fact that she didn't ask for more than I was willing to give. Liked that she kept it light. I don't have to like or care about the women I take to bed," he told her without turning around, voice a gritty rasp of sound. "In fact, I rarely do."

She swallowed the thick feeling in her throat. "I see."

His eyebrows lifted as he turned to look at her over his shoulder. "Do you?"

Molly nodded. "Emotional safety. You don't get too close. I wonder if Kendra felt the same way, or if she hoped you'd fall in love with her."

Tossing back the dark amber liquor, he wiped the corner of his mouth with the back of his wrist. "Why the hell are we talking about her like she's dead?"

His question startled her, and with it came a nauseating sense of certainty. Molly didn't know why she'd started referring to the woman in the past tense—but she feared the heavy knowledge settling like a sickening bulk of reality in her gut. Her brow broke out with a clammy sheen of sweat and she pressed one hand over her heart, its rhythm rapid and light against her palm. "I warned you something would happen, Ian. I have a horrible feeling that it already has."

He didn't say anything. Just settled his lower back against the counter and stared, probably thinking she was the biggest freak alive.

"Why do you think Elaina picked you?" he rumbled, his deep voice low and rough.

"What?" she asked, caught offguard by the change in topic.

He stared, hard, as if trying to figure out a problem. "Why *you?*"

"Oh, I don't really know. I don't know why any of

the voices I hear come to me. Maybe I'm able to draw them in some way. Maybe she couldn't find anyone else who would do something this crazy." Her words came faster, cut with frustration. "Right now, we have something much more important to talk about. Were you even listening to what I said?"

"Yeah," he said, his voice raspy. He took another drink. "I was listening."

"Then will you try calling her?" Panic was crawling its way up her spine, making her dizzy…nauseous. God, she'd been sitting here arguing with him, and a woman was dead. Murdered. She didn't know how she knew, but she was certain of it. Just as she was certain it had something to do with the man standing before her, glaring at her as though she was something he wanted to scrape off the bottom of his shoe and be done with.

When he didn't immediately respond—just kept staring—she added, "Please, Ian."

Sighing, he slammed his glass down on the counter, went to the phone hanging on the wall beside the softly humming refrigerator and quickly punched in a number. He held the receiver to his ear for a moment, then set it back into the cradle. "She isn't home," he muttered, glaring at her. "Which means she probably hit her favorite haunt tonight and made a new friend."

"Or maybe something terrible has happened," she argued, lifting her chin.

A rude sound of impatience rumbled in the back of his throat. "Christ, you just don't let up, do you?"

"I don't have time to sit around and beat you over the head with this. I need you to listen to me, to believe what I'm telling you and help me make things right, and then I need to get back home." Where she might have to beg for her job back, if they'd decided to fire her for leaving so suddenly, and hope that the voices in her head would finally stay quiet, leaving her in peace. Giving her a goddamn break for once in her life.

"Where's home?" she heard him ask through the pity party she was throwing in her mind.

"Not important," she snapped, frustrated with herself and the whole horrible situation. "Will you come with me to check on Kendra?"

He slowly shook his head from side to side. "You've got to be kidding."

"I'm not."

"There's no way in hell I'm going to go skulking about in the dark because you think the bogeyman's out there. Get real."

"Fine. If that's the way you want it, then I'll go alone."

She stood, walking toward the living room, and he grabbed her arm, his long fingers biting into her flesh as he gripped her in a tight hold and spun her back around. "Are you crazy?"

"You don't believe me. Think I'm out of my mind. So fine. What's it to you if I go wandering about in the dark?"

"You're not going anywhere," he growled, anger roughening the edges of his speech, "except back to wherever you came from."

"Wrong. I'm doing whatever I damn well please. Whatever it takes to get your mother out of my head so she can move on to wherever she's meant to go!"

"Christ," he grunted under his breath, releasing her arm. He rubbed his palm against the scratchy edge of his jaw, then quietly said, "The sheriff's going to laugh his ass off when he finds out I let myself get dragged out into the night by a little pain in the ass like you."

"Don't worry," she whispered, struggling to hold back her relief that he'd caved. She wasn't exactly thrilled to be spending more time with him, when he insisted on being such a jerk, but she couldn't deny that she'd rather deal with his crass rudeness than handle things alone. Especially when she still didn't have a clear understanding of exactly what she was up against. "If I'm wrong and she's okay, then you can laugh in my face and tell me to get lost. The sheriff will never have to know."

IAN SHOOK HIS HEAD at her softly spoken words. The woman was unbelievably naive if she thought they could go wandering about town and keep it from Riley.

Not likely.

He was aware of her slim figure following behind him as he walked into the dark living room, the press of her eyes on his back as she watched him through the long shadows. Grabbing his cell phone off the coffee table, he turned back to her, saying, "He'll know." He grimaced with a wry twist of his lips. "Trust me. He's like Santa Claus. He *always* knows."

Her brows pulled together in a quizzical frown. "Are you friends with the sheriff?"

"You could say that," he muttered, pulling on his shoes before scanning the room for the keys to his truck. "I'm surprised Elaina hasn't mentioned it."

"It's not like we have chats," she said with a sigh. "Basically she just nags me about coming to find you and delivering the warning I gave you this afternoon."

"Huh. That sounds like her. God knows that woman loved to nag," he grunted as the phone he'd stuck in his pocket began to buzz. Flipping it open, Ian couldn't believe the name glowing on the screen. "Speak of the devil."

"Who is it?"

A low laugh rumbled in his throat as he held up the phone, waggling it in the air. "The sheriff."

"That's not funny," she murmured, frowning.

He snorted, another wry smile kicking up the corner of his mouth. "Tell me about it." Hitting the call button, he put the phone to his ear. "Yeah?"

"Get dressed," Riley's deep voice grunted over the line. "I need you to meet me."

His smile faded, replaced by a rising wave of apprehension. "What's going on?"

"It's Kendra."

Ian screwed his eyes closed, a sharp, guttural curse jerking up from his chest. No. Hell no. This so wasn't happening.

"Where are you?" He couldn't bring himself to ask why his brother was calling.

Riley shouted for someone to hold on, before saying, "Out on Marsden Road."

"I'm on my way."

There was a heavy pause, and then Riley said, "Aren't you going to ask what happened to her?" When he didn't respond, Riley growled, "She's been killed, Ian. Murdered."

He swallowed, unable to scrape up so much as a grunt. "I'll be there in fifteen," he finally managed to choke out, before disconnecting the call. Fury crawled its way through his system, sickening and thick, consuming his body heat along its way, until he was standing there, shivering, his skin cold and clammy. Not wanting to look at Molly, he scanned the room, finally eyeing the flash of his keys on the TV stand by the window.

"The sheriff's your brother, isn't he?" she asked softly. "Riley?"

He tried to nod, but the movement came out too jerky, like a spasm. "Yeah. Like I said, I'm surprised Elaina left that little bit of information out."

"She told me that you had a brother and sister, but that's all." She took a deep breath, then quietly said, "Something's happened, hasn't it?"

Ian turned to look at her over his shoulder, wondering what the hell she was, what the hell was happening. "Kendra's dead."

She flinched, shaking, the color draining out of her face as if she were bleeding out, leaving her pale and ghostly, like the damn voices she apparently heard in her screwed-up little head.

"I have to get out there. Riley's waiting for me." His gut felt as if it'd been stripped with acid, and he struggled to keep down the scotch. "Where are you staying?" he asked, heading for the door.

"Out at the Pine Motel." She moved through the front door as he jerked it open, standing beside him as he quickly locked it.

"The Pine Motel? Christ," he muttered, "That place is a dive."

"Thanks for that remarkable observation," she said thickly, and he could hear the threat of tears in her voice as she followed him down the rickety stairs. He headed toward his truck, her dark blue rental parked beside it, the moonlight no kinder to it than the sun had been.

Giving her his meanest glare, hoping it'd make her listen, he said, "Get back there, then lock the windows and door and don't answer it for anyone. You understand?"

She lifted her chin, opening her car door and sliding behind the wheel. It struck him that she looked too small within the run-down rental, too fragile and easily breakable. "Don't worry. I know how to take care of myself."

Ian could tell that the low sound of doubt he made in response grated on her nerves more than any snide comment he could have delivered.

"When will I see you again?" she burst out, when he started to turn away.

He shook his head, jamming his hands into his front pockets before he did something stupid, like try to touch her. "You won't."

"Ian—"

"I want you to stay away from me," he growled, cutting her off. "Tomorrow, when dawn hits, you get your ass in your car and go back to wherever it is you came from. You hear me?"

"There's nothing wrong with my hearing."

"No," he rasped, "just your sanity."

"I'm not crazy. I wish I was. And I'm also not running. Not until we've set things right."

"Get out of town, Miss Stratton." He punctuated the order with a hard look of warning, then slammed her car door. Ian waited until she'd started the engine and driven out onto the street, her taillights disappearing down the road, before turning around and climbing into his truck.

He sat for a moment, staring at nothing, lost in thought, wondering if he'd ever see her crazy little ass again, hoping that she was smart enough to do what he'd told her before things got any more screwed-up than they already were. She could end up hurt. Hell, if she was right, if something was gunning for him with murder on its mind, she could even end up dead.

With a low growl of frustration, he jammed the key into the ignition, hit the gas and headed into the night.

CHAPTER FIVE

Saturday Afternoon

WHAT HAD BEEN a shitty night turned into a grinding, bitch of a day, every lead they followed slamming into a frustrating wall of nothing. By the time Ian finally made it back to his apartment, it was late the following afternoon. While the forensics team had dealt with the gruesome crime scene, he'd spent the hellish hours helping Riley retrace Kendra's steps, talking to everyone they could find, while getting the third degree about her personal life. It was almost embarrassing, how little he was able to tell his brother about the woman he'd known for almost six months. And the crowd at Kendra's favorite bar knew even less. A couple of people remembered her leaving with some blond guy, but no one could provide his name. One cocktail waitress coming back on shift had called him "tasty," and the bartender was able to describe his eyes.

"Like a husky's. That cold, ice-blue. Know what I mean?"

There'd been an odd moment when Riley had finally pulled up in front of his apartment building to drop him off, his brother's expression one of intense frustration, as if he couldn't decide what to say. Or how to say it. Then he'd scraped one hand back through his shaggy hair and asked, "Did you ever head out to that storage place over in Mountain Creek?"

After Elaina's funeral, Riley had shipped their mother's personal belongings back to Colorado, storing them in a nearby facility. Instead of selling the small house where she'd lived, which had been in Elaina's family for generations, he had left it in working order, along with some furniture—since, according to Riley, Saige was thinking of spending some time there when she wasn't wandering all over the world, searching for her bits of junk. Everything else had been brought to Colorado, including some things that Elaina had apparently wanted Ian to have. Not that he'd been interested. He'd told Riley to throw whatever it was into storage, along with the rest of her stuff, which his brother had done. Then Riley had turned around and given him a set of keys to the storage unit, warning him that he might want to get his hands on whatever she'd left him someday.

Considering what they'd just been through, it had seemed an odd thing to bring up, but then Ian had given up trying to figure out how Riley's head worked a long time ago.

"I told you I wasn't interested in anything of Elaina's," he'd muttered, opening his door.

Before he could climb out of the truck, Riley had reached over and grabbed hold of his arm. "I think maybe you should go out there."

"What the hell for?" he'd growled, pulling free of his brother's grip.

Riley had scowled as he'd slumped back against his seat. "If I told you, you'd never believe me," he'd said with a hard sigh, sounding worn out. "Hell, I don't even believe it myself. But if things…if things get weird, I'll go out there with you. Help you find what she left for you."

Shaking his head, Ian had climbed out of the Bronco, slamming the door behind him. As he'd walked around the front of the truck, Riley had stuck his head out the driver's side window and shouted for Ian not to go anywhere until he'd heard from him.

Huh. As if he had the energy to go anywhere. Frustration had gnawed him down to the bone.

Slamming his backside down on his sofa, Ian tossed his cell on the battered coffee table, wondering if he should try Molly at the motel, then shook off the irritating thought. If she had half a brain, she'd have already hit the road by now, and what would he say anyway? *Hey, you were right. Some jackass mangled Kendra, leaving her body scattered over a field for an unlucky group of teenagers to come across when they stopped to take a leak. It was pretty sick and the kids are probably going to need therapy. Guess I really should have listened to you.*

Naw, he could save that useless conversation for…never. He already hated himself enough at the moment—he didn't need to add her scorn on top of it. She'd tried to warn him, but like the arrogant know-it-all his brother always accused him of being, he hadn't listened. Seemed he'd spent years fine-tuning the worthless talent of shutting people out, ignoring them, even when they were trying to help him.

Scrubbing his hands down his face, Ian struggled to get his mind on something useful, something that would help Riley nail that murdering bastard's ass, but his brain just kept buzzing with the images of Kendra's broken body and the blood-soaked field that he knew he was never going to be able to fully erase from his memory. Hell, they couldn't even be sure it'd been a human who killed her, the damage was so extreme.

If you can't be honest with anyone else, jackass, at least be honest with yourself. You know what it was, his conscience taunted him, scraping against his nerves like a jagged blade. *You've known all along.*

Ian clenched his jaw, doing his best to ignore the snide asshole in his head, wishing he could just get his hands on whoever…or whatever was responsible. He might not have been in love with Kendra, but he'd respected the hell out of her, and at the start of their affair, he'd enjoyed the time he spent with her. Kendra Wilcox had been a good person. Funny, beautiful, independent. She hadn't deserved what she'd suffered. Christ, no one deserved to die like that.

Riley was going to come back for him the second something came up, and he needed to rest before things started rolling, but he was too angry to sleep, adrenaline still pounding through his system, keeping him on edge. If he couldn't get some rest, food would be the next best thing to keep him going, but he couldn't face another nuked dinner. Everything tasted stale to him these days, his appetites bored with the usual fare.

Muttering under his breath, Ian made his way into the kitchen, grabbed the bottle of scotch and a glass, then headed back toward the sofa, picking up the remote for his flat-screen TV; the only thing in the apartment worth lifting, if anyone ever bothered to break in. Flicking on a Rockies game, he sprawled out over the cushions, trying to focus his mind on RBIs and pitching averages, rather than the gruesome images he'd witnessed—trying not to think of Kendra and the strange little blond who'd warned him that someone close to him was in danger.

Like an idiot, he'd spent the entire damn night and day trying to convince himself that Kendra's murder had nothing to do with him, that he couldn't have prevented it from happening. But he knew better. There was a burning, gnawing sensation in his gut that felt too much like shame for him to buy his own bullshit. He made an attempt to drown out the unwanted, sour emotion by hitting the scotch, but it didn't work worth a damn. Instead, he just kept sinking deeper into the guilt, like standing on the muddy banks of a river, his bare feet sinking farther and farther into the thick layers of sludge. Riley had pressured him all night for anything he could offer up, but he'd lied through his teeth, claiming that he didn't have any information. He didn't tell him about Molly, much less the fact that she'd delivered her strange little warnings straight to his face, begging him for his help.

And he sure as hell hadn't mentioned the dream they'd shared. Instead, he'd done his best to avoid thinking about it, though it was always there, lingering at the edge of his consciousness…waiting for the moment to strike.

Like now, his conscience whispered, and he drained the glass, the liquor hitting his gut with a hot, fiery burn.

Exhaustion finally overtook him in the seventh inning, his last thoughts centering on Molly Stratton as he drifted into a restless sleep. He wondered where she was, what she was doing. Wishing he could get her out of his goddamn mind. Hating the grinding frustration… the illogical panic that burned like acid in his chest every time he faced the maddening possibility that he might never see her again.

Despite the oppressive heat of the evening, he slept hard, thanks to the booze. Until the dreams began again. Ian had half expected the fertile heat of the forest and the erotic frenzy of the gypsy campfire, and he'd been prepared to do everything he could to keep his focus on the first woman he got beneath him. If he went with it, then maybe he wouldn't find himself drilling Molly into the damp forest floor, taking more of her than he had any right to.

But as always, fate had a way of turning around and biting him on the ass.

As Ian pulled himself up from the deep, murky levels of his subconscious, he opened his gritty eyes to a soft, flickering light—and instantly knew something was wrong. Something even more messed-up than before. Than the twisted nightmares that had been plaguing him for weeks.

There was no forest…no gypsy campfire…no sloe-eyed provocative brunette to slake his lust.

Instead, Ian found himself kneeling on a soft, intricately woven Persian carpet, the air around him filled with the intoxicating scents of woman and wood smoke as a fire roared somewhere in a distant hearth, the heat of the flames warm against his naked body. And sprawled before him on her back, her pale thighs spread indecently wide, lay Molly.

"What?" he heard her gasp, surprise softening her husky voice, blurring the edges of her speech, as if she'd only just realized it was happening again. She'd probably been snuggled up in one of the lumpy motel beds, carrying on some warped conversation with his mother's ghost, only to suddenly find herself there, with him. Her gaze flicked its way down the pale line of her body, velvety brown eyes going wide with shock as she took in the unadulterated intimacy of their positions.

She moaned, and quickly covered herself with her arms.

Lust thickened in Ian's throat, choking off his ability for speech. He gripped her wrists, pulling her arms away from her body, pinning them at her sides. The red-and-black swirl of the rug accentuated the warm, luminous glow of her skin, while her honeyed scent grew stronger with the rise of her pulse. Atop the delicate swell of her breasts, her nipples hardened like tender berries, lush and beautiful and ripe. He wanted to draw them into the heat of his mouth, suck on them until she came undone. Wanted to run his lips across her fever-warm skin, so smooth and soft and delicious, and work his way down the mouthwatering length of her body.

"Ian?" she whispered, her voice hushed...shaky. "How?"

He shook his head, unable to pull his heavy gaze away from the provocative details of her figure, each exquisite discovery making him ache just a little harder, a little deeper. "I don't know."

"Where are we?" she asked, her breasts rising and

falling as the cadence of her breathing grew shorter and sharper.

"Don't care. Just don't move, don't cover yourself," he growled, a grittier edge to his voice than he'd ever heard before, graveled and rough. He released his hold on her wrists and shifted, rubbing himself against her, against those perfect breasts and the soft, slick folds nestled between her splayed thighs, her sex so tender and wet he damn near lost it then and there. There were so many things he wanted to do to her, to *take* from her. Harsh, explicit intimacies that had no place between strangers—and yet, he'd have taken them if he had the time. Hell, he'd have given her more of himself than he'd ever given any other woman in his entire life— have lost himself in her, content to spend days on end exploring the sensual secrets of her body, drowning in the discoveries…in the breathtaking details.

But time was the one thing he didn't have.

He knew that with each harsh, erratic breath, the seconds he'd been granted with her were slipping away. Trying to grab hold of them would be like struggling to trap rushing water within his hand. Pointless, futile, and a waste of his time.

The scene was just too perfect to last. At any moment, Ian expected to have it ripped out from under him, leaving him completely destroyed.

He only hoped he didn't crash and burn when it happened—when he lost her.

Pointless apologies for being such a jackass jammed painfully in his throat, leaving a bitter taste in his mouth. He choked them back as he caught the hazy, burnished glow of her gaze, saying, "I want to go down on you. I want it so bad I can taste it, Molly. But I don't know how long this is going to last, and no way in hell am I missing the chance to fuck you again."

She didn't recoil at his crass honesty or try to roll away from him. She just lay there against the carpet, beautifully supplicant, arms bent, palms open either side of her flushed face, her hair a tangled fury of golden curls around the violent bloom of color in her cheeks. The luminous depths of her eyes pulled on him, dragging him deeper, as if he were falling into her, completely under her spell.

A log popped, crackling in the fireplace while an ominous bellow of thunder rumbled somewhere in the distance, the harsh pulse of the oncoming storm echoing the violent pounding of his heart. Taking her softly panting silence for consent, Ian pressed closer, wanting to cradle her hands within his own, to rub his thumbs into the humid cups and stroke her skin, but he fought the urge, afraid of where that closeness would take him. It was already scary enough, this wild, unknown emotional no-man's-land he kept finding himself in every time he got close to her.

Settling deeper between her spread thighs, Ian braced his weight on one elbow, then greedily opened his mouth over the succulent tip of her left breast, so hungry for her, he wanted to eat her alive. He rolled the exquisite, berry-red nipple against his tongue…and fit himself against her. Their gazes locked. Held for a single, smoldering instant. Then he lifted his head and drove his body into her with a thick, grinding motion, having to work at her as hard as he had the night before. Her eyes went wide, white teeth sinking into the pansy-soft cushion of her lower lip…and Ian shoved deeper.

Locking his jaw, he slowly pulled back his hips, the sensations so acute they bordered on that intense precipice of pleasure and pain. When he'd almost pulled completely out of her—his muscles tensed, skin sweat-slick and burning—he shoved back in, harder this time, somehow giving her more of him. His left hand came up to fist in the pale curls that haloed her head, holding her steady as he came down over her. Needing her taste, he claimed her mouth in an urgent, eating kiss, savoring her throaty moans against his tongue like a breathless stream of promises. Wrapping his other hand around her hip, his fingers biting into her flesh, he powered himself into her as if his life depended on it. Each heavy, possessive thrust fed a part of his soul that was greedy for every part of her, as if he could break her open and claim the pieces for his own.

"Look at the reflection," he commanded against her lips in a dark, husky whisper, sharing her breath, her nipples hard against his chest, dragging against his skin as he moved over her, inside of her.

She panted, shaking her head.

"Look at the goddamn reflection, Molly."

His fingers tightened in her hair, turning her head for her, and she stared at the explicit image emblazoned upon the wall of windows that took up an entire side of the room.

"I bet you've never had that particular look on your face before," he rasped with a low, wicked rumble of laughter. "Not Little-Miss-Molly-Do-Right. You're too shy. Too buttoned-up. Except with me. You know how hot that makes me?"

She shook her head again, gasping, and he said, "I get off on knowing that I'm the only man who can crack that cool, pristine surface of yours and make you go wild. Make you scream and claw at me, completely out of control."

And it was true. At the moment, her small nails were dug into his biceps so hard, he knew crescent marks would be left behind on his skin, a testament of her passion.

Her eyes drifted closed as the intensity cranked higher, her body writhing, drawing closer…and closer to the edge, before she suddenly turned her face away from him. She was holding it back, denying her body what it wanted. Fighting it. Hiding from it. Hiding from him.

Grasping her chin, Ian pulled her back. "Eyes open, Molls. I want to see it happen. Want to watch your face when you go over."

"*No…*"

"Oh, yeah." The words were gritty and thick with lust, with pleasure. "Stop fighting it."

"You'll leave me again," she said quietly, her lashes lifting, revealing eyes that glistened with tears, the look in their mysterious depths making his breath catch, while something in his chest clenched with pain. In that moment, Ian had the strangest feeling that even though she was the one pinned to the floor, she held all the power, and there was nothing he could do to reclaim it.

Lowering his mouth to the moist hollow of her throat, he told her, "I won't. I won't leave you."

She drew in a deep, shivery breath, clutching his back, her hands cool against the scalding heat of his body, and broke with his next down stroke, the tight, rhythmic pulses of her orgasm pulling him in, holding him, refusing to let him go. His tongue flicked against the damp heat of her skin, wanting the salty sweetness of her flesh, needing it…craving it, and the next thing he knew, his fangs were buried deep in the side of her throat, near her shoulder. A sharp, hoarse scream pierced the air, the roar of his heartbeat deafening and fast in his ears, while the warm, heady spill of her blood filled his mouth, thick and hot and seductively rich. *This* was what he craved. This claiming of both her blood and her body. It was the one thing that satisfied that gnawing emptiness in his soul. The one thing that made him feel almost at peace, as if he was right where he belonged.

The thick pleasure slipped down his throat, his mouth working with greedy intent against her skin, needing more…and more, the hunger growing more insatiable than it had been before, suddenly frightening him with its power, its urgency. Ian fought himself for what seemed like endless, drugging moments. Wicked, decadent pleasure pulsed heavily in every cell of his body. Finally, he managed to rip himself away, terrified he would drown in that dark, destructive burn of gratification and drain her dry.

Can't… Can't lose her.

Ian screwed his eyes shut against the haunting beauty of her blood spilling gently from the puncture wounds, slipping across the translucent glow of her skin.

"Shit…*shit,*" he hissed, his fangs heavy within his gums, her taste exquisitely hot in his mouth, while his body slammed into her harder…faster. He wanted to run, to escape the uncomfortable knowledge sinking into his bones, but he kept his word, staying with her until the hot, blistering friction shoved him into his own raging explosion. He pulled free at the last second, erupting onto her pale stomach in hard, violent surges, the intensity of the orgasm all but destroying him, turning him inside out. He looked everywhere and nowhere—anywhere but at her face, in her eyes. He had no idea what'd he see there, and he was terrified of finding out.

"Ian," she said softly, her voice hitching with emotion. "Don't leave. Please. Not yet."

He ground his jaw, not knowing what to say, how to give her what she needed. Comfort. Warmth. Caring. Those things were as foreign to him as color to a blind man.

You have to give her something, jackass.

"Molly," he rasped, forcing himself to meet her gaze. "I…" He tried to choke out an apology, an explanation, the words somehow strangled inside of him, and she lifted her hand, cupping his cheek in her cool, soft palm.

"Shh, it's okay," she whispered, the look in her eyes so strangely tender, it scared the ever-loving hell out of him. "You don't have to say anything, Ian. Just hold me."

"Yeah. All right." The simple words came out alarmingly shaky, his eyes suspiciously hot, the strange buzz of emotions slamming through him as terrifying as they were unfamiliar. There was more than just a beast awakening within him. The very fabric of his being, his personality, was being shifted, altered, molded into something new beneath the power of her hands.

He loathed it as much as he hungered for more, for everything she could give him. The rational part of his mind wanted to retreat, to escape the gauzy web of emotional overload closing in around him like a suffocating fog, but he held firm, unwilling to leave before giving her this one thing. He owed it to her after she'd given of herself so freely, so beautifully.

"Come on," she teased, holding out her arms to him. "I promise I don't bite."

The corner of his mouth twitched with bitter humor, and he lowered himself over her, letting her take his weight, the delicious cushion of her body pressed against his own making him hiss, his fangs still heavy within his mouth, the exquisite taste of her blood lingering like a gift.

But it was her arms closing around him that undid him. That, and the way she suddenly smiled at him. Beautiful. Sweet. Shy and serene. So trusting, it blew his goddamn mind.

He should have known it was too good to last.

Her breath sucked in on a sharp gasp the second the dream began changing on him, the room melting away, like an acid trip gone bad. A blistering wind swept through the swaying pines, replacing the warmth of the fire, the carpet giving way to the fertile soil of the forest. The air was heavy, electric, the storm rolling in hard and fast.

"Ian!" Molly cried, her small nails digging into his arms, eyes huge within the startled expression of fear creeping over her face, the damp flush of satisfaction paling to ghostly white.

Ready to reassure her that everything was going to be okay, that he wouldn't hurt her…that he'd protect her, he opened his mouth, when something cried out in the distance, like a wolf's howl, but different. Harsher, thicker, grittier. Guttural and terrifying as hell.

"Fuck," he snarled, sweeping his gaze from side to side. The hairs on the back of his neck were standing up, his body tense, ready for battle. Something was out there. Something evil. Something hungry.

Hating the helpless feeling of inevitability creeping over him, slimy and cold and slick, Ian scrambled to his feet, spinning in a circle. Panic clawed its way beneath his skin, digging painfully deep, shredding his confidence. "Go!" he barked at Molly, when she stumbled to her feet. Her pale body gleamed like a pearl beneath the ethereal streams of lavender moonlight, and it terrified him, how delicate and fragile she was. "Get the hell out of here!" he roared, knowing they were running out of time…that every moment she stayed with him put her life in danger.

Whatever was out there, it was closing in. Fast. And it wanted him.

She shook her head, chin lifting, and then her eyes suddenly went huge as she looked over his shoulder. He braced himself for the blow before it came, survival instincts surging into focus. Something heavy and thick slammed into him, taking him to the ground, knocking the air from his lungs at the same time Molly let out a bloodcurdling scream of terror.

"She's going to scream like that when I fuck her stupid little brains out, just like that other useless bitch," a grizzled voice rasped in his ear, the heavy weight of it pinning him to the ground, and Ian felt the stirring of that thing inside of him. Felt its growl breaking out of his chest, bleeding out in a feral sound of outrage and fury as the darkness rose beneath the fevered surface of his skin.

"*Casus*," he snarled, the word surging up from the depths of his subconscious without any direction from his brain.

"Come on, Merrick," it whispered huskily in his ear, the rank, meaty stench of its breath filling his nose, sliding down his throat, gagging him. "Give me a run for my money."

And in the next instant, Ian awakened.

CHAPTER SIX

WITH A STRANGLED GASP, Ian opened his eyes, blinking against the shifting shadows of his living room, the low buzz from the TV drowned out by the hammering beat of his heart, the colors from the screen painting the room in a hazy, psychedelic glow. "Christ," he hissed, scrubbing his hands down his face, struggling to get his breathing under control, his body slick with sweat, chest so tight that for a moment he almost believed he was having a heart attack.

But then a strange, fertile scent hit his nose, and he pulled his hands away from his face, squinting at the dark smear of dirt on his palms.

What the hell?

Suspicions mounting, he started to roll up into a sitting position when a cramp hit his gut, vicious and sharp, doubling him over. His lips pulled back over his teeth, body curling into a fetal position there on the sweat-damp sofa, muscles tensing as spasm after torturous spasm coiled through him, contorting him like a seizure. It felt like something inside of him was trying to force its way out, punching against his insides.

A raw, graveled cry of pain ripped out of his chest, and he struggled to hold himself together, afraid to let go and surrender to the thing inside that was doing everything it could to tear its way through, struggling to take control of his body. It scared the shit out of him, the possibility of what he might become, the things he might do, if the darkness battled its way to the surface.

Cursing, Ian twisted as another violent spasm shot through him, fiery and hot and painful, and the silver casing of his cell phone lying on the coffee table flashed at the corner of his eye. *Riley!* That was it. He needed to call his brother. Needed him there. God only knew what would happen if he couldn't hold it in, couldn't keep it together. Horrific images from the scene of Kendra's murder flashed through his mind, ripping through the landscape of his terror like a scythe, thrashing and destructive. Gritting his teeth, he lunged for the phone, reaching out with his right hand, shouting when he saw that the tips of his fingers were bleeding. Razor-sharp talons slowly pierced through his callused fingertips, the bones in his hand expanding, musculature thickening, exactly the way it had in his nightmares. With horrified eyes, he watched as the blood ran down the back of his hand, over the heavy veins pumping beneath his skin, down his thick wrist, matting in the hairs on his arm.

Christ, he was turning into a goddamn, son of a bitching monster!

No. Not monster. Merrick.

No sooner had Ian thought the word, than his last dream came rushing back at him, and he remembered what the creature had said. Remembered its threat against Molly. And if he'd been able to slip into a dream with her again, fucking her, feeding from her, then she was probably still in Henning. Still close. And in a shit-load of danger.

"He's going after her," he gasped, panting, seething…knowing only that he had to get to her first.

He lifted his head, his lip curling as a low, aggressive snarl broke from his throat. The next thing Ian knew, he was rushing from the apartment, out into the unusually humid night, the air close and damp against his skin, a faint scent of electricity in the air. Thunder rumbled in the distance as a violent summer storm rolled its way in, eerily reminiscent of the dream with Molly. Vaulting over the banister of the second-story walkway, he landed in a low crouch on the warm asphalt of the apartment parking lot, knees bent, one hand flat against the ground between his legs for balance. The gritty tarmac was damp against the bare soles of his feet, the thick shadows of the night mysteriously brightened with a faint, luminous glow. The rational part of his brain knew that he shouldn't be able to see so clearly, just as it knew that the leap from the second story should have injured him, but he sprang into motion. His body felt more alive, more powerful than ever before, the adrenaline pumping through his system as addictive as it was empowering.

Speeding across the empty street, Ian raced toward the thick, looming rise of trees, hurtling himself into the thicket of the forest, knowing it was the quickest way to reach Molly. Branches scratched at his arms and face, but he didn't let it slow him down. The heavy muscles in his thighs powered him forward, just as they had in his dreams, where he was running toward the heat of the gypsy campfire. Lightning crackled like the earsplitting blast of a shotgun, echoing through the forest, while he raced through the dense woods, somehow managing to see with only a silvery thread of moonlight to guide him, as if it were merely the beginnings of dusk and not the dead of night.

He'd already covered a good half mile with amazing speed, when a stark, familiar cry pierced the air, coming from up ahead. He stopped running, slowing to a halt beneath the milky weight of the moon, the night closing in around him like a curious swarm of specters, slithering against his skin, slinking around the backs of his ears…across his nape. Pulling back his shoulders, aware that the thing inside of him wanted to respond to that bestial howl, wanted to claw its way to the surface and battle the enemy itself, he waited. Knowing it was on its way. Tilting back his head, Ian pulled in its rank stench with senses more powerful than they should have been, sharp and precise, revealing the pulse of the forest to the predator that lurked within him.

Electricity flashed across the ink-black sky with the fury of an explosion as the first drops of rain began to fall. It soaked into his shirt, wetting his hair, running over his face and arms in cold, wet trails, and still he stood there, waiting, unmoving. And then finally, he saw it, stalking out from between two gnarled pines. Terror settled heavily into his gut. In that moment, the helplessness of childhood fears wrapped him in a cold, suffocating hold, just as they had when he was a kid, waking at night to the creaking of the old house he'd grown up in. He'd always been certain there was a monster hiding in his closet, and too afraid to confront his demons, he'd spent restless hours huddled beneath his covers, shaking with terror.

Pathetic, that at the age of thirty-two, after everything he'd been through, he could be so easily transported back to that time. That after all the hard years of rough, desperate living—of trying to hide from what he'd always feared was inside of him—it'd all caught up to him in the end.

"I can smell your fear, Merrick," it growled, stalking closer, the rain slipping off its furless body in a silvery stream, giving a slimy cast to the grayish skin beneath, when Ian knew, from his dream, that it was actually dry to the touch. The physical details of the creature perfectly matched the ones from his nightmare. Ridged spine topped by broad, hunched shoulders. Thick muzzle and long, curving claws. Wolflike head, with a tall body covered in leathery, pale gray skin. At nearly seven feet in height and packed with dense, powerful muscle, it lived up to every expectation of evil he'd ever had, complete with piercing, ice-blue eyes.

His heart clenched at the thought of Kendra, knowing how terrified she must have been during the minutes she'd spent with this monster, before she finally drew her last breath.

"I'm surprised you have the balls to face me," it rasped in a gritty, demonic drawl, the garbled words distorted by the muzzled shape of its mouth. "Especially after seeing what I did to sweet little Kendra."

Choking back a low growl of outrage, Ian set his feet and braced himself against the inevitable attack he knew was coming, the razor-sharp talons piercing his fingertips his only weapon—and one he planned on using. He wasn't going to give the bastard the satisfaction of chasing him down. Even if it ripped him to pieces, he was at least going to die holding his ground.

Lightning cracked again, striking a nearby tree, and the Casus leaped into the air at the same instant, kicking out at him with both feet, the powerful blow connecting with Ian's chest and knocking him backward. The air burst from his lungs as the jarring, dizzying strike slammed him into the rain-soaked ground, the pine needles beneath his back in no way cushioning the impact when the beast landed on top of him, pinning him with its crushing weight. It immediately went for his throat, jaws gaping, saliva dripping from those long, lethal fangs set within pale pink gums.

Determined to fight as dirty as he needed to, Ian lifted one knee, slamming it into the bastard's balls, at the same time he reached for its eyes, ready to sink his talons deep. But it reared back, snarling, and Ian was able to lift his right leg enough to kick at its head, knocking it off balance. He rolled across the soggy ground, quickly scrambling to his feet, its claws slashing across his left bicep as it came at him in a blur of preternatural strength and speed. He fought with everything he had, but it wasn't enough. It was too strong, too powerful, weathering his blows with little effort.

He was only holding it at bay, prolonging the inevitable, unable to inflict as much damage as it delivered with ridiculous ease, another swift claw strike catching him along his ribs, down his right-hand side. Ian knew, instinctively, that the only way he could hold his own was to release the thing inside of him. Desperate to confront the Casus on its own, it punched against his resistance with enough force to leave him feeling as battered within as he felt without. But he couldn't do it, too afraid of what he would become…of what he might do if he gave in.

The sky rumbled, the rain coming down in a driving sheet as the creature came at him in another swift flurry of blows that he struggled to deflect, barely avoiding the long, lethal slash of its claws as they swung toward his throat. Suddenly throwing its weight against him, it slammed him into the rough trunk of a thick pine. Chuffing its foul breath in his face, it leaned forward, going nose to nose with him, his own mysteriously glowing eyes reflected back at him in the clear black depths of its dilated pupils.

"You're not wearing the talisman," it muttered, lowering that ice-blue gaze to his throat, as if looking for something. Ian struggled against its hold, and its gaze lifted as a slow, syrupy smile spread across the grotesque horror of its mouth. "You know, the brunette bitch called to you for help. When I was buried deep inside her, she cried and begged for you…but you weren't there."

"You son of a bitch," he snarled, rage engulfing him in a black, murderous wave that seeped through his pores, coating his insides. Ian tried to shove against its shoulders, but its skin was too slippery and smooth, the rain-slick surface impossible to hold.

"Wonder if your new little blond will beg for you the same way? Pathetic, when you think about it. How can you be expected to save them, when you can't even save yourself?"

"You won't fucking touch her!" he roared, struggling to break free as it pinned his shoulders to the trunk.

"Oh, yeah, and who's going to stop me? You?" It threw back its head and laughed, closing one claw-tipped hand around his throat, a fraction away from cutting off his air. "Please. The second I decide she dies, she dies. It's as simple as that. She'll bleed out, screaming for you, and there's nothing you can do to stop it."

Ian drew in a short, shuddering breath, clawing at its wrist, while a red haze clouded his vision. It was building inside of him, a vile, vicious fury unlike anything he'd ever known, surging up from the darkest, deadliest depths of his soul. He could feel it rushing up through him, gaining speed, gaining power. This time, instead of fighting it, he went with it, releasing the air from his lungs just as he felt the moment of transformation drawing nearer…almost there.

With a deep, guttural growl vibrating under his breath, he eyed the silvery stretch of the bastard's throat, his tongue curling around the deadly point of one elongating incisor as his fangs slipped free. He could already taste the kill, his blood surging at the thought of tearing out that exposed flesh, the darkness inside of him rising so close to the surface he could feel it stretching beneath his skin.

But before he could strike, the Casus suddenly stepped away from him, releasing its hold. Its massive head tilted back, the rain splattering across its hideous face, nostrils flared as it sniffed once…twice. The black smear of its upper lip pulled back in a snarl, the sadistic rumbling of sound surging up from the depths of its chest.

It looked back toward Ian, and shook its monstrous head, a garbled laugh that made his skin crawl slipping through the muzzled snout. "You won't be so lucky next time, Merrick," it rasped, and then with a slow, taunting smile, it turned and disappeared into the thick sheets of rain drowning out the midnight sky.

CHAPTER SEVEN

Sunday, 1:00 a.m.

ON THE EDGE OF COLLAPSE, Ian pushed himself to keep moving through the storm-ravaged forest, determined to reach his destination before he gave in to the overpowering wave of fatigue. The moment the creature had retreated, Ian's deadly talons had receded back into his fingertips with an intense burst of pain; muscles, teeth and bones also returning to normal, to the way they'd been before he'd awakened from the dream. But with their loss came a devastating state of exhaustion, the wounds from the Casus's claws searing like liquid fire beneath the lashing fury of the storm. It seemed to take forever, each step costing him more than the last, but he finally stumbled out of the woods. Squinting through the driving rain, Ian found himself on the outskirts of town, the weatherworn building looming before him none other than the run-down facade of the Pine Motel.

For better or worse, he'd made it to Molly.

After the confrontation with the Casus, he knew he should have gone anywhere but there. If it was following him, he'd just led it right to her, and yet, he had to warn her about the threat it had made. Had to make sure she was all right. Had to make sure it hadn't already made a move against her.

And you want to be near her. Want her comfort. Her touch. Want to be close enough to protect her.

Cursing under his breath at the irritating voice in his head, he crossed the empty highway. The smell of the asphalt seemed sharper than usual, the thick scents of gasoline and tire rubber filling his nose, making him dizzy. He wove his way across the parking lot, left hand pressed against his injured side, staunching the flow of blood from the cuts that striped his flesh. Moments later, he stood at the motel-room door that had Molly's rental parked in front of it. A soft, yellow light glowed behind the faded curtain.

Lifting one battered fist, Ian knocked on the door, its green paint peeling away to reveal the brittle wood beneath. He didn't know what he planned to say when she opened up…if she even bothered to open it for him.

You were right, there's some bloodthirsty monster living inside of me and another one tried to chew my head off.

Help me before I bleed out.

Why did my mother have to send you?

The words turned themselves around and around within the chaotic frenzy of pain and fury grinding him down, but in the end, he didn't say a goddamn thing.

Instead, the instant she opened the door, her golden hair pulled back in a sloppy ponytail, pale face pinched with worry, he was on her, against her. His mouth took full, aggressive possession of her own. His much larger body covering her front, hands gripping her arms, lifting her off the floor. All it'd taken was seeing her…scenting her, and his injuries and fatigue were forgotten, his body coming alive, revving into overdrive. There was no other word for it. Heart pumping. Adrenaline surging. Chest heaving.

She made a startled murmur of surprise in the back of her throat, the soft, sexy sound vibrating against his tongue, driving him wild. Ian answered it with a primitive growl, at the same time he pushed her into the room, slamming the door shut behind him. He broke away only long enough to throw the lock, and then he was on her again, pushing her against the nearest wall and covering her with every part of him that he could. His cold hands lifted to cup the tender heat of her jaw, thumbs tilting up the dainty point of her chin as he captured her mouth in another long, breathtaking, eating kiss, tasting…feasting on every part of her, from the pansy-soft inner swell of that lush lower lip, to the sleek surface of her teeth, the kittenish stroke of her tongue.

Spearing his fingers into the silken warmth of her hair, he pulled it free of the elastic band, thinking she was too good to be true, to be real. She tasted like sunshine, like something that he needed to live, to counter the seething darkness inside of him, softening that bloodthirsty rage with warm, gentle pulses of light. Ian kissed her harder…deeper. Wanting to just crawl inside of her. His desperation—this gnashing, maddening need—knew no bounds, no logic, no restraint, his body suddenly searing with fever, skin burning so violently, he half expected to see steam rising from the cold chill of his rain-soaked clothes.

He'd gotten the hazy impression of a long, sleep-rumpled shirt before he'd shot the bolt, her legs slim and bare beneath the frayed hem. With biting urgency, Ian slipped his hands down her sides, over the gentle outer swells of her breasts, her rib cage, over the feminine flare of her hips, until he was grazing the trembling, baby-soft length of her thighs. Slipping beneath the hem of the shirt, he worked his way back up, taking the threadbare cotton with him, his mouth keeping hers too busy to protest, not that she would have. No, she was kissing him back now, her small, sweet mouth moving under his, trembling and delicious, like something warm and wild and decadent, meant to be devoured with the first taste, then savored for hours on end. Delicate, slender fingers bit into his shoulders, her body vibrating against his with a high, sexual frequency of need that damn near matched his own.

With another feral growl rumbling deep in his chest, Ian shifted his right hand, stroking her stomach with the backs of his fingers, and his breath caught at what he found there. Her soft, supple skin was slightly sticky to the touch, and he knew the cause. The source. Cursing under his breath, he broke away from the kiss, reality slowly intruding through the crazed fog of lust as he wondered what other souvenirs she carried from their dream. With his fingers on her chin, he tilted her head to the side, staring at two fading puncture wounds—as well as two fresh ones, lower on her throat, near her shoulder.

Taking a step back, Ian ran his gaze over her body, twisting the now-damp shirt around his fist and wrenching it to the side, exposing her hips, lower belly and thighs, as well as a minuscule pair of pink cotton panties. Faint smudges marked one hip, and he knew they had formed there when he'd gripped her too tightly. He stroked the developing bruises with his fingertip, making her breath draw in on a sharp gasp. "Did I do this?" he rasped, his voice thick with lust and a surprising thread of regret.

She blinked up at him, looking as if she might cry, the shadows under her eyes only accentuating the impact of that softly glowing gaze. "It's okay, Ian. They don't hurt." She gave a dainty sniff, swiping her fingers under her eyes, long lashes glistening with tears. "When I woke up, I was so terrified that something had happened to you. I wanted to go to your apartment again, but after the dream, I didn't know if that thing was out there."

"It's okay," he rasped, the words coming out shivery and raw as he skimmed his fingertips across the gentle, feminine swell of her belly, unable to believe how soft her skin was, how smooth. Hardening his jaw, he stroked one fingertip along the top edge of the panties, and she stopped breathing, knees shaking, barely holding her up. Unable to stop himself, Ian slipped his fingers just under the elastic. "I'm here, Molls. I'm not going anywhere."

She moaned, tilting back her head, her eyes hazy and soft and heavy in the ethereal glow of light spilling from a bedside lamp on the other side of the small room, the slashing of the rain against the window providing a steady backdrop of sound to the harsh, provocative rhythm of their breath. She looked like some kind of wood-nymph stolen from the forest, curls wild around her fey face; mouth red, swollen, impossibly beautiful;

cheeks flushed with a wild, vivid bloom of color. He wanted her so badly it was a physical ache, more painful than the stinging wounds striping his flesh.

"If you want me to stop, you'd better tell me now." The words scraped past his lips, graveled and rough with hunger.

Her lashes lowered, and Ian held his breath, his lungs burning, waiting for her answer.

"I'm sorry," she finally whispered, rolling her lips together. "But I...I can't do this, Ian."

He forced himself to step back, putting distance between them, until the backs of his knees hit one of the beds and forced him to sit down. As if she didn't realize the danger—the temptation she posed—she followed after him, drawing closer until she stood between his legs, her fingers in the damp strands of his hair. Ian placed his hands low on her hips, grasping handfuls of the shirt, and pressed his forehead against the cushion of her breasts. He loved how soft she was. Slender, but not bony. Just endlessly female and tender. Her mouth-watering scent filled his head, making him clench his teeth against the visceral urge to lift the threadbare T-shirt and put his nose to her pale curls, breathing in headier gulps of that warm, womanly fragrance that did crazy things to him.

Looking up at her face, capturing that burnished gaze and claiming it, he couldn't help but ask, "Are you sure about that?"

Her mouth twisted with regret, at the same time her skin flushed brighter with desire. "I have a rule about... That is, I don't get involved with men who I meet this way."

There was a story there—one he didn't want to hear. Not now, when he was too on edge. He knew he could bend her to his will, use her desire against her, and change her mind. But she'd hate him for manipulating her when it was over—and he was already working with a big enough deficit when it came to the personality department. God only knew he didn't need to dig himself any deeper.

Still, he wasn't giving in without an argument. "You didn't have a problem with me touching you before," he rasped, holding her with his stare.

Her cheeks burned brighter, lashes shielding her gaze. "That was a dream," she whispered. "It wasn't real."

Ian eyed her throat with a meaningful glance and lifted his brows. But he didn't argue. Reason, though slow, was finally returning, and with it an uneasiness, a mounting fear, that he couldn't ignore.

Face it, Buchanan. You pose as much of a threat to her safety as that murdering-asshole-monster, his conscience snarled, pissing him off.

His sudden anger must have bled into his expression, because she shivered, her gaze sliding away, shifting lower, and she gasped. One slender hand moved to his arm, hovering over the claw marks slashing his left bicep, the angry slices mottled with drying blood. "Those need to be cleaned," she whispered.

Ian rolled his shoulder, trying to dispel the sexual hunger still riding him hard. He cleared his throat, and there was a gruff, frustrated edge to his voice as he said, "They're not serious. Bled a lot at first, but they're about done."

Her gaze lifted back to his. "You need to tell me what happened, but right now it's more important that we get you cleaned up. The hot water doesn't last long in this place, but there should be enough for you to take a shower. Then I'll get something on these cuts."

"I'd argue about you managing me," he replied in a low rumble, the corner of his mouth twitching with a reluctant grin, his hands still clutching her hips, "but I'm too tired."

Her slender brows lifted in challenge. "Good, because I'd win."

Ian studied her for a moment, recognizing an inner core of steely, stubborn strength that he wouldn't have expected from her, though he supposed he should have, considering she'd stood up to him from the moment they'd met—even faced him down after that first dream. And she was still here—proof that he hadn't been able to intimidate her into leaving town. Shaking his head, his grin slowly shifted into a wry smile. "Yeah, I have a feeling you would. So I'll be a good boy and do as I'm told."

Reaching for the hem of his tattered shirt, he winced when the cuts on his side pulled with the movement. "Here," she said, brushing his hands aside and taking over the task, "let me help you get this off."

"Thanks," he groaned, his voice muffled beneath the wet shirt that covered his face.

The moment it cleared his head, he saw that her eyes had darkened with concern, that lambent gaze focused on the claw marks cutting across his ribs. "God, it really got you."

Ian snorted, looking forward to that hot shower, needing it to relieve the stiffness in his muscles that he suspected came more from the fight he'd put up against the darkness…against the beast inside of him, than the one he'd had with the Casus. "I was lucky it didn't take my head off."

Concern sharpened her gaze. "That bad?"

"Yeah," he muttered, the exhaustion crowding in on him again, weighing heavily around his shoulders like a yoke. "And it's still out there somewhere, so I don't suppose I have to tell you not to go near the window or door without me."

"I know. And if I hear anything, I'll knock on the bathroom door and let you know." Stepping back, she gestured toward the small kitchenette attached through a narrow archway. "I have a first-aid kit that I always carry when I travel. I'll set it up in there while you shower."

"Thanks." He reached out to grab her wrist when she started to move away, and before he could stop himself, Ian heard himself saying, "Which one did you like better?"

She shook her head, silken curls grazing her shoulder. "What do you mean? Which one what?"

"The dreams?" he pressed in a low, husky voice. "Which one was better?"

MOLLY TOOK A QUICK, inaudible breath, and his gaze slipped from her eyes, to the base of her throat, where her pulse fluttered to a wild, chaotic beat. "What kind of question is that?" she whispered.

"Do you always answer questions with a question?" he asked, arching one ink-black brow.

She tore her gaze away from his, focusing on a distant point against the faded, pale green walls. "Neither one was particularly likable."

"Ouch." With a gruff chuckle, Ian rubbed at his chest with his free hand, acting as if he'd been wounded. "This night's proving hell on my ego."

Her gaze shot back to his, her tone sharp with frustration as she said, "You know I don't mean it like that. It has nothing to do with you. With what happened between us. I was just too frightened in both to—"

"Bullshit," he suddenly grated, narrowing his eyes, and for the first time since she'd opened the door to him, she saw that dark vein of bitterness that was so much a part of him rise to the surface. "Maybe in the second one, yeah, after we ended up in the woods. But you weren't afraid in the beginning, when you were under me, in that room. And you weren't afraid in the first dream, either."

"How do you know?" she demanded, the heat in her face so intense, she knew she probably looked sunburned.

Molly didn't think he was going to answer, until he hardened his jaw and gave her two simple, husky words. "The smiles."

Her voice was stuck in her throat as he let go of her wrist and rolled to his feet. "You smiled at me. Both times." A gritty edge roughened his words—one that sounded suspiciously like…she couldn't quite put her finger on it. Not embarrassment. She doubted anything could ever embarrass a man like Ian Buchanan. No, it was more vulnerable than that…almost breakable.

She watched him shake it off, his cocky arrogance rising back to the fore. His mouth curled with a boyish grin, a devilish dimple flashing in his shadowed cheek that made him look younger. Less harsh. "At least that second dream answered one question."

There was a soft catch to her voice as she said, "I'm almost afraid to ask."

He reached out, tweaking the end of her nose in a playful gesture completely at odds with the hard-edged hunger still lingering in those raging blue eyes. "I definitely didn't imagine how good you felt the first time, Molls. Because this time, you felt even better."

Molly swallowed, unsure of how to respond. *Thank you? My pleasure? How can you be the same man who ordered me to stay the hell away from you not twenty-four hours ago?* Her indecision didn't matter, because in the end, all she could manage was a breathless, red-faced silence.

Cupping her jaw, he stroked his thumb against the corner of her mouth once…twice, his gaze focused with sharp intensity on her trembling lips, their surface extra sensitive after that incendiary kiss. "I'll go grab that shower now."

Swallowing the shaky feeling in her throat, Molly watched his backside as he walked away, thinking it was entirely unfair for a guy to look that gorgeous from the front *and* back. It was the first time she'd ever seen him from behind when he wasn't shrouded in shadows, and she couldn't help but admire the view. The wet jeans were streaked with dirt, but they still hugged his muscled backside to perfection, as well as his powerful thighs.

Her gaze traveled higher, over the sleek, stunning beauty of his back, the deep furrows of muscle that lined his spine, higher, lifting to his broad shoulders, and she suddenly gasped, unable to believe what she was seeing. Shock slammed through her with whipcord strength the instant she spotted the dark, intricate tattoo between his shoulder blades. She didn't know why the image affected her so strongly—she only knew that she felt its power like a physical touch thrumming against her senses, intimate and deep. It was uniquely beautiful. A thick cross, like a Maltese, with four equal arms, the surface covered in what looked like tiny, intricate symbols.

"Ian," she whispered, her voice soft with amazement.

He slanted a curious look over his shoulder from the bathroom doorway. "Yeah?"

Heat crept up into her face like mercury rising in a thermometer, setting her on fire, leaving her breathless and flushed. "Where did you get that tattoo?"

A strange expression crossed his face, those deep blue eyes darkened by shadows. "The tattoo? In L.A."

"No, I mean, the design. Where did it come from?"

He held her stare for a moment, then muttered, "No idea," and walked into the bathroom, shutting the bathroom door behind him.

Dropping down onto the edge of the nearest mattress, Molly stared into blank space, unable to process such a strange, unsettling sense of premonition. That design *meant* something. She was sure of it. She just didn't know *what*. The answer hovered just beyond her reach, like smoke that kept slipping through her fingers when she tried to grasp hold of it. She didn't think she'd ever seen a cross like that anywhere before, though it might have been in one of the collector's books at The Paper Mill. She'd been working at the bookstore for several years now, and often spent her breaks in the paranormal section, looking through the thick, leather-bound texts. Had she seen the tattoo in one of the pricey tomes? Was it from a dream? Her imagination?

Or was she simply out of her mind...as crazy as the gorgeous bulk of studliness using her shower thought she was?

Groaning under her breath, Molly leaned forward, braced her elbows on her knees and dropped her head into her hands.

Even after what he'd been through tonight, even after the strange shared dreams, the bite marks, the horrifying monsters—even after all that, she still didn't know if Ian believed her about the voices. If he believed his mother really spoke to her from beyond—believed she could truly hear the dead.

Why do you even care? her inner voice of reason whispered. *It doesn't matter what Ian Buchanan thinks of you, so long as you do what you came here to do. So long as you see it through to the end. You have no business getting involved with him. Didn't you learn your lesson the first time?*

Lifting her head, Molly narrowed her eyes, thinking that she really hated that damn little voice, no matter how right it was.

And it *was* right. There was a reason for the old saying *What we want isn't always what we need.* The adage certainly proved true when applied to her. She might have wanted Ian Buchanan with more intensity than she'd ever wanted anything in her entire life—but he was the last thing in the world she needed. Rude, crude and ruthless. Hard and distrustful. Sneering and snide, when the mood suited him, able to bruise her with nothing more than his blunt way of saying things. Molly had no doubt that he would take her beneath his heel and grind her into dust when he was through with her, if she wasn't careful.

Wadding up the ruined shirt, she moved to throw it in the wastebasket, listening to the running of the shower while taking a moment to collect herself. She was still rattled, not only by the dream and that beautiful, compelling tattoo, but also by the kiss he'd laid on her when she'd opened her door.

He'd kissed her as if he was starved for her, and need had exploded through her system like a cataclysmic event, while he'd explored her mouth with a raw intimacy that made kissing feel like something so much more. Wicked and wet—like the actual act of intercourse, of sex itself.

She'd been kissed. And she'd lost her virginity years ago, before she'd decided to give up on the idea of a healthy, happy relationship with a man who could accept her as she was, crazy voices and all. But what Ian had done to her mouth was more intimate than anything any other man had ever done to her body. He'd possessed it, *possessed her,* his hands rough and shaking as they'd clutched at her jaw, and then her body, his taste as wickedly delicious as in her dreams, hot and rich and impossibly male.

Amazing, to think that after the shocking intimacy they'd shared the past two nights, that kiss was the first time his mouth had actually touched hers.

The shower stopped, and a moment later, Ian opened

the door, steam billowing out around him, a white towel wrapped around his lean waist, powerful arms crossed over the muscled width of his chest. The rugged angles and hollows of his face seemed more pronounced, accentuating his masculine perfection, storm-blue eyes even darker beneath those thick black lashes. For a moment Molly was speechless, her tongue stuck to the roof of her mouth. She'd seen him undressed in the dreams they'd shared. Had felt his body covering her, penetrating her. But she was still unprepared for the incredible beauty of his dark, powerful physique.

Her heartbeat fluttered like a flock of startled birds, the moment stretching out endless and long as they stared at one another across the distance of the shabby motel room. Outside, the storm continued to rage, violent and vicious and loud, and then he finally said, "As impossible as this all seems, I really don't have a choice anymore. I wish like hell that you weren't involved, but I guess I'm ready to believe you."

CHAPTER EIGHT

"YOU BELIEVE ME about Elaina?" Molly whispered, staring at him as if she'd never before set eyes on a man wearing nothing but a towel. "About your mother? The things she's told me?"

Ian glanced down at the raw slices slashing across his rib cage and snorted. "Yeah, I believe you. You know, when my mother started talking about how the Merrick were still alive, she'd always say that one was right under my nose. That when the darkness called, I'd find him. Guess I should've listened to her."

"Well, the important thing is that you're listening now," she murmured with obvious relief, before heading toward one of the suitcases stored in the corner of the room. "We can talk while I get those cuts cleaned. You don't want to risk getting them infected."

"You're not going to ask why I came here? Why I came to you?" he questioned, watching as she pulled out her first-aid kit.

She didn't look at him as they moved into the shabby kitchenette, as if purposely avoiding his mostly naked body, her intense stare focused on the supplies she was setting out over the small table. "I heard what it said about Kendra in your dream. Heard it threaten to go after me, as well. I imagine you came here to make sure I was all right." Gesturing toward one of the rickety chairs, she said in a soft voice, "You can tell me what happened while I work."

Sitting down in the chair, Ian tucked the towel between his legs and leaned back, feeling remarkably well, considering the events of the night. The hot shower had helped, but more than that, it was the woman. There was just something about her— something he'd noticed when they first met. Something that eased the tension he'd carried inside for so long, calming him, at the same time she made him feel insatiable and out of control, ready to fight to protect her, defending her to the death. Odd, unsettling sentiments for a man who had always prided himself on detachment—on never caring about anyone but himself.

Releasing a rough breath, he ran his fingers through his wet hair, slicking it back from his face. He'd have given a limb for a cigarette at that moment, but he'd left his pack back at his apartment and he knew from the taste of her mouth that she didn't smoke. "When I woke up from the dream," he told her, getting on with his explanation, "I knew something was wrong. I could feel… Hell, I don't know how to explain it. It was like there was this thing inside of me, and it wanted out. And unlike the nightmares I've been having, it was damn painful."

Her brow knitted with concern. "It hurt?"

"Like a bitch," he sighed, watching as she went to the sink and washed her hands, then came back to the table and opened an alcohol swab.

"You fought the change, didn't you?"

"Yeah," he muttered, grimacing at the first touch of the medicated swab against the deepest of the cuts on his arm.

"Maybe that's what accounted for the pain."

He grunted and drew in a deep breath that smelled of Molly and the lemon hand soap she'd used to wash her hands. "Maybe."

Ripping open a fresh swab, she asked, "What happened then?"

"I remembered that it'd threatened you in the dream, and the next thing I knew, I was running out into the night, into the forest. I ran through the woods like a friggin' madman, until I heard it. I stopped, and it was there. Waiting for me. Calling me. Who the hell knows?"

Her hand stilled, the expression in her eyes hidden beneath the thick fringe of her lashes. "Was it… Did it look the same as in the dream?"

"Oh, yeah." His mouth twisted with a bitter smile. "Scared the ever-loving hell outta me."

Working her way down the shallow wounds, she paid meticulous attention to her task as she said, "And yet you fought against it, faced it down. You didn't run like most people would have."

His head tilted a fraction to the side as he studied her, wanting to reach out and hook the fall of her hair behind her ear, just so that he could watch the shifting angles of her expression. Maybe then he'd be able to understand her. Get a read on her motivation, since it was clear by now that this wasn't a con. He wanted to find out what made her tick—made her willing to risk her life by coming there and delivering her strange little messages from beyond, though it was still hard to get his head around the idea that she talked with his mother's ghost. "How do you know I didn't run?"

Pausing, she gave him a quick, soft smile that melted something in the center of his chest, making it burn with a slow, sweet fire. "I just know. No matter the odds, I can't ever see you just giving in without a fight."

Ian rolled his shoulder, aware of an odd heat climbing up the back of his neck. "Yeah, well, it did a pretty good job of kicking my ass."

"So you didn't change then, either?" she asked, carefully rubbing a slick antiseptic ointment over his bicep, her fingers cool against the heat of his skin. "Not even when you fought it?"

"Something happened," he grunted, working his jaw as the cold salve seeped into the wound. "It threatened you again, told me it was coming after you, and after that, I was pissed enough to let that thing…to let whatever the hell's inside of me have a go at it. But then it seemed to pick up on something else in the woods."

Frowning, she met his stare. "Like what?"

Ian shrugged. "No idea. Maybe it was an animal. Bear. Mountain lion. Whatever it was, it scared the bastard off."

"And then you came here." The words were hushed, almost solemn.

"Yeah. I…" His voice trailed off as she placed one hand low on his side, holding herself steady while switching her attention to the ugly cuts on his rib cage. Ian noticed that her fingertips were now smeared with his blood, and the jarring intimacy of that strange, unsettling sight slammed into him like a physical blow. "You don't have to worry about that," he murmured under his breath, jerking his chin toward her fingers. "I've been tested."

Her hand stilled, and then she resumed her task with a gentle touch, hiding behind the fall of her hair again. "Thanks," she whispered. "With everything that's been going on, I wasn't even thinking about that."

Ian grasped her wrist, waiting patiently for her to look him in the eye. When she did, he asked, "What about you?"

She ran her tongue over the sleek swell of her lower lip. "What about me?"

"Been tested?" he drawled in a quiet, husky rasp, as her gaze grew deeper, making him feel as if he could fall into those warm brown depths and find her soul.

She arched one slender brow in a cynical lift and pulled free of his hold. "That's a pretty personal question."

"These are pretty personal circumstances," he shot back, his breath suddenly hissing through his teeth as she returned to her task, applying a fresh swab. Ian took advantage of her absorption with his injuries to lose himself in the study of her features, lingering over the individual details that when put together, created a face that if not the most beautiful, was certainly the most fascinating he'd ever seen. Soulful, big brown eyes. Pink, full mouth that somehow managed to look sinfully angelic. Feminine nose and jaunty chin. Masses of thick, silky curls that begged for the touch of a man's hand.

The details were pretty, delicate, sweet…even innocent in their purity. She could have been a Sunday-school teacher. A college student going for her master's degree in humanities. The kind of girl who married a high-school sweetheart, raised 2.5 kids with a white picket fence and a flurry of schedules to coordinate, from gymnastics to soccer practice, living the Norman Rockwell equivalent of the American Dream.

And yet…the way she made him feel was none of those things. Dark. Edgy. Desperate. The explicit things he wanted from her, wanted to do to her, wanted to make her do, they had no business in that world of innocence and happily-ever-afters.

"I had blood work done when I went on the Pill two years ago."

"What?" Ian shook his head, trying to find his way back to the conversation, his body buzzing, head foggy, reminding him of his drug-hazed days. Molly Stratton was that potent, like a narcotic, jacking him up, making him crave a fix. He'd fought so hard to get beyond that kind of need—that kind of dark, addictive craving—he almost could have hated her for dragging him back there.

"I said that I had blood work done two years ago, when my doctor put me on the Pill."

"That's a long time to go without getting tested," he managed to mutter, shifting in the chair.

"Not if you haven't had sex," she replied casually, gaze still focused on her task.

Ian went completely still for the span of ten seconds, then cursed something hot and foul under his breath. "Are you telling me that you haven't had sex in *two* years?"

"Well, I had the test done two years ago. But I think it's been more like three since I've been to bed with anyone." She flicked a quick glance at his face. "You know, it's not like being celibate is a crime."

"It should be," he grunted, unable to get his head around it. He'd known, instinctively, that she wasn't very experienced, but three years! How was that even possible? "Abstinence or celibacy or whatever the hell you want to call it isn't natural. If it was, we wouldn't have been given all the working parts that make fucking so much fun."

"That's such a guy thing to say," she snorted, shaking her head.

"Thank God," he drawled, completely deadpan. "If I start sounding like a chick, do me a favor and shoot me."

"Can't," she said lightly, and he could just glimpse the grin she was hiding in the corners of her mouth. "No gun."

"Me, neither. Don't believe in them. But we could always borrow Riley's."

There was a question in her eyes, but she didn't comment, and he didn't bother to explain. Instead, he caught one of her curls, twining the honey-colored strand around his finger. "Seriously, no sex for three years is just…wrong."

"So says the man who confesses to sleeping with women he doesn't even like, just so he can get his rocks off."

"Careful," he murmured, studying her through his lashes. "You sound jealous."

She rolled her eyes, smoothing on the antibiotic ointment. "Of nameless women you've used for meaningless sex? Hardly."

Ian shifted in the chair, not liking where this conversation was headed. "It's been a two-way street, Molly. They've used me as much as I used them."

"If it makes you feel better to believe that," she murmured, frowning as she stuffed the swabs and empty packets into a small plastic bag, "then go ahead. But I think you're selling yourself, and them, short."

She started to step away, but Ian reached out, grabbing her wrist again, careful to control his grip. "Speaking of selling people short, I should have listened to you before," he told her. "It would have made a difference. If I had, Kendra might still be alive."

MOLLY COULD SEE the sincerity in his eyes, the pain, and knew his regret was genuine. Knew that though he might never admit it, Ian was mourning the loss of the woman who'd been so brutally murdered. It'd been all over the local news that day, speculation rampant as to what could've carried out such a brutal attack. Pulling out of his hold, she kept her tone soft as she said, "I'm just glad you're willing to believe me now."

Leaning forward in the chair, he braced his elbows on his spread knees, the rugged angles of his face hard with tension, the mouthwatering muscles beneath all that dark golden skin attesting to the power, to the strength, that few men could claim. He drew the eye like a fascinating, provocative work of art, making it impossible to look away.

"So talk to me," he said. "Tell me what you know."

She tossed the bag of rubbish into the trash bin, washed her hands again, then turned, leaning back against the counter, arms crossed over her chest. "I almost don't know where to start."

"You said you came here because you didn't have a

choice," he prompted. "I assume that was because of my mother. That you couldn't ignore her…requests that you come and find me."

"That's one way of putting it." The corner of her mouth twitched. "Elaina is definitely stubborn, as well as persistent."

"And you just believed her?" he questioned, the lingering shadow of doubt still visible in his eyes.

Shaking her head, Molly quietly said, "I gave up the luxury of disbelief a long time ago, Ian."

"So something like this has happened to you before?"

She nodded, hooking her hair behind her ear. "I can talk to spirits—to ghosts, as most people call them—when I'm sleeping. Or rather, they can sometimes talk to me. But this, what's been happening here, between us these last two nights. This is way out of my league. Way beyond normal, even for me."

He absorbed that for a moment, then quietly asked, "When did you first talk to Elaina's ghost?"

"A few months ago, not long after her death. She made contact then, but it took a while for her to come through clearly enough that I could understand her." She paused, and the attentive look in his eyes encouraged her to continue. "It's difficult to explain how it works. Most of the time, it just sounds like someone shouting at me through water. But if they're persistent, the messages become clearer with time. It wasn't until a few weeks ago that I finally understood what Elaina was trying to tell me. That she wanted me to find you, warn you about the danger here, and find a way to make you believe. The bad news is that that was the easy part. The hard part, now that you *do* believe, is going to be learning how to survive."

"And just how am I supposed to do that?" he grunted, scrubbing his hands down his face.

She blew out a shaky breath. "Honestly, I don't know. I don't even know why this is happening or what's caused it to happen *now*. All I can tell you is that that monster won't stop hunting you. Not until one of you is dead. That's one of the things Elaina wishes she'd been able to tell you before she died. I guess she began to fear this might happen—that those creatures, the Casus, might return. And she believes that's the reason why the Merrick is finally awakening inside of you. Because of your bloodline, it's always been there, dormant. Lying in wait. Now that one of its enemies is near, it will want to protect you from it."

"What about my brother and sister? Are they awakening, too?"

"Elaina believes they will, with time. But for now, you're the one that it wants. You're the beginning, but of what, she hasn't told me. I'm not even sure that she knows."

He leaned back in the chair, watching her. "And is this…this thing, this Merrick that's inside of me…is it evil?" he rasped out of a dry throat, the words scratchy and raw, and Molly knew what it cost him to ask her that question.

"No," she answered softly, honestly. "But…"

"It's not good, either," he said flatly, cutting her off. "They may be enemies of the Casus, but they're still killers. Predators."

"I wasn't going to say that. I was going to say that

they're not…tame," she argued, frustrated with him for putting words in her mouth. "They're more primal than humans. More visceral. But they're inherently good. There's no way you would ever do anything to hurt anyone unless they deserved it."

Shaking his head, he rubbed one palm against the scratchy surface of his jaw, his expression saying that he wanted so badly to believe her, but was afraid. "Do you honestly believe that?"

"Yes." But Molly understood the power of his fear. Self-loathing worked in much the same way. Like acid in your veins that slowly consumed you from the inside out, leaving nothing but a rotten skeleton in its wake. She knew all about that kind of torture. She'd been living, writhing, within its cold, clammy grasp for years. "You could never hurt anyone, Ian," she said in a gentle voice, wishing he'd believe her…trust her.

Lowering his head, he turned over his right hand and stared at his upturned palm, rubbing the thumb of his left hand against its center, as if working out an ache. She knew he'd decided to change the subject when he said, "From what I remember of Elaina's stories, the Casus were a nasty piece of work. They get off on pain and fear. On agony and torture. That's what makes them tick."

"And this one is drawn to you," she told him, shuddering at the memory of the foul creature from his nightmare. "Elaina believes that it needs you, but she's not sure why."

The violent cracks of lightning from the rumbling storm were the perfect complement to the hard strain of his expression, and she wanted to walk to him.

Wanted to take that ruggedly beautiful face between her palms, stroking the hollows of his cheeks with her thumbs, and press a comforting kiss to his knitted brow. But she didn't dare—and not because she didn't trust him.

No, it was her own irrational needs that she didn't trust.

He fisted his hand for a moment, then flexed his fingers, stretching them out, as if the simple gesture could release the heavy tension riding the rigid lines of his body. "So what now?"

"If you want to live, you need to learn how to bring it out. How to accept the change without fighting it."

His gaze flicked back up to her face, brows drawn in a deep V over those impossibly blue eyes. "And you think that's a good idea, after what I dreamed tonight? Whatever the fuck that thing was, Casus or not, what happened while I was fighting it wasn't pretty, Molly. This thing inside of me wanted to tear its throat out."

"You don't have a choice," she whispered. "You *will* fight it again, Ian, and when you do, you'll need to be on even ground. Your mother says that until you're able to accept what you are, you won't be able to defeat it. And who's to say that more won't come after him? I know this isn't what you wanted, but sometimes—sometimes we just have to accept the life we're given and learn to go on."

His gaze narrowed, piercing and dark. "And when I bring it out—if I'm even able to bring it out—how do we know I'll be able to control it? What if this thing, this Merrick, is hungry?"

Heat climbed its way up from the center of her chest,

over her throat, into her cheeks, impossible to hide from him. "I don't think you would try to feed from me again," she said hoarsely. "Not unless we were having sex, like we were in the dreams."

He made one of those cocky, arrogant snorting sounds that only a guy could pull off. "You sure about that?"

"No, I'm not sure about anything right now. But what are you so afraid of? It didn't kill me in the dreams. So what makes you think it would try to hurt me in reality?"

He scrubbed his hands down his face, as if he could wipe away the bleak expression falling over him like a shadow. "You didn't see what that thing did to Kendra."

"But you're not like the Casus," she argued, wishing she could make him understand. "You're one of the good guys, Ian. One of the ones who saves the day, not destroys it."

His smile was bitter. "Trust me, Molly. I've never been one of the heroes."

"Your halo may be a little tarnished," she whispered, her mouth twisting with a wry smile, "but you're not bad. I'd be willing to bet my life on it."

She could tell, instantly, from his grim expression that she'd said the wrong thing.

He stared at her for a long, hard moment, then suddenly surged to his feet so quickly that the chair crashed over backward behind him. "Christ, what is it with you?" he growled. "We only just met! You *don't* know me. I hardly know myself right now!"

"I know you came here tonight to make sure I was okay," she pointed out in a calm, quiet voice, "even though you don't like me."

He growled low in his throat, his muscles bulging beneath the golden sheen of his skin as he shoved his hands back through his hair, then let them fall loosely to his sides. "And after that dream, maybe I only came here because I wanted the chance to get in your pants again."

"Considering the shape you were in when I opened the door," she murmured, unfazed by his anger, "you're going to have a tough time selling me that one."

"And what if I *do* hurt you?" he demanded, crossing his arms over the broad width of his chest. "What then, Molly?"

"You won't."

He ground his teeth so hard that a muscle ticked in his jaw, then finally said, "That's a helluva risk you're willing to take for a total stranger. I can't help but wonder why."

She hesitated, her gaze sliding away for a moment, before she forced herself to meet the dark primal intensity of his stare. "Why isn't important. What's important is that I'm staying to see this through to the end."

"Even though the Casus threatened you?" he rasped, studying her determined expression. "You're the one in danger now, Molly. That changes everything."

She lifted her chin, refusing to back down. "I knew the risk when I came here, Ian. It doesn't change anything."

"It damn well should," he muttered, his jaw clenched, head lowered as he cut a sharp glare toward the floor. Another jarring, violent crack of lightning shook the thin walls of the motel, and she jumped, drawing his shadowed, heavy-lidded stare back to her face. Slowly, he shook his head, as if he didn't know what to make of her. "I think you're out of your mind, Molly, but it doesn't matter. Even if you wanted to run, I wouldn't let you. Not now. Not after tonight. There's no telling how far this thing, this Casus, would go to get his hands on you. Until this is over," he told her in a dark, angry slide of words, "I'm not letting you out of my sight."

CHAPTER NINE

Sunday Morning

MALCOLM DEKREZNICK, the Casus who had stolen tall, blond and blue-eyed Joe Kelly's body strolled down the empty sidewalk in Henning without a care in the world. He enjoyed the warmth of the hot summer day, a new pair of designer sunglasses protecting his sensitive eyes from the bright glare of sunshine raining down from above. The summer storm had moved on with daybreak, the rustic mountain community quiet and still, but then it was Sunday morning, many of the residents attending religious services. His mouth twisted with a wry smile at the thought of all their pious prayers and earnest devotion, knowing that if he were to choose them, he could end their pitiful existence with such ridiculous ease it was hardly worth the effort. Like blowing out a flame. *Poof.* And the light was gone.

They could pray all they wanted for Kendra Wilcox's immortal soul, but it wasn't going to change her fate. It wasn't going to bring her back. Malcolm had made sure that once he got his hands on her, there'd been little left to put in the ground.

Crossing the street, a low rumble of satisfaction warmed his throat as he thought of the kill.

The brunette bitch had been so much more exciting than the coarse animal fare that had sustained him since his return. She'd not only tasted sweeter, but he'd been able to "blood fuck" her, which had always been Malcolm's favorite way to feed. And the way she'd fought him had only made it that much more satisfying.

It'd been so long, an eternity, since he'd enjoyed a proper meal. He'd almost forgotten how empowering it was, that perfect, breathtaking moment when the light finally dawned. When his prey realized they were staring death in the face, and he was able to feed on that sweet flood of fear as deeply as he fed on their flesh. Almost forgotten the hot burn of pleasure he took when they refused to give in, so potent and addictive.

And Kendra had fought hard.

Still, she hadn't been enough. Had failed, in fact, to give him the power he needed to bring his brother through that metaphysical prison gate that trapped his kind within the holding ground they'd named Meridian. To bring him back from the hell that had imprisoned his kinsmen for century upon century, while their enemies continued to walk the earth.

Only now did they have hope. Hope that Anthony Calder had given them. The first of their kind to establish order among the imprisoned Casus, Calder had mysteriously discovered a way to send a Casus through the gate and back to this realm. It was a difficult, draining process for Calder and his followers, and though there'd been serious doubts that it would actually work,

Malcolm had been ecstatic when Calder accepted his petition to be the first.

But his freedom wasn't the same without his brother, Gregory, there to share it with him. While Calder would eventually try to send others through the gate, Gregory would never be chosen. His brother was considered too unstable—too much of a risk—which meant that Gregory's freedom was up to him.

Malcolm had been told that once he'd gained enough power, he should be able to bring a shade back on his own, ripping him back from the bowels of Meridian. Kendra had been an inspired kill, as well as a pleasure, but he wasn't surprised that she'd failed to provide a strong enough feeding. After all, Calder had warned him that it would most likely take a Merrick to do the job.

That was why he needed Buchanan. Malcolm could have killed him last night, with little effort, but it'd been obvious that the bastard was still too green. Though he'd enjoyed scaring the shit out of him, until Ian Buchanan was fully awakened, there was no point in feeding from him. He hadn't even had the first talisman that Calder had charged Malcolm with finding—the one thing that could provide him a bargaining chip for Gregory's freedom, should Calder's theory prove wrong.

Impatience rode him hard, but he had to hold firm and show restraint. Traits not common to his kind, but Malcolm knew his brother's freedom could very well hinge on his success, and the rules were simple. Kill the bastard too early, and the feeding wouldn't be enough to get the job done. To get the full dose of power he needed, the Merrick living within Buchanan had to be at full strength at the time of his death.

Shoving his hands into the pockets of his slacks, Malcolm pulled in a slow, deep breath and shook off his frustration.

Yes, he could wait. It would be worth it. And in the meantime, he could always keep entertaining himself with the local fare. He'd been cautioned endlessly about the need to be careful in these modern times—that their kills couldn't be as rampant as before, when the Casus had ruled the night with fear, as powerful as bloody kings. But he'd been determined to leave the Wilcox woman out in the open, just so he could screw with Ian Buchanan's mind.

Witnessing the bastard's rage over her death had been worth the risk of a little exposure.

For now, he'd enjoy tormenting Buchanan for as long as it took, tightening the screws, while waiting for the perfect moment to strike. He'd even make a point of getting his hands on that particularly tasty little blond.

And, of course, there was that pesky matter of the interruption last night that he needed to look into. That had been unexpected, and he needed to be better prepared before he made his next move.

Until then, Malcolm planned on enjoying his newfound freedom. The body he'd taken wasn't half-bad, though the life attached to it could be described as nothing more than embarrassing. You would think someone with Casus blood running through his veins would have amounted to more in this world, but Joe Kelly's accomplishments were as mundane as his name.

Not that Malcolm was complaining. He still couldn't believe his luck that he'd been chosen as the first of his kind to return. Nor could he decide if it was because his kinsman had been sure he would succeed—or because Calder considered him expendable if things didn't initially go according to plan. And in truth, he didn't care. Whatever Calder's reason for choosing him, there wasn't a chance in hell he'd have turned down the opportunity. Meridian held no life—and without life, how could you feed on the pleasures of death? That was why the Casus had grown weak, wasting so many pointless years fighting amongst themselves. It wasn't until they'd finally begun listening to Calder that they'd been able to unite and work together toward a common goal. That goal being freedom, as well as revenge.

And this first taste of revenge was going to taste, oh, so sweet.

Tilting his face up to the sun, Malcolm basked in its warm glow, a deep breath filling his lungs with the fertile scents of the forest, such a refreshing change from the cold, rotting decay of Meridian. Turning at the end of the block, he continued making his way through the center of town, humming softly under his breath. When he reached the next street corner, an elderly woman wearing a Help Kendra's Family T-shirt, a donation bucket clutched in her frail hand, approached him with an appropriately somber smile.

"We're collecting money for Kendra Wilcox's funeral expenses. Her mother's a widower and is in desperate need of the kindness of strangers."

"I'd be happy to help out," Malcolm murmured, searching in his front pocket and pulling out a roll of bills. He enjoyed a silent chuckle, appreciating the irony of the situation. After all, he'd taken the money off Kendra Wilcox's broken, bleeding body. Or at least what was left of it.

"Thank you, sir. It was such a tragedy, what happened to the poor girl. If ever there was a time to be neighborly, it's now. God bless you."

Glancing at the photograph pasted to the side of the bucket, Malcolm shook his head with mock sympathy. "She was a beautiful girl. That picture doesn't really do her justice."

The woman's gray brows knitted with compassion. "You knew Kendra?"

"Oh, yes," he drawled as he started across the street. Looking back over his shoulder, Malcolm struggled to conceal his slow, satisfied smile. "You could even say she helped make me what I am today."

CHAPTER TEN

Sunday, 10:30 a.m.

STANDING WITH HER BACK propped against the counter in the small kitchenette, Molly took a fortifying sip of coffee, thinking she could drink an entire pot and still feel weary. She'd slept like hell, but at least the storm had finally moved its way through by dawn. Eventually, she'd managed to catch a few hours of rest, before Elaina had contacted her with another message. After that, she'd awakened to the bright burn of morning sunshine glowing around the dark green curtains that hung over the lone window, unable to fall back asleep.

As she'd rolled over to climb out of bed, she'd been met with the breathtaking sight of Ian Buchanan sprawled facedown over the neighboring queen bed. The intricate tattoo at the top of his spine had instantly caught her eye, somehow calling to her. She'd wanted to reach out and stroke it with the tips of her fingers— the oddest sense of certainty rushing through her blood that it would have been warm to the touch, pulsing with heat, with a strange, latent power—but she'd resisted, out of self-preservation more than anything. Because once she'd put her hands on him, she didn't think she'd have been able to stop. He was too beautiful, his dark shoulders gleaming against the white sheets that swept low across the sleek contours of his back, his powerful arms clutched around his pillow, partly shielding the rugged perfection of his face, thick lashes lying like dark smudges of ink against his cheeks, while he slept like the dead.

Not that she blamed him. He'd barely had time to rest the past few days and it was obvious the fight with the Casus, as well as the internal struggle he'd waged against the Merrick side of his nature, had taken its toll on him.

After his stunning declaration that he intended to keep her under his protection, they'd made a silent truce in the face of exhaustion and gone to bed. Ian had crawled between the sheets wearing his towel, then pulled it off and tossed it on the end of the bed, leaving Molly torn between a keen sense of regret that she didn't get to see him in the raw…and piercing relief that she wasn't being faced with that kind of devastating temptation. Borrowing her cell phone, he'd left a quick message for his brother, Riley, telling him that something had come up and he'd be in touch when he could, along with a strong warning to watch his back and be careful. Then she'd turned out the light and crawled into her own bed. For long minutes, she'd lain there, listening to the quiet sound of Ian's breathing and the hypnotic rhythm of the pounding rain against the thin roof of the motel, while wondering if they would share another dream…worrying over what the next day would bring.

And now that she'd received Elaina's latest directive,

she couldn't help but speculate as to how cooperative he would be.

She was still standing beside the sink in the kitchen when he finally came in, wearing nothing but his dirty jeans, the top two buttons undone, revealing a compelling shadow that drew her gaze. His chest was bare, skin dark and bronzed in the low glow of light spilling in from the bedroom.

"Coffee?" she asked a bit hoarsely, noticing that his beard had grown in thicker during the night, darkening his jaw, accentuating the mesmerizing color of his eyes. He nodded, sinking his long, rangy body into one of the chairs, the cuts on his arm and rib cage looking remarkably better. Molly poured him a cup, then grabbed the pack of cigarettes and matchbox off the counter and took everything to the table, where an ashtray already sat in the center.

"Where did those come from?" he grunted, eyeing the cigarettes, his voice still rough from sleep, sounding warm and rich and scratchy, not to mention incredibly sexy.

"Don't worry. I didn't leave the room," she told him with a slight smile, taking a chair on the other side of the small table as she tucked a wild strand of hair behind her ear. She'd already taken her shower and thrown on jeans and a shirt. Her face was freshly scrubbed, and she'd left her hair to dry naturally, hoping it'd behave, but the damn curls had a mind of their own. "I called up to the front desk a while ago and asked if they could put them on my tab, then just leave everything outside the door."

"That was awfully *nice* of you," he drawled, the low,

silken words just shy of being snide. His gaze slid away from hers as he reached for the pack and stripped off the plastic outer wrapping. Molly's smile slipped at his tone.

Huh. Maybe he's just cranky in the morning…

She watched as he placed one of the cigarettes between his firm lips, then lowered his head and lit the tip, immediately taking a long drag, while the distinct smell of the sulfur burned her nose. A deep, rumbling groan of pleasure vibrated in his throat, and in spite of her unease, her mouth twitched at the corner. "I really shouldn't encourage such an unhealthy habit, but I thought you might wake up desperate for a cigarette."

"You could say that," he muttered with a noticeable dose of bitterness, after exhaling a hazy stream of smoke. Leaning back in the chair, one hand resting across the firm cut of his abs, his dark eyes found hers, delivering a look that was somehow wary…distrustful even, as if he wanted to know what the hell she was up to.

Despite his indolent posture, Molly could feel the tension in all those long, lean muscles and corded lines of sinew, his body tight…hard, as if ready for a confrontation. Jerking his chin toward her, he muttered, "Do you always look like that in the morning?"

She wet her lips, aware of the warmth climbing up her throat, the nerves twisting in her belly. "Like what?"

"Like you've just had sex." He leaned forward, resting his elbows on his spread knees, his cigarette pinched between his thumb and his forefinger, blue eyes holding hers in a challenging stare. "Cheeks flushed, mouth swollen, all those wild curls tousled around your face, like a man had his hands buried in them, even though I know we didn't share another dream last night. Doesn't matter how tired I was—there's no way in hell I'd have slept through *that*." He paused for a moment, taking a lazy drag off the cigarette, before adding, "Is that your little game, Miss Molly? You get a kick out of mind-fucking every guy you meet?"

Ready for a confrontation…or maybe looking to start one.

She knew a response was in order to put him in his place, but the words were jamming up in her throat, vibrating with a flustered combination of anger and confusion and lust. Saying nothing, she watched as he lifted the cigarette and took another deep drag, the burning ember at the tip a fiery spark of color against the burnished perfection of his body. It caught the light, like his eyes, and she stared, transfixed, aware that she could feel the coursing of her blood as it surged through her veins, vibrant and heavy and strong.

She was caught in time—held, suspended, trapped.

And he knew it. Knew just what his words had done to her. Knew just how easily he'd unraveled her composure. Knew the images his provocative words had planted in her mind like a seed.

Molly was ready to call him a jerk for playing with her emotions, when she caught a shadow flicker within that angry blue stare. She finally realized what he was doing—trying to start an argument as a way to avoid facing his feelings. He needed to release the emotional buildup after everything he'd been through…and she was the nearest outlet.

She could understand it—but it didn't change the fact

that she needed to learn how to handle him without freezing up every time something provoking fell from that firm, sensual mouth. Molly was discovering first-hand that it could be as dangerous as it was beautiful.

"You're upset," she murmured, taking a sip of coffee, thankful that the mug didn't shake in her grip.

For a moment he just stared, and then he slouched back in the chair, shaking his head as if he didn't know what to make of her. "Men don't get *upset*," he finally informed her in a slow, precise drawl. "We get pissed. But don't take it personally. I woke up angry at every-thing this morning. Merricks. The Casus. Women being raped and murdered and threatened. I'm pissed off about this entire goddamn situation."

"Be careful," she cautioned. "Your anger…it can lead to other things."

He snorted, sending her a tight smile. "Don't worry, sweetheart. As tempting as you look, I'm not going to attack you."

"It's not me I'm worried about," she told him, refus-ing to let him rattle her any more than he already had. "I meant what I said last night, Ian. I'm not afraid of you. But until you learn to accept what you are, you're waging an internal battle against yourself. I don't think anger's going to help that."

He didn't make a response. Just kept staring at her, as if waiting for some kind of answer…a revelation.

Feeling a desperate need for a change in the subject, Molly set her coffee on the table and said, "I talked with Elaina again last night. Or rather, she talked to me."

Rocking the chair onto its back legs, Ian absorbed those strange words, wondering how the hell he'd ended up here. Wondering how in God's name he was going to keep his hands off the woman sitting across from him, wrapped up in soft jeans and a tight coral-pink T-shirt that hugged the delicate shape of her breasts, making his mouth water. She looked too warm and soft and giving, and *that* made him as angry as all the other whacked-out shit going on. He hated this need for her itching beneath his skin. Hated the fact that all he wanted to do was just reach out, rip off those hip-hugging jeans and pull her over his lap, pressing his mouth to the warm, tender patch of skin beneath her ear. Breathe in her mind-drugging scent, while trailing his right hand up the smooth expanse of her inner thigh…

Rolling his shoulder, Ian shook off the provocative image and refocused his gaze, scanning the small kitchen, thinking the cheap motel room was all wrong for her. Cracked linoleum, scarred table. Stale air smelling of acrid smoke from his cigarette. Molly Stratton was like something from a different world that had just landed there by accident, so vibrant and real and fresh, but alien…completely out of place.

She shifted beneath the piercing intensity of his stare as it swung back toward her, and ran her tongue over her bottom lip, drawing his eye. Her mouth was too sweet looking for a man not to want to violate. To take and capture and dominate. The violence of his kiss the night before had left it swollen and dark with color— the normally soft pink replaced by a crimson rose that looked good enough to eat.

And she hadn't had sex in three years. Unbelievable.

God only knew he'd be lucky if he lasted another

three minutes without touching her. Only two things stopped him in his tracks. The fact that she'd told him no last night. And the dark, seductive knowledge that once he'd buried his body in hers, thick and hard and deep, his fangs would quickly follow, seeking that rich, dangerously addictive rush of blood.

Rubbing his tongue against the roof of his mouth, as if he could recapture that wild, decadent flavor, Ian lifted his gaze. "So what did she have to say?"

She wet her bottom lip with her tongue again, a nervous gesture of hers, her fey face flushed with color. He knew it was from the way he was watching her. "What?" she asked.

"My mother," he prompted, clearing his throat. "You said you'd heard from her."

"Oh, uh… She gave me a name."

"Yeah?" He slowly exhaled. "A name for what?"

Shifting in her chair again, she curled her fingers around the mug of coffee sitting on the table in front of her. "Elaina said that there are those nearby who can help us. She gave me a man's name, but when I called information this morning, they didn't have an available listing."

"What's the name?"

"Scott. Kierland Scott. Does it sound familiar to you?"

Ian snorted. "I've never heard of him, but he sounds like a prick."

She frowned at his tone. "Is your first instinct always to dislike someone before you even know them?"

"Pretty much," he rumbled, reaching for his coffee and taking a heavy sip.

"You know," she ventured cautiously, warning him

that he wasn't going to like what she was about to say, "if you want, we can talk about things. It might make you feel better if you just get it off your chest."

He cut her a narrow-eyed look, suspicious and wary. "Get what off my chest?"

"The fact that you're mourning her." He opened his mouth, but she rushed on, saying, "Regardless of how you would categorize your relationship, I know you're upset about Kendra. That isn't just going to disappear with a good night's sleep, Ian."

He put one hand over his eyes, holding up the other in a gesture of entreaty. "Please, just shut up. I have no desire to sit here and listen to you analyze my *feelings,* especially over another woman. Not now. Not ever."

"All I'm saying is that it's okay to feel remorse, to be upset over her loss."

Feel remorse? Be upset? Christ. As if either of those platitudes even came close to the self-loathing eating away at his insides like acid. "What the hell do you want to hear, Molly?" he exploded in a low, seething rush of words, the front legs of the chair slamming back on the floor with a sharp crack of sound as he leaned forward. "That I feel bad about what happened? That if it wasn't for her knowing me, she wouldn't be dead? Yeah, I admit it. Now can you just shut the hell up about it?"

"You didn't kill her, Ian," she said softly, the look in her eyes even softer, making him feel dangerously close to the edge.

"I didn't warn her, either," he growled. "If I'd listened to you—"

"She might have laughed in your face and told you

that you were as crazy as you told me I was on Friday afternoon."

"Yeah, maybe," he grunted with a heavy sigh, stubbing out his cigarette into the black plastic ashtray, the set of his mouth grim, his fury like a living thing within his body. "All I know is that I want to make that bastard pay."

"And you will," she murmured. "I have no doubt of that."

He took another sip of coffee, ran one hand back through his hair, and finally said, "So what's the plan?"

"The plan?" she repeated, as if she didn't know what he was talking about. "What makes you think I have one?"

Hah. He wasn't buying that innocent expression for a second. "You're a woman, right?"

She frowned, moving to her feet and taking the empty coffee cups to the sink. "Meaning?" she asked over her shoulder.

"Meaning a woman *always* has a plan," Ian drawled, going for the most insufferable tone he could deliver.

"Well, as a matter of fact," she said, turning and leaning back against the counter, her arms crossed over her T-shirt-covered chest, the coral color accentuating the fairness of her complexion, "There *is* something that we need to do."

Taking another cigarette out of the pack, he perched it between his lips and reached for the matches. "Let's hear it."

"Last night, Elaina asked me…*us*…to do something." She hesitated, then went on. "She wants us to go to the storage unit where her things are being kept.

I guess Riley is keeping them in a town called Mountain Creek. She didn't say where it all came from, but I'm assuming it was shipped there from where she lived."

"Let me guess," he muttered, lighting his cigarette while Riley's strange mention of the storage facility burned through his brain, making him uneasy as hell. "I'm betting there's something she wants us to pick up. Something she *left* for me."

"How did you know?" she asked in a surprised voice.

"I have a key to the place. Riley gave it to me. He told me that she'd left me something."

"Do you know what it was?" she asked, her tone hopeful.

He stared at the glowing tip of the cigarette, then shifted his gaze back to her curious expression. "Not a clue."

"Can't you call Riley and ask him? He could probably let us know what we're looking for."

"If I call him, he'll show up," he said, flicking his cigarette over the ashtray. "And I'd rather not have to explain who you are and what I'm doing with you."

"All right," she agreed, though she still sounded determined. "We'll just have to go and search through everything on our own, then."

"And how are we supposed to know what we're looking for?" he grunted, his uneasiness mounting. Whatever the hell was out there, it probably wasn't going to be anything he wanted a part of. "That place has to be full of crap. I don't think Elaina ever threw anything away."

Her brown eyes shimmered with a spark of amusement, and he knew he wasn't going to like her answer.

"Well?" he snapped, inhaling an impatient stream of smoke.

"I know it sounds crazy—" she paused, a wry smile twisting the corner of her mouth "—but she said we'd know what we needed when we found it."

AFTER DECIDING that they'd have more privacy if they stayed at the motel, they made a quick stop by Ian's apartment so that he could shower, change clothes and throw a bag of stuff together. He also grabbed the key to the storage unit that Riley had given him, and then they were finally on their way.

Leaving her rental car at his apartment, they loaded into his truck, then picked up an early lunch of burgers and fries from a fast-food restaurant. Now, as they headed down the two-lane highway toward the nearby town of Mountain Creek, Molly broke the heavy silence by saying, "Can I ask you a personal question?"

"Let's have it," he drawled, picking up his soda and taking a sip through the straw. Sunlight poured through the front windshield, glinting blue off the thick, ink-black strands of his hair, the warm, radiant glow of sunshine highlighting the rugged beauty of a face that looked as wickedly sinful as it did divine, too gorgeous to be merely human.

Which you know he's not.

The small bite marks that she'd managed to cover with a light layer of concealer pulsed like a memory against the side of her throat, and Molly shivered, forcing her mind back to her question.

"Exactly what went wrong between you and Elaina?" she asked, twisting in her seat to face him.

His expression shifted to one of…regret?…edged by that customary bitterness that was so much a part of him.

"Let's just say that I was anything but her golden child," he said after a moment, his left hand braced on the top of the wheel, while his right curved around the top of the soda cup he had perched on his thigh.

"She loved you," she said simply. "Very much."

He rolled his shoulder, as if throwing off an unwanted touch. "Yeah, well, that didn't stop her from accusing me of throwing my life away, of being just like my old man, who was the biggest loser to ever walk the planet. The hell of it was, she was right. She always said she expected more from me, but all I ever did was disappoint her. By the time I was sixteen, I'd dropped out of school and had started running with a rough crowd—" a gritty burst of laughter rumbled in his chest "—which was putting a nice spin on what they really were. Eventually I just got tired of her bitching and hit the road."

"Did you ever go back?" she asked, fighting the urge to reach out her hand and trail her fingertips down the masculine perfection of his arm. Over the bulging power of his bicep that stretched the sleeve of his gray T-shirt. Across the corded strength of his forearm. Against the thickness of his wrist.

"Once I left, I never set foot in her house again."

"And yet, when she needed your help, you gave it," she said softly. "I know you paid for most of her medical bills while she was sick, up until the time of her death."

He cut her a dark, sudden look of surprise, his brows pulled together in a deep scowl over the furious blue of his eyes. "Who the hell told you that?"

Molly lifted her brows. "Who do you think?"

Shifting his gaze back to the road, he cursed under his breath. "I told him to tell her the money came from him," he growled, thumping his palm against the steering wheel.

"You asked Riley not to tell her?" she murmured, fascinated by the play of emotions shifting over his profile, his anger like a living, breathing thing, trapped there in the cab of the truck with them.

"No, I didn't ask him," he ground out. "I *told* him. But he never could keep a damn secret to save his life."

"Well, for what it's worth, I think what you did was very admirable, Ian. Elaina told me it cleared out the savings you'd accumulated since moving to Colorado and starting your business. That's quite a sacrifice."

He shifted his shoulders, clearly uncomfortable with her praise. "Money's money," he muttered. "I do what I do because I enjoy it. Because it keeps me outside. Allows me to work with my hands, set my own schedule. Not because it's gonna make me rich someday."

"I can respect that," she told him, wondering if he had any idea how amazing it was, the selflessness and pure generosity of what he'd done in a world whose very pulse centered on the mighty dollar. "And from what I've heard, you're incredibly good at what you do. She's very proud of you."

He grunted under his breath in response, and they fell into another heavy silence, until he eventually said, "Now it's my turn."

Molly had been staring out the front window, but she shifted her gaze back to his profile. "Your turn to what?"

"To ask a personal question."

She knew what he was going to say, but she asked anyway. "What do you want to know?"

"I want to know why you're here. Why you couldn't just tell Elaina to take a flying leap and pretend you never even heard about us crazy-assed Buchanans. Why you're willing to put your life on the line for people you don't even know."

"It isn't a pretty story," she warned him in a low voice, her gaze focused on her lap, where she smoothed a thumb over the dark denim of her jeans. She was aware of a cold, slick sensation curling around the back of her neck, beneath her hair, and knew precisely what it was. The chilling burn of guilt. The kind you could never outrun. Never undo.

He took another sip of his soda, set it back in the cup holder, and reached for the pack of cigarettes that sat between the seats. When his hand brushed her knee, she shivered, the reverberation of the slight touch shimmying through her body like a tremor. "Go ahead," he prompted her, lighting the cigarette with the truck's lighter. "I can take it."

Staring at the narrow highway that stretched out before them, Molly took a deep breath and searched for a way to start. "It wasn't always like this…the voices in my sleep. It started my freshman year of high school, when one of my best friends, Sara, committed suicide. I went to her funeral, and the next thing I knew, she was talking to me every time I fell asleep."

"That must have been pretty scary." His tone was low, thoughtful, without any of the derision or disbelief she'd encountered on the few occasions she'd tried to tell this story before.

"Yeah, it was. I was terrified and I didn't want to listen, but she wouldn't stop. Each night, she came to me, begging me to tell someone that her stepfather had been abusing her. Before she died, she'd tried to tell her mother, but the woman accused her of making it up for attention, claiming that Sara was jealous of her happiness. The abuse continued, and that's…that's why she finally took her life."

He cursed something foul under his breath again, and then said, "Jesus, you guys were only kids. What the hell did you do?"

A bitter sound jerked from her throat, that sickening wave of guilt pouring over her like thick, sticky tar, binding her in place. "I did nothing. I was too afraid everyone would think I was crazy. Out of my mind." Her hands fisted in her lap, jaw tight as she scraped out the shameful words. "I wanted so badly to tell my parents, the police…" Her voice trailed off, her throat tight, and then she forced herself to admit the truth. "But I didn't."

"Did she keep contacting you?"

"Yes." Her smile twisted with bitterness as she turned toward him, catching his shuttered gaze when he cut a quick glance in her direction. "And pretty soon, I learned the hard way that I wasn't crazy, after all."

Staring at the muscle ticking in his jaw, Molly explained. "Sara's stepfather was a powerful judge in our county, and I knew no one would ever take my word over his. So I did nothing, and a few months later, a young girl who was in the class beneath us was brutally raped and murdered. Sara came to me, telling me that the judge was responsible." She swallowed against the bile rising in her throat, blinking away the hot sting of tears burning at the backs of her eyes. "And I…I finally found the courage to do something, and went to the police. They thought I was crazy, until I was able to tell them where he'd hidden the rope he'd used to bind the girl. They found it in his basement, along with a bloody lock of her hair that he'd kept as a souvenir, sick bastard that he was."

He cut her another quick, piercing glance, and she could tell by the look in his eye that he knew there was more to the story than what she was telling him. But instead of pushing her, he quietly said, "And so you've listened to the voices ever since." It wasn't a question, but a statement.

"I've tried, and I've managed to help people. But this…this is the first time that lives have been on the line. I wasn't brave enough to make a difference then, but I can't make the same mistake this time. When Elaina first told me what she wanted me to do, I was sick with fear. It took me days to build up the courage to come and find you, but I finally realized that this is it—my chance for atonement. Ever since that first time, I've been nothing but a messenger for the dead, asked time and again to pass on their words from beyond. *I'm sorrys* and *I wish I'd told yous*. Apologies. Explanations. But this is the first time since Sara that I've been given the opportunity to truly make a difference." She paused, sending him a sad smile as she said, "That's why this is so important to me, Ian. After all these years, you're my chance to finally do what's right."

CHAPTER ELEVEN

AN HOUR LATER, Molly and Ian were standing waist-high in boxes, the summer heat wave stifling within the small five-by-ten storage unit, the only ventilation the door they'd left open at the far end. They'd been working their way through from front to back, opening boxes and shuffling through the contents, inspecting each one, before moving on. So far, they'd found everything from clothes to dishes to books—but nothing that had caught their attention. Nothing that jumped out at them and screamed, "I'm it! I'm what you're looking for!"

"Exactly how much time are we supposed to waste rummaging through this crap?" Ian grumbled, wiping the back of his arm over his face. His shirt was damp from the heat, as was the hair around his temples, his dark blue eyes narrowed with frustration, accentuating the tiny, sexy lines that creased the corners.

"This isn't crap. It's someone's life," Molly grumbled right back at him, tired of his pissy attitude, since he'd started complaining not five minutes into the task. The only boon was the fact that his rich, vital scent rose with the heat of his body, filling the cramped space, adding a sensual dimension to a job that was slowly wearing her down. "And don't forget that you're the stubborn ass who won't call his brother to find out what it looks like."

Grunting in response, he propped his broad shoulders against the wall at his back, and watched as she knelt down to search through another box. From the corner of her eye, Molly could see him glaring at the ponytail she'd pulled on top of her head. "What?" she asked.

"You look like a kid when you wear your hair like that," he muttered, sounding as if it was a criminal offense.

"Gee, Ian. I'm really sorry you feel that way," she drawled, blowing a wayward curl out of her eyes. Her shins hurt from kneeling on the floor, and she was just as hot and sticky and as frustrated as he was, but she wasn't going to give up before they'd found what they'd come there for.

Whatever the hell it is.

She understood how difficult it was for Elaina to communicate with her. She really did. But there were times when Molly wished the woman was just a little more precise with the information she doled out.

Like the way she failed to mention that he'd take your blood, a disgruntled voice drawled sarcastically in her mind. *Or that whole dream sharing thing. Would've been nice to have had some warning about those two tasty little tidbits. Having a little beforehand knowledge never hurt—*

"I still think this is a waste of our time," Ian suddenly growled, interrupting her private rant. "Whatever she left me, I don't see how it's going to save our asses. Knowing Elaina, it's probably some superstitious, hoodoo-voodoo charm. Something that smells rank, made out of snake eyes and lizard tongues."

With her head and shoulders buried in the box, trying to see what was packed beneath an extra-thick layer of Bubble Wrap on the bottom, Molly called out, "Why don't you just sit down and try to stop complaining for five minutes? I know what I'm looking for."

"Yeah?" He snorted, the sarcastic sound setting her teeth on edge. "What is it, then?"

She finally dug her way through the Bubble Wrap, only to find what looked like a snow-globe collection, of all things. *Dammit.* Satisfied that this *wasn't* the box, Molly pushed her upper body free and turned to glare up at him, baring her teeth in a hard smile. "When I find it," she offered sweetly, "I'll be happy to tell you."

"Women," he muttered under his breath, at the same time as she looked for another box to search. A second later, he added, "If you need me, I'll be outside having a smoke."

Molly gave him a friendly little wave goodbye, just to push his buttons, and watched as he made his way through the boxes, out the open door, enjoying the view of his tight backside in the dark jeans. Grumbling to herself about the impossibly sweet, warm sensation of longing in the center of her chest that kept growing with each moment she spent with him, whether he was bitching at her or flirting with her—knowing that it was eventually going to land her in nothing but trouble—Molly turned back to her task. With a groan for her aching muscles, she shoved aside the heavy box of photo albums she'd already gone through, in order to get to the smaller one behind it.

When she'd first found them, Molly had been tempted

to open the quilted albums, though she knew Ian would have objected. Still, she would have liked the chance to look through the photos and satisfy her curiosity about the Buchanan family—specifically, the complicated, irritating, thoroughly fascinating man staring at her through the open doorway at the far end of the unit. He had his back propped against the opposite building, a smoldering cigarette dangling from the corner of his mouth. Molly knew she would have known he was there, watching her, even if she hadn't caught a glimpse of him as she'd pushed the box of albums aside. She could feel the press of his stare. Its heat. Its hunger. Its frustration.

He'd been watching her like that all day, keeping her on edge, driving her out of her mind.

Using Ian's truck key to cut through the tape on the unopened box, Molly flipped back the top halves, and almost instantly felt a strange shiver travel up her arms. Her breath quickened with excitement, and she swiftly grabbed several handfuls of wadded packing paper, revealing a sleek, black wooden case that sat on top of a slightly wider cardboard shoe box. Heart pounding, Molly tossed the handfuls of paper onto the floor, reached inside and took hold of the case, carefully transferring it to the top of a nearby packing box. "I think I've found something!" she called out.

"What is it?" Ian rasped at her side, and she knew he must have hurdled a box or two to have gotten there so quickly.

"I don't know," she said unsteadily, lifting the latch and opening the case. A second later, she gasped, the swift intake of air strangely audible in the stifled silence of the close space, while Ian remained quiet at her side. Nestled inside, on a bed of bloodred velvet, lay an intricately etched Maltese cross fashioned from some type of shiny black metal, attached to a length of black velvet cord.

"Ohmygod," she whispered, at the same time the man standing beside her cursed something hot and gritty under his breath. "I think this is it, Ian. What Elaina wanted us to find. What she left for you. She said I would know it when I saw it. This *has* to be it."

"There's something taped inside the top of the case," he said in a low voice.

"You're right." Carefully pulling the small square of paper free, she offered it to Ian, but he gestured for her to go ahead. Unfolding the handwritten note, she read aloud.

My Dearest Ian,
I've asked Riley to give you this box upon my death. It's my hope that you'll use the contents wisely and take care of yourself. I know, when the time comes, that you won't give in without a fight. Please wear this talisman for protection. The cross will lend you the power to set things right, when the time of the awakenings begins.

Always know that I love you. I've missed you, but I'll forever be watching over you.

                                    With love,
                                    Mom

Folding the letter back to its original size, Molly laid it inside the top of the case and looked up at Ian. He gazed down at the necklace…the talisman…with fierce intensity, as if its secrets would be revealed the longer he stared, like fog rolling back from a shrouded coastline to reveal the contours of the shore.

His chest stretched the cotton of his shirt as he drew in a deep, audible breath, tension pouring off him like heat, burning and prickly against the surface of her skin. "God," he muttered, rubbing his palm against the hard angle of his jaw. "That woman never changes."

"What do you mean?"

"She thinks some necklace is going to save me," he explained with a wry, shaky burst of laughter that sounded somehow damaged. "That's so like her. Always one bizarre, crazy-ass idea after another."

"It's very beautiful," she said, the words hushed, almost solemn. Molly could feel his bitterness…his resentment, as if the cross somehow signified something important—something that had stood between him and his mother—though she still didn't understand what that was.

"Yeah, well, it may be beautiful, but that doesn't mean that I want it." He clenched his jaw, shoving his hands deep in his pockets as he slanted her a narrow look, his blue eyes glittering and dark. "I know lots of beautiful things that I'd rather not be stuck with at the moment."

Her gaze slid away, focusing back on the necklace, a blush crawling its way up her face like heat building up from the bottom of a pan, pulsing in her cheeks. The way he'd looked at her made it more than clear that he was talking about her.

"Molly," he rasped in a hesitant tone, the low, graveled sound of his voice making her shiver with awareness. "Hell. I didn't—"

Not wanting to hear an explanation, she cut him off, saying, "You know where I've seen this design before, Ian?"

He breathed out a rough sound of impatience at the change in topic. "I wondered how long it would take you to mention that."

"It's an identical match to the cross on your back." Tilting back her head, she stared up at the hard cast of his features. "When you got the tattoo, did you show them a picture of this one?"

"Hell no," he grunted, jerking his chin toward the necklace. "I've never even seen that thing before."

Confused, Molly lifted her shoulders as she asked, "Then how did you pick the design?"

"I didn't. At least not that I remember. I got blind drunk one night, eight or so years ago, when I was about twenty-four, and the next morning it was there." A rough burst of laughter rumbled in his chest, though his expression remained strained. "The woman I woke up beside swore up and down that I walked right into a tattoo joint on Wiltshire, drew the guy a detailed picture, and told him I wanted it at the base of my neck."

"Wow," she said softly, feeling as if they were being spun in a bizarre web of fate that grew increasingly stranger by the moment. "That's…odd."

"You're telling me," he grunted, slanting a wary look at the cross. "And you wanna know what's even creepier? When I was fighting the Casus last night, the bastard said something about how I wasn't wearing the talisman."

Her eyes went wide with surprise. "The Casus must know about it somehow," she murmured, reaching for the necklace. Molly carefully lifted the cross from its bed of bloodred velvet, surprised by its heavy weight, as well as its warmth. Shifting to her feet, she turned toward Ian. "If you bend down, I'll slip it over your head."

"Not a chance," he rasped, eyeing her with a cautious stare as he took a step back.

Molly frowned. "Ian, your mother wants you to have this. I don't think she would have gone to all the trouble if it wasn't important. She even says it will help protect you. You can't just leave it packed away."

He stared down at her with eyes so dark they looked black beneath the thick shadow of his lashes, the moment stretching out painfully long, until he finally said, "If you don't want to leave it in the case, then *you* wear it."

"What?"

"I'm serious. Here," he muttered, taking the necklace from her grasp. "It'll look a helluva lot better on you anyway."

"Ian," she breathed out on a soft burst of air. "I…I couldn't. This is…dammit, it was meant for *you.*"

"Either you wear it or it stays in the case," he told her, his deep voice cut with stubborn determination. His fingers closed around the gleaming black metal in a fist, the long velvet cord falling gracefully over the powerful thickness of his wrist. Molly stared, unable to look away, the simple image of the sensuous velvet draping his dark golden skin somehow painfully erotic, and she pressed her hand against the jarring burst of awareness burning low in her belly, its deep, rhythmic pulse spreading through her, until she had to fight the urge to reach out and grab him.

She wanted to ask him if he could feel the cross's warmth, its power, but didn't want him to think she was any crazier than he already did.

"I mean it, Molly."

"Fine," she snapped, frustrated at him for being so stubborn.

"Turn around," he instructed, his voice husky and low as he stepped up behind her, and she shivered from the heat of his body. He didn't touch her…but came close enough that she felt his size, his forceful masculinity, so strong and vital and overwhelming. It made her feel small, vulnerable, endlessly feminine. Melted her insides with a hot, smooth glow of warmth. Made her breath catch. Made her ache for his touch.

And yet, he didn't touch her at all. He simply slipped the necklace over her head, its warmth settling between her breasts. Then he murmured for her to turn around, the erotic rasp of his breath teasing the sensitive shell of her ear as he spoke.

"Ian, you should really be the one wearing this," she said unsteadily, turning to face him.

He gave her a tight smile. "It's not my style," he said quietly, his gaze appreciative as he eyed the way it rested against the swell of her chest. "But it looks hot as hell on you."

A part of her wanted to smile in response, but the part that was worried and frightened had her frowning instead. "You can't keep running from what you are, Ian. Trust me, I know."

He arched one brow at the whispered words, his sensual mouth curved in a purely wicked, utterly male expression of arrogance. "I'm not running, Molly. If I was, you could bet your sweet little ass that I wouldn't be here right now. And since we got what we came for, let's get out of here."

"Wait," she said quickly, bending down to pull out the shoe box that had been stored beneath the black case. "We haven't opened this one." She set the box beside the smaller case, then pulled off the lid.

"What's in it?"

"These," she said, turning toward him with a small, leather-bound journal in one hand, a framed snapshot in the other. Molly held the journal out to him, but rather than take it, Ian stepped closer, staring down at the photograph in the carved wooden frame.

"That's me and Elaina," he said in a quiet voice, his thick lashes shielding his gaze as he studied the image. "Man, I was a scrawny little thing."

Her mouth curled with a ghost of a smile. "You were adorable, Ian. And you're actually grinning. I almost didn't recognize you without a scowl on your face."

"Very funny," he drawled, rolling his eyes.

"Look at this…at the edge of the frame. The pattern's been worn down where someone has held it." A terrible sense of sadness bloomed deep within her chest as she smoothed the tip of one finger against the worn patch, wondering how many times Elaina must have clutched the frame in her grasp. Lifting her gaze, she caught his guarded expression as she handed him the photograph. "Elaina must have missed you very much."

"Christ," he rasped, rubbing his thumb against the smooth patch of wood.

Blinking, Molly fought the hot glow of emotion burning at the back of her eyes and throat. She could see the regret etched into the rugged, beautiful angles of his face.

For all his macho blustering, there was a scarred, tender core at Ian Buchanan's center. He might have been tarnished and battered and a little rough around the edges, but he was still solid and strong and good. She knew there had to be something more behind his rift with Elaina—something deeper than teenage rebellion and arguments. Whatever it was, it'd been enough to keep them apart—a fact that he now regretted. And in that moment, something inside Molly shifted into a sharper focus.

She'd been touched by his reaction to Kendra Wilcox's death—but the depth of emotion revealed in his expression as she stood there beside him—God, it melted her. Made him so much more real to her. Changed him from the surly, too-gorgeous-for-his-own-good womanizer, the cynic she needed to guard herself against, to a man with incredible depth and compassion. And that made him dangerous to her in a way that no amount of physical desire could ever do.

He'd already been a threat to her defenses—now he was a threat to her heart.

Holding out the journal, she gently said, "You should take this, Ian. There must be something in here, something important, for her to have left it with the cross."

"Just put it back in the box with this," he rasped, handing her the photograph. "We can take the whole thing, along with the case."

"And you'll read the journal?" she pressed, replacing the lid on the shoe box, then stacking the cross's black case on top.

Rubbing at the back of his neck, Ian gave a low, shaky laugh. "Naw, but you should. Maybe there'll be something in there that we need."

"I don't know," she told him, feeling uneasy as he picked up the shoe box and case. "They weren't left to me. It feels like it would be an invasion of privacy."

"Hell, she's been sneaking into your head for months now, Molly," he drawled, heading for the open door. "Don't be such a Girl Scout. Seems only fair that you would get to read her journal."

"Ian, you don't really think she can…"

"Read your mind?" he finished for her, shooting her a teasing look over his broad shoulder, the regret that had carved his features only moments before hidden, as if it'd never existed, behind a wickedly sexy grin. But she wasn't about to forget.

No, Molly was on to him now. She'd have even returned his smile, if she wasn't feeling quite so uncomfortable about the idea of his mother snooping around in her mind, especially considering the way she'd been thinking about his body last night. Gaack. Talk about embarrassing.

"Ian, I'm serious," she said, her tone dismal as they stepped out into the bright glare of afternoon sunshine, the heat rolling up from the asphalt in a searing, stifling wave. "Do you think she can really do that?"

"Hmm, I dunno." He shifted the items under his arm as he locked the door behind them. "Anything interesting in there you wouldn't want her to know about?" he asked in a suggestive drawl.

The blush firing beneath her skin said more than any words, and his shoulders shook with a soft, husky rumble of laughter. But instead of teasing, he took mercy on her and changed the subject, saying, "After we get back to the motel, we need to try and figure out who this

Scott guy is. I'll put a call in to Riley and see if he can get us an address."

Molly almost managed a grin as she climbed into the truck. "That would be wonderful."

"Yeah. It doesn't happen often, but there *are* times when ol' Saint Riley comes in handy." He laughed drily, and a minute later, they were on the road, traveling beneath the brilliant glare of a lemon-yellow sun, surrounded by the rugged beauty of the mountain forest that hugged the narrow highway. It was a peaceful, idyllic setting, oddly comforting, as if it was the most natural thing in the world for her to be doing, driving down the road with Ian Buchanan, the radio playing softly in the background. But as Molly rubbed her fingers against the intricately etched surface of the cross, its power thrumming against her skin, warm to the touch…she couldn't help but worry about the darkness that lay ahead.

CHAPTER TWELVE

THE SECOND IAN OPENED the weathered door of Molly's motel room, he knew someone was there. Throughout the day, he'd had the strangest sensation of acute awareness, as if he were sensing everything with an intensity that wasn't normal. Sounds. Sights. Smells. Each of them amplified and sharp.

Though the Merrick wasn't trying to fight its way out of him, its presence was lingering, heightening his abilities.

His nostrils flared as he breathed in the dark, clean, woodsy scent of the trespasser, and he scanned the room, looking for anything that was out of place. Reaching behind him, he grabbed on to Molly's wrist, holding tight, a gentle squeeze warning her to be silent as he slowly pulled her into the room. He pressed her against the wall just inside the doorway, his back plastered to her front.

He could tell by its scent that the intruder wasn't Casus—but that didn't mean that it wasn't dangerous. Wasn't a threat. Because the scent definitely wasn't human.

Cutting a quick look over his shoulder, he mouthed the words, "Don't move," to Molly, then slowly moved toward the center of the room, bitterly aware of the

Merrick shifting within him, demanding more information. Like an animal, it wanted to lift its nose and sniff at the air, its bright eyes alert to danger. It was letting him know that it wasn't docile—that it intended to do its part to protect their woman.

Whoa. Their woman?

The jarring thought slammed into Ian's brain like a hammer, stunning him, and he scowled, choking off a vicious curse when a light thread of sound came from the small kitchen. Keeping his arms loose at his sides, he flexed his hands, ready to take down whatever the hell was about to come through that doorway.

"You needn't try to sneak up on me," came a deep, lazy drawl from the other room. "I already know you're there, and as corny as it sounds—" there was a slight muffled sound, like someone snickering under their breath "—I come in peace."

Stopping in the center of the room, Ian rolled his head over his shoulders, keeping his weight light on his feet as he muttered, "If that's so, then get your ass out here and show your face."

A chair screeched against the linoleum, and then a dark shadow fell across the floor, through the archway, seconds before a tall, dark-haired man filled the space.

"Who the fuck are you?" Ian growled.

The stranger arched one dark brow, his hard mouth twitching just a little at one corner. "Charming," he murmured.

Jerking his chin toward the intruder, Ian said, "You know this guy, Molly?"

"Um…no," she whispered. "I've never seen him before in my life."

If she had, Molly knew she would have remembered him. He was too striking to ever forget, and if asked to describe him, the first word that would have come to mind was *dark*. Dark hair, shorn close to his scalp, his features…perfect, like something that had been sculpted from marble. Dark eyes burning within thick black lashes, beneath the dark slash of his brows. Even his skin was dark, burnished a deep gold with a slight reddish undertone, attesting to what had to be a Native American ancestry, especially with those striking cheekbones. He wore a plain white T-shirt and dark blue jeans, with brown hiking boots on his feet.

"What the hell are you doing in her room?" Ian demanded in a strained voice, while the stranger hooked his thumbs in his front pockets and leaned his shoulder against the side of the archway.

"No need to get your back up. I'm not here about the woman, as tempting as she is. I'm here because of you, Merrick."

Molly choked back a gasp, thankful she'd slipped the cross inside her T-shirt before they'd climbed out of the truck. Whoever this guy was, he was somehow involved in the nightmare closing in around them. Until she knew which side he was on, she wasn't about to reveal their secrets.

"My name is Buchanan," Ian snarled, his voice unusually guttural, and for a moment, Molly wondered if the darkness inside of him—*the Merrick*—was about to break free.

As if impervious to the danger of that possibility, a low, coarse burst of sound that could have been a laugh rumbled in the stranger's throat. "Ah, but you're more

Merrick than anything else. Even more than you're human. So let's not play word games," he drawled with the barest inflection of a Western twang.

Crossing his arms over his chest, Ian demanded, "And what exactly do you want with me?"

"Kierland Scott sent me. I believe you might be familiar with the name."

"You know Scott?" Ian grunted, and Molly wondered if his shock matched her own.

The stranger inclined his dark head with a fraction of movement. "You could say I work with Kierland. He's asked me to bring you to Ravenswing. Both of you."

"Ravenswing?" Molly repeated, at the same time Ian snorted, saying, "And what in God's name makes you think we'd go anywhere with you?"

"Those marks on your arm," the man remarked in a quiet rumble, gesturing with one sun-browned, long-fingered hand toward the scratches revealed beneath the edge of Ian's short sleeve. "I know what made them. They're called the Casus, mortal enemies of the Merrick. If you come with me, we'll teach you what you need to know in order to survive."

"We?" Ian rasped.

"The men I work with. We're called the Watchmen."

Ian made a rude sound under his breath. "The Watchmen, huh? Sounds like some kind of eighties rock band."

A slow, hard smile spread across the stranger's mouth. "I can assure you we're not, though Aiden's been known to play a mean Mozart on the piano. If you're as smart as we've been led to believe, you'll realize how lucky you are to have us on your side."

"Is that right?"

The stranger lifted his dark brows. "Who do you think ran off the Casus last night in the woods?"

"That was you?" Molly whispered, moving to Ian's side, which earned her a hard, intimidating glare as he uncrossed his arms. "If you're here to help, why now? Why not before he got ripped to shreds by that maniac?"

"*Molly*," Ian growled, obviously taking exception to her words, but she merely grabbed hold of his hand, the surprising gesture startling him into silence. For a moment, his hand remained rigid in her grasp, but then his long, warm fingers curled around her smaller ones, holding tight. Smiling to herself, she wondered if he'd ever actually held hands with a woman before, then jerked her attention back to the stranger, who watched them closely, his dark eyes taking everything in.

"Interference is not our way," he explained. "Our purpose is to remain neutral, to keep watch over those who are not human and report our findings to the Consortium. But we've broken the rules, I guess you could say, in this case, because the battleground is no longer an even playing field. Until you know how to protect yourself, the Casus is at an advantage, which became clear last night. These are strange, unprecedented times, and our unit has decided that allowances have to be made, whether the Consortium gives their consent or not."

"The Consortium?" she asked, her questions mounting as she thought over what he'd said.

"It's a complicated story," he murmured, "and one I'm certain Kierland would rather explain himself."

"You know," Ian muttered at her side, "I've never

trusted anyone who claims to be neutral. Usually means they're just too chickenshit to pick a side."

"I assure you, Merrick, we are not cowards," the stranger responded with a sharp smile, the look in his onyx-colored eyes even sharper. Molly shivered in reaction, and Ian gave her hand a comforting squeeze.

"I still haven't heard a good reason why we should go with you," he said in a quiet rasp, the gritty tone as challenging as his body language.

"Because if you don't, you'll die. It's as simple as that. And once the Casus kills you, he'll start in on your woman. You've been safe so far during the day, but what about tonight? Or tomorrow night? The night after that? Do you trust yourself to be able to protect her when it makes its next move?"

Turning his head, Ian stared down at Molly, knowing he didn't have a choice. If it was just his life on the line, he probably would have taken his chances. But he couldn't roll the dice where Molly's life was concerned. She didn't deserve it, just as she didn't deserve getting dragged into the middle of what was turning out to be a living, breathing nightmare.

Looking back toward the dark-eyed stranger, Ian held the man's stare as he said, "You still haven't given us a name."

White teeth flashed in a hard, satisfied smile. "My friends call me Quinn."

AFTER GRABBING ANOTHER round of burgers and fries for their dinner, it took nearly an hour of traveling on the winding mountain roads, climbing to a higher elevation, before they finally reached the place Quinn called Ravenswing. There was no doubt that the Watchmen compound, as he'd described it, had been aptly named. Nestled between the base of a sheer cliff and a smooth lake that gleamed like black oil in the moonlight, the compound's largest building possessed a sweeping roof that resembled the fluid arc of a bird's wing, flaring up at the far end as if curved in flight. Reflecting the infinite, star-studded darkness of the sky, the surface of the large, three-storied structure glittered like black diamonds.

"Ohmygod," Molly breathed in a stunned murmur of awe.

"Beautiful, isn't she?" Quinn rumbled from the backseat of Ian's truck, an unmistakable thread of pride in his deep voice.

"It's magnificent," she replied, while the massive gates that blocked the private driveway swung to a close behind them.

"The entire compound is fenced," Quinn explained. "We have surveillance equipment running 24-7. Whoever is manning the control room tonight recognized your truck. Otherwise, they wouldn't have opened the gates."

"How long have you been watching Ian?" Molly asked, staring with wide-eyed fascination out the window as they drove up the winding drive that led to the main building, an array of smaller structures just visible through the inky darkness. As they'd made the journey, Quinn had confessed that the Watchmen knew about her conversations with Elaina and the reason she'd come to Henning, Colorado, since they'd been watching Ian closely, monitoring his awakening. But he hadn't explained how long Ian had been under their surveillance.

"The Buchanan line has always been one of our top interests," Quinn murmured, avoiding a straight answer. Molly was ready to press him for more information, when Ian pulled to a slow stop near what appeared to be the entrance into the building…or house…since she still wasn't certain of its function. Opening the back passenger's side door, Quinn climbed out, leaving them alone within the intimate cab of the truck.

Aware of the warmth of Ian's stare on her profile as she leaned forward, still gazing in awe at the beautiful structure through the windshield, Molly turned and found herself captured in the glittering depths of his eyes. There was a silent message in that mesmerizing blue gaze—for her to be careful, to stay close to him. She wondered if he felt the same nervous certainty that she did—that they were getting ready to embark upon a new leg of this…she stumbled over what to call it. Journey? Quest? Whatever it was, they were drawing nearer to the end…to the moment when Ian would have to face what was inside of him, as well as the evil hunting him down.

Lowering her gaze to his mouth—to the hard, sculpted perfection of his lips—she sent him a small, trembling smile that bloomed up from that shaky knot of emotion churning deep inside of her. A low sound lost somewhere between a groan and a visceral growl slipped from his lips, and he reached out, capturing her chin in the callused hold of his fingers.

Before Molly could prepare herself, he leaned across the center console and pressed the hot, damp, delicious heat of his mouth against hers. The warm, shivery sensation in the pit of her stomach sparked into a fiery burst of craving, and she moved her mouth under his, undone by the rough-silk texture of his lips. By his warm, rich scent and intoxicating taste. With just the simple touch of his mouth, he held perfect, complete mastery over her body, her will—and the fading bite marks on her throat began to slowly pulse with heat. She would have gone anywhere with him—*done anything with him*—just to get more of that dark, decadent pleasure.

Thankfully, Ian had the frame of mind to realize that now wasn't the time or place. Breaking the kiss, his breath surged against her mouth, gritty and rough, as if it'd taken a physical effort for him to stop. The air closed in around them, lust-thick and heavy with warmth, despite the cool burst of the air conditioner blowing in from the vents. "No matter what happens, you stay close to me," he breathed against the sensitive surface of her lips.

"I will," she whispered. "I promise."

He stamped the impression of his mouth against hers one last time, hard and fast, then pulled away. Shivering from the inside out, Molly forced herself to turn and open her door, then climbed out into the lingering heat of the evening.

THE MOMENT he came around the back of the truck, Ian stepped closer to Molly's side, surprising both her and himself as he settled his hand at her lower back in a silent, yet unmistakable gesture of possession.

Quinn stood just outside the opened double doors that led inside the building, talking with another man. Moving closer, Ian could see that the guy's dark, windswept auburn hair fell over his brow, his pale green eyes sharp with awareness as he watched them make their way toward the door. He was as tall as Quinn, the lean muscles stretching the seams of his blue T-shirt attesting to the fact that he lived a hard, physical life.

It didn't escape Ian's notice that Molly couldn't take her eyes off the pretty-faced asshole, and it pissed him off. All of it. All the ways in which this woman affected him. But what irritated him the most was the fact that he even noticed her reaction to another man. That had *never* happened to him before, which seemed to be some kind of warped theme in their bizarre relationship, this constant discovery of new ways she could get to him.

He didn't like the uncomfortable feeling in his gut, either—the one telling him to throw off his jackass-of-the-year routine and just play nice with her. Playing nice with women like Molly Stratton gave them ideas—expectations he didn't have a chance in hell of ever meeting. Not that he wanted to meet them. He just wanted to have sex with her. To take hold of her sweet little body, lay it over the nearest flat surface he could find, and learn how she tasted from the top of her head down to her dainty little feet. Then he'd get this infuriating itch for her out of his system once and for all.

And he'd have done it, too, if he'd been able to dredge up so much as an ounce of faith that once he got her under him, spread and penetrated, he'd be able to control himself. That he wouldn't slip over into that dark, slick pool of hell lurking beneath his skin, and end up hurting her. End up sinking his fangs into her pale little throat and accidentally killing her.

Molly could sit and tell him he was one of the good

guys until she turned blue in the face, but it wasn't going to change the fact that he didn't trust himself with her, that he feared what he'd do to her if he got her beneath him.

By the time they reached Quinn and the redhead, Ian's jaw was clenched, his expression pulled into a tight, hard scowl. The stranger's pale green eyes met his, and Ian sneered, "Let me guess. Kierland Scott?"

"At your service," Scott murmured with just the trace of a British accent rounding out the edges of his speech. The bastard had the audacity to send Molly a flirtatious grin as he took hold of her right hand, leaning down to press a kiss against the delicate ridge of her knuckles.

"Watch it," Ian warned, the words so low, they were barely audible.

Scott merely arched a brow in response, and Molly pulled her hand from his grip with a soft, nervous murmur of sound.

"Let's take this inside," Quinn said, shaking his head at their male posturing. "I could use some coffee."

"This way," the redhead drawled, the corner of his mouth kicking up at one corner as he flicked a quick glance at the possessive hold Ian had on Molly's waist. Gritting his teeth, Ian held her tighter, pulling her more closely against his side as they followed after the jackass, while Quinn shut the doors behind them.

The rich, intoxicating smell of cedar and wood polish filled the air, and Ian glanced upward at the exposed beams that crossed the high ceiling of the wide hallway, then down at the thick stretch of burgundy carpet running along the center of the gleaming hardwood floor. Despite its modern exterior, the inside of Ravenswing conveyed nothing short of wealthy, rustic comfort, warm and inviting. It seduced the senses, the colors as soothing as they were bold.

Opening a thick, double set of intricately carved pine doors, Scott led them into a massive, equally high-ceilinged kitchen, complete with terra-cotta tiling, gleaming black appliances, rows of cabinets that matched the doors, and a mass of gleaming copper pots hanging from three wrought iron pot racks.

Two long tables ran down the center of the room, but Scott gestured them toward a smaller oval table that sat in a windowed alcove off to the left, the glinting surface of the lake visible beyond the glass. "I'll grab the coffee," Quinn said to Scott. "You go ahead and get started. I think they've got some questions they'd like to ask you."

Ian snorted under his breath, thinking that must be the understatement of the year. He was about to pose the first of what he expected would be many when Molly slipped into one of the high-backed wooden chairs and immediately said, "What can you tell us about the Merrick?"

"How much do you already know?" Scott asked, folding his tall body into a wide chair on the opposite side of the table, while Ian did the same with the chair at Molly's right.

Tucking her hair behind her ears, she ruefully admitted, "I'm afraid we don't know much, really."

Leaning back in his seat, Scott rubbed his hand against the bristled surface of his jaw, slanting a shuttered look toward Ian. "I assume your mother talked to you about the Merrick."

Pulling his pack of cigarettes from his shirtfront pocket, Ian took one and wedged it between his lips; at the same time Scott reached toward the counter behind him and grabbed an ashtray. Using his lighter, Ian lit the tip of the cigarette and took a slow drag before replying. "She talked of ancient ancestors who she claimed once walked the earth. Said they were more than human. Powerful. Primal. Something that existed between man and…and something darker…more visceral in its nature."

"She was right," Scott murmured, eyeing his cigarette with a hungry intensity that made Ian wonder if the guy had recently quit.

"Where did they come from?" he asked, flicking his cigarette at the ashtray.

Scott took a deep breath, as if collecting his thoughts, then slowly began. "No one really knows where they came from or how they came into being. But it's believed they lived throughout Europe, easily blending in with humanity when they needed to, which enabled their numbers to thrive. They consumed blood in order to feed the primal parts of their nature, though they didn't kill their victims. Instead, they lived in peace, respecting their human brothers and feeding only from other Merrick and gypsy tribes who were aware of their existence. The gypsies traded their blood for the protection the Merrick offered from those clans who were sometimes aggressive toward the tribes."

Molly slanted him a meaningful look, and Ian knew she was thinking of that first dream they'd shared on Friday night, when he'd taken her on the ground in the middle of a gypsy campsite. Her cheeks flushed with color, and she delicately cleared her throat, cutting her gaze back to Scott. "So there were other clans?"

Scott nodded. "The Merrick, though one of the most powerful, were only one of many, the abilities of the various clans differing as widely as their physiology. Some only partially altered when in their primal forms, like the Merrick. Others fully transformed, able to take the shape of an animal, similar to those of us who make up the Watchmen today. Others couldn't venture out into the light, living only from blood. Some had talents that involved telepathy, others the ability to live underwater or to master the skies. The variety was as rich as it was diverse. And for the most part, the clans lived in peace with one another, hidden among the humans, until the Casus came on the scene sometime during the second half of the first millennium."

"Were the Casus also one of these ancient clans?" Molly asked, murmuring a soft thank-you to Quinn as he placed a mug of coffee before her on the gleaming surface of the table.

Taking a heavy sip from his own cup, Scott shook his head, the golden gleam of the recessed lighting glinting off the auburn strands of his hair. "At first, yes. They came from an isolated clan that roamed the European continent. Several of the ruling families, believing their bloodlines were not only the purest but also the most powerful in terms of physical strength and ability, became fanatical about breeding for the purity of their species. They matched brother with sister, parents with offspring. At first, because of their isolation, their actions went unnoticed by the Consortium. But within a few generations, it became apparent that the inbreeding had brought about dangerous, unforeseen consequences. Rather than keeping the purity of the line intact, their biology mutated. They had bred themselves into immortal beings of incredible strength, but their power came with a price. They became slaves to an intense, overwhelming hunger, evolving into what we know today as the Casus, meaning *violent death*."

"An appropriate name," Molly whispered, wrapping her arms around her middle, as if to ward off a chill, though the room remained pleasantly warm.

"Yes, it was," Scott agreed, his gaze lingering on her face in a way that made Ian want to snarl at him. Biting his tongue, he took another drag on his cigarette, listening as the Watchman went on with his explanation. "The Casus began hunting humans as their main food source, discovering that they grew stronger when they not only fed upon their victim's blood, but their flesh, as well. All they knew was death and destruction, like a black plague that annihilated everything within its path."

Exhaling a short stream of smoke, Ian said, "My mother would often talk about the Casus hunting the Merrick."

"And she was right. They soon learned that the stronger their victim, the greater their rush of pleasure and power when they fed. The Merrick, being one of the strongest of the ancient clans, soon became their favorite food source, though they continued to sustain themselves on human kills, also. Intent on protecting both humanity and their own species, the Merrick went to war against the Casus, with the blessing of the Consortium. The two clans battled for years, until, with the help of the Consortium, a plan was finally devised to imprison the Casus."

"What the hell's the Consortium?" Ian asked, stubbing out his cigarette, then immediately taking another from the pack. "I've never heard of them before tonight."

"The Consortium," Scott explained, "is a body of officials drawn from each of the original ancient clans, like a preternatural United Nations. Their purpose is to settle disputes, to keep peace among the differing species, while working to preserve the secrecy of the remaining clans from the human world. They're a bureaucracy, more than anything, often bogged down in politics and personal agendas—though they do help keep the lines of communication open between groups that would otherwise avoid interaction. The Watchmen were formed from various shape-shifting clans as the Consortium's eyes and ears around the world. Now we monitor the different species and known bloodlines that are still in existence, like the Merrick, and then report back with our findings. If action is required, the members of the Consortium vote on how to proceed."

"So then after years of war, this Consortium finally got off their asses and decided to help the Merrick capture the Casus," Ian rumbled, taking a sip of the coffee Quinn had placed on the table in front of him, wishing like hell it was a beer. "What changed their minds? And how did they do it?"

"And where exactly did they trap them?" Molly added.

"No one knows for sure," Quinn answered, his tone dry as he turned down the lights in the kitchen, leaving only the alcove in a warm glow. Slipping into the far seat on Molly's left, he sat with his back to the bay window. "But it's believed that toward the end of the Dark Ages, the Consortium decided to take action against the Casus when it became obvious that their rampant, violent attacks against humanity threatened the exposure of the other clans. Despite internal bickering and opposing beliefs, they agreed to construct a prison, or holding ground, for the Casus. Realizing that the future of their bloodlines depended on the imprisonment of their mortal enemy, the Merrick leaders offered themselves up as bait in order to set the trap.

"The Casus, believing they were about to embark upon what would prove their greatest victory and the end of the Merrick, gathered all their clansmen and women together to witness the momentous event, never suspecting what was coming. Once the trap was sprung, the Consortium was able to create some sort of metaphysical gate to hold the Casus inside, but no one knows where. Some believe they were buried deep within a mountain somewhere in Eastern Europe, others in an underground cavern. There are even claims of the holding ground being beneath the sea. But the one certainty that no one could dispute was that the Casus *did* disappear and their reign of terror came to an end."

"But how can no one know where or how it happened?" Ian muttered, his tone thick with disbelief.

Scott sighed, locking his arms behind his head as he leaned back in his chair. "You have to remember that these were chaotic, violent times. They weren't called the Dark Ages for nothing," he drawled. "The Consortium's plan was to hold the Casus trapped in this holding ground until weapons could be created that would not only kill their immortal bodies, but their spirits, as well. Once these weapons were fashioned, they'd planned to go back and destroy the Casus once and for all, purging the earth of their existence."

Lowering his arms again, Scott reached for his coffee. After taking a swallow, he continued in a grim tone. "But dark times fell over the clans. The Casus's mindless killing had spread paranoia throughout the human world. A group named the Collective was formed, comprised of mankind's most fearsome warriors, their purpose to hunt those who weren't human and destroy them. Many of the clans were massacred, including the Consortium itself. Their records were believed lost in the gruesome battles that were waged between the clans and the Collective for centuries afterward, until most of the surviving clans finally disbanded, blending completely into human society. Many even bred with humans, generation after generation, until the primitive blood of their ancestors became so diluted, it was all but forgotten. The Merrick, whose numbers had been severely decimated after so many years of war, were one of those clans who eventually took human mates."

"And so the Casus were never killed," Molly murmured, her hands wrapped around her mug, brown eyes shadowed with fear. "They were left trapped in this holding ground?"

"That's exactly what happened," Scott rasped, setting his own mug back on the table. "Everyone who knew where it was, how to find it, how to open the gate, how to kill the Casus, was slaughtered. And the answers died with them. Even after the new Consortium was formed, they couldn't discover the truth. They searched for the records, or archives, that had been collected by the original Consortium for centuries, as did the Collective, believing they would hold answers to these questions, as well as information about all of the ancient clans—but as far as anyone knows, neither group has ever managed to find them. The only thing everyone agrees on is that the Casus never died. It's believed that though their flesh-and-blood bodies would have eventually decomposed without a proper food source to sustain them, their shades, or spirits, would continue to be trapped within the Consortium's prison."

Quinn leaned forward, bracing his crossed arms against the table as he picked up where Scott left off. "But that's not the end of the story. There was a gypsy legend that was passed through the European tribes, foretelling of a time when the Casus would escape and once again walk the earth."

"Escape how?" Ian grunted.

Quinn lifted his shoulders. "Again, the details are unclear. But it's said that the day will come when the Casus, eager for revenge, will figure out a way to send a shade back into this realm, in search of its mortal enemy, the Merrick. And in keeping with the balance of nature's order, the gypsies believed a Merrick would rise to battle the Casus. Because of this legend, the Watchmen have been responsible for monitoring the most powerful Merrick bloodlines, waiting for the time of the awakenings to begin. There are compounds scattered over every continent, each of them manned by Watchmen who are running surveillance on the Merrick, monitoring their status. We'd hoped the legend would prove untrue, but as you know, the time has finally come. You're the first."

"Why me?" Ian questioned in a gritty rasp.

"It makes sense you were awakened first," Scott explained. "The Buchanan bloodline has always been believed to be one of the strongest. And you're the eldest son. So we've watched you closely, from the moment you were a boy."

"You're fucking kidding me," he snorted.

Scott's mouth twitched at his tone. "Not at all. We followed after you when you left home. Watched you during all those unsavory years in Los Angeles. For a long time we wondered if you wouldn't simply self-destruct, but then you finally pulled it together and moved closer to your brother. That decision saved your life," he murmured. "No one could have kept going down the path you were on and survived."

"But why wait until now?" Molly asked, a hint of frustration in her words. "If you've known where Ian was, known what was coming, why not contact him earlier and prepare him?"

Scott sent her a slow, arrogant grin. "And would he have believed us?"

"I don't know," she told him, and Ian could tell from the subtle change in her expression that she was upset. "But if you'd tried, it might have saved a woman's life."

Scott's grin bled away, and the rugged line of his jaw locked, one broad shoulder rolling in a hard gesture. He looked as if he wanted to curse, but in a calm voice, he simply said, "Interference is not our way."

"So you don't care that an innocent woman died?" Molly demanded, all but bristling with fury.

"I didn't say that," Scott countered in a gritty rasp,

his mouth grim. "But we're governed by rules. Specific ones. Ones that we're already breaking by bringing you here, risking the safety of this compound, as well as reprimands by the Consortium for acting without their approval. And even if we *could* act, we don't even know where the Casus is. Quinn could have followed him last night, but he was more interested in making sure Buchanan made it to safety."

"Rules, huh?" Ian drawled. "Funny, but I never was much for those."

"We noticed," sneered a deep, rasping voice from one of the far, shadowed corners of the kitchen. Looking over his shoulder, Ian could just make out the outline of a giant hulk of a man, his golden eyes glittering in the dim light.

"Allow me to introduce our colleague," Scott murmured. "This is Aiden Shrader. Aiden, this is Ia—"

"I know who they are," the shadow rasped in an angry snarl.

Ian was about to ask what the guy's problem was, when Molly, who'd obviously decided to ignore the intrusion, said, "So then you think it's an actual Casus shade who's hunting Ian, and not just a Casus awakening inside one of their living offspring, the same way the Merrick part of Ian is awakening?"

"Unfortunately—" Quinn sighed "—that's exactly what we believe. It also accounts for why the Casus is so much more powerful than Buchanan." Cutting his dark gaze toward Ian, he said, "The Merrick inside of you is slowly awakening to what it is, realizing its potential. But the Casus, he's one of the originals, the body he's existing in stolen from some unsuspecting bastard who was just unlucky enough to have a drop of Casus blood running through his veins."

"I know how he feels," Ian muttered.

"Is that right?" the man they'd called Shrader growled from the shadows. "Tell me, human. What's so unlucky about finding out you're not a complete asshole?"

Scott and Quinn both groaned, and the man stalked from the room, his angry strides echoing on what sounded like a distant set of wooden stairs. "You'll have to ignore Aiden," Scott murmured. "He doesn't care much for humanity."

"I never would have noticed," Ian drawled with a heavy dose of sarcasm, wondering how much of a problem the Watchman was going to be.

"Some grudges are easier to let go of than others," Quinn explained.

"I don't care what his issues are. I don't want him coming near her while we're here," Ian told them, tilting his head toward Molly.

"He won't be a problem," Scott assured him. "Aiden agreed that bringing you here was the right thing to do. It's just going to take him some time to…adjust."

"I don't give a damn if he adjusts or not," he snapped. "I don't want him coming near her."

As if sensing that the conversation was taking a turn for the worse, Molly quickly said, "You mentioned before that the legend speaks of one Casus escaping and making its way back to this world, in search of a Merrick. But then you mentioned awakenings, as in more than one. Do you believe more Casus will escape?"

Quinn leaned back in his chair, shaking his head. "To be honest, we aren't sure how it will work. But there are many who believe that once one Casus shade makes his way through, others will follow. If the gypsies' belief that nature will work to keep balance among the species is true, then with each Casus that escapes, a Merrick will awaken. And each time a shade enters our world, they will seek the Merrick, not only for a powerful feeding, but to satisfy their thirst for revenge. Only a few Casus bloodlines are known to exist—the product of human victims who were raped by those monsters, and by simple acts of chance, managed to escape with their lives. Several Watchmen compounds have been watching those bloodlines closely, but so far there's been nothing suspicious to report, which leads us to believe they must be using a line we're not familiar with." Staring at Ian, he said, "And of all the Merrick bloodlines we monitor, you're the only one we believe has awakened so far."

Exhaling a rough breath, Ian asked, "What about my brother and sister?"

"If more Casus escape, we have no doubt that your brother and sister will be hunted…and the Merrick parts of their nature awakened."

"Christ," he hissed. "We don't even know where Saige is."

"Fortunately," Scott drawled, "we do. Each of the Buchanan siblings has been under surveillance since the time you left home. Your sister, at this time, is on another one of her archeological digs in South America. Though she doesn't know it, one of the Watchmen tails her every move."

Ian opened his mouth, ready to pose a question, when Molly suddenly asked, "And this Casus that's hunting Ian…it won't go after them now?"

"Killing either of them at this point would be a waste of an energy source," Quinn responded, drawing their attention. "Better to leave them alive until they've awakened and can provide a full dose of power. Kill them too early, and it's like picking fruit before it's ripe. But they *will* need to be warned of what's to come."

"And can these things be killed?" Ian asked, cutting a sharp look toward Scott.

"Yes…and no," he rasped, the fingers of one hand curled around the mug of coffee sitting on the table. "According to the legend, you can't destroy its spirit by killing its host body, though you *can* send its shade back to the holding ground. But first you have to be powerful enough to defeat it, which won't be easy. As one of the original Casus, it's going to be stronger than you. Your only hope of survival is to learn to fight with the true power of a Merrick, which is why we've brought you here."

Molly's voice quivered as she said, "Will he be able to become a Merrick whenever he needs to? How will it work?"

Scott's gaze shifted, his green eyes warming as he met Molly's stare. "The darkness calls to the Merrick, so it's easiest to make a full change at night. But as he grows stronger, traits will materialize when needed—especially when provoked by hunger."

Ian watched as the bastard's gaze slid to the faint marks on Molly's throat, and he got the message loud and clear. If the Merrick wanted blood, it could take it whether it was night *or* day, which meant that sex with Molly in the middle of the afternoon wouldn't be any safer than sex with her at night.

So much for that loophole.

"You know, the more I learn here, the less I care for this goddamn legend," he admitted.

"The matter, however, is now out of your hands," Scott stated quietly, his gaze lingering on Molly for a moment longer, before finally making its way back toward Ian. "You must let go of your anger and accept that things are now beyond your control, Buchanan. These monsters, they have no conscience. As soon as the Merrick part of you is ready," he murmured, "you must confront the Casus, before it destroys everything that you care about."

Scraping the words past the anger and frustration bottled up in his throat, Ian growled, "So then you're saying my only chance of surviving is to let this thing inside of me free?"

Quinn nodded. "Only the Merrick part of your nature will be powerful enough to defeat the Casus."

"But even if Ian kills the body of its host," Molly pointed out, "you said he could only send its spirit, its shade, back to the holding ground. And if they can get out once, surely they can make it out again. Can the spirit not be killed, as well, ensuring that the Casus is destroyed forever?"

Scott shook his head. "Not without one of the Dark Markers."

"The what?" Ian rasped.

"It's the name given to the weapons created by the Consortium—the ones meant to hold the power to kill the Casus, body and soul. But no one knows for sure if they're just another part of the legend, or if they actually exist. The weapons were meant to be used as a talisman for those who wore them, offering protection from the Casus so that they could get close enough to make the kill. But the Markers were lost, if they even existed to begin with, when the Collective's wave of terror began. It's not even known what they looked like. Some believe they were shaped like daggers, but—"

"No, that's not right," Molly murmured, cutting him off. She cast a questioning look toward Ian, who nodded for her to continue, suddenly aware of what she was thinking…and looking forward to their hosts' reactions. Shifting her gaze back to Scott, she said, "You told us they protected those who wore them, right?"

Scott's pale green eyes narrowed. "Yeah."

"The talismans, the Dark Markers," she said softly, her breathless words shivery with excitement, "they weren't daggers. They were crosses. And they did actually exist."

Scott's expression turned doubtful, while an arrogant smile began to curl the edge of his mouth. "And how do you know that?"

"Because," she told him, her cheeks flushed with a wild bloom of color, "Ian's mother left him this one." And then, reaching inside the top of her shirt, Molly grasped the velvet cord and pulled out the mysterious cross they'd found that afternoon.

CHAPTER THIRTEEN

As THEY MADE THEIR WAY up to the third story, where Scott had directed them to a suite of rooms set aside for their use, Ian thought about the last moments down in the kitchen. His mouth kicked up at one corner as he recalled the Watchmen's reaction to Molly's announcement about the cross they were certain was a Dark Marker. They'd been nothing less than stunned, nearly turning the damn table over as they'd lunged forward, wanting a closer look.

Molly had taken the cross off and let them hold it, while explaining about Elaina's note and how she'd referred to the necklace as a talisman, as a way to "set things right." Quinn had stood up to switch on a bright overhead light, and the two men had spent long minutes simply turning it over in their large hands, studying its intricate designs. Noticing the heavy look of fatigue in Molly's eyes, Ian had finally asked if they could be shown to their rooms, and Scott had reluctantly handed the cross back to Molly, who'd slipped it over her head once more. Before they'd left the kitchen, Ian mentioned the fact that the Casus had spoken of the talisman to him, which had earned a new round of surprised reactions. According to the two Watchmen, the Dark

Markers weren't created until *after* the Casus had been imprisoned, which begged the question as to how the one hunting Ian even knew of its existence.

His brow drawn with concern, as well as confusion over the strange development, Scott had told them their bags had already been taken from the truck and up to their rooms. He'd said they would meet again in the morning to further discuss the talisman over breakfast, after which they'd get started with Ian's training.

Reaching the top of the stairs, Ian turned the strange story of the gypsy legend around and around in his mind, not sure what to think of it all. There was still a part of him standing back, shaking its head, thinking this must all be some kind of cosmic prank. But the cuts on his arm and ribs were proof enough that it was real.

As was Kendra's death.

And now this son of a bitching Casus wanted to get its hands on Molly.

Not in this life.

"Scott said the rooms were at the far left end of the hallway," Molly murmured at his side, her tone distant, as if she were lost in thought, same as him.

"Not too shabby," Ian drawled, eyeing what looked like a recessed library off to their left as they made their way down the wide hallway, toward the double doors at the end. The library sported floor-to-ceiling bookshelves on two of its walls, as well as three large coffee-colored leather sofas, a hi-def LCD TV and an assortment of low tables in dark wood placed throughout the spacious alcove.

"This place is pretty amazing," she said as they reached the doors of their suite. Grabbing the thick wrought iron handle, Ian opened the door, a rough curse jerking from his throat at the sight that met his eyes. Beside him, Molly gasped, one soft hand clutching on to his arm as if she needed him to hold her upright.

They both stood eerily silent and still, staring at the red-and-black pattern of the Persian carpet spread out over the hardwood floor, identical to the rug in the second dream they'd shared. The dream where they'd been in a firelit room, with a wall of windows, while the storm outside had raged as violent and thunderous as the pounding of Ian's heart.

"I don't believe it," he rasped.

"This…this is unexpected," Molly whispered, sounding dazed.

"Unexpected?" He made a rude sound in the back of his throat, shaking his head. "It's insane, is what it is, Molly."

She tilted her head back to look up at him, her delicate face caught somewhere between an expression of awe and fear. After pulling her lower lip through her teeth, she quietly said, "Ian, I think it's time we accept the fact that the things happening here…between us…that they must be for a reason. One that's beyond our control."

He scowled, moving away from her, onto the edge of the carpet. The familiar wall of windows loomed before him, while two open double doorways stood on either side of the room, revealing matching bedrooms within. Assorted pieces of expensive-looking furniture caught his attention—a small love seat, dark table, tall entertainment center—though he didn't recall any of them from the dream. But behind him, in the corner near

the door, sat the empty fireplace that had been crackling with flames.

Their luggage, he saw, had been left at the foot of the
bed in the room to his right, as if they'd be sharing it
together. Which they wouldn't.

Shoving his hands deep in his pockets, Ian struggled
to get control of his anger. "Beyond our control?" he muttered under his breath. "God, you sound like *him* now."

"Him?"

He shot her a dark look over his shoulder. "The British asshole downstairs."

"You don't like him, do you?"

Instead of answering, he shifted his gaze back to the
rug and drawled, "He certainly liked you."

"What are you talking about?" she asked at his side,
closer than he wanted her at the moment. Ian ate her up
from the corner of his eye, noting the fact that she
looked somewhat irritated. Not that he wasn't used to
having that effect on women.

"Don't play stupid," he replied in a low, gritty slide
of words, turning to face her. He dug his hands deeper
into his pockets, just to be smart, in case he decided to
do something stupid now that they were alone, like grab
on to her…and never let her go. "The guy couldn't take
his eyes off you."

She didn't say anything right away. Just chewed on
the corner of her mouth, head angled slightly to the
side as she studied him through her lashes. He fought
the uncomfortable urge to shift his feet, as if he was five
and had been caught doing something he shouldn't
have. "I never would have believed it was possible, but
you actually sound jealous, Ian."

He glared down at her, then turned away with a disgusted grunt and stalked toward the wall of windows. "Maybe I am."

"But…why?" Stepping to his side again, she tilted her face up, a husky tremor to her words as she said, "There's nothing for you to be jealous of. After everything that's happened between us, I would've thought that was obvious by now."

Ian locked his jaw. "Shut up, Molly," he ground out through his clenched teeth.

"I'm not trying to make you angry," she whispered. "I'm just trying to talk to you."

Pressing his forehead to the cool glass, he braced his forearms above his head and stared out at the darkness, doing his best to ignore her presence…his uncharacteristic jealousy…the ravenous, primitive craving coursing through his veins, pulsing in every cell of his body, demanding he *take* her…*feed* from her.

Christ, he didn't want to be there, but what choice did he have? After hearing Scott's explanations, he knew there wasn't a chance in hell he could beat that Casus jackass as a man—and it scared the shit out of him, the thought of becoming something that wasn't human.

Staring out into the night, he slowly became aware of a cold sensation on the back of his neck, slipping down his spine like a trickle of moisture, and he narrowed his eyes, wondering if it was out there. Was *it* watching him…waiting for the moment to strike? Would it feed again, and if so, on who? He hadn't dated anyone in Henning other than Kendra, though there'd been a few women in nearby towns. But no one he could imagine the Casus finding out about. They'd been low-profile arrangements, like all his relationships. Simple, short-term, based on mutual exchanges of pleasure. Hell, he could hardly recall their faces, one as easily replaced by another, which he supposed made him one of the biggest jackasses around.

And now, here was this woman who tempted him like no other ever had, and he couldn't touch her, couldn't put his hands to her body…his mouth to her flesh, for the sickening fear of what would happen when he did. Was he being punished? Tested? Or was his luck really just that screwed up?

"Ian?" Her voice was soft and husky, with an unmistakable thread of lust that made him want to explode.

Grinding his jaw so hard that his teeth ached, he screwed his eyes shut, as if that could block out the sound of her…shelter him from that warm, lush scent that was making his damn mouth water. "Christ, Molly," he breathed out on a ragged, guttural groan. "Don't tempt me."

She touched the rigid bulk of his bicep, her fingers cool against the searing heat of his skin. "Is this about the bites? Are you still afraid of hurting me?"

He made a gruff, choked sound in the back of his throat, which was all the answer he could give her.

Quietly, her voice a little breathless, she said, "I've told you that I trust you, Ian."

Opening his eyes, he turned his head to stare down at her, wondering how in God's name he was going to survive this. He was cracking apart inside, raging on the verge of something terrifying, and she just stared up at him with the softest look in those big brown eyes, her mouth curled the barest fraction into a tender, inviting smile, as if she didn't fear him at all.

And in that moment, the thought burned through his brain that he wanted to crack that infuriating shell of calm serenity that always surrounded her. Just smash it, break it open…break *her* open, and watch her go wild on him, screaming and clawing and begging for everything he could give her. Just watch her shatter and fall apart on him, while he sent himself so deep inside of her that she felt him everywhere, down in her bones and her blood and her secrets. In her dreams and her thoughts. He wanted to be that thick, burning presence that forged its way into her deepest hollows, deeper than any man had ever been before.

But you're forgetting that she doesn't get involved with men she meets this way.

Ahh…right. So then what was she offering with that soft, hazy look in her eyes? Did she think he could cuddle up with her, hold her, keep her safe through the dark hours of the night, and not be buried a mile inside of her within five minutes?

Hell, he'd be lucky if he lasted two.

"Even if I ask you to, you won't stay with me tonight, will you?" she whispered.

THE SOFTLY SPOKEN words falling from her lips surprised Molly, but then, in a way, she felt as if the entire past twenty-four hours had been building up to them. Moments in time that finally led to the stunning realization that she needed to be close to this man. Needed to stay close to him. The pain in his eyes when he'd looked at that photograph in the storage unit had probably been the most significant. Then there'd been the way he'd clutched her hand when they'd first met Quinn, as well as his unexpected jealousy over the ruggedly gorgeous Kierland Scott. Even his grief over Kendra Wilcox's death…and the way he'd come to her at the motel, injured and on the verge of collapse, just to make sure she was okay. Each of those instances had forged the change, like the ebb and flow of the tide, sweeping through her, rearranging the landscape of her emotions with each surging, powerful wave.

She still feared the emotional damage he could wreak on her life, but her caution had been overwhelmed by her need. It didn't matter what came later. Scott's warnings of what was to come had left her staring at a bleak dose of reality, and for the first time in…well, in what felt like forever, Molly didn't want to base her decisions on the events that had shaped her past. She wanted to be in the moment—to live for it. Take from it all the pleasure and happiness that she could, for however long it would last.

And at that moment, Molly knew that if she didn't get close to Ian now, while she still could, she was going to regret it for the rest of her life. They were beginning a new chapter in this drama, and she wanted to be by his side during it. Wanted to help him…hold him…not knowing what would come when he was forced to confront the evil bearing down on them.

And she had no doubt that day would come, probably sooner than any of them were ready for it.

He didn't respond to her question, but Molly could see the answer written into the lines on his face. Could see him withdrawing, closing himself off, probably pissed that he'd revealed as much as he had. She knew her own demons, but what were his? "Why are you still so afraid of getting close to me, Ian? After listening to what they had to say down in the kitchen, you know the Merrick aren't evil. They don't kill the innocent."

"You've been in my dreams, Molly," he muttered, his expression savage, eyes the color of a stormy sea, raging and beautiful and dangerously wild. "It can't be that hard for you to figure out."

"Yes, I know all about your needs," she said evenly, unwilling to back down. "You're right. I *have* been in your dreams…seen the things that excite you. Felt them. Experienced them firsthand. And I'm still here, standing at your side. Doesn't that tell you anything?"

"It tells me that you're too goddamn trusting for your own good," he sneered. "In case you don't realize it, there's a helluva big difference between dreams and reality, Stratton."

"There doesn't have to be," she told him, her tone calm, which seemed to anger him even more. She could see the muscle ticking in the side of his jaw, feel the furious waves of energy pulsing off him, violent and intense, and yet, she wanted to push him further. Wanted to push him past that infuriating control of his, until he finally let go and gave in to what they both wanted. The moment reminded her of standing before a roaring, raging fire, the intensity of the flames burning her face, while its primal beauty entranced her…enthralling her mind. She'd never experimented with drugs—not once, in her entire life—but Molly wondered if this was what it felt like…this insatiable craving to feel that hypnotic burn against her skin, all the while knowing that it could end up destroying her in the end.

"Jesus, don't you get it?" he growled, the viciousness of his tone pulling her from her reverie, making her flinch. "There's nothing *nice* about what I want from you, Molly. The smartest thing you can do is stay the hell away from me."

"That's such bullshit," she shot back, the sharp, husky words heavy on her tongue. Emotion tingled in every cell of her body, prickly and hot, a dizzying combination of frustration and longing, combined with the icy burn of fear that she'd never be able to get through to him. "You don't frighten me, Ian. The only thing that scares me is knowing that, no matter what happens between us, you're going to walk away when this is over. And you *will* walk away, won't you? Even if you want to stay, you'll make yourself turn away from me, the same way you've turned away from every other person in your life who's ever cared about you."

"Yeah, running's my specialty," he retorted in a low, ugly tone, taking a step closer, the heat of his chest touching hers, the furious power of him all but a living, breathing thing against her body. "But then I'm sure Elaina's told you all about that. Riley, he's the stand-up guy in our family. Always doing the right thing, walking the straight and narrow, like a goddamn saint. But me, I'm just the self-centered screw-up, who runs as good as his daddy did. Don't ever expect me to be there or to do the right thing, to stick around and save you, because you'll end up disappointed, Molly. Hell, at this rate," he snarled, "you'll probably end up dead."

Molly bit her tongue, fighting the urge to scream in

his face. She was so damn tired of hearing him put himself down, when she knew he was so much more than the selfish jerk he made himself out to be. Not perfect, no. But then she'd always been wary of perfection. Perfection wasn't real. Wasn't honest. Perfection was an illusion that could turn on you at the drop of a dime, like a still, pristine beach just hours before the ravaging fury of a hurricane.

Ian Buchanan was angry and rough and bruised inside, but he was also brave and strong and honest. He'd had the strength to pull himself up out of a hellish existence and make something of himself. Had given freely to the mother he'd done his best to forget, without wanting any recognition in return. And now he was determined to keep Molly by his side, to protect her, even when he feared the attraction between them…feared the darkness he carried inside.

No, he wasn't perfect. But she had the strangest, most shocking sensation glowing in the center of her chest that told her he might…*just might*…be hers.

With a faint tremor to her words, she finally managed to say, "You might not have faith in yourself, Ian, but I do."

He turned away from her, toward the window again, hands shoved back into his pockets as he stared out at that endless pitch of night, the lake water lapping at the shore like something trying to crawl its way out of the inky darkness. "Christ, Molly," he rasped, his voice so low, she could barely hear him. "You have faith in everybody."

"That's not true," she argued, her anger rising like lava building up within a volcano, readying itself to erupt with explosive fury. "I stopped believing in other people a long time ago. I didn't tell you before, about everything that happened when Sara died."

Turning his head sharply to the side, he stared at her through the heavy weight of his lashes.

"I was dating her older brother. Sara's stepbrother. He was my first boyfriend, first kiss, first love," she told him, the hoarse words tumbling out in a choppy, breathless rhythm. "He was my first everything. When Sara's spirit came to me, telling me about the judge, I made the mistake of confiding in him. He acted so worried for me, so concerned. And he talked me into keeping quiet, not saying anything, convincing me he was afraid of what people would do…that they might even try to have me committed." A low, brittle laugh jerked from her throat, and she wrapped her arms around herself as she lowered her stare, focusing on the strong muscles of his throat, the dark silk of his skin. She swallowed, then nervously wet her lips, hating the shame that still flavored her memories, knowing she'd never be able to wash it away.

"He played on my fears perfectly," she explained, forcing herself to get the story out. "And in the end, after everything blew up and the judge was arrested, he came to me, calling me a freak and a stupid little bitch. And then he told me that he'd known all along about the fact that his father was abusing Sara, but had kept it to himself. Said he blamed Sara for acting like a slut and tempting his father, who was only a man. I guess he'd blamed Sara's mother for breaking up his parents' marriage, and he figured her daughter was getting what she deserved."

"Christ."

"So a girl lost her life because I was so gullible," she whispered, her words thick with disgust. "Because I was scared and stupid and wasted all those weeks keeping my mouth shut, doing what he wanted me to do."

"And that's why you told me last night that you don't get involved with men you meet like this." It wasn't a question. He knew he was right.

She nodded, turning her head to stare out at the infinite stretch of night, the moon barely visible through the tall reaches of the swaying pine trees that lined the far side of the lake. "I learned an ugly lesson about trust the day he told me the truth, and I've never forgotten it."

Taking a deep breath, she looked back at him, the confession falling softly from her lips as she said, "And I've used that lesson as an excuse to close myself off for years, living in my own little world, where nothing can hurt me. Where I don't have to rely on anyone or expect anything from them. Where their actions can't affect me. That's why I told myself I had to fight what was between us. But I can't, Ian. I don't even want to anymore."

Shifting closer to him, Molly put her hand on his arm, wishing he'd turn toward her. Take her in his arms. Hold her. "I've dated since then, but it's always been difficult. Guys aren't exactly understanding about someone like me. And the more I tried to hide it, the bigger the blowup when the truth came out, until I finally just gave up. That's why I haven't had a relationship in so long. But you already know my crazy little secret. And yet you're still here. You still want me. Don't you think that means something, Ian? That maybe all of this is happening for a reason? Your mother? The dreams? I don't know how to explain it, but it's like…"

"Fate?" he snorted.

She shook her head at his tone. "I'm serious, Ian. Call it whatever you want. Fate. Kismet. Stupid blind luck. I don't know what it is, and I don't care. I just know that as scared as I am of messing this up—I can't keep trying to convince myself that you're a mistake. You don't *feel* like a mistake. In some strange, wonderful way, you feel like the best thing that's ever happened to me."

For a long time he just stood there, staring at her, the longing in his dark eyes so intense, so deep and wild and powerful, that she wanted to scream for him to grab on to her. The corner of his mouth twitched with emotion, his blue eyes brightening with the soft glow of wonder, and he lifted his right hand, touching her face, catching a teardrop on his thumb.

And then, from one breath to the next, his expression hardened, like a storm cloud blotting out the promising warmth of the sun, and he took a step back, his deep voice chilling, cutting her to the bone. "I've never been the best thing that's happened to anybody," he muttered. "So don't go wasting your chance on me, Molly. You're going to regret it if you do."

CHAPTER FOURTEEN

Ravenswing, Monday Afternoon

TRAINING WITH THE WATCHMEN was a bitch. For the past seven hours, Ian had been getting his ass slammed again and again, until he'd finally hit the ground so many times, he suspected his backside was now a gnarly shade of black and blue. He was also hot and hurting, and in a seriously pissed-off mood. One that was getting worse with every pounding kick and punch he received from the bastard fighting him.

Once Quinn had finished with him, Aiden Shrader took over, making the last two hours some of the most painful Ian had ever experienced. Unlike Quinn, who'd been more interested in showing Ian how to fight against something that wasn't human—as well as preparing him for the time when his own body would be *altered* in its Merrick form—Shrader seemed determined to beat the ever-loving hell out of him. At least two inches taller than Ian, the guy was massive, with muscles poured on top of muscles, and a smart-ass attitude that he directed at everyone around him. His caramel-colored hair fell in shaggy waves below his chin, hazel eyes piercing within a face that probably got him laid whenever he wanted.

Both of Shrader's corded forearms were tattooed from wrist to elbow, the designs a blend of Celtic and pagan symbols that also covered the backs of his knuckles. Ian knew them by memory, because he'd had those knuckles shoved in his face too many times to count. The only bright spot in the afternoon had been when he'd not only busted Shrader's lip, but had managed to blacken one eye.

They'd been dancing around one another for the last minute or so, getting their breath back, when the Watchman suddenly came at him hard and fast, the bulk of his body knocking Ian to the ground. A cloud of dust swallowed them, their limbs tangling as each man fought for dominance, their bodies rolling over the sandy lot they used for training. It was hidden out of sight of the main house, behind a long L-shaped garage that housed an impressive collection of cars.

The world spun as they rolled side over side, and the next thing Ian knew, he had a vicious set of jaws clamped on to his forearm. He roared at the fiery burn of pain, unable to believe the bastard had actually bitten him.

"What the hell was that?" he snarled, staring at Shrader as the guy moved to a crouch beside him, wiping the back of one tattooed hand over his mouth. The Watchman sent him a slow, arrogant smile, the bright glare of afternoon sunlight glinting off the pointed tips of what appeared to be a sinister set of fangs. "Just giving you a taste of what you're going to be up against," he drawled in a gritty rasp.

"By going wolf on my ass?" Ian muttered, pulling himself up into a sitting position. After inspecting the damage, he wiped the bloody bite-wound against his jeans, all the while cursing a hot, foul string of words under his breath. Quinn had tried to show him how to transform his fangs and hands for training, allowing the Merrick's talons to slip free, but Ian hadn't been able to make it happen at will—which meant he couldn't retaliate in kind.

"I'm not a wolf," Aiden grimaced with disgust, curling his lip. "Do I look like a bloody wolf to you?"

Ian studied him through slitted eyes. "If not wolf, then what the hell are you?"

"Aiden's a cat," Quinn offered with a throaty chuckle, suddenly appearing off to their right, about fifteen yards away, as if he'd just dropped out of the sky. He'd obviously grabbed a shower, the dust and grime of the training field washed away. His jeans were clean, as was the loose white shirt that hung open in deference to the heat, revealing the hard, muscled slab of his torso.

Ian was on the verge of asking him where he'd come from, when Aiden shot Quinn the finger, drawling, "That's *big kitty* to you, flyboy."

"Idiots," Ian grunted, thinking they were both crazy. "It's like a goddamn zoo around here," he added under his breath.

"Minus the bars and cages, of course," Quinn offered with a quiet snicker.

Scowling, Ian cut him a sharp look. "How the hell did you hear what I said from all the way over there?"

"We're not human, Merrick," the Watchman murmured, arching one midnight brow, his dark eyes glittering with amusement. "What makes you think we'd hear or see or move like one?" He cast a meaningful glance at Ian's wounded forearm. "Or fight like one, for that matter."

Moving to his feet, Ian gritted his teeth against the pain in his ribs, wondering how many Shrader had managed to crack. "So you're saying that you have…what?" he grunted, "Superhuman hearing?"

"It's definitely better than a human's," Quinn agreed, walking toward them, his long gait making short work of the distance. "How else do you think I knew why Molly came to Colorado? I was watching you last Friday at the building site."

Pushing his hands back through the sweat-damp strands of his hair, Ian thought back to that first conversation he'd had with Molly. "You heard her tell me about Elaina?"

"That's right."

"Were you listening to our conversations at the motel?" he demanded, his irritation rising, considering those had been some pretty personal conversations.

The corner of Quinn's mouth twitched and he shook his head. "I may have better hearing than most humans, but I can't hear through walls."

Grunting in response, Ian scanned the area, looking for his shirt, remembering that he'd taken it off at one point during the afternoon. "If you weren't listening in, then how did you know we were familiar with Scott's name?"

"We've been monitoring her cell phone," Quinn told him, pushing his hands into his pockets. "We know she called information for the listing." There was a curious gleam in his dark eyes as he said, "Am I right in assuming your mother gave her the name?"

"Yeah." Ian finally spotted his shirt by the garage and went to pick it up, wiping the salty beads of sweat from his face as he made his way back toward the two Watchmen. Shrader—who, like Ian, wore only his jeans—had sprawled his big body out over the dusty ground, one hulking arm thrown over his eyes, his bare feet crossed at the ankles, looking for all the world as if he was sleeping. Ian grinned with grim satisfaction at the sight, hoping he'd worn the bastard out.

He'd just finished using his shirt to wipe the oozing blood from the bite marks Shrader had left in his arm, when Quinn gave a quiet rumble of laughter, saying, "You should have seen Kierland's face when we told him Molly knew his name. After what I'd heard at the building site, we kinda figured your mother was the one who'd passed it on. He definitely wasn't too keen on the idea of a ghost keeping tabs on him."

A hard smile broke over Ian's mouth, but his satisfaction faded as soon as Quinn went back to the original topic of conversation. "Haven't you noticed your senses improving? Becoming more intense? Sharper?" At his scowl, the Watchman added, "It's because your Merrick is now a part of you. Even though you're still not able to accept the full change, it's altering your physiology, improving your abilities, making you stronger…more perceptive than a human male."

"That's what you meant last night," he muttered, throwing his bloodstained shirt over one sweaty shoulder. "At the motel. When you said I'm more Merrick now than human."

Quinn nodded. "That's right."

"How far is it going to go?" he asked, hating the cold

touch of fear creeping up his spine. He wanted a cigarette, but had left his pack up in the room he'd slept in last night. Not that he'd actually slept. He'd been too afraid to fall asleep, half terrified that he would dream of Molly again…knowing exactly what would happen if he did.

"Don't worry. You'll still look like a man when not in Merrick form," Quinn assured him, as if he cared what he looked like, when he couldn't have given a rat's ass. That wasn't the problem. It was the idea of constantly walking around with this ugly burn of hunger in his gut, stripping his insides raw, that scared the hell out of him. "But you'll retain much of the strength and heightened abilities of your primal bloodline," Quinn went on to say, "at *all* times."

Son of a bitch.

"Enough gabbing," Shrader suddenly muttered, shifting to his feet in an effortlessly fluid move that made Ian wonder if the guy was even feeling a twinge of pain. With a deliberately taunting look in his eyes, he flashed Ian a sharp, predatory smile. "Now that I've had my catnap, I'm ready to beat down what's left of you, Buchanan."

"As entertaining as that sounds, I think he's done for the day," Quinn offered in an aside, after glancing at Ian's savage expression.

Shrader pushed his hair back off his face, then laced his fingers together and cracked his knuckles. "And I think he needs a good meal or he isn't going to be worth shit out here on the training field, either today, tomorrow, or the day after that. This is just a waste of our time."

"What does that mean?" Ian demanded in a graveled voice, while something uneasy twisted in his gut.

Rolling his eyes, Shrader explained. "No matter how bloody good you are at fighting, you're too damn weak. Until you've properly fed, you won't be able to go two rounds with that Casus prick."

"Fed?" he grunted, knowing damn well what the man was talking about.

"Isn't there something you crave?" Shrader drawled, his hazel, catlike eyes glittering and bright as he held his stare.

"You're talking about blood," Ian said flatly, his throat tight, mouth dry...while the sound of his pulse roared in his ears. It'd been almost two days since he'd shared that second dream with Molly, and he'd felt every minute that had gone by, the hunger growing stronger with each passing second.

"The blood's part of it," Quinn offered at his side.

"What do you mean *part of it*?"

"You can't just drink," Shrader muttered, sounding disgusted by his ignorance. "Well you *could*, but you're not a vampire, so you probably wouldn't want to."

"Then explain it," Ian growled, forcing the words out through his teeth.

"You crave blood *and* sex. When you're Merrick, the hungers are combined into one primitive need, so you'll want them together. That's why, in the old days, the un-mated Merrick males had agreements with the gypsies. Just bedding a woman isn't going to do anything for you but get your rocks off. But if you feed while riding her—" a gritty burst of laughter rumbled deep in Shrader's chest "—let's just say your Merrick is going to be a really happy boy."

"And until you feed properly," Quinn added, "you're

not going to be strong enough for your Merrick to completely break free. Your fangs will still release, if there's an opportunity for nourishment, but otherwise, you'll be unable to make the transformation. Food is only going to sustain your body. The Merrick, it lives off the blood."

"He's right." Scott's deep voice suddenly rumbled at his back. "It needs to happen, and it needs to happen now."

Turning around, Ian fisted his hands at his sides as he took in the sight of Scott and Molly standing together, side by side, as if they were the best pals in the world. While he'd spent the day outside getting his ass kicked, Scott had been cozied up in the library with her, going over his mother's journal and examining the cross. The idea of the two of them alone together in the house had heat crawling up the back of his neck that had nothing to do with the record-breaking temperatures scorching the mountains…and everything to do with possession, while his gut twisted with the raw, caustic burn of jealousy.

Molly stared at his face for a long, breathless moment, then trailed her heavy, luminous gaze down his body, as if he were something tasty that she wanted to slip in her mouth and savor for hours on end. He reminded himself that he wasn't the kind of man to be brought to his knees by a woman. But when her tongue touched the plump center of her upper lip, her focus centered on his hard, dust-covered abdomen, he damn near hit the ground. And he knew precisely what would happen if he did. With his knees buried in the sand, he'd reach for her, pulling her to him, and bury his face in the plump V nestled there between her sweet little thighs, gulping in desperate lungfuls of her warm, womanly scent.

Hell, in another lifetime, he'd have groveled at her feet, begging for whatever she was willing to give him. Sex. Love. Companionship and compassion. Even commitment…trust. Things he could never accept from her in this world, no matter how badly he wanted them.

And aside from the sex—things he wouldn't even know how to offer her in return.

It drove him crazy—the fact that he couldn't trust himself to touch her, when he wanted it so badly he actually hurt. The destructive pain lingered in his gut, in his muscles—God, even his skin itched for the feel of her against him, under him, wrapped around him.

"How's he doing?" Scott asked the Watchmen, the quiet words jerking Ian out of his personal hell.

"He's good, I'll give him that," Shrader admitted, surprising him. "All those years of boxing made him strong and quick on his feet for a *human,* but he's still got a lot to learn."

"And he's still trying to fight with his fists," Quinn added, "instead of keeping his fingers loose, the way they'd be with his talons."

"You used to box?" Molly asked into the brief pause, blinking up at him in surprise. She lifted one hand to shield her eyes from the bright glare of sunshine, and Ian knew they were all watching her, as captivated as he was by the feminine lines and movements of her body. His gaze dropped to the sight of her breasts pressed against the dark blue cotton blouse she wore, the outline of her nipples tight against the soft material, making him want to growl. The primitive, predatory sound rumbled deep in his chest, and it took everything he had to choke it back and hold it inside.

Instead of answering her question, Ian ground out one of his own. "What are you doing out here?" he muttered, when what he really wanted to ask was what she'd been doing inside all day with Scott.

Reaching out to him, she grabbed his right hand, turned it over and laid the cross across the sweaty heat of his palm. "You're going to need this," she said softly.

Ian scowled, the expression born from his trembling reaction to her touch as much as it was from the cross. "I told you that I don't want the damn thing."

"The training is important," Scott said, "but you need to figure out how to use this Marker as a weapon. I've tried everything I can think of, but it won't work for me."

"I don't know what to do with it," he argued.

Scott's pale green gaze narrowed. "Maybe not, but you're never going to figure it out if you don't try. For all we know, it only works for a Merrick, which means I can study the bloody thing all day long and it isn't going to do anyone a damn bit of good."

"Elaina's journal entries reveal that she'd heard fragments of the legend, as well as stories about how the Casus were trapped," Molly explained, squinting against the afternoon sunlight, the vivid rays glinting off her hair, making his hands itch to reach out and touch its silken weight. Fist his hands in it, and then pull her against his sweat-covered body, taking her to the dust-covered ground.

He could see her lips moving, and gave himself the

equivalent of a mental slap, forcing his mind to pay attention to what she was saying. "Ian, she also explains how she came into possession of the cross."

It was obvious from her expression that she expected him to be surprised by the answer. Wondering what it was, he nodded for her to go ahead and tell him.

"Saige gave it to her."

"My sister?" he rasped, realizing that of all the possible scenarios, that was one he hadn't expected.

"Elaina writes of how Saige studied anthropology because she shared her passion for the stories about your bloodline, about the Merrick and the Casus. Saige has been researching the subject for years now, a fact which Kierland can confirm, since they've been watching her. According to your mother, your sister came into possession of the cross last year, after being on an archeological dig in Italy."

He cut a questioning, suspicious look toward Scott. "Then why didn't you guys know about it?"

The Watchman rolled his shoulder and winced. "My brother, Kellan, was assigned to her at the time, but he was…let's just say easily distracted by the local attractions."

Ian snorted, shaking his head. "So instead of watching my sister, the way he was supposed to be doing, he was off getting laid?"

Scott nodded. "Which is why we took him off the assignment and brought him back home, once we realized he was being remiss in his duties. But we didn't know until now that he'd missed something this important."

"Where is he now?"

"In Henning, watching your brother."

"And who's watching Saige?" Ian demanded, wondering just how much his sister knew about what was happening. She'd always been as headstrong as she was willful when they were kids. It'd been years since he'd seen her, but he could only imagine she'd turned out to be hell on wheels.

"A Watchman by the name of Paul Templeton is in South America with her. He's not part of our compound, but he's one of the best there is. She's in good hands."

"You better hope she is," he warned. "And with everything that's happening, this Templeton had better be a damn sight better at his job than your brother."

"Kellan's still young." Scott sighed. "He still has a lot of maturing to do, but he's good at what he does."

Shrader snorted, which earned him a hard glare from Scott, as well as a cuff on the arm from Quinn.

Grinning, the Watchman lifted his arms in a gesture of surrender. "Hey, lay off. I didn't say a word."

"Ian," Molly murmured, drawing his attention back to her fey face, the freckles sprinkled over her nose more prominent in the sunlight, making her look impossibly young and fresh and innocent. "Your mother believed the cross was the first Dark Marker to be found. She also talks about stories that she remembers her great-grandmother telling her, about a divine 'Arm of Fire' that held the power to destroy a Casus for all eternity."

Rubbing at the stiff muscles in the back of his neck, he asked, "How did it work?"

She lifted her shoulders in a baffled shrug. "That's the thing. She didn't know. And neither her nor Saige could ever find anyone who knew how it could be used."

Ian slanted a look toward Scott. "Any ideas?"

"Beats me. Like I said, I've been studying it all day, but I haven't come across anything useful."

"Arm of Fire?" Ian repeated, trying the words out on his lips while he stared at the cross, as if the answer would be revealed in its detailed designs. It was hot against his palm, the way it had been yesterday, when he'd taken it from Molly before slipping it over her neck. But it wasn't hot like fire. The sensation was more like pressing your hand against sunbaked sand. Warm, but tolerable.

He glanced back at Scott again. "And you really have no idea what we're supposed to do with it?"

Scott shook his head, the deepening lines around his eyes and mouth revealing his frustration. "Believe me, I wish I did."

"Looks like you're going to have to figure it out," Quinn murmured at his side, staring at the cross, same as Ian. Even Shrader stalked closer for a look.

A wry, pained smile twisted Ian's mouth. "I hate to cultivate negativity here, guys, but I don't have a god-damn clue what to do with this thing."

"You'll figure it out," Molly said softly, the gentle smile playing at her lips making him grit his teeth.

"Why don't you go on in and get cleaned up," Scott said a moment later. "We'll have dinner in an hour and talk things over then."

Closing his fingers around the cross, Ian gave them all a curt "Later" and set off toward the house, half-terrified that Molly wouldn't follow him, staying behind with Scott…while even more terrified that she would.

And then, drawing in a deep breath, he caught her

scent just behind him, though she remained silent, not saying a word. It wasn't until he'd entered their suite, and was just about to head into the room he'd taken, that she touched his back, her fingertips cool against the searing, sweaty heat of his skin.

"Ian?"

"What?" he grunted, aware of the fact he sounded like a total bastard.

"Are you going to keep avoiding me?" she asked softly. "You walked out on me last night, and we haven't talked all day."

He choked back a snarling sound of frustration. "I haven't been avoiding you, Molly. I've been busy getting the shit beat out of me."

She pulled his stained shirt away from his body and stroked his shoulder, her touch gentle, tender, conveying a depth of longing he was surprised he even recognized. He'd never before been in tune with a woman enough to notice or even comprehend such things, until Molly. There was something connecting him to this woman—some kind of primitive, intense, piercing awareness—that magnified every sensation. That made him hyperaware of her every breath, every gesture, every shadow of emotion that crossed her face, the powerful need conveyed through the simple touch of her hand against his body.

Quietly, she said, "Will you talk to me, then?"

"I'm not trying to be a jackass, Molls. It just isn't a good idea," he muttered, slipping the cross into his back pocket. She touched a sensitive place on his spine, and just like that, he went hard.

"Why not?" she asked.

Yeah, why not? his conscience taunted.

Ian turned around to face her, his gaze settling hungrily on the pink swell of her mouth, remembering how it tasted. How she felt beneath his lips, and he wanted to shout…to seethe…to rage against the maddening injustice of finding that the one thing he needed to make his world right, he couldn't have. He wanted to put his fist through the wall. Wanted to rip something apart with his bare hands. But most of all, he wanted to drown himself in her, in that pulsing glow of heat that burned inside of her, that he could feel ignite every time he got close to her. That smoothed its way into his body through the touch of her skin, her breath, her taste…melting things inside of him that had been frozen solid for too damn long.

He started to move forward and grab hold of her, when Shrader's words rushed back at him, making his breath hiss through his teeth.

You need blood and sex. When you're Merrick, the hungers are combined into one primitive need, so you'll want them together.

Craving crawled through him, thick and meaty and raw, like a physical thing inside his body that had substance…that had its own agenda. Ian closed his eyes, trying to block out the physical temptation. But he could still see it in his mind's eye. Her lush mouth. Flushed face. The tender stretch of her throat as she tilted her head back to stare up at him. Could remember how the hot, drugging flavor of her blood slipped over his tongue, burning like pleasure in his belly.

You're losing it, asshole. Big-time.

"I'm trying to understand, Ian," she told him, her

tone sharper than before, and he opened his eyes to watch the slow spill of frustration wash over her expression. "To give you the space you need without pressuring you into something you're not ready for. But you can't keep avoiding me. This is ridiculous. I heard what they said out there…about you needing blood in order to release the Merrick. What am I even doing here if you won't let me help you?"

"What do you want from me?"

"I want you to stop running every time you see me," she burst out, her velvety brown eyes glittering and bright with a constantly shifting well of emotion. "To talk to me, to tell me what's going on in that thick head of yours, because I swear to God, Ian, I don't have a clue!"

"I can't," he suddenly snarled, stepping back from her, the wild, furious look in his own eyes warning her not to follow. "I mean it, Molly. I can't deal with this right now."

Looking like an enraged she-cat, she moved closer, forcing him to retreat a step…and then another. "Like hell you can't. You're going to deal with it, because I'm not letting you walk away from me again. I don't get it, Ian. What are you so afraid of?"

What was he afraid of? Christ, the list was growing longer each day, every time he had to be in her presence, every second that he wasn't. He was terrified of the way she looked at him. Of the way she made him feel. Of the infuriating fact that he couldn't control himself with her. He owed her the explanation, dammit. He knew he did. But all he could say was, "It's not going to happen."

He turned away from her, ready to escape and slam

the door behind him, when she said, "Then you're the biggest coward I've ever known."

"Is that really what you think?" he asked without facing her, his hands fisting and flexing at his sides, while his pulse echoed through his skull like a deafening, primal roar.

Softly, she said, "What else am I supposed to think, Ian?"

"Dammit, I know you're not stupid," he growled. "You know I'm trying to protect you."

"Is it me you're trying to protect? Or is it you?"

He turned back around slowly, with deliberate purpose, his gaze, once again, settling hungrily on that pink, provocative little mouth. *A taste,* a raspy voice whispered through the hazy fog of lust in his mind. *Just a taste. It won't hurt her. She'll be perfectly safe. You won't even go anywhere near her throat.*

Ian lifted his hand, cupping her jaw, his thumb pressed against the corner of her lips, stroking her skin. "Do you even know what you're asking, Molls?"

She blinked up at him, her breath coming in a hard, sweet rush. "I just want you to let go and do what feels right. I want you to stop fighting me. To stop fighting what you need."

See? It's time to stop denying yourself. Time to stop...

Before he'd even made the conscious decision to act, he was on her, against her, claiming her mouth with a dark, aggressive, eating kiss, taking her to the floor...pinning her there with the heavy weight of his body against hers. His hands found the delicate hollows of her inner elbows, sliding up the tender stretch of her forearms, until he'd captured her fine-boned wrists, trapping them against the gleaming shine of the hard-wood floor. She urged him on with her breathless cries, her thighs parting, inviting him against her body, silently begging him to press closer…closer.

"*Molly,*" he panted against the damp, tender heat of her mouth, lost in it, unable to stop…to slow down. Something was rolling over him, through him, as unstoppable and fierce as a powerful force of nature. All he knew was that he needed the feel of her beneath him, the softness of her skin, the decadent heat and taste of her flesh as he kissed her cheek…her temple…the delicate point of her jaw.

"Yes, Ian. God, yes."

"No—no talking," he ground out, somehow finding the strength to force himself away from the dangerous terrain of her throat, where her pulse beat to a heavy, rushing rhythm. He released her wrists and moved back, straddling her thighs, so that he could run his hands down the front of her body, over the feminine swell of her breasts, the shivering stretch of her belly. "Just shut up, Molly. Just…don't say anything. I have to concentrate…to keep it together."

Sound words, but even as they left his lips, Ian knew he was playing with fire, tempting fate, like dangling a raw steak through the bars of the lion's cage with your bare hand and hoping you came away unscathed. You could hope all you wanted—but the odds weren't in your favor.

And the hell of it was, he wasn't the one who would pay the price—she would.

It's okay. You're in control. You can do this.

She stared up at him, her eyes heavy and dark…but

without fear…without anger, that wild, smoldering gaze simply reflecting his hunger back at him, magnifying it, expanding it until it surrounded their bodies, spreading outward, filling the room like a thick, searing presence. Helpless beneath its power, Ian turned his attention to getting her naked—to baring her body to his burning, avid gaze for the first time outside of his dreams. Fisting his hands in the dark blue material of her blouse, he wrenched, ripping it apart, sending buttons flying, skittering across the floor, then immediately did the same to the delicate white lace of her bra.

And that quickly, he had her.

Her breasts were…perfect, the sight of her plump, dark pink nipples hitting him like a vicious kick to the chest, knocking the air from his lungs. Shaking, Ian bent down and pressed his damp face to her quivering stomach. His hot breaths rushed against her skin, a low, steady stream of carnal swearwords falling soundlessly from his lips, while she ran her fingers through the sweat-damp strands of his hair, petting him…gentling him, making him want to snarl in arrogant defiance, at the same time as he silently begged for more.

Her scent was growing stronger, making him crazed, his mouth watering for the taste of her beneath his lips, and he suddenly loomed over her, bracing himself on his bent arms, as he caught one of those raspberry thick nipples between his lips, suckling it, working the hardened flesh against the roof of his mouth. Desperate to taste all of her, he eagerly moved to the other, leaving it wet…swollen, then trailed his mouth lower, over the delicate span of her ribs, across the shallow indentation of her navel, until he nipped at the tender curve of her hip.

His callused hands clutched at her waist, stroking the petal-softness of her skin, and then he was working frantically at her jeans, ripping them open, pushing them down along with a white, lacy pair of panties, each action driven by a primitive urgency that should have scared the hell out of him, but he was already too far gone to care. He managed, with her help, to get one leg free, then quickly slipped lower, his shoulders forcing their way between her slender thighs, spreading them, demanding she open to him…make room for him.

A breathless, keening cry broke from her chest while her hands stroked the slick, burning heat of his shoulders, then the corded tendons in his neck, before finding the sensitive places behind his ears, as she softly panted his name again and again. She touched as much of him as she could reach, her body writhing beneath him with sensual, carnal abandon, and Ian pressed his forehead against her lower right hip bone, the words breaking out of his chest in a graveled, gritty rush. "Christ, Molly, you're killing me."

"No," she whispered brokenly, sounding dazed. "No…I just want…I want—"

"You just want to drive me out of my mind," he groaned, his lips moving against the smooth curve of her hip, then lower, to the tender flesh of her inner thigh. "I've tried so hard to get you out of my head, but I can't stop thinking about you. Can't stop wondering what you're doing. Can't stop thinking about every goddamn thing I want to do to you. It's driving me crazy."

"It doesn't have to, Ian. Don't you understand that?

You're the only one making this hard. I'm right here, offering whatever it is you need…whatever you want."

He lifted his head, snagging her heavy gaze over the pale, shivering length of her body, the golden shafts of sunlight spilling in through the far wall of windows painting her skin in a luminous glow. It made her shine like a pearl, dazzling and smooth, the most intoxicating, beautiful woman he'd ever seen.

"I won't fuck you," he told her, his voice thick with lust. "God knows I want to, but I can't. Not when I don't trust what I'd do to you. But that…that isn't going to stop me from taking this."

She blinked, looking equal parts wary and intrigued. "Taking what?"

Despite his fury and frustration that he couldn't have everything he wanted from her, the corner of Ian's mouth twitched at the nervous excitement smoldering in her heavy-lidded gaze. She wanted it…whatever it was—but she was still shy. He could see it in her eyes, hear it in the erratic cadence of her breathing, and it ramped his own need up that much higher, when he already wanted her more than anything he'd ever wanted before.

Slowly…quietly, he said, "You ever had a guy go down on you, Molls?"

Her eyes went comically wide, and she nodded jerkily, a warm blush rising up from her chest, over her throat, blooming wildly in her face. "O-once."

"Like it?" he asked in a low voice, holding her with his gaze, silently commanding her not to look away.

She shook her head, wetting her lips, the color in her face burning hotter. Brighter. "Not…not really."

"Why not?" he asked, his tone casual, completely at odds with the intimate way he braced himself on one elbow between her indecently spread thighs, and placed his fingertips against the soft, golden curls at the top of her sex, stroking them with a slow, possessive touch.

She blinked, panting, and finally managed to stammer out a reply. "I can't b-believe I'm telling you this, but it was…um, k-kind of awkward…and a little…a little embarrassing."

The corner of his mouth twitched again, her innocence melting him with tenderness, at the same time it pushed him perilously close to the brutal, dangerous edge of hunger he was doing his best to avoid. "If you had time to think about being embarrassed, then he wasn't doing it right, angel."

She pulled her lower lip through her teeth, gasping when he deliberately swept his thumb lower, against the damp, knotted heat of her clit. "What do you mean?"

"I mean, if a man knows how to do it right," he explained in a deep, rasping murmur, struggling to keep himself together, "then his woman won't be able to think at all while he's doing it."

He shifted lower, settling himself on his elbows until that lush cleft was only inches from his mouth, glistening and pink and unbearably exquisite.

"God, look at you," he said thickly, his shoulders keeping her from closing her thighs when she stiffened with shyness, an incoherent murmur of panic falling from her lips. Pulling in a deep breath of her mouthwatering scent, Ian used his thumbs to open her wider, revealing that candy-pink center that he remembered so vividly from his dreams. Then he gave in to the driving urgency that had been riding him hard since the moment he'd first set eyes on this woman, and greedily put his mouth to her warm, drenched center.

Her pure, salty sweet taste exploded over his senses, somehow even better than he'd imagined, and all his years of experience and acquired skill were lost in that stunning, jolting moment beneath an overpowering flood of hunger and instinct and insatiable, clawing need. Through the primal roar in his brain, Ian could hear the small, choked cries of pleasure breaking out of her, while her pale body thrashed, twisting beneath him. His mouth worked on her, desperate for her flavor.

Once he heard her scream, he needed it again…and again, until she couldn't hold them in, the choppy, erotic cries spilling from her lips in endless succession, each one only cranking up his own need to a dangerous, deadly degree.

The first climax slammed into her without warning, arching her like a live wire when it hit, crashing over her, flinging her into some dark, infinite unknown and damn near taking him with her. Ian knew he was tempting fate in daring to take her in such an intimate way— but he couldn't stop…couldn't deny the savage, sharp-edged craving in his blood that demanded he get as much of her as he could, before it all came crashing down around him. There was no doubt that she deserved more than that—more than a man who could only give in half measures. Who had to control himself like an animal on a leash—and the bitter knowledge caused regret to coil heavily around his shoulders, weighing him down.

Time to retreat, jackass, before you go too far.

Right, right. Just a little bit more, he promised himself, his tongue pressed hard against her clit as he suddenly thrust two thick fingers up inside of her. She convulsed around him in another long, wrenching climax, and Ian shut his eyes, promising himself that he'd move…he'd leave…in a moment. He just needed the feel of those lush muscles gripping his fingers for a little longer. Just needed that warm, intoxicating scent filling his head. Needed that sweet, exquisite taste against his tongue.

Just a little longer…a little longer… And then he suddenly knew that it was too late—that he'd taken it too far. His fangs exploded from his gums in a fiery, burning rush, and he froze, afraid to even breathe as he slowly opened his eyes.

"Enough…enough torturing me with orgasms," she gasped, oblivious to the danger as she sluggishly lifted herself up on her elbows, her pale curls hanging over one eye, chest heaving with the force of her ragged breathing. She looked as adorable as she did seductive, and it amazed him that he didn't combust then and there. Wetting her lips with the pink tip of her tongue, she stared at him with a ghost of a smile playing at her provocative mouth, and teasingly said, "You've proven you're the master, Mr. Buchanan. I surrender. I'm officially wrecked. Destroyed. Utterly and completely at your mercy, and if you don't get inside of me right now, I won't be held responsible for what I do to you."

He shuddered, carefully shifting back on his knees, his movements slow…calculated…carried out with excruciating control, while his muscles shook from the ungodly strain of holding himself in check.

"No," she whispered, suddenly seeing the panic in his eyes, her own darkening with a myriad of emotions. "Don't leave me," she said brokenly, sitting up in a clumsy rush of motion, her tattered blouse hanging limply from her shoulders, framing the feminine weight of her delicate breasts and quivering torso. She reached for him, cupping his hot face in her small, cool hands, her magnificent eyes swimming with tears. "Trust me, Ian. It's going to be okay. Just let me prove it to you…let me take you inside of me. Please…"

A little bit more, Buchanan. Just a little bit more.

The words were guttural and low, coming from someplace deep inside of him that was dark and deadly, and he suddenly understood what was happening.

His Merrick was luring him in…tempting him to take what it needed, like a stranger crooning, *Here child, try a piece of candy.*

"Goddamn it, no!" The words burst from his throat like the blast from a weapon, and she flinched, stiffening as her hands fell slowly from his face.

"Ian?" Her eyes flooded with tears, and she clutched on to the ragged panels of her blouse, crossing them over her breasts. "Please…don't do this. Don't turn away from me. We have to find a way through this. I can help you. I know I can."

She was wrong. No one could help him—especially not her. But he couldn't get the words out to explain. Hell, he couldn't even look at her. Not without tempting the devil. Without freeing that part of himself that he didn't trust. That scared the ever-loving hell out of him.

In the end, all he could do was turn his back on her. And run.

CHAPTER FIFTEEN

Henning, Thursday Morning

SHAKING HER HEAD at her foolishness, Rachel Potter moved farther into the forest, the pine needles crackling like a bed of broken shells beneath her booted feet. Seconds earlier, a rabbit had rushed from its hiding place behind a thick, towering tree, making her jump, her hands lifting before her as if to ward off an attack. Not that she'd actually been in any danger, unless the mangy little puffball had planned on nibbling through her boots and assaulting her toenail polish. She'd have laughed at the absurdity of her reaction, if she wasn't so insulted by her loss of dignity. After all, she wasn't one of those brainless ninnies who traipsed off into the woods by herself, not knowing her compass from a compact.

Still, after the gruesome attack last Friday night, Rachel hadn't planned to come alone today, but the so-called friend who'd arranged to accompany her hadn't shown at the coffee shop that morning. She would have just gone another day, but there'd been a problem with her film and this was her last chance to get the pictures she needed for her summer photography course.

The ancient, twisted bristlecone she'd fallen in love

with on her last hike was going to be the crowning centerpiece of her assignment, and the lighting today was perfect. Ominous, shredded storm clouds scarred the horizon, while radiant beams of golden sunlight fought their way through the oppressive gloom, painting the forest with dappled shafts of color. If she could capture the atmospheric effect, the photographs were not only going to get her an A, but more than likely a coveted scholarship to the art institute she'd applied to.

Considering how important that scholarship was to her future, Rachel hadn't had any choice but to go it alone this morning. And at any rate, she wasn't really afraid. Maybe a little spooked, but she still felt safer there than she did when surrounded by the hustle and bustle of town. Nature was her sanctuary—where she felt safe, protected, at peace. It was around people that she always kept up her guard, looking over her shoulder, wondering what psychotic thing they were going to do next. People were the unpredictable powder kegs in this world, but nature…nature was a refuge. It wasn't always gentle, but it never let you down. Sure, it could be dangerous if you didn't respect its power, but it wasn't cruel. It didn't kill for the simple pleasure of killing.

At least…that's how she'd always felt, until now. It was those damn stories swarming through the mountains like a brush fire, putting everyone on edge, that were messing with her head. She'd thought herself above the media's determination to breed fear into the minds of the masses, but it was obvious that the propaganda had managed to worm its way into her subconscious, catching her up in its frenzied grip. She'd heard whispers that there was a missing teenager who might turn out to be the second victim, although a body still hadn't been found. And there were even some who believed that it was some kind of monster that had massacred Kendra Wilcox, but Rachel didn't buy into any of that supernatural hysteria.

At least, she hadn't thought she did, until a sudden rustling sound off to her left had her flinching, jerking a girlie squeak of fear from her throat. Hiking her camera strap higher onto her shoulder, she chastised herself for allowing her imagination to get the better of her, and forced herself to keep moving deeper into the forest.

Five minutes later, she'd made her way to the tree, a relieved smile curling the corner of her mouth, and was just reaching for her camera bag when a twig suddenly snapped behind her. Spinning around, Rachel nervously scanned the area, searching for the source, while her heart about beat its way out of her chest—her panic instantly flaring back to life. But nothing was there. Stepping backward, she looked from side to side, that strange feeling of being watched growing stronger, engulfing her.

Icy tendrils of fear clamped around her throat, making it difficult to breathe, until her lungs were working in hard, sharp gasps. Another snap, this one from a different direction, and she spun again, quickly reaching into her back pocket and pulling out the small knife her father had given her when she began hiking on her own.

"Whoever the hell you are, I'm not afraid of you!" she called out, though the vibrato of her words said otherwise. A rush of air came from behind her, like the movement of a body close to hers, and she screamed, spinning around, nearly stumbling as she searched the woods with wild, frantic eyes.

"I swear to God, you had better stay away from me or I'll call the cops!" she shouted, knowing it was a bluff. She'd lost her stupid cell phone at a party the week before and had been too busy with work and school to get a new one.

"Go ahead and try it," a deep, velvety voice suddenly drawled from just behind her, "and let me know how it works out for you."

Spinning, so scared she nearly lost her breakfast, Rachel found herself face-to-face with a...man. He wasn't a monster. No slathering beast or creature from the terrifying dead of night. He was just a tall, easy-on-the-eyes, golden-haired Adonis type. The kind who'd have snagged her notice if she'd passed him on the street, even though he was a little too *GQ* for her tastes. He didn't even hold a weapon in his hands. No ominous-looking knife or scalpel clutched maniacally in his grip.

"You're...you're just a guy," she whispered, before noticing the strange, icy blueness of his eyes. They were the kind you saw on an animal, not a human, and shock crawled over her body like a thick, slimy ooze, sinking into her pores. She took a clumsy step back, followed quickly by another, careful to keep the knife in front of her. "Just a guy," she repeated, as if saying it out loud could somehow make it true.

"You sure about that, angel?" His head tilted slightly to the side as he spoke, while he matched her steps, slowly stalking her, those oddly lit eyes glittering with something that looked horrifically like joy.

"I'm n-not an angel," she stammered, shaking so badly that her teeth chattered.

"Wanna know a secret?" he asked, slanting her a slow, sensual smile that made her whimper. As if he enjoyed the childlike sound, a low, husky chuckle slipped from his beautiful mouth, and he whispered, "Neither am I."

She knew he was the one, then. Knew exactly what he would do to her. So many questions flooded her mind, but all she could say was, "Why?"

His hands lifted to the front of his crisp, expensive-looking shirt, the material snowy white against the deep golden tones of his complexion, and he slowly began undoing the top button, then the next, as he calmly explained. "Because I'm the hunter, and you, sweet one…you're the prey."

Rachel opened her mouth to shout, to call for help…but before the first sound escaped her throat, he'd lunged forward, catching her in a deadly grip, one hand plastered over her mouth, while he made low, soothing sounds in her ear. She wanted to fight him, to cut him, but it took no more than a handful of seconds before he'd easily stripped her of the knife. Her camera slipped off her shoulder as he forced her to the ground beneath the gnarled branches of the tree, its ancient limbs reaching toward the heavens like a multitude of arms uplifted in prayer, though she knew no one could save her now.

As her ravaged screams rang out through the forest, a startled flock of birds took flight in the morning sky, but there was no one else to hear her.

CHAPTER SIXTEEN

Ravenswing, Thursday Afternoon

IT'D BEEN THE WEEK from hell. Not that Ian had been expecting tea and roses. But, Christ, at this point, there wasn't going to be anything left of him for the Casus to kill. He hurt from his head to his toes, his body one aching, throbbing pulse of pain, with a noxious mood to match.

Wiping the sweat from his eyes, he choked back a guttural growl, determined to ignore a slick, visceral slide of jealousy slipping through his system as he thought about how much time Molly was spending with Scott. He blew out a sharp breath, rolling his neck and focused instead on his grinning opponent.

Big kitty, my ass, he thought with a silent snarl. He'd learned for himself exactly what kind of shape-shifter Aiden Shrader was when he'd walked outside late Monday night for a smoke. He'd found himself face-to-face with a four-hundred-and-fifty-pound tiger, its golden eyes glittering with humor when he'd stumbled back in shock and landed on his already bruised ass like an idiot.

Now, as Ian faced off against the arrogant Watchman, he was aware of his Merrick seething beneath his skin, furious that it couldn't get its hands…or its talons…on the guy. Shrader came at him in a blur of speed, but Ian was ready. Balancing his weight on the balls of his feet, he swiveled at the last second, grabbing the Watchman's upper body as he shot past. Holding as tight as he could, considering they were both drenched with sweat, Ian used all his weight to propel him headfirst toward the garage wall, hoping to knock him out.

"You can keep trying to bash his brains in, but it won't do any good," Quinn called out from the garage rooftop, where he'd been sitting for the past hour, observing the training. "I've been telling Aiden for years that he hasn't got any."

A low snarl surged up from the Watchman in his arms, and Ian could feel the power building inside of Shrader, his muscles coiling, rippling beneath his skin. He struggled to get a better grip on him, but in the next instant, Shrader twisted out of his hold, swiveled around, and kicked his knees straight out from under him.

Ian went down. *Hard.* Pain exploded through his head as his skull cracked against the dusty ground. He expelled a harsh burst of air, and before he even knew what was happening, Shrader had one hand over his mouth. Then, with a quick flick of his wrist, the Watchman jerked his head to the side.

The next thing Ian knew, he was blinking his eyes open, squinting against the bright glare of sunshine raining down from the crystal blue summer sky, the morning storm clouds long since burned away, leaving another record-breaking heat wave in their wake. He was surprised to find Shrader, Quinn and Scott all standing around his prone body. They stared down at him with varying expressions that ranged from disappointment and disgruntlement, to sheer unadulterated disgust.

"What did you do to me?" he croaked, wondering how long he'd been out.

"It's a simple enough trick, if you know how to do it," Shrader drawled. "And by the way, you lose. *Again.*"

"No shit," he grunted, struggling to pull himself up into a sitting position. His head spun, his stomach roiling as if he hadn't eaten in days.

"I would've thought someone who's done as much fighting as you have would be able to give me more of a contest," Shrader added, curling his lip. "But you're proving as weak as every other human I've ever come up against."

Rubbing at the knot on the back of his head, Ian snapped, "Are you trying to piss me off?"

Quinn's drawl was as dry as the mountain wind. "Is he that obvious?"

"What's obvious is that you're the most stubborn jackass I've ever known," Scott muttered, speaking up for the first time.

"Go to hell," Ian grunted, moving slowly to his feet. Dizzy, he braced one hand against the wall of the garage, wondering if he was going to lose the lunch he'd eaten five hours ago.

"He could be watching you right now," Scott lectured him in a low voice. "Seeing you get your ass kicked. He's going to think you're so easy to kill, it's pathetic. You're supposed to be getting better, not *worse.*"

Ian wanted to argue, but it was true. He'd been growing weaker every day, until he felt like something that'd been tied to the back of a car and dragged through the desert.

Though he'd finally slept out of sheer exhaustion—thankfully without any of the recurring dreams like those he'd experienced over the weekend—he felt sluggish inside, weighted down, the way he did after a bad case of the flu. His arms were heavy, same as his legs, his muscles cramping with each punch and kick he delivered during the long days of training.

You know what you need, you obstinate bastard. And she's up in that big ol' house…just waiting for you.

Shaking off the dangerous, destructive thought, Ian tried to draw in a slow, calming breath, but he could feel the violent fury of the Merrick part of his nature punching at his insides, raging and wrathful, demanding release. More than ready to take matters into its own hands. It wanted free, that very instant, but was too weak to fight its way out. It had been so long since the last dream, when the Merrick had taken her blood, that the need had become like a parasite, draining them both…and Ian knew something had to be done. He just didn't know what. He'd fought the hunger for so many days now, there wasn't a chance in hell he could get his fangs into Molly and not turn into a ravenous, raging maniac on her.

So if that's the case, you need to find another woman….

The jarring thought slithered through his system like something slimy and cold, but it wasn't the first time he'd heard it. There'd been a few moments over the course of the last few days that Ian had actually considered getting into his truck, driving into a nearby town, and finding a bar. Picking up a woman. Slinking back to her place with her, all the while hoping like hell that the Casus wasn't following him, when he'd already been warned that it was "tuned" into him, like some kind of preternatural tracking system. And then what would he do? Cross his fingers and hope that she didn't notice when he sank a set of fangs into her throat?

Yeah, great planning, Buchanan. You're a helluva strategist.

"Shut up," he muttered under his breath, wondering if the fact that he was now talking to the voices in his head was an indication that he'd truly lost his mind.

Pushing away from the wall, he muttered, "I'm done out here."

He hadn't taken more than a step before Scott grabbed hold of his shoulder, spun him around and slammed him back against the garage. "You're not going anywhere until we've talked," the Watchman grunted.

Furious that he was too freaking tired to go head-to-head with the asshole, Ian snarled, "We've been talking all goddamn week. What the hell do you want from me?"

Scott shifted forward, getting right in his face, his usually easygoing expression pulled into a vicious scowl. "I want you to stop fighting what you are, because it's not only wasting our time, it's putting the lives of innocent people on the line. If you don't stop the bullshit and get it together, you'll never be able to defeat the Casus. He'll rip you to pieces before you even know what hit you, and then he'll go to town on Molly. Is that what you want?"

Rage built up within him so swiftly, Ian was amazed the top of his head didn't come off. "Leave her out of this."

"Why should I?" the auburn-haired bastard demanded in a challenging snarl.

"Because she's not your problem!"

"No, you just…" Scott's voice trailed off as he suddenly cut a sharp look over his shoulder, and Ian shifted in his hold, trying to see what had captured the man's attention. His eyes narrowed, blood rising, when he spotted Molly coming their way from the far side of the L-shaped garage. She looked too soft and sweet to have landed in the midst of this macabre nightmare, like a delicate pansy being tossed into a valley of nettles, or a lamb thrown heartlessly to the wolves. That vulnerable core of tenderness called to him, made something inside of Ian clench with pain. Made him want to take her in his arms and protect her to his dying breath—if it weren't for the fact he wasn't the hero in this little drama, but one of the very things she needed protection from.

And yet, she truly didn't fear him. He could sense it—scent it—and that was what fascinated him most of all. The way she could be so undeniably delicate, and yet, so bloody strong and fearless.

By some kind of silent agreement, Quinn and Shrader moved away to intercept her, leaving Ian alone with Scott. It looked as if she was arguing with them, her worried gaze cutting again and again to where he stood with the Brit, who had released his hold on him and was now casually propping his shoulder against the wall at Ian's side. Molly searched his face for any sign that he wanted her to come to him—her hope and worry achingly obvious—and he worked to keep his expression neutral, though he could feel his facial muscles twitch beneath his skin. After what had nearly happened on Monday, he'd been avoiding her for days, going out of his way to make sure he was never alone with her, and he could sense her frustration, as well as the bruised shadows of hurt she tried so hard to conceal. She'd given him nothing short of wrenching, brutal honesty, and he'd repaid her by turning away from her. Not once, but twice. He kept expecting her to storm into his room late one night, slap his face and tell him to go to the devil. But she did none of those things.

Ian didn't know whether to be relieved…or irritated that she wasn't demanding he stop acting like an asshole.

You never know. Maybe she's changed her mind and opened her eyes to what you really are. Maybe she doesn't even want you anymore. Maybe she's found someone else.

Locking his jaw, he fought the urge to go to her, while his Merrick howled its fury so loud within his mind, the fractured sound echoed against his skull. It wanted nothing more than to run to her, take her to the ground, and feed from that delicious little body. Feed until it was powerful enough to break its way out of him and finally face the Casus, putting an end to this nightmare once and for all.

She glanced his way one last time, her eyes shadowed and dark, while pulling that juicy lower lip through her teeth the way she did when she was upset. Or when she was coming, he remembered, damn near exploding from the swift, savage burn of lust that ripped through him. Then she shifted her gaze back to Shrader, who'd already become chummy with her, and nodded at whatever he was saying. A moment later, she turned away, letting the Watchmen escort her around the end of the garage and back up to the house.

"If you want to keep your eyes," Ian grated under his breath, when he noticed the direction of Scott's gaze, "stop staring at her ass."

Despite his simmering anger, the corner of Scott's mouth twitched. "Yeah?" he drawled. "And just what are you going to do about it, Buchanan? If I wanted her, you couldn't stop me. You're so weak right now, you couldn't punch your way out of a paper bag."

"Wanna try me?" he grated, almost hoping the guy would say yes. Despite all the hours he'd spent training that week, Ian had yet to face off against the arrogant Brit, and he couldn't help but wonder why that was.

With the wind whipping the dark auburn strands of his hair over his brow, Scott slanted him a cocky smirk. "I won't say I'm not tempted, but we have more pressing matters."

Ian arched his brows. "Yeah? Like what?"

"Be a smart-ass all you like. It isn't going to save you from hearing this."

"So spit it out already."

For a long, tense moment, Scott simply glared at him, and then he finally got to his point. "When you got here, there were bite marks on the side of Molly's throat, though I'm assuming you didn't take enough of her blood, if any, considering how weak your Merrick is. Because they were made by the Merrick part of your nature, they healed quickly. And since then, despite everything we've told you, despite us making it clear that you have to feed the Merrick in order for it to break free, and that only *after* that happens will you be powerful enough to face the Casus and take it down, putting an end to its killing spree—despite all that, I haven't seen any new bite marks on her. I asked Molly why that was."

Fury curled around the backs of Ian's ears, clawing up the inside of his throat. "It's none of your damn business," he ground out through his clenched teeth.

"That's exactly what she said," the Watchman rumbled, rubbing his palm across the ginger bristles on his chin, a brief flicker of amusement in his eyes, "though in politer terms."

"And I'm still wondering why you think this topic has anything to do with you," he muttered, wishing that he had a smoke in the worst way.

Scott's green eyes narrowed with impatience. "You *have* to feed from her. If you don't, one way or another, you're going to end up losing her. Either to the Casus, or because you've had to take what you need from another woman. You don't want to go through that."

Ian shoved his hands in his front pockets, drawling, "And here I thought you just might be hoping you could have her all to yourself."

"I'd like nothing better," Scott admitted in a graveled slide of words, his gaze shuttered. "God knows she deserves better than you, but I'm trying to do what's best for everyone."

Ian's lip curled. "Yeah, you're a real saint."

"And you're a real bastard," Scott shot back. "A dead

one at that, if you don't get your head out of your ass. I know you don't want any of this, Buchanan, but it isn't something you can just run away from. It's time to accept it. To do the right thing."

He dug his toes into the sandy ground, the gritty texture hot beneath his bare feet, and struggled to wrap his mind around the answer. The right thing? Jesus, he didn't even know what that was anymore. Keep his hands off her, no matter how insane it drove him? Or sink his fangs into that warm, beautiful throat and risk taking her life?

"It's obvious you bit Molly before," Scott grunted. "Do it again, and this time take what you need. Then face this thing and put an end to it."

Ian rolled his shoulder in a tight gesture, surprised to hear himself saying, "You don't know what the hell you're talking about."

"Yeah? Then enlighten me."

Wanting to get the conversation over and done with, he forced out a gritty, "I haven't."

The Watchman scowled. "I saw those marks on her throat. It wasn't my imagination."

"They were there because of a dream," he grated, pushing the words through his clenched teeth.

Scott eyed him with wary suspicion. "What dream?"

Ian hesitated…and the Brit made an impatient sound. "If I'm going to help you, you've got to come clean."

"Molly and I…when we first met," he ground out, "the first two nights, we shared dreams. Intense ones."

"Go on," Scott murmured, jerking his chin forward.

"What do you want to hear?" he snapped. "We had sex, I bit her, drank her blood and damn near couldn't stop myself the second time it happened. I'm not about to risk it again. I won't be the thing responsible for her death."

Scott stared at him for a moment, studying his face…his eyes, then quietly said, "You're going to have to trust me when I tell you that won't happen. I may not be Merrick, but we deal with our own hungers. Believe me, I know how destructive the craving can be, but…you *will* be able to control it."

Right. He'd never been able to control anything in his entire life, which was why he'd become so damn good at running. He wasn't about to believe he could do it now, when something as important as Molly's life was on the line. "Have you ever heard of anything like that happening before? Two people sharing dreams like that?"

Deep in thought, the Watchman slowly shook his head. "No," he finally admitted, sounding defeated. "Never."

Ian's impatience flared with blistering force, hot beneath his skin. "Then what does it mean?"

"Who knows? It could be her powers. She obviously has some psychic ability, to be able to listen to the dead the way she does. Then again, it could be something that comes from you. Your mother had…special gifts. Hints of precognition, it was believed. What many refer to as 'the sight.' Or it could be a combination of the two. Hell, it could even be linked to the Merrick awakening inside of you. Until more of the awakenings begin, there's no way to say for sure."

"Great," he muttered, lifting his arm to rub at the corded tension gathering at the base of his neck. "You're a lot of help."

"I'm trying to be," Scott grunted, "if you'd just listen to me. I know it's difficult to take something like this on faith, but I'm telling you the truth. You're not going to hurt her. The smartest thing you could do is to go to Molly right now, grovel at her feet for treating her so badly all week, and then take her to bed and feed from her before it's too late."

"Thanks for the advice," he sneered, "but I'll do it when I'm damn good and ready."

"Yeah, well, you let me know how that dumbass plan is working out for you," the Watchman drawled, the harsh words cut with a quiet, seething rage. "And in the meantime, just pretend there aren't consequences to your actions. The longer you wait, the more innocent people will pay with their lives because of your stubbornness."

"What are you talking about?"

Scott crossed his arms over his broad chest, his tone grim as he explained. "I came out here to find you for a reason. Kellan called me a little while ago. Your brother's got another murder on his hands. A teenager was reported missing by her father a couple of days ago. They'd thought she might be a runaway, but this morning some hikers found her remains in a canyon, about ten miles from Henning. The story is only just now breaking on the news, and the authorities are calling it another possible animal attack. But Kellan said it looks like a Casus kill."

Ian could feel the color drain from his face, while gruesome images from the scene of Kendra's murder kept playing through his mind. "Why would he go after a kid?" he croaked. "I don't even know any teenage girls, and no way in hell would I ever get involved with one."

"That doesn't change the fact that this thing needs to feed. Just because you and Molly have been hiding out here, where it can't get to you, doesn't mean it's going to just sit back and wait for you to make an appearance. It's probably been using animals for the most part, but it needs human flesh to keep it sustained, to build its strength, the same way you need blood. If it can't get its hands on someone who's connected to you, it'll take what it can get."

Ian started to pace away, but Scott grabbed hold of his tensed bicep, pulling him back around. "Don't you get it, Buchanan? You're trying to control a situation that can't be controlled, and it's all going to blow up in your face. It's time to deal with it, before your entire life ends up getting fucked."

"Open your eyes!" he shouted, suddenly shoving at the bastard's shoulders, wanting a fight…needing it. "It's already happened. And you're all sitting around here like a bunch of jackasses, doing nothing!"

It was obvious Scott wanted to shove him back, but he fought it down, his hands fisted at his sides as he growled, "We have our job to do, and you have yours, Merrick. Don't think these killings aren't going to draw the notice of the Collective. When it does, when they come here, we're going to have our goddamn hands full dealing with them."

Ian started to scrape out a scathing response, when he caught Shrader's scent drawing near again. Turning, he watched the man make his way toward them, minus Molly and Quinn. Shrader wore a bleak expression, and Ian knew more bad news was on its way.

When the Watchman reached them, he met Ian's hard

gaze and muttered, "Molly sent me with a message. She napped for a few hours after lunch, and heard from your mother again. That's what she came out here to tell you."

"And?" he rasped, wondering what the hell Elaina had told her.

"Molly said it was difficult to understand. She doesn't know if Elaina's connection is weakening, but she could only make out part of the message. Something about the Marker coming into power when the Casus is near."

Scott moved to Ian's side. "If that's true, then it would explain why you haven't been able to get the cross to work."

Ian nodded his agreement, while staring at a dusty patch of ground, a hazy idea flickering at the edges of his mind, slowly taking shape like an image materializing out of mist.

"There's more," Shrader muttered, the gruff words cut with a brutal, foreboding edge.

"What is it?" Scott asked.

"Kellan just called in on the secure line again," the Watchman explained. "A woman has been reported missing in Henning. A young art student. She went out in the woods this morning to take some photographs, and was supposed to be back for her shift at one of the local markets by noon, but no one's heard from her. After the breaking news about the teenager, the whole town's suddenly in a panic, believing this art student is the third victim."

The idea that'd begun brewing in Ian's brain suddenly vanished, replaced by a sickening wave of horror that swept through his system, obliterating everything in its path. He couldn't think, couldn't speak. All he could do was stand there, his muscles coiling and flexing as the summer sun beat down on his face. A vile, blistering wave of rage roiled up from the soles of his feet as he thought of the women who'd lost their lives, and all because of him. Because of this thing inside of him.

Shrader shoved his hands in his pockets, then slanted a shuttered look in Scott's direction. "Kellan also said that the meeting's set. Whenever you're ready to head into town, all we have to do is give him a call."

Scott appeared no less happy with this second bit of news, his mouth compressed in a hard, flat line, the unforgiving sunlight accentuating the shadows beneath his eyes, as well as the deep grooves bracketing his mouth.

"Is it a go?" Shrader asked, at the same time Ian grunted, "What meeting?" His eyes cut back and forth between the two men, not liking the strange feeling creeping up the back of his neck, like a cold hand against his skin, holding him in place, warning him that whatever they were hiding, he wasn't going to like it.

Scott stared at him for a moment, his dark gaze shadowed with anger and frustration and some indefinable emotion, and then he finally shifted his attention back to Shrader. "Yeah," he said, his voice low…graveled. "We're getting nowhere here. I didn't want it to come to this, but I don't think we have any other choice. Call Kellan back and tell him we're heading in now."

"For the last goddamn time, what meeting?" Ian ground out through his clenched teeth, hating the way they kept talking around him, making it obvious that he was being left in the dark on purpose.

"I'll explain when we get there," Scott called out, already walking away. "Grab a shower and be ready to go in fifteen."

Ian stood his ground, determined not to move until they told him what the hell was going on. "I'm not going anywhere until you tell me what this is all about."

Looking back over his shoulder, Scott squinted against the bright glare of sunshine. "I've called in someone who can help us."

"Someone? What kind of someone?" he pressed, ruefully aware that this was freaking the shit out of him. "If they aren't an enemy, then why aren't they coming up here?"

"Because it would be a really bad idea," Shrader snorted, before casting a questioning look toward Scott.

Ian took a deep breath, struggling to keep it together, the fiery burn of the sun against his bare shoulders the perfect complement to the anger smoldering through his veins. "Why?"

Walking back toward him, Scott didn't stop until he was right in his face, nose to nose with him. "I know you're not going to like it, Buchanan. I know you'd like nothing better than to tell us all where to go, but you're just going to have to trust me."

"Not in this lifetime," he snarled, his mouth twisting in a snide smile.

The seconds stretched out slowly as Scott stared him down, both of them refusing to budge…to back off, until the Watchman took a step back, his chest rising and falling with a series of hard, deep breaths. When he finally spoke, he didn't make any threats—didn't offer any explanations. Instead, he played the one card that he knew Ian didn't have a chance in hell of resisting, and quietly said, "If you want her to live, then do it for Molly. Because this just might be your last chance to save her."

CHAPTER SEVENTEEN

WHILE QUINN AND SHRADER stayed behind with Molly at Ravenswing, Ian drove his truck down to Henning along with Scott, who insisted on riding with him. He hadn't wasted any more of his breath pressing the Watchman for answers he knew he wasn't going to get, and Scott hadn't offered him any information, simply telling him where the meeting was set to take place. While the Watchman leaned back in his seat and closed his eyes, Ian spent the drive working things over in his mind, searching for a solution…for some kind of way to put an end to it all without sinking his fangs into someone's throat. He knew he needed to do something, dammit…but what? What was the answer? He felt as if it was hovering right in front of him, taunting him, but no matter how hard he tried, he couldn't grab hold of it.

Despite the winding mountain roads, they made good time down from Ravenswing, the sun still hanging in the sky like a smoldering ball of flame beyond the lavender twilight when they pulled into the parking lot shared by Nate's, a local Henning hangout, and the Mountain Inn Motel. There were a few uneasy moments when he climbed out of the truck and found Aubrey

Rodgers, a woman he'd briefly dated the previous year, heading toward him with a bright, flirtatious smile painted on her cherry-red mouth. Knowing that every second she spent in his company put her life in danger, Ian did his best to get rid of her quickly. He was a marked man, like the kiss of death, and though he could tell she was hurt by his curt dismissal, it was better than taking the chance she'd be seen with him.

Thankfully, there'd been no one else in the parking lot to witness their brief discussion, but as he followed a brooding Scott over the sun-warmed asphalt, toward the motel, and up the painted metal staircase that led to the second-story rooms, Ian couldn't help but worry over the shitty luck that had put Aubrey in his path. She didn't even live in Henning, so what were the odds? He hadn't seen her in months, and then *Bam!* There she was. His wary gaze scanned the thick ridge of forest that began on the far side of the motel, and he wondered if the Casus could be out there. Ian hoped like hell he was just being paranoid, but he couldn't quell the uneasy feeling in his gut that told him Aubrey Rodgers had just been screwed by the fickle finger of fate.

You're overreacting, man. No one saw her. No one's watching.

They reached the railed landing and Scott turned right, heading down the smooth concrete walkway, then turned left at the corner. Stopping in front of the second doorway, he raised his fist to give the dark green door a hard knock. Ian stood with his hands shoved in his pockets, wondering what they were heading into as he cast an uneasy look over his shoulder, toward the forest again, unable to shake the eerie feeling they were being watched. At the sound of the lock turning, he swung his head back around in time to see the door being opened by a darker, slightly younger version of the man at his side. The guy had thick, dark red hair that looked almost black, his eyes an unusual blend of blue and green, and Ian knew he must be Kierland's brother, Kellan. The resemblance between the two men was unmistakable, and while Kierland might have had an inch on him in height, Kellan was brawnier than his brother, with a build that could have belonged on a professional football player.

With his odd-colored eyes flashing with curiosity, the younger Watchman stepped aside to allow them in, then shut and locked the door as he said, "Morgan'll be out in a minute." He turned and held out his hand toward Ian, his grip firm as they shook, and with the same trace of a British accent as his sibling, he jerked his head toward Scott, drawling, "I'm this asshole's younger brother, but don't hold it against me. Name's Kellan."

Before Ian could respond, Scott asked, "Any problems getting here?"

Kellan turned his attention to his brother and shook his head. "None so far. Everything's been quiet."

Ian moved away from them, glancing around for clues that might reveal what was going on, but the room looked untouched, the only luggage he could see a battered backpack propped beside the far wall, next to the closed bathroom door. He could hear the sound of running water coming from within, revealing the presence of the third person—the individual named Morgan that Kellan had mentioned—and could only assume that was who they'd come to meet with.

Moody shadows dwelt like a gothic presence within

the confined space, the only furniture a queen-size bed, dresser and matching nightstands, along with a desk and chair. Though there were two lamps, they remained off, the only source of light coming from the fading spill of twilight that made its way in through the slanted blinds; revealing a breathtaking view of the thick forest that stretched its way up the side of the mountain.

Reaching for the pack of cigarettes he'd stuffed in the pocket of his T-shirt, Ian slanted a wary look toward Scott, who had taken up position against the closed door, as though to block the only escape route. Did they expect him to run, then? And if so, why?

Digging in the front pocket of his jeans for his lighter, he said, "Don't you think it's time you told me what's going on here?"

Before the Watchmen could answer, the bathroom door opened, and a woman appeared. She paused in the doorway when their gazes caught, one arm lifted, pressing a white hand towel to her cheek, her skin dewy, as if she'd just washed it. Ian drew in a deep breath and knew, instantly, that she wasn't human. She smelled similar to the Watchmen…only softer, sweeter. Tall and slender, with shadowy gray eyes and a heart-shaped face that looked as if it'd been carved from fine porcelain, she was undeniably beautiful. Though she had a killer figure, she wore a simple T-shirt and jeans, hardly dressed for seduction—and yet, all it took was one look at her and Ian knew precisely what was going down.

Driven by a swift, staggering rise of fury, his unlit cigarette fell from his fingers, forgotten, and he lunged for Scott, catching him by the front of his shirt. Twisting his fist in the soft cotton, Ian lifted the Watchman off the ground, then slammed him into the door with a hard, resounding crack. "You son of a bitch," he snarled.

Scott's green eyes stared back at him with unblinking intensity, his expression strangely blank, as though a veil had been pulled over his face, removing any trace of emotion. "Be as angry with me as you like, Buchanan, but you've left us no choice. You won't feed from Molly, and the body count is climbing."

"I won't do it." The dark, graveled words were torn from his throat with no conscious direction from his brain, born completely from instinct—from a part of him that he refused to look at too closely. He didn't want to think about *why* he couldn't go through with their plan. God only knew the woman was beautiful, and apparently willing, but it didn't matter.

Forcing himself to take a deep, shuddering breath, Ian clawed onto his rage with what was left of his control and released his hold on Scott. He stepped away, and stared round the room, gauging the other two, trying to get a read on their emotions, while doing his best to conceal his own. While Kierland struggled to hide his simmering anger beneath a mask of indifference, his brother simply appeared intrigued, as if he were watching some fascinating drama playing out for his entertainment. Even Kellan's stance was casual, his broad shoulders propped against the wall at his back, muscled arms crossed over a faded Led Zeppelin T-shirt. But it was the woman, Morgan, who was the easiest to read, her obvious relief evident in the softening of her expression, as if she'd just been granted a reprieve.

"This is your last chance to do what's right," Scott said in a low voice, breaking the breath-filled silence.

"Unless you want the blood of more innocent women on your hands."

"I know it'll be hard for a self-righteous prick like you," Ian sneered, "but do me a favor and lay off the fucking lectures."

"Open your eyes, Merrick. I *am* trying to do you a favor."

Kellan whistled softly under his breath, his eyes wide as he looked back and forth between them, while the woman simply remained in the doorway, listening intently to the argument.

"All I'm asking is that you be sensible and think about what you're being offered here, before you let your temper get the better of you," Scott added, his tone setting Ian's teeth on edge. "Morgan traveled a helluva long way to come here, and you owe her that much."

Pulling out another cigarette, Ian quickly lit the tip with his lighter and took a sharp, hard drag, doing his best to ignore the way his goddamn hand shook.

"I don't believe this shit," he muttered, taking another deep drag, not stopping until the smoke burned his lungs. He needed that sharp burn of pain to center himself, focusing on it in order to keep his rage and frustration from overpowering him. "I didn't realize you guys were pimps on top of everything else."

"I brought you here to *feed* from her," Scott grunted, his air of calm indifference slipping a notch, allowing his own frustration to bleed through. "You're so bloody terrified of hurting Molly, but Morgan is one of us. You can take what you need from her without worrying about hurting her, and then go after that bastard and put an end to this thing, once and for all, before any more innocent people lose their lives."

Despite its weakness, Ian could feel his Merrick rising within him, starved for blood, undeniably tempted by the offer that was being laid at their feet, and yet, painfully aware of what it would mean to go through with it. There was no doubt that Kierland knew just how to twist the knife—knew, just as Ian and the Merrick did, that his options were limited. Either take Molly…and risk the unthinkable, or feed from someone else, and in doing so, cut all ties with her forever. Because once he did, there wasn't a chance in hell that Molly Stratton would ever want to come within a God-given mile of him again. Not after she'd offered herself to him so freely, and he'd refused, turning his back on her.

"I'm not the one who killed them," he seethed, needing an outlet for his visceral, animalistic rage, unable to hold it in. Stubbing out what was left of his cigarette in a plastic ashtray, he took an aggressive step toward Scott, who still stood with his back to the door.

"Maybe not," the Watchman rasped, watching him closely, his brow drawn in a deep V over the pale green of his gaze. "But you haven't done a helluva lot to save them, either, have you?"

The next thing Ian knew, he was slamming his fist into Scott's jaw and watching as the man's head snapped to the side. With lightning reflexes, Scott responded with a powering jab that cracked against Ian's already bruised ribs, tearing a guttural roar from his chest at the same time Ian connected with a swift uppercut beneath the bastard's chin.

"Goddamn it! You two need to chill!" Kellan grunted as he entered the fray and tried to pull them apart, while the punches continued to fly, the sound of a fist connecting with cartilage making a thick snapping sound that had the younger Watchman shouting for them both to go to hell. They slammed into the desk, sending the lamp crashing to the floor, then banged into the far wall, knocking down a framed landscape when Scott missed Ian's face and sent his bloodied knuckles straight through the drywall.

They were too evenly matched in their anger, and in the end, it was Morgan who finally managed to shove her way between them, pushing them apart, her outstretched arms pressed against their heaving chests. Neither man swung, afraid of hitting her by accident, and so she was able to hold them back from one another, while shouting for them to stop acting like a pair of adolescents.

"All right, all right," Scott panted, backing away until his shoulder blades came up against the wall, his breathing ragged as he hunched forward, bracing his hands on his knees. Looking up through the dark strands of hair falling over his brow, he finally said, "This wasn't my first choice, Buchanan. Trust me. I've tried over and over again to get you to do the right thing this week. I told you today to get your ass up in the house and take Molly to bed. But you refused, said it's never going to happen, and I accept your decision. I don't agree with it, but I finally realized you're never going to change your mind. So that makes this your only option. Take what Morgan's offering, what she's willing to give, because if you don't, you'll never be strong enough to face him, and that maniacal bastard is just going to keep picking them off, one by one."

Ian shifted his gaze to Morgan, her gray eyes huge as she stared…studying him. There was no doubt that she was one of the most beautiful women he'd ever seen—but it didn't change the fact that she wasn't the one he wanted. "Why?" he muttered, while a cold sweat that felt uncomfortably like panic broke out over his skin. "Why did you come here?"

"I don't whore myself out for the Watchmen, if that's what you're thinking," she told him, her voice soft…but strong. "I'm a soldier, same as these two. I do, however, happen to be a woman, which is what you need. I also happen to understand just how important you are—as well as how important it is that you're given every possible advantage when dealing with the Casus. That being the case, I wanted you to have the choice."

Christ. So she was there to sacrifice herself for the cause. Pushing his sore fingers back through his hair, Ian silently cursed under his breath, thinking their good intentions were going to be the fucking death of him.

Morgan was offering him the perfect answer to a shitty situation, and yet, he simply couldn't take it, for the simple fact that touching her meant losing any chance he could ever have with Molly. And no matter how improbable that future seemed, it was something he wouldn't—*that he couldn't*—throw away.

Clearing his throat, he tried to explain. "Not that you're…that this isn't appreciated, but I'm afraid you've wasted your time by coming here."

Instead of arguing, she surprised him with a slight smile. "I won't say that I'm surprised. After he explained the situation between you and your woman," she said, jerking her chin toward Kierland, "I told him you wouldn't go through with it, but the jackass never listens."

"You agreed to come here," Scott grated, glaring at her as he shifted position, leaning his shoulders against the wall at his back again.

"But *not* for you," she drawled, taking a seat at the foot of the bed. With her slender arms crossed over her chest, she turned toward Scott. "I agreed because there's a war coming, and I'm willing to do what needs to be done to ensure the right side wins."

"Trust me, I know just what you're willing to do. Why else do you think I called *you*, and not some other woman," Kierland sneered, his bitter tone surprising Ian, making it obvious that these two had some kind of history.

"Ooh," she drawled, pitching her voice seductively low. "That was below the belt, Scott. Even for you."

"Just ignore him." Kellan sighed, flashing her an apologetic look. "You know he loves to push your buttons, Morgan."

"He isn't ever getting anywhere close to my buttons," she muttered, switching her attention back to Ian, her expression softening. "And for what it's worth, I think you should have a little more faith in yourself. Your feelings for the human are strong enough to keep you faithful to her, even when you know it could mean your death. I'm not a betting kind of woman, but I'd place everything I own on the fact that you could never hurt her. But no one can give you proof of that until you discover it for yourself. It's something that you're just going to have to accept on blind faith."

Pacing across the room, Ian moved to the window, staring through the blinds at the darkening sky, his attention focused on her words, working them over in his mind. There was something there that jarred his memory, reminding him of the moment on the training field, during his argument with Scott, when a hazy idea had begun to form at the edge of his consciousness.

Scott's voice came from the far side of the room, interrupting his thoughts. "I know you don't want to, Buchanan, but it's time to face what has to be done."

Ian ground his jaw, while the image in his brain slowly began to crystallize, growing clearer…sharper, various fragments of conversation looping round and round in his mind.

The Marker will come into power when the Casus is near….

Accept on blind faith…

Time to face what has to be done…

When the Casus is near…

Son of a bitch! He'd known there was something significant in the message Shrader had delivered from Molly, but it wasn't until that instant that it finally hit him, the jolt of understanding jerking a low grunt from his chest. He had the answer, dammit, and it was the simplest solution of all.

Simple? More like suicide, his conscience snarled.

True, but it was better than doing this day after day, fighting the constant temptation to take Molly, scared out of his mind that he'd end up killing her, with no logical solution in sight. He wasn't going to feed from her, and he wasn't going to feed from anyone else. Which meant he could stand around and do nothing or he could finally get off his ass and take some action.

And he finally knew exactly what to do.

Turning around, he pushed his battered hands into his pockets and quietly said, "I'm leaving."

Scott made a low sound of frustration, his green eyes flashing with impatience. "Running back to Ravenswing isn't going to solve anything," he snapped.

Ian pulled back his shoulders, knowing, without a doubt, that the Watchman wasn't going to like his plan. "I'm not going back to the compound."

Scott looked at him as if he'd gone crazy. "You're going home?" he growled. "If you go back to your apartment, she'll still be in danger. Molly knows where you live, Buchanan. She'll come after you."

He shook his head. "You're right, but that's not where I'm headed."

"Then where are you going?" Kellan asked, rasping his palm against his bristled jaw.

Taking a deep breath, Ian said, "I'm going back to the beginning."

Kellan sent a comical look of confusion toward his brother. "What the hell does that mean?"

But Ian could tell Scott knew exactly what he meant. That pale green gaze drilled into him with piercing intensity, and then the Watchman slowly said, "You're going back to Elaina's. Back to South Carolina, aren't you?"

Ian nodded. "Molly doesn't know about the house there, so she can't follow after me. And you told me the other day that this thing is tuned in to me. That it would know I was here, would know if I left, would know where I went. That wherever I go, the Casus will follow me. That's what I'm counting on. And when it does, I'll use the Marker to put an end to it."

To make this work, he needed to get far enough away that Molly *couldn't* get to him—needed to draw this thing onto his own ground, and face it there. Though they'd talked about his childhood, he'd never told her where he'd grown up. And he knew from their conversations that Elaina hadn't talked to her about his upbringing, much less about where they'd lived, which meant that she didn't know about the house. Riley had said that Saige was planning on using it, but thanks to the Watchmen, he knew that she was still down in South America. Which meant that his childhood home was empty…just sitting there, waiting. So he'd go back to the place where he'd first heard the stories of the Merrick and the Casus, and wait for this thing to come to him.

Something in Ian's gut told him that it wouldn't take long.

And maybe…just maybe, the Marker he carried in his pocket would be enough to save his ass, even without the strength of his Merrick.

Scott ground his jaw, forcing his words through his clenched teeth. "Even if you can get the cross to work, you'll be easy for him to kill in human form, and you won't be able to change because you still haven't fed. You may kill it, Buchanan, but he'll end up taking you with him."

"If you don't hear from me in a few days, then you'll know that's what happened," he rasped. "And no matter what, keep an eye on my brother. Don't leave him hanging out in the wind. He's a tough son of a bitch, but if more of these things are on the way, then he's going to need your help."

With that said, Ian turned to head for the door, until Scott's next words brought him to a stop. "And what are you going to tell Molly?" the Watchman asked.

Hunching his shoulders, Ian shoved his hands deeper into his pockets. "I can't get near her right now. I'm not going to tell her anything."

And she's going to hate you for that.

Most likely, but he couldn't think about that right now. He couldn't think about her *at all,* or he was going to go out of his mind.

"Then what am *I* supposed to tell her?" Scott growled.

Working his jaw, he said, "Tell her I said to go home."

"That's it?" the Watchman scoffed, shaking his head.

Ian could think of about a million *other* things he wanted to tell her, but couldn't. "Tell her I said that she did what she came here to do, and now it's time to get on with her life."

Trite, he knew, but what else was he going to say?

As if sensing his determination, Scott cursed something foul under his breath, then quietly said, "You better hope you know what you're doing, Merrick. If not, you're going to find yourself in hell."

"Then I'll be right at home," Ian drawled, and with a hard smile, he turned, opened the door and walked out into the falling night.

CHAPTER EIGHTEEN

Thursday Night

WITH A COLDPLAY SONG playing softly on her radio, Aubrey Rodgers made her way home down the narrow stretch of highway, her headlights cutting two stark beams through the inky darkness. She sang softly under her breath, one hand thumping against the wheel of her Honda in perfect rhythm with the music, her mind miles away, stuck on the man she'd run into earlier that evening on her way into Nate's. When she'd first spotted Ian Buchanan in the parking lot of the local hangout, she'd been so sure he was on the prowl. He'd had that predatory look in his dark blue eyes—the one she'd learned to recognize and had come to love during the two months they'd dated last year. Two months that had left her wilted with pleasure—her body sore from his ravenous sexual appetite, but more alive than she'd ever felt in her entire life.

Aubrey hadn't been surprised to see him at the bar tonight. If anyone had a reason to drink, it was Ian. She'd heard about what had happened to Kendra Wilcox, and she'd been more than ready to console him, even knowing he wouldn't want her for more than the time it'd take him to work out his tension and grief.

He'd sent her a tight smile when she'd approached him, her uncomfortable heels clicking against the gritty asphalt, hoping she wasn't about to make a fool out of herself—and that's when the second man had climbed out of Ian's truck. Aubrey had faltered for a moment, knowing Ian wasn't one to socialize. When he went to a bar, he went alone, though he rarely left that way. The stranger had been more than easy on the eyes, though no friendlier than Ian, as if she was interrupting something important. He'd walked away a few steps, making a call on his cell phone, affording her and Ian some privacy, and though they'd chatted for a moment, the conversation had been awkward and flat. It'd been painfully obvious he wasn't interested in any solace she had to offer, and she'd wanted to kick him in the shins for being such a jerk, but had stifled the impulse. Instead, she'd tried to play it cool when he'd told her they had to meet up with some friends. She'd said goodbye, walked into the bar, and then watched through one of the tinted front windows as he and the auburn-haired man had headed next door, toward the motel.

Bastard. She could imagine just what kind of "friends" they'd met up with.

"Arrogant jerk," she muttered under her breath, hating that he still held the power to make her weak in the knees. When their brief affair had ended, she'd decided, over a bottle of shared tequila with a group of girlfriends, that men like Ian Buchanan were the sexual equivalent of chocolate. Even when you knew they were bad for you, when faced with the temptation, you couldn't help but crave them.

Following a long bend in the road, Aubrey had just

reached down to crank the music louder, when a man stepped into the middle of her lane, only a handful of meters in front of her car. Screaming, she jerked the wheel in reaction, sending the car onto two wheels as it careered off the side of the road. The front end hit the shallow ditch that lined the highway, sending the car tumbling end over end, before it slammed to a jarring stop against the heavy trunk of a tree.

Hanging upside down, pinned by her seat belt, Aubrey slowly opened her eyes, aware of a pain unlike anything she'd ever known filling her up inside, pulsing from one end of her body to the other. She wanted to scream, but there was too much blood in her mouth, dripping down her face, into her eyes, staining her vision with crimson strips of terror. The engine was still running, the stringent smell of gasoline filling the mountain air. She knew she had to get out of the car before it burst into flames, but she couldn't move.

Do it! she silently screamed. *Move your goddamn arms!* But they remained limp…useless…broken, the messages lost somewhere in the deep recesses of her mind. She'd have feared she was paralyzed, if it wasn't for the excruciating pain seizing her in a pulsing clutch of agony.

And then she saw something crouch down onto the ground, just beyond the shattered driver's side window. Blinking from the blood dripping into her eyes, Aubrey stared into the palest gaze she'd ever seen. Angel's eyes. Perfect and beautiful and blue.

"Help me," she whimpered, giving a silent prayer of thanks that she'd been saved. "It h-hurts."

"Not for long," purred the gorgeous blond, reaching

his hand toward her, a slow, tender smile melting across his sensual mouth, just seconds before his hands transformed into terrifying, deadly claws. They ripped through the seat belt, the expensive silk of her new dress, before slicing effortlessly through her right breast. The scream that had been buried inside of her forced its way out, painful and scraping against her throat, pouring out of her mouth as she felt him grab hold of her hair.

In the next moment, Aubrey Rodgers was pulled from her car, into the fertile heat of the night, and delivered into hell.

CHAPTER NINETEEN

Laurente, South Carolina, Saturday Morning

IAN SAT on the hardwood floor in nothing but a pair of jeans—his back propped against the wall, long legs bent at the knee—and stared through the dingy living-room window. Though the humidity was climbing, the floor was still cold on his ass as he watched the depressingly gray cut of sky bleeding orange, the sun rising in the distance like a Phoenix soaring from the flames. It struck him as a strange, ill-fitting analogy, considering nothing was being reborn here. No second chance at life. This was an ending, a conclusion, the final act in a macabre nightmare that had, looking back, no doubt been a long time coming.

A cold beer was perched on his abs, the bottle icy against his hand—and yet, a thick layer of frustration covered his body, sticky and damp against his skin. No matter how many beers he downed, reality was still a blunt, dull blade hacking its way through his gut, relentless and without mercy.

He knew he'd done the right thing by coming here—coming home to the house he'd grown up in—but he still felt bad over the way he'd done it. He should have told Molly goodbye rather than leaving Scott to deliver that lame-ass, cop-out message. But, God, he didn't think he could have handled facing her. Not when he knew it probably would've been the last time he'd ever see her.

Crazy, that after spending so many years feeling nothing, a riot of fractured emotions now stormed through his system, as ruthless as they were cruel, leaving him sucking wind while he struggled to deal with them. No, he knew he couldn't have told her goodbye—because if he'd tried, he never would have done it. He'd have grabbed hold of her, and that would have been it. He'd have ended up taking her...and no matter how much he cared about her—and he knew that he *did* care about her—he still didn't trust the seething darkness inside of him. So he'd taken off like a thief in the night, just like his old man.

And now you'll never see little Miss Molly Stratton again. Happy, jackass?

A sharp curse hissed past his lips, and Ian hurled the beer bottle against the far wall, the violent shattering of broken glass the perfect complement to his foul mood.

Leaning his head back against the wall, he pushed his hands into his hair. Gripping the sweat-damp strands, Ian closed his eyes, but instead of peaceful nothingness, visions of Molly's soft, radiant smiles kept screwing with his mind. Of that luminous look of longing in her big brown eyes every time she'd glanced at him. He hadn't wanted to hurt her, dammit, but he hadn't had a choice.

Still, he hated that it felt like a betrayal—the heavy, sour feeling of guilt sitting in his gut like something rancid, making him ill. Scrubbing his hands down his battered face, as if the simple action could wipe away his bitter frustration, Ian accepted that he didn't know what the future would bring, but he had to face the fact that he'd thrown away the best damn thing that had ever happened to him.

Not that it mattered. Hell, he probably wasn't going to survive the weekend, so what difference did it make that he wasn't ever going to see her again? Even if he did make it through alive, he wouldn't know where to look for her. Like the stubborn bastard he was, he'd made it a point, once he'd realized she actually *meant* something to him, not to ask where she lived. He hadn't even looked in her purse and glanced at her driver's license.

No, he'd known, right from the start, that this woman was dangerous to his peace of mind—that it was best not to tempt fate and ensure that when they cut their ties, whether it was her or him, he wouldn't be able to go crawling after her later on.

Sitting on the floor a few feet from his hip, his cell phone suddenly vibrated with a low buzzing noise that grated on his already frayed nerves, but Ian ignored it, same as he'd been doing since he'd left Colorado. It would be another message from Riley, ranting and raving, wanting to know why he hadn't been in touch. He could deal with that later.

He'd been listening to the radio on his way to the airport on Thursday night, and had heard the breaking news story about another victim in Henning. With a sick feeling in his gut, Ian had called the Sheriff's Department for information, and though Riley was at the crime scene, he'd talked to the dispatch operator, who told him that the woman's name was Aubrey Rodgers. Barely able to speak over his rage, he'd left a message for Riley with the operator, saying that if he didn't hear from him by the end of the weekend, to contact a man named Kierland Scott. He knew, if something happened to him, that Scott would be able to give his brother the answers he needed.

Not that Ian planned to go down without a fight. He'd brought his knife, the one he'd carried with him in L.A.—in the circles he'd moved in while out there, you didn't tread without a weapon—and he was good with a blade. If the cross didn't work and he couldn't send the bastard to hell, he at least planned on gutting it, returning its sadistic ass back to the Casus holding ground. But even then, even if he survived the weekend and managed to take down the Casus, he didn't know what the future would hold. He hadn't fed, didn't plan on feeding, so where did that leave him? Would his hunger eventually drain him to the point that he just faded away? Or would it overtake him completely, turning him into something as ugly and vile as the monster he'd come there to kill?

The craving hadn't lessened with the distance he'd put between himself and Molly. If anything, he craved her even more. It was always there, at the back of his mind, like an ulcer in his mouth that he couldn't stop prodding with his tongue. A constant, grating reminder.

He shut his eyes again, but not to sleep. He hadn't slept all night, too worried that he might dream, though he hadn't shared a dream with Molly in almost a week. He could only thank God that he'd taken the time in that second dream to make love to her.

The stunning words stumbled into his brain, making him tense, but he kept his eyes closed, determined to ignore the unsettling realization that he'd never used that particular term before when referring to sex. And the hell of it was, he couldn't deny it. If he didn't care about Molly Stratton, he'd have fed from Morgan, let the Merrick face the Casus with the Dark Marker, and maybe had a chance of surviving. But he hadn't. He'd chosen to face it as a man.

And it's too late now to look at why you did, idiot.

"Shut up," he muttered, convinced he'd really gone off the deep end, if he could sit in a lonely old house and talk to himself. He forced his mind to go blank, existing in that hazy state between pure, numb exhaustion and wired alertness, when a sound from outside caught his attention. Scowling, he opened his eyes and rolled to his feet, the lingering bruises from his days training with the Watchmen pulling a graveled groan from his throat.

He cut a sharp glance out the window but the front yard was clear. The house sat in the middle of what had once been local farmland, with nothing but fields and shade trees for neighbors. The road came up the back, and he could hear an engine as a car came closer. Scowling, Ian wondered who the hell would be coming out there. He doubted the Casus was just going to drive up to the front door in broad daylight, but then with the week he'd been having, he supposed stranger things could happen. He was about to turn back and get the knife he'd brought, as well as the cross, just to be safe, when the car pulled to a stop. He heard a door slam, and a second later, he caught sight of pale blond curls coming around the side of the house.

No. Hell no.

Ripping open the front door so hard he about pulled it off the bloody hinges, Ian stepped out onto the rickety front porch, his heart all but pounding its way out of his chest as he watched Molly make her way toward him. Her eyes were hidden behind a dark pair of glasses, mouth set in a hard, firm line that looked delicious, despite its obvious anger.

Crossing his arms over his chest to keep from reaching for her, he growled, "How did you find me?"

"I'll be happy to answer your questions," she told him, her soft voice edged with a low, simmering rage, "but can we go inside first? I'm not comfortable being out here in the open. The Casus…Kierland said it would follow you."

He didn't comment on the news, but he stepped aside, saying, "Get inside."

She moved past him, and he had to grit his teeth to keep from leaning down and capturing that beautiful, angry mouth. Her scent filled his head as he shut the door, threw the flimsy lock, and turned back to face her. Shoving his hands in his pockets, he asked again, "How did you find me, Molly? Did Elaina tell you?" he snarled, furious that his mother would have put her in the path of danger not once, but twice.

"She didn't have to."

"Then explain it. Now!"

She slipped off the glasses, hooking them over the top button of her blouse. Ian could tell she'd been crying, and guilt curled like a viper in his belly, ready to strike. "You wanna hear something funny, Ian? No one, this entire week, has ever bothered to ask me where

I live. Not you. Not Kierland. And then I come downstairs for dinner on Thursday and find out that you're gone. Just like that." She snapped her fingers with a sharp, angry movement. "Not a word from you, or even a note. Not anything. And all Kierland can say is that you want me to go home. I'll be safe if I go home. Everything will be fine if I just go home!" She was shouting, the anger pouring out of her in a raging, molten rush that had her trembling from her head down to her toes. "Well, guess what, Ian? I know this is going to come as a great bloody shock to you, but I am *home!*"

He stared at her as understanding slowly dawned, and shook his head. "You're kidding me."

She closed her eyes, pulling a deep breath into her lungs, her skin so pale she looked like a ghost. When she lifted the thick weight of her golden lashes, she said, in a soft, throaty voice, "I moved to Laurente three years ago."

"I don't believe it."

"It's true. I work in a local bookstore. That's where I met Elaina."

"You knew her!" he ground out through his clenched teeth, his fury like a dark, blistering heat burning him from the inside out. "You *knew* her before she died and you never told me!"

Her smile was small and infinitely sad as she sniffed, and then began to explain. "I didn't know her well. Just as a customer. She would come in and buy books. Sometimes I'd suggest titles. We'd chat, but never… never about any of this. I didn't even know she had children. Then, a few weeks after I heard that she'd died, she visited me for the first time in my dreams."

"Christ," he hissed, unable to get his head around it. When he'd told himself to expect the unexpected, this sure as hell wasn't what he'd had in mind.

"I don't know how she knew about my dreams. We never talked about them, I swear. I just thought she was this sweet, kinda quirky woman who was lonely."

Molly might have been clueless about Elaina, but Ian would've bet his right arm that his mother had known about Molly's…talent or power or whatever the hell it was. Was that why she'd sought Molly out? Had she known he wouldn't be able to resist her? That he'd fall completely under her spell?

"Why didn't you tell me?"

"I don't know," she whispered, slowly shaking her head, her hurt revealed in her liquid gaze. "You never asked, for one. Not after that first night, when I was still trying to convince you to believe me. And I thought if I told you that I'd known her, then you'd believe I really *was* trying to scam you. But then later, I still kept it to myself, because deep down, I think I always knew you were going to run," she said unsteadily, looking around the living room. "And I guess I hoped, that when you did, that maybe…just maybe, you'd come here." She paused, then lifted her chin, saying, "Have you fed yet?"

"No," he muttered, wondering if Scott had told her about Morgan.

"For what's it worth, not that I expect it to mean much to you, I'm glad."

She was wearing her heart on her sleeve, standing before him, so strong and so damn vulnerable. Ian wanted to run to her, sink to his knees, and beg her to give him another chance. But he couldn't. Even if he wasn't terrified of hurting her, he wouldn't have known how…how to give her what she needed. What she wanted. Something inside of him had been locked up, seized, shut down, for too long, and now he couldn't open up. Couldn't access that part of himself that would show her warmth, tenderness. That would enable him to treat her the way she deserved to be treated. Instead, he snapped, "There's nothing to be glad about, Molly. If I had been able to go to another woman, things would be a lot simpler now."

"Why? Because you trust yourself with one of them but not with me?" she demanded. "That doesn't make any sense, Ian."

"Because I wouldn't want them the way that I want you," he admitted in a shaky rasp. "Trust me, Molly. That makes a hell of a difference."

She looked around the small, Spartan living room again, the sofa and end table the only furniture that remained. When her gaze landed on the shattered beer bottle, she shook her head, wrapping her arms around herself. "And so you came here to do what? Sacrifice yourself?"

"I don't plan on going down without a fight. I'm going to do everything I can to make the Marker work, even though I still don't have a clue what to do with it. If I can't, then I'm going to gut the bastard and send him back to wherever the hell he came from."

"When I told Shrader to tell you about the Marker working when near the Casus, I didn't think you were going to do something this stupid!"

"This is the only thing *to* do. People are dying. You're in danger. This needs to come to an end."

"Then you should have fed from me and dealt with it back in Colorado."

His jaw worked, and he muttered, "You know I can't do that."

"No, Ian. No one knows that. You're the only one who believes it. Everyone else understands exactly what needs to happen here."

"I want you to leave, Molly."

"Yeah, well, guess what? I'm learning pretty quickly that we can't always get what we want."

WONDERING HOW she managed to hold herself together, Molly stared at the man who'd reduced her to this shaky, trembling state of emotional chaos. He looked tired, haggard, the rugged lines of his face stark with strain. And yet, he still took her breath away, he was so impossibly beautiful. But there was a haunted quality to him that hadn't been there before, and she knew it was the hunger wearing him down. She was so angry at him, but she hurt for him, too.

The hot, salty burn of tears on her cheeks had her gritting her teeth. She swiped at the wet trails, wishing she could control the emotion tearing her up inside, stripping her raw—but it was impossible. Looking back, it was hard to believe how strongly she'd reacted after Kierland had told her Ian was gone. She'd screamed, hysterical, throwing things and hitting him when he'd tried to pull her into his arms and calm her down. She'd battered him with her fists—hoarse, choking sobs breaking out of her that had sounded like a wild, wounded animal—until she'd finally collapsed against him, exhausted. But the tears hadn't stopped, and she'd continued to cry for what felt like hours.

When she'd finally managed to pull herself together, Scott had delivered Ian's message to her. Then he'd told her that Ian said he was going back to the beginning, never suspecting she'd understand what that meant. The dry burst of laughter that had broken out of her chest had startled him, but she'd been too weary to explain. She'd simply asked him to book her a cab for the airport first thing in the morning. Then she'd gone upstairs, curled up in her bed and gone to sleep.

When she woke up at six, she'd found Quinn ready to act as her chauffeur. Her rental car had already been picked up at Ian's apartment during the week, so it was either Quinn or a cab, and she'd been too wrung out to argue. Before they'd left, she'd tried talking to Kierland, begging him to go to Ian, to help him, but the Watchman remained as stubborn as ever, giving her the old "interference is not our way" speech again. She'd been so furious she'd slapped him—something she'd never done before and then she'd called him an asshole and walked out of the room, leaving with Quinn. They'd made the long drive down from Ravenswing in stilted silence, and she'd flown home on an early afternoon flight, then caught a taxi from the airport to her apartment.

Back to the beginning. She'd have known exactly what it meant, even if Elaina hadn't come to her in her sleep and told her that Ian was going home. His mother was terrified for him, not that Molly blamed her. She was terrified herself.

But she was also angry. Her pride wanted her to march past him, get back in her car and leave him to deal with this nightmare on his own. It was what he deserved for being such a blind, stupid fool.

But her heart wouldn't let her, and her anger was bleeding into something more powerful…impossible to deny.

"So did you and Kierland have an emotional parting?" he asked, slanting her a dark look.

"Why would you even care?" she responded with a shaky laugh. "You left me there with him, Ian. You hardly have the right to be jealous. This whole attitude of yours sucks."

"Yeah, well, just remember that you went looking for me, Molls—not the other way around. You could have ignored those crazy little voices in your head and said to hell with it. Could have never set foot in Colorado, but you didn't."

Her temper flared, white-hot and raging. "I should have known you were going to act like a total ass."

He took a step forward, and she could tell by his expression that he was going to try and intimidate her into leaving. "I'm not going to stand here and argue with you. I don't want your help, and I don't need it. All I want is for you to turn around, get back in your car and find somewhere safe to stay until this over."

"As much as you deserve it," she told him, "I'm afraid it isn't going to happen like that."

"I can make you go, Molly," he warned in a low, gritty rasp. "Trust me. It won't be pretty and you won't like it."

She forced a slow smile onto her lips, knowing that if she let him push her away now, she was going to lose him. Forever. "Go ahead, Ian," she whispered, standing her ground as he came closer. "Do your best to be big and bad and scare me away. But I could save you the trouble and warn you right now that it isn't going to work."

His lashes lowered over the raging blue of his eyes, his voice a grating whisper that she knew was meant to frighten her, but only made her shiver with sensual awareness. "I could force you."

He meant he could force her to leave, though she chose a different meaning, determined to break through to him. "You could try, Ian. But it's hard to force someone to have sex with you when they're more than willing."

Taking his hands from his pockets, he fisted them at his sides. "I want you gone. Now," he growled, and Molly could feel the predatory force of his anger blasting against her face. But she could also feel his torment…his frustration.

"If you want me to leave, I'm afraid you're going to have to carry me out of here," she warned him, trying for her sexiest, most provocative tone. "And that means you're going to have to touch me."

"Goddamn it," he seethed, looking ready to explode with fury…with lust. His muscles were so rigid, she could see their perfect definition beneath the golden sheen of his skin. "Don't do this, Molly."

"I'm not doing anything," she murmured. "At least not anything that shouldn't have been done a hell of a long time ago. I should have gotten naked and crawled into bed with you back at Ravenswing. But I was trying to respect your decision. Waiting for you to come to your senses. Hoping like crazy you'd realize that the right thing to do was to take me to bed, and take what you need from me. But no, you had to go and decide to be the noble jackass who doesn't want to risk hurting me. Well, guess what, Ian? You don't have a choice anymore. I'm making the decision for you."

"Don't you get it?" he snarled, throwing up his hands in an aggressive, purely male gesture of rage. "There isn't a goddamn single thing about me that's noble!"

She shook her head, saying, "Shut up and waste that sorry-ass story on some other idiot. I'm on to you, Ian. I know all about you. And if you're not going to touch me, then I'm sure as hell going to touch you."

In the next instant, Molly closed the remaining distance between them, and with trembling hands, she curled her fingers around the frayed waistband of his jeans, ripping at the top button of his fly.

"What the hell are you doing?" he grunted, grasping her wrist in a biting hold that was just shy of hurting.

Molly glared up at him, ready to scream. "What does it look like I'm doing? I'm taking matters into my own hands, Ian. You won't touch me? Fine. But I'm going to touch you." Her gaze lowered, staring at the massive bulge behind the worn denim. "Better yet," she said, the words thick…husky, "I'm going to do *more* than touch."

"NOTHING'S CHANGED," Ian snarled, lifting his hands to either side of her head. He held her like that, pressed between the heat of his palms, and leaned his forehead against hers. "Christ, Molly. Don't you get that?"

"I don't need you to lie to me," she said softly, grasping on to his thick wrists as the words poured out of her in a trembling, emotional rush. "I know you. I've been inside your head. I know what you're willing to give. I know what you need to take. You want sex, and I want to give it to you. You need blood, and I'm willing to give that, too. Because unlike you, I know there isn't the slightest chance you could actually hurt me. I care about you, and I need to be here to help you through this, Ian."

"You're not helping me." He lifted his head, and forced himself to take his hands off of her. "You're distracting me. There's a hell of a difference."

"I could be useful, if you'd let me," she argued, blinking up at him, her eyes bright with tears.

"What do you want from me, Molly?"

"I want you to stop fighting me," she told him. "I want you to *take what you need.*"

What he needed? He *needed* everything—all that she had. He wanted her laid out and bared, spread, defenseless in every possible way there was. Wanted to take her under his body, and take her blood into his mouth, while he drove himself into her. Wanted her begging for him, beating his shoulders, clawing at his back, her passion wild and limitless and out of control.

He wanted to get inside of her, unlock her and break her open, forcing her to give him something that he craved even more than her body...*more than her blood.* Something that he couldn't even put a name to—and yet, Ian knew that when he found it, he would grab hold of it, clutch it in his iron grip and kill anything that dared to take it away from him.

"I want everything, Ian. Everything you can give me," she added in a breathless rush.

Christ, she actually meant it.

Shaking apart inside, Ian stared down at her, seeing the truth in her eyes, scenting it, absorbing it through his senses, and something suddenly snapped inside his head, as if he could hear the last bonds of his restraint breaking.

Before she could draw her next breath, he was claiming her mouth, kissing her as if his very life depended on it. Hot. Damp. Delicious and breathtaking and so goddamn good that he couldn't get enough of it…*of her.* With his hands cupping her face, the kiss turned almost angry, edged with fury and dark, dangerous craving. She gasped, her small hands clutching at his sweat-slick shoulders, and he nipped her lower lip, forcing himself to stop before he drew blood.

But he knew, in that moment, that he'd finally been pushed past his limit.

CHAPTER TWENTY

HIS BREATH JERKED from his lungs in a hard, panting rhythm as he picked her up, clutching her high against his body, and Molly wanted to scream from the wild rush of anticipation; at the same time she melted with relief. A week's worth of longing that felt like years sizzled through the touch of his mouth against hers. Poured into her like a slow, sweet spill of honey, while craving flashed like an arc of electricity, furious and fast, the dual assault against her senses dizzying and breathtaking. His hands gripped her waist, his long fingers biting into her flesh as he held her against him. She wrapped her legs around his hips, a husky cry breaking from her throat as she pressed against that impossibly hard, thick ridge behind the fly of his jeans.

"You could end up getting hurt," he panted against her mouth, carrying her down the shadowed hallway, while a rumbling bellow of thunder sounded far in the distance. "Dammit, you know that, Molly."

"I know exactly what's going to happen," she gasped, the dark stubble on his cheeks scratchy against her palms as she held his face. "So do your worst. You won't scare me away."

"You keep pushing me," he growled, "and that's not a good vibe right now. Trust me."

"Why?" she countered, nipping his jaw, kissing her way to his ear. "If I push you, you're going to crash right over the edge. And guess what? That's where I want you. So just shut up and take me to bed."

"I'm filthy," he grunted, stepping through a door on their left, into a murky bathroom, the only light spilling in from a small, rectangular window that sat high on the wall. "I have to get clean. I'm not going to cover you for the first time drenched in sweat."

"Fine, but we're just going to end up sweaty again," she told him as he set her on her feet. With trembling fingers, Molly pulled her blouse off while he reached past the flower-printed shower curtain and started the water. Her glasses were nowhere in sight, probably somewhere on the floor between the bathroom and the living room, but she didn't care. All she cared about was getting her hands on him before he could change his mind. "I'll get in with you."

Kicking off her sandals, she stripped off her bra, and was reaching for the zipper on her jeans, when he turned and caught sight of her half-naked body. Hunger sharpened the rugged angles of his face, making him look dangerous in a dark, predatory way. But she wasn't afraid. With a coarse growl vibrating deep in his chest, he pulled off his jeans. She stared, fascinated…dazed, at the shocking, primal beauty of him, and he grabbed hold of her, pulling her into the shower, jeans and all. Warm steam swallowed them in a hazy vapor, making him look like some primordial satyr who'd stolen away from the forest to ravish her, though she planned on doing some ravishing of her own first.

With his back turned to the pounding spray of hot water, Molly dropped down to her knees. She ran her hands up the strong, corded muscles of his hard thighs, and blinked up at him while her breath rushed in violent bursts, her pulse roaring through her ears. "Come here," she whispered, curving her hands around his hips and pulling him toward her.

"*Dammit*," Ian snarled…but he jerked forward, and the swollen, heavy head of his cock nudged the corner of her mouth, hot and delicious and nearly bursting with need. He was so unbelievably beautiful that for a moment she could only stare, smoothing her trembling fingers over the thick, rigid length, awed by its power…its heat.

"Christ, don't tease me," he gasped, and Molly took mercy on him, opening her mouth as he choked off a dark, guttural shout, the provocative sound the most erotic thing she'd ever heard.

And then she lost herself in the feel of him…in the warm, salty, sweet taste. He was thick…impossibly large, the blunt, plum-sized tip massive and smooth, barely fitting as she stretched her lips wide. He tasted earthy and rich, like primal male perfection, and she stroked her tongue over the slick opening in that broad head, desperate for more of his taste—for more of those snarled gasps of pleasure breaking from his throat that he tried so hard to hold in. Moaning, she took another inch, and his hips bucked, big feet spread wide for balance, his hands braced against the wall at her back as he pitched forward, while the shower rained down on his back.

Even though she knelt before him in a blatantly submissive position, Molly had never felt more powerful…or more beautiful, as she did in that moment.

"Dammit," he growled for the second time, and she lifted her gaze, watching his jaw work as he stared down at her through the dark shadow of his lashes, the vivid blue of his eyes burning with an unearthly light, taking her breath. His palms found the sides of her face, holding her, gripping her, and he pushed forward, giving her another wide, thick inch…then another. They both knew she couldn't take all of him, but she was desperate for as much as she *could* take. She pushed forward, pulling him in deeper, stroking him with her tongue. His hands flexed against her face, and Molly could feel the wave of power that roared through him, violent and intense.

"I wanted this the second I set eyes on you," he confessed in a gritty voice, the words so low, they were almost silent. "When you first slipped out of that car at the building site." He stroked his thumb against the corner of her mouth, rubbing the tender stretch of her lips, and whispered, "Can you take more?"

She nodded, ravenous for him, and he trembled, the shiver moving through his hard, rangy body driving her wild. Molly wondered if this was how Ian felt; at the same time, she marveled at his ability to fight it for as long as he had.

"Relax your throat," he rasped, and his warm hand trailed across her jaw, the backs of his knuckles stroking the quivering column of her throat, coaxing her to do as he said. His eyes squeezed shut as she worked her mouth over him, moving into a decadent rhythm, his lashes thick, dark against the rugged beauty of his face.

He made a low, purely male sound that shuddered through his big, powerful body, and opened his eyes, staring down at her with a fierce expression of need. And then she watched the need bleed into something darker…more primitive, seeing the panic flare in his eyes at the same time as it surged through his body. He slammed his hands against the tiles, pulling back his hips as he growled, *"Enough!"*

"No," she gasped, pressing her lips against the swollen, bruise-colored head. He made a low, roaring sound, and the air filled with the piercing screech of something sharp grating against the tiled walls of the shower.

Molly knew, without even looking, that the Merrick's talons had slipped free from his fingertips. Flicking her gaze upward, she watched his lips pull back over his teeth, the long points of his fangs blindingly white in the low spill of early-morning sunlight. Steam beaded on his skin, the heat of his body like a fever, burning against her lips, and his head fell back on his shoulders, into the misty spray of water. The position arched the strong, corded column of his throat, its muscles trembling, and a feeling of such profound longing broke open inside of her, she had to choke back the hot, liquid rush of tears.

"Later. I'll come in your mouth later," he grunted, shaking the water from his face as he looked back down at her, his stark, intense expression making her shiver. "Need you in bed. Now."

He didn't say anything more, though his eyes were wild with emotion, revealing everything he couldn't put into words. His fear. His craving. His need. He drew in a series of slow, deep breaths, and then he pushed away from the wall, reaching for her, and Molly realized he'd pulled the talons back into his body, though she could still see his fangs through his parted lips. Picking her up, he clutched her against his chest and took her to the bedroom, tossing her, wet jeans and all, onto a mattress that had been covered with an open sleeping bag, the tag still dangling from its corner.

"Isn't this the part where you run, screaming?" he rasped, kneeling on the end of the bed. He ran his heavy gaze up the shivering length of her body, devouring her with his eyes, at the same time he ran his tongue over the sharp point of one deadly incisor.

Run screaming? Did he honestly think she would run from him?

As if.

"Honestly, Ian. Do I look like I want to run away from you?"

He trembled, his breathtaking muscles coiling and flexing, as if he was about to explode into action. "Then take off your jeans," he growled, "or you're not going to like what I do to them."

Molly hurried to do as he said, struggling with the damp denim, kicking them away with her panties. The combination of lust and tenderness coursing through her veins was so overwhelming, she felt light-headed.

"God, just look at you." He placed a hand on each ankle and bent her knees, forcing her legs out wide at her sides, until she was splayed in the most erotic pose she could have ever imagined. Staring at her sex with a searing, hungry intensity, Ian ran the blunt tip of one finger through her folds, slipping through the slick moisture. Then he twisted two thick fingers up inside of her, pressing them deep as she writhed beneath him, the heavy sensation of being filled pulsing through her system, jerking a sharp cry from her throat.

With dazed eyes, Molly watched him pull the long digits from her body, his skin shiny, glistening with her juices, and he touched his tongue to them. A dark, graveled sound rumbled in his chest, and he took the slick fingers completely into his mouth.

"Ian," she gasped, her voice trailing off in a breathless sob as he lowered his head between her legs.

"Open wider," he growled, and then he licked her, slipping his tongue through the drenched folds, circling her tender opening, before thrusting into her, eating at her with a hungry avidity.

Arching, Molly cried out, "I want you inside of me. Right now."

He took another long, lingering lick, collecting more of her juices on his tongue, then moved higher, licking her clit…higher, dipping his tongue into her navel. His head turned, and their eyes met in the antique mirror that sat above the dresser on the far wall. It was such an erotic sight, her pale skin contrasted against the dark sheen of his body. Soft curves to hard, powerful muscles.

When Molly caught her reflection, it was almost like staring at a stranger. That woman couldn't be her. Eyes wild, skin flushed, mouth swollen and red. She looked…exotic. Even…sexy. Not like a shy little mouse. That woman in the mirror looked like someone who could take on the world and make it come to heel at her feet.

"You're beautiful," Ian said with a low moan, and as she turned to stare into his eyes, his mouth at her breasts, lips touching one sensitive tip as he spoke, she knew that he meant it. He licked greedily at her nipples with slow, savoring strokes, before taking one deep in his mouth, shocking her with his heat. "Christ, Molly. I've been craving the taste of your skin for days."

"Ian...*now*," she pleaded, completely undone by the depth of emotion revealed in his smoldering gaze—by the reverent touch of his lips against her hungry flesh. She didn't care that she was begging, knowing only that if she didn't get him inside of her right then, at that very second, she was going to scream like a banshee—like the wild, primitive creature that had surfaced up from the darkest, deepest depths of her soul.

STRUGGLING TO KEEP some shred of control in his grasp, Ian crawled over her, caging her beneath his body. He'd tried so hard to hold back, but he couldn't. He held his breath as he went in, pushing against her resistance, unable to believe it could feel so good. The reality was even better than he'd dreamed. She was hotter. Tighter. More perfect than anything he'd ever known. Ever imagined. Delicate muscles clutched at him in a possessive, greedy hold, and yet, she was endlessly soft...tender.

"You okay?" he growled, the physical effort of speaking almost impossible. The Merrick's deadly fangs were heavy within his gums, and he could feel that deep, inner well of darkness roiling beneath his skin, its senses starved for the sensory intake...for each intense, explicit detail.

"I'm wonderful," she whispered, the soft, shy sound stroking down the length of his spine like the feather-light touch of her fingers.

"You can barely take me," he grunted, putting his strength behind the relentless push of his thick shaft into the tiny, delicate opening of her sex. She was warm and slick, easing his way, and yet, he knew he had to be careful not to hurt her.

"That's not true," she argued, breathless. "I can take all of you, Ian. Whatever you want to dish out."

"Liar," he drawled affectionately, nuzzling the smooth curve of her shoulder. She was so soft, so warm and sweet and giving, and he wanted to sink his teeth into her so badly he could feel the craving living inside of him, like a breathing, snarling entity. It was his Merrick. Awake and ready to come out and play, slowly stripping him of control. "Whatever happens, Molly, don't be afraid to tell me if I hurt you."

MOLLY GRABBED his beautiful face in her hands, forcing him to meet her gaze again, the torment in his eyes ripping at her heart. "You won't, Ian. It's going to be okay. I promise."

He shook his head even as his hips jerked, driving that thick, burning heat deeper into the core of her body, the sensation so sharp, it was a wild, wonderful blend of pleasure and pain.

"You're so small," he groaned, his voice raw… strained. He lowered his head, rubbing his mouth against hers, his chest against the hardened tips of her breasts, grazing her nipples. His hips rolled, and he shoved in harder…faster, his muscles flexing beneath the burnished, sweat-dampened heat of his skin. *"Molly."*

She turned her head, exposing her throat, knowing

what he needed…what he was still so terrified of taking.
With her hands threaded through the thick, damp
strands of his hair, Molly pulled him to her. His tongue
lapped hungrily against the sensitive stretch of skin,
and her sheath contracted in response, rippling around
him, making him buck.

"I can't control it," he rasped, the words barely audible in the seductive thickness of the morning. Shaking, he dragged the points of his fangs against her
vulnerable flesh.

"Please," she panted, begging…pleading, consumed
by her own raging need. "Please, Ian."

A sob broke from her throat, her body writhing, on
fire, desperate for completion, and he clutched her
tighter, a low, primal vibration shuddering through his
hard, heavy form. "*Molly,*" he breathed against her skin,
nipping at her throat. His chest heaved, hips shoving
against her, his body thrusting powerfully into hers,
and then he made a rough sound against her throat and
sank his fangs deep.

She cried out, the pleasure rising so violently, it made
her scream. She was distantly aware of the sound of
rending fabric, and realized he'd buried his talons in the
sleeping bag, the power of his Merrick rippling beneath
his skin. He thrust into her so hard that he shoved her
across the mattress, his movements primal and wild. The
friction was so slick and hot and breathtaking, she
couldn't find her way through the chaotic frenzy of
pleasure.

His mouth worked on her with hot, hungry intensity,
the deep pulls tugging on her womb, the tips of her
breasts…and he sobbed against her throat, the stark

male sound completely undoing her. Clawing onto the slick surface of his shoulders, Molly struggled to hold on in a world that was spinning violently out of control.

He pressed down on her, anchoring her in place, and she loved it. All of it. Loved the provocative power of him covering her…consuming her. Loved the searing burn of his fangs in her throat, adding a deeper level to the shattering, relentless waves of ecstasy crashing through her. Pleasure poured over her skin like a shimmering, dazzling summer rain.

It coalesced into a liquid glow of bliss in her belly, then shot outward, swelling, rising higher and higher, rolling through her in a thick, stunning wave that kept growing…and growing. Suddenly he pulled his fangs free, throwing back his head as a deep, guttural roar surged up from his chest, his hips shoving him deep, driving him fully into her. Molly stared up at him, watching the dark, raging beauty of his orgasm wash over him as he came deep inside her. Then she was thrown into the most violent, mind-shattering climax of her life. For long, endless moments, the dark waves of pleasure coursed through her, and she thrashed beneath him, screaming and sobbing, holding on to him as he covered her with his hardness and heat, every lean muscle in his body rigid with the force of his release, his chest heaving as he gasped against her temple.

TREMBLING FROM HIS HEAD to the soles of his feet, Ian clutched her against him, unable to let go. The wave of relief pouring through him was so strong, chills broke out over the surface of his body, while the residual pulses of pleasure trembled in his muscles. He knew it was wrong to keep her here with him, but he couldn't let her go. He wanted just a few more moments with her. Just a few more…

Taking mental stock of his condition, he was forced to accept that she'd destroyed him—annihilated his barriers and those scarred, impenetrable walls that had kept him together for so many years. She hadn't scaled them—she'd powered right through them, leaving nothing but broken rubble in her wake. Leaving him wide-open to her, completely undone.

He'd never felt anything that explosive in his entire life, and he suddenly realized that he'd come inside of her. It had been brutally intimate. Incredible, if he were completely honest, like something he had to do again…and again, which should have terrified the living hell out of him. And yet, with Molly it had felt…*right*.

It had been perfect. And now he had to send her away.

Both man and Merrick snarled their fury, but Ian knew he didn't have any choice.

As if sensing his tension, she stirred beneath him. "What's wrong?"

Rolling to his side, he pulled her against his chest, pressing her head beneath his chin, knowing he had to get the words said without getting lost in the luminous depths of her eyes. "I've…fed," he rasped, struggling for his words. "It's done. The Merrick…he's in me, Molly. It can come out now, when the time comes to face this thing. But I have to do it alone. I want you to leave. Get out of here. Go somewhere safe until this is over."

Her curls brushed his chin as she shook her head. "No," she whispered.

"Dammit. You have to trust me to know how to handle this."

"I'm sorry, Ian," she said softly, "but I can't do that."

Tangling his hand in her hair, he pulled back her head, saying, "You told me that you trusted me."

She blinked up at him, so beautiful it hurt just to look at her. "That was before you ran away from me."

"You know why I left," he grunted, struggling to find the words to explain the way he felt. "I...I care about you, Molly. God knows I tried not to, but I couldn't stop it. I *can't* stop it. And I can't let you stay here, where you're going to be in danger."

MOLLY HATED DOING it to him, but she wasn't above playing dirty to get what she wanted. Not when his life was at risk. "And if I leave, how do you know it wouldn't find me? Wouldn't come after me first?"

He glared, staring down at her with an angry fire in his eyes.

"Staying with you, it's the right thing to do," she told him, stressing the point, knowing he wouldn't want to send her away when he couldn't go with her. He was damned if he did, and damned if he didn't. And she was terrified, but no matter what, she knew she was safest there with him.

His jaw worked, and then he groaned, pulling her back against his chest. She could feel the angry tension in him, as well as the worry, but there wasn't any other possible choice. No way in hell was she going to drive away and leave him there alone, with no idea if he'd live or die.

She snuggled against him, content to stay pressed

against the heat of his body for the rest of her life. Lifting her hand, she placed it over his heart, capturing the beat with her palm. "Can I ask you a question, Ian?"

He threw one heavy thigh over her legs and pulled her closer against him. "What do you want to know?"

"What really happened between you and Elaina? And I don't want to hear about what a problem child you supposedly were. I want to know what was so important that it kept you away for so many years."

He was silent for so long, she didn't think he was going to answer. And then, he finally said, "She was always a little out there. Just a little…off center, with her wild stories and strange beliefs. But when I hit my teens, she got…"

His voice trailed off, and she stroked his chest, waiting for him to find the right words.

"She got intense. Started spending all her time researching stuff about our ancestors, bringing people around that she thought could help her get the answers she needed. Some of them were just kooky, but some…some were downright freaks, and we started butting heads. I didn't want her bringing these strangers into our home, around my brother and sister. And Elaina, she just kept sinking deeper, taking it to the point of obsession. I warned her to leave me out of it, but she just wouldn't let up."

He paused for a moment, stroking one hand down the length of her spine, and she could sense the tension mounting in him, his heart thundering beneath her palm. "When she brought a group to the house one night," he rasped, the words low…gritty with emotion, "begging me to let them hold some kind of ceremony to contact the 'darkness' inside of me, I'd had it. I asked Riley and Saige to come with me, but they both refused, too afraid to leave her." A harsh, brittle laugh broke from his throat. "And I was selfish enough to leave them behind. I sneaked out with my stuff in the middle of the night, and I never came back. Never set foot in this house again, until yesterday."

Shifting back, Molly looked up at him, lifting her hand to stroke the hard line of his jaw. "I know it must have scared you," she whispered. "It would have scared me, too. She must…all I can think is that she must have been afraid for you, as you started getting older. Afraid of what the future would hold."

"Maybe. All I know is that I had to get away from it or I was gonna go crazy."

"So you left," she said simply, and he snorted in response.

"For all the good it did me. Guess it just goes to show that no matter how far or how fast you run, it all catches up to you in the end."

"Fate?"

"Or hell," he rumbled. "I just…I can't believe she never told me that she feared the Casus would return someday."

"Maybe she just didn't want you to live in fear."

Regret darkened his eyes as he sighed. "Maybe."

"So what now?" she asked, listening to the rain as it began to fall in a steady rhythm against the old roof. The hazy morning was melting into a rumbling storm, the air thick with humidity, sticky and close.

Ian rolled to his back, his head resting in one palm, the other pulling her into his side. He stared up at the ceiling with a sharp intensity, as if he could find the answers in the shimmering, rain-dappled shadows. "Now we wait," he said.

"For how long?"

"Not long," he murmured, and she knew he felt it, too.

Something was coming, rolling in with the storm.

He pulled her closer with his arm, and she snuggled her head onto his warm, firm shoulder. "I love sleeping to the sound of a storm. For some reason it's soothing, no matter how violent it is."

"You should try to get some rest," he murmured, brushing her hair back from her cheek.

"Not a chance. I'm too nerv—"

Before she'd even finished the word, he'd rolled her to her back. Shifting between her legs, he pushed back into her with a deep, urgent thrust, as if he couldn't stand not being a part of her.

"I don't think I can sleep like this," she teased, loving the feel of him beneath her hands as she ran her palms down the strong, sleek muscles of his back. Loving the feel of him buried so deep inside of her even more.

He pulled back, then surged in again with a slow, grinding thrust that made chills break out over her body. "Don't worry, Molls," he whispered, the husky words hot within the sensitive shell of her ear. "By the time I'm done with you, you'll be so tired, the only thing you'll be able to do is pass out."

Her soft spill of laughter bled into a gasping moan, and then, moments later, into a crying, sobbing shout as the ecstasy rolled through her once again, driven into her body with ruthless, mind-shattering skill.

They made love throughout the long hours of the morning and afternoon, while the storms rolled overhead, both of them lost in the scorching, breathtaking burn of passion that bound them together, doing their best not to think of what lay ahead.

But they knew that with each moment that passed by, evil was coming closer…drawing nearer.

And when it hit, someone—*or something*—was going to die.

CHAPTER TWENTY-ONE

Laurente, Saturday Evening

WHILE ITS FROTHY LEAVES blew gently in the humid breeze, Malcolm DeKreznick rested his shoulders against the sturdy trunk of an ancient weeping willow…and ran the back of his hand across his mouth. His lips were moist…slick, and looking down, he could see the crimson smear of blood they'd left on his wrist. The Southern-fried farm girl he'd just killed had been sweet—and if he tried, he swore he could still taste her screams lingering on his tongue, just like candy.

He'd discovered, firsthand, that Southern hospitality really was as charming as they claimed.

Malcolm had found her skinny-dipping out in her daddy's pond a few hours ago, and had been unable to resist, knowing he needed his energy for the coming battle. Chuckling softly under his breath, he licked his lips, realizing he'd never even gotten her name. But it didn't matter. Who she'd been was no longer important. She belonged to him now, forever, same as the others. That warm, heady wash of life flowing from her—taken so effortlessly—to become something all his own. It'd been like raping her soul, as well as her body, and he'd loved it. Craved it. It was what his kind had been born for. What Malcolm had fought so hard to come back for, just so he could experience it again…and again.

Only one dark spot marred his pleasure. He hadn't realized he would have competition for the Markers so soon. But he'd recently learned that two more of his kind had already been sent through the gate, back from Meridian, in exactly the same way as him. The knowledge didn't sit well with Malcolm. He wanted Buchanan's Marker, and had no qualms about killing his kinsmen for it, should they try to take it from him. Calder would be furious, but then Calder was already going to be angry with him for killing so many, so quickly. Malcolm had been incessantly lectured about the need to be conservative—but the choice had been taken out of his hands.

After Kendra Wilcox, his hunger had grown too strong, too quickly. It'd swelled up inside of him each time a woman had caught his eye, spurring him on, impossible to resist.

This is yours…take it…take it. It's what you were made for. It's your right, your due. Haven't you gone without for long enough?

Still, he'd tried to control it. He'd taken down a deer on Sunday, but that had been before he was forced to watch Buchanan and his woman leave with that Watchman, snatched from his reach, when he'd had such inspired plans for them. Even from his place within the woods, Malcolm had sensed the talisman on the delicate little blond as they'd left her motel room, and in his frustration, the hunger had consumed him. To satisfy his craving, he'd needed the full, gratifying effect of his power, his domination, over his prey. Needed a woman under him, whimpering, begging for her life. Needed to see that perfect moment spill over her face when he showed her his true, beautiful self. There was nothing in the world quite like it.

Afterward, he'd hidden the teenager in the canyon, making it look like a wild kill, but he'd known Buchanan would realize the truth when he heard about it. Malcolm had wanted the Merrick slime to understand that he wasn't going to just sit around and twiddle his thumbs.

The wind picked up, blowing the low clouds across the ethereal glow of the Carolina moon, darkening the sky, and his blood-covered lips curled in a welcoming smile. The sweet sinful night was his favorite hour, when darkness fell…and fears arose. When shadows stroked their chilled fingers down the length of a spine…at times causing the most hardened souls to peer over their shoulders for fear of what lurked within the midnight black.

Mankind was so much fun to play with when afraid—and yet, Malcolm was growing tired of easy prey. He wanted the Merrick, and tonight he was finally going to get him.

Lurking within the nighttime shadows, Malcolm had watched as Buchanan packed up his truck on Thursday night. A nosey neighbor had stepped outside her doorway, wanting to know where he'd been all week, telling him his brother had been looking for him. Buchanan had shouted back the words South Carolina, and Malcolm had smiled, thinking how sweet it was that the man was running home for a change.

Not that he'd needed to be told where Buchanan was headed. The bastard could have tried to run and hide at the far reaches of the earth, and Malcolm would have been able to track him down. But he was happy with his choice. He'd never been to South Carolina, but he'd imagined he was going to enjoy a change of scenery—and he had.

After he'd watched the Merrick drive away and had dealt with Aubrey Rodgers, he'd decided to go back to Joe Kelly's condo…pack a bag, and head to the airport himself. He could have driven Kelly's truck, but he didn't want to waste the time it would take. Calder had assured him that he'd know how to function in the modern world once he found his host—and he'd been right. Malcolm had retained all of poor Joe's mundane memories, as pathetic as they were. He could have even walked into his office and plodded away at that worthless job of his. Not that he needed to. Money was never going to be a problem for him. Calder had already seen to that, and quite nicely, too.

Drawing in a deep breath of moist, fertile-scented air into his lungs, Malcolm could barely contain his excitement as he considered his prospects for the future. The anticipation was so ripe in his gut, he could almost taste it. Once he finished destroying Buchanan and had possession of the Marker, he would free his brother. Then, with Gregory at his side, he planned on burning a path of destruction through this buttoned-down, stiff-lipped modern world the likes of which had never been seen.

And no one would be able to stop him.

CHAPTER TWENTY-TWO

As THE LAZY AFTERNOON bled into evening and darkness fell, thunder rumbled in the distance, signaling the beginnings of another summer storm. That was normal for this time of year, Ian knew, and yet, it had still felt like a warning of things to come.

He had no doubt the Casus would arrive tonight. And he knew Molly could feel it, too, like something heavy and thick settled in the center of his chest that made itself known with each slow, deep breath.

After sharing an easy meal of sandwiches and chips, they sat on the floor in the living room, each with a cold beer from the cooler he'd picked up in town yesterday when he'd gone shopping for essentials, listening as the latest storm rolled away. Staring at her profile from the corner of his eye, Ian recalled how he'd spent so much time over the course of the past week wondering what it was about her that made him so hungry—and not just in a physical sense. Not just for her blood, as mouth-watering as it was. And not just for sex, though sex with her was beyond anything he'd ever experienced.

When he'd taken her beneath him for the second time that morning, he'd paused to savor, to slow down, to enjoy each decadent, pulsing sensation. He'd pushed up on his arms and watched as he thrust into her, staring at the way he penetrated the tender mouth of her body, his cock dark and brutal-looking, her drenched folds tender and glistening and pink. He'd lost himself in the cadence of her breathing, in the touch of her hands…the taste of her mouth and the softness of her skin.

And in the quiet hours of the afternoon, as the storms had raged overhead, when she'd slept, cradled in his arms, exhausted from the hours of physical excess he'd put her through, he'd finally come to an understanding of what made her so special…so different.

He had the answer—he was just too terrified to acknowledge it. But he knew, deep inside, where it counted, what had happened to him. And now that he understood, he wondered if maybe he hadn't been running all those years, so much as he'd been searching for something. For this. *For Molly.* For the one person who had the ability to settle him inside, making sense of the darkness…of the chaos, while exciting him in ways he could have never imagined, taking him to levels of pleasure he hadn't even realized existed.

Funny, how he'd had to come full circle, returning to his childhood home, for this miracle to happen. That he had his mother, of all people, to thank for bringing Molly into his life and showing him what it meant to truly care for another person.

"You can still smell the honeysuckle in this place," he murmured, pulling in a deep breath of the faint, familiar scent that he'd always associated with home.

She sent him a curious smile, and he explained. "Elaina's favorite scent was honeysuckle, and she drowned the house in it. Candles and little pots of dried flowers. Lotions and perfumes. I swear to God, Riley and I would go to school smelling like girls half the time."

She laughed, making him want to pull her into his arms and kiss her, just so he could taste that sweet, sexy sound on her lips. But he resisted, wondering what she was thinking, what was going through her mind. She hadn't pressed him for anything. No explanations about his feelings…no promises. No talk of the future, and he was ready to explode. What was she waiting for?

Needing to touch her, Ian reached out, taking hold of her hand, marveling at how small and delicate it felt in his grasp, his fear for her like a living thing inside of him, seething beneath his skin.

"You're afraid for me, aren't you?" she asked, her voice soft…hushed.

"Christ, Molly. Why the hell do you think I came here in the first place?" he grunted. "I was drawing this bastard away from you, and then you go and show up." Cutting a dark look at the swollen, darkening sky through the front window, he said, "It's coming. Tonight. I can feel it."

"I can feel it, too. But it's going to be okay. I know it is. No matter how powerful the Casus is, it's still no match for you."

Ian shook his head at her faith in him, a harsh burst of laughter rumbling in his chest. "I've ruined your life, Molls. Don't you get that? You should be trying to get away from me as fast as you can, not standing up for me, cheering me on."

"IAN, YOU HAVE IT all backward," Molly told him, squeezing his hand. "You didn't ruin anything. You *gave* me my life back. No matter what happens, I belong here with you, so don't waste your time trying to get rid of me."

"I already tried," he drawled, his tone wry. "You can see how well it worked."

A playful grin curved her mouth. "So what are you going to do now?"

"I dunno," he murmured, leaning his head back, watching her from beneath his lashes, the teasing look in his beautiful blue eyes one of the most beautiful sights she'd ever seen. Molly loved seeing him look so…comfortable, so at ease within his skin…as well as with her, as if he were that much closer to being at peace. "Who knows? Maybe, if I get lucky, I'll be able to fuck some sense into you."

"You're welcome to give it a shot," she quipped. "I doubt it'll work, but God knows I'll enjoy your efforts."

A sharp bark of laughter surged up from his chest and she smiled, wondering if he'd ever been at ease like this before with a woman. She doubted he ever had, and it made her insides light up with a warm, incandescent glow.

"What?" he asked, rubbing his thumb over the delicate points of the hand he still held in his grasp.

Molly set her beer down and lifted her free hand, hooking her hair behind her ear. "I was just thinking that this isn't the way you normally spend your time with women. Talking. Teasing."

He stared at her for a long, breathless moment, then reached out, touching her face with the tips of his fingers. "You're right," he rasped in a deep, velvet-rough voice. "And I'm a selfish bastard for enjoying having you here with me when I know it's putting you in danger. But I can't help it. I want to have as much time with you as I can, Molly, but I'm scared of losing you."

"Won't happen," she whispered, completely undone by his stunning words. She wanted to throw her arms around his neck and beg him to love her, but she fought back the impulse, too afraid of how he'd react. Instead, she plastered a teasing smile on her face. "But I don't suppose you have a hidden arsenal anywhere around here? Maybe a Beretta I can unload in him? Shotgun? Uzi?"

He snickered under his breath, shaking his head. "Not that I know of."

"ELAINA DIDN'T BELIEVE in guns, either?" she asked, her tone casual, when Ian knew that what she was really asking was why *he* didn't believe in them.

"Let's just say that my daddy, before he ran away, was *overly* fond of them. Which probably wouldn't have been so bad, if he hadn't been as equally fond of Wild Turkey."

Even now, Ian could still remember the terror he'd felt when he'd awakened one night to the sounds of an argument between his parents. Peeking through his bedroom door, he'd witnessed his father holding a gun to his mother's head, screaming for the "demons to be gone."

Ian had known she'd been talking about their ancestors again, which always threw his father into a rage. Elaina's face had been covered in tears, the look in his father's eyes as cold as the metal of the gun he'd held jammed against her temple.

He'd wanted to run to her rescue, but he'd been terrified, standing there frozen with fear, as if his feet had been nailed to the cold hardwood floor. Finally, his father had pushed Elaina away and grabbed his truck keys, storming out of the house. He'd driven away that night in a blind, drunken rage…and they'd never seen him again.

And from that day forward, Ian had never been able to stomach the sight of a gun…and neither had his mother.

"Hey, you in there?" he heard Molly ask softly, and he gave himself a mental shake as the sweet, womanly weight of her body settled over his lap. Her arms lifted around his shoulders, lips pressed to the hard point of his jaw, and he bit back a husky moan. She felt…incredible, as if she'd poured herself over him, covering him in a warm, sweet wave of longing. Wrapped him up in something beautiful and tender and pure. His throat jammed up with emotion, but he wrapped his arms around her, pulling her closer, lowering his head so that he could bury his nose in the warm, silken mass of her hair, breathing her into his body…into his heart…his soul.

He was so goddamn terrified of losing her, that he never wanted to let her go.

They stayed like that for long, endless moments, rocking gently together, the rumbling thunder the only backdrop of sound, until a sharp, guttural cry tore across the night, the eerie sound coming from the front of the house. Molly stiffened in his arms, and Ian grabbed her shoulders, setting her away from him.

Moving to his feet, he said, "It's time."

"OH, GOD," Molly gasped, her voice thick, eyes damp with a sudden wash of tears as she watched him move toward his duffel bag. He looked so calm…so focused, as if he weren't about to face the most frightening experience of his life.

He leaned down, taking out the cross and a long, wicked-looking knife that he held out to her, saying, "When I came here, I didn't plan on things working out the way they have. Now that I've fed, the Merrick should be able to hold its own with this asshole, and God willing, the cross will kill it. But if something goes wrong, the Casus is going to come after you. Use the knife, Molly. Do whatever you have to do, and then get the hell away from here."

"The cross will work, Ian. It has to."

"I meant what I said," he grunted, waiting for her to take the knife, before slipping the cross over his head. It glittered against the center of his chest, his only clothing the low-slung jeans that hung on his hips. His body looked lean and dark and dangerous, golden skin stretched tight over the hard, rippling power of his muscles. "If something goes wrong," he told her, "you go out back, get in your car and get out of here. Drive straight to the airport and go back to Scott. He'll take care of you, Molly."

"Ian," she breathed out softly. He looked so vital, so strong and powerful, even more so than when she'd first set eyes on him only a week ago. And yet, she was terrified for him, knowing that he was about to face something so evil and vile it didn't belong in this world.

"Just do it, Molly. The only thing that matters here is that you make it out of this alive. That's why I brought this bastard here. No matter how this plays out, I want you safe."

She nodded, trembling with fear, and watched as he

made his way toward the door. He reached for the handle, and his name burst from her lips. "*Ian!*"

He looked over his shoulder. "Yeah?"

"I don't care what it takes," she whispered, "just kick his ass and make sure you come back to me."

For a moment, he just stared at her, those dark eyes swirling with devastating emotion, while he held completely, utterly still. Then he took a deep, shuddering breath, and quietly said, "For what it's worth, Molls, I want you to know that I love you."

He held her gaze, reading the overwhelming rush of astonishment in her tear-drenched eyes, in the shivering of her body, and then he gave her a slow, wicked smile, and walked out into the night.

STEPPING OUT ONTO the front porch, Ian drew a deep breath into his lungs, and immediately found the Casus's foul, thick stench hanging on the air. Closing in. But he was ready. Ready to fight to save the life of the woman he loved.

And he *did* love her, more than he could have ever imagined. Her faith had changed him, and he could see now that it wasn't his control that had kept her safe when he'd fed from her that morning, enabling him to stop before he'd taken too much blood. It was because she meant something to him—because she meant *everything* to him—and he was going to do whatever it took to protect her.

Rather than fight the darkness that dwelled within him, as he'd been doing for so long, Ian was finally ready to embrace it. To surrender to its power, trusting it not only with his life but with Molly's, as well.

Rolling his neck across his shoulders, he moved down the porch steps, into the front yard, the cool blades of grass damp beneath his bare feet. A strange, eerie calm spread through him, his body hard…tight, senses perfectly attuned to every sound…every fraction of movement in the trees ahead. The Casus's scent thickened, and he could tell it was drawing closer. His fingers flexed at his sides…and he waited impatiently for the Merrick to rise within him, the cross warm against his chest, thrumming with power. And yet, when the creature stepped from the shelter of the woods, an evil, malicious smile curving its muzzled mouth…Ian still stood there as a man.

What the hell? Taking a deep breath, Ian reached for that primitive part of his nature, digging deep into the darkest recesses of his being. He could feel it there, roiling through his system like some primordial creature racing through an ancient loch, but no matter how desperately he tried, he couldn't reach deep enough to grab it. Couldn't get hold of it and rip it to the surface.

What in God's name was it waiting for?

"Anytime now," he growled under his breath, giving a frustrated roll of his shoulders, and the Casus came closer, its gray, grotesque body moving like something torn straight from the chilling depths of a nightmare. Ian stood his ground as it stalked forward, its pale, ice-blue gaze burning bright within the shadowed darkness, and it was like looking into hell itself, feeling its flames blistering your skin, melting you piece by piece in a slow, torturous burn.

Lifting its nose to the storm-damp air, it pulled in a deep, searching breath, and a guttural sound immediately vibrated in its throat like a demonic purr.

"Mmm. I can smell your little blond bitch inside the house," it rasped, the grated words strange within the muzzled shape of its mouth. "I have to admit, I was hoping she'd follow you here, Buchanan. I've had so much fun tearing your women to shreds, I wasn't about to let this one slip through my fingers. I'd planned to track her down once I finished with you, but this is going to be so much sweeter, with you here to watch our playtime."

Ian's lip curled as a deep, inhuman growl surged up from his chest in response to the bastard's taunting, and with a piercing burst of relief, he realized the Merrick was finally breaking free. He almost smiled with feral satisfaction, until the first wave of pain ripped through him, tearing and sharp, like being turned inside out. His back arched, arms flung out wide at his sides, his muscles jerking in spasms, as if he were being electrocuted—and then it tore free in a violent, explosive force of rage.

Blood trailed over his hands as long, razor-sharp talons pierced through the tips of his fingers, his gums stinging as his fangs released with a sibilant hiss. He shook violently, teeth gnashing as the change rolled up from the soles of his feet, altering his body in an agonizing clutch of pain. Bones expanded, muscles bulging…enlarging, the ferocity of the transformation as terrifying as it was freeing in some strange, wonderful way. His chest heaved as the final stages of the change flowed through him, his facial bones cracking, altering the shape of his nose, flattening it against his face like an animal's.

"Merrick," the beast growled, and with a primitive

roar of rage, Ian leaped through the air, slamming into its body so hard that they crashed to the ground and rolled across the slick grass. Snarling, he dug his talons into its ridged back, a stark howl erupting from the Casus's throat as it slashed out at him with its claws. He should have been ripped to pieces, but they slid over his skin without breaking the surface, and Ian shook his head, stunned to discover the cross was actually protecting him.

"Talisman," it sneered, eyeing the Marker as it pushed to its feet. It watched as Ian did the same, flexing its long, sinister claws at its sides, its ice-blue gaze burning with hatred.

Ready to bring this thing to an end, Ian grasped the heat of the cross, then tugged, breaking the velvet cord. He held the hot metal clasped tight between his thumb and fingers, wondering how he was supposed to make it work. How was he meant to use it as a weapon? He'd half expected it to transform into some kind of dagger or Ninja star. Something he could throw. Even burst into flames like a fireball. But it did none of those things.

Arm of Fire? Like hell.

"There's no way you can win," the creature hissed, its deformed body moving around him in a slow circle, and Ian mirrored its movements, careful to keep it in front of him. Gritting his teeth, he wondered how long he was supposed to wait before shoving the Marker in his pocket and relying on his talons and fangs to rip the monster to pieces.

"I've waited too long for this," the Casus snarled, its long fangs gleaming in the pale shafts of moonlight breaking through the heavy storm clouds. "Centuries of time to prepare…to think about nothing but how good it was going to feel to take you down, Merrick. Don't think that little bit of metal is going to stop me now."

*Come on…come on…*Ian thought, rubbing his thumb against the etched surface of the cross, hoping for a miracle.

"But I won't kill you right away," it went on, its thin lips twisted in a malevolent smile. "I'm going to leave you bloody and broken, but breathing, just long enough for you to watch me get acquainted with your blond. Then you're going to give me what I need."

Ian's rage mounted in a vicious, visceral wave, magnified by the power of the Merrick, and a deep, guttural growl ripped from his chest, at the same time as the Casus charged him. It came at him in a flurry of hammering blows, striking him with its clawed hands as he fought to hold his ground.

Slashing back at it with his free hand, Ian sliced at its gut with his talons, drawing a hot spray of blood, but it just kept coming. Needing both his hands to fight off its attack, he tried to slip the cross in his back pocket, when the Casus aimed its long, curved claws at his wrist. Though the stunning blow didn't break Ian's skin, it hit with enough force to knock the cross out of his hand, onto the grass. In the next instant, the Casus's claws tore deep across his chest, making him cry out in pain.

"Mine," it snarled, taking him to the ground, the jarring impact jerking the air from his lungs. Ian struggled to hold it off, but it was almost impossible. Despite the strength of his Merrick, the Casus was bigger…stronger. It snapped at his throat, his arms shaking as his Merrick used all its power to hold it at bay, but it wasn't enough. Its fangs sank deep into his shoulder, ripping flesh…muscle, cracking the bone. He roared as excruciating pain exploded through his system, white-hot and ravaging, while those lethal fangs tore at him again…and again.

With wide eyes, Ian stared death in the face, holding the creature's gaze, while his heart shattered at the agonizing knowledge that he'd failed to protect Molly. And then the Casus suddenly threw back its head and let out a bloodcurdling howl of suffering. Unbelieving, Ian watched as Molly slowly backed away from them, her eyes huge within her ghost-white face, the knife he'd left with her now buried in the beast's broad shoulder.

"Get inside!" he shouted, at the same time the Casus turned and backhanded her with a powerful swipe of its long arm, sending her flying onto her back. Ian roared her name, fighting to get his feet beneath him, while blood poured down his body, his shoulder a mangled, bloodied mess. The Casus leaped for Molly, pinning her to the ground, and Ian lurched forward, gnashing his teeth against the pain, but the world upended before he could reach her and he found himself sprawled facedown across the yard.

Molly's screams filled the air as the monster trapped her beneath its horrific body, and the Casus looked over its shoulder, sending him a slow, malicious smile. "Don't die yet, Merrick. Not yet. I want you to enjoy the show."

Gritting his teeth, Ian dragged himself over the rainsoaked grass, determined to reach her…to protect her or die trying. He'd covered no more than a handful of feet, when a flash of metal glinted at the corner of his eye and he reached out with his right hand, his bloodied fingers clawing desperately at the damp earth. When his fingertips touched hot metal, he grabbed hold of the cross, clutching it in his fist, trapped against his palm…and the power of the Marker finally released. A blistering sensation, like a stunning jolt of electricity, instantly arced through his arm and radiated out through his body, the cross turning fiery hot as Ian roared at the sickening burn of pain. In the next instant, a fierce burst of energy shot through him, and he surged to his feet on an explosive wave of rage that propelled him toward the creature, his Merrick's powerful body crashing into the Casus and slamming it to the ground.

The burn in his palm grew hotter, melting his skin, as Ian used his talons to strike at the Casus's leathery flesh. It twisted away from him, slinking to its hands and feet, its gray body hunched as it scrambled away from him like a cornered animal, its pale eyes shocked wide with fear.

"Get back here, you bloody coward," Ian growled in a voice too deep and guttural to belong to a man. From the corner of his eye, he watched Molly stagger to her feet, the devastating flood of relief pouring through him so intense that he nearly went to his knees. He was going to take her into his arms and never let her go, holding on to her for the rest of his goddamn life—just as soon as he'd dealt with the bastard trying to sneak away from him. The night winds surged, carrying the thick scent of the Casus's fear to his nose, and Ian stalked toward it, the heat in his palm radiating up through his hand, into his forearm, as if liquid fire had been poured beneath his skin.

Gritting his teeth against the fierce burning sensation, he drew in a deep breath, and could have sworn he smelled…honeysuckle. What the…

You wear the mark, Ian.

The soft words whispered through his head like a cool, soothing breeze, and he pulled back his shoulders, keeping his eyes on the Casus, struggling to understand.

You wear the mark….

The mark? The cross was called a Marker. And he held the cross in his hand. But wearing it? What did that mean?

And then the answer suddenly slammed into his brain with a staggering jolt of awareness, and he had it…knew exactly what he had to do. Charging toward the Casus, Ian tackled it to the ground, their bodies rolling over the grass, while Molly's screams for him to be careful filled the night. The beast snapped at him with its deadly jaws, but they no longer broke his flesh, its claws simply sliding across his skin, the protection of the talisman once more keeping him from harm. But even more amazing was the fact that his injuries no longer throbbed with pain, as if they didn't even exist.

Snarling, the Casus fought to break his hold, scrambling to its feet, but Ian was quicker. As it twisted away from him, he aimed for the base of its thick, leathery neck, at the exact point between its shoulder blades where Ian bore a tattoo of the cross, and slammed the Marker against its body. A sizzling, popping sound filled the air, like oil hitting a hot pan, and then a scorching ball of fire engulfed his arm as his hand broke through the Casus's skin and sank into its body.

Arm of fire. Holy shit.

Holding his burning arm out before him, Ian watched, amazed, as the Casus's gray body began to glow from within, as if lit with molten lava, the brilliant blaze burning orange beneath its skin, while bubbling blisters formed on the surface. Its limbs jolted with violent spasms, as though it'd been struck by lightning, and Ian braced his feet in the damp grass, working to keep his balance. The scorching wave of heat poured through his body, but he was locked against the Casus, unable to pull away, the intense flames growing hotter…brighter. Its unearthly screams tore from its chest in an endless, garbled stream, gruesome and stark, and then its body finally erupted in a stunning, pulsing explosion of light.

The battering shock wave knocked Ian back with the force of a cannon blast. Thrown through the air, his body crashed against the ground, a staggering crack of pain ricocheting through his skull.

And then everything went black.

CHAPTER TWENTY-THREE

WHEN HE CAME TO, the smell of sulfur and burned flesh filled Ian's nose, while a strange cacophony of sounds buzzed through his pounding head.

"Ian, dammit. Wake up," a deep voice grunted above him, followed by a large, rough hand slapping his cheek. "Come on and open your eyes."

The graveled voice sounded oddly familiar, and he struggled to crack his eyelids. Grimacing against the dull, throbbing pain, he stared up into a pair of blue eyes a shade darker than his own. "Riley?" he croaked, wondering if he was hallucinating. What was his brother doing in South Carolina?

The wind whipped Riley's dark hair over his brow, his gaze shadowed with concern as he asked, "You okay? Anything broken? That was a hell of an explosion."

"Molly?" Ian gasped, unable to get the rest of his question scraped past the choking knot of fear in his throat. He tried to sit up, but Riley held his shoulders against the ground. "Easy, easy...she's going to be okay." His brother cast a quick look over his broad shoulder then turned back, saying, "She just hasn't woken up yet."

Oh, shit.

"Get the hell off me," he tried to shout, but the angry words came out as nothing more than a hoarse grunt of sound. Terror was pressing in on him, like a staggering weight against his chest, making it difficult to breathe…to think.

"Ian, just take it easy, man."

"Now!" he finally managed to growl, swinging his fist toward Riley's face. His brother jerked back, cursing under his breath as he barely managed to evade the blow.

"All right, just chill. She's going to be okay," he heard him mutter, but Ian was already crawling toward her, his head swimming, while his right hand burned like the devil. But all that mattered was reaching her…holding her. He tried to get to his feet, but slipped on the damp grass, slamming to his knees, and through the hazy cloud of smoke still lingering over the front yard, he made out Kierland Scott's dark red hair.

Ian crawled across the grass on his hands and knees, his movements clumsy and disjointed while his breath jerked from his lungs with a painful, scraping cadence. It seemed to take forever to cover the distance, each second shredding his insides with fear, and then he was finally there, kneeling beside her. She lay curled on the ground, lifeless and still, the auburn-haired Watchman kneeling at her other side, one hand pressed to her throat, checking her pulse. Scott's mouth was moving, but Ian couldn't make out what he was saying. The sound of his own heartbeat filled his head, raging and violent, like a lashing storm, and he reached out for her, his unsteady hands hovering over her body, afraid to touch…afraid he'd accidentally hurt her if he did.

"*Molly,*" he rasped, the single word cracking with emotion. Ian couldn't understand what was wrong with his voice, until he realized he was choked with tears. They were hot in his throat, burning in his eyes, the salty trails slipping down his cheeks, mixing with the grime and sweat and blood.

Scott reached over her body and grabbed his shoulder, shaking him, and Ian jerked his tormented gaze back to the Watchman's face, straining to hear him. "She's going to be okay, Buchanan. She was knocked out by the blast, but she's coming to now. She's coming to."

That's good…that's good. So get a grip, man. Stop bawling and pull it together.

He didn't know if the words were coming from the resident asshole in his head or if it was Riley grumbling at him again, but he jerked a deep breath into his lungs, focusing on her face…and suddenly she was blinking up at him with a slow, sweet, kinda wobbly smile playing over her tender, precious mouth.

"Ian," she whispered, her voice scratchy from the smoke, and then she lowered her gaze and the smile instantly fell, replaced by a horrified look of panic as she saw the crimson smears of blood that covered his upper body. "Ohmygod, you're hurt!"

"No, I'm okay…I'm okay." Falling back on his ass, Ian reached for her, pulling her into his trembling arms, holding her too tight, but he couldn't help himself. It was crashing down on him—all the fear and anger and pain that he'd been through—until she curled against his chest, pressing her lips to the side of his throat, where his pulse raced to a fierce, hammering rhythm. And in that moment, everything in the world that had

slipped into such terrifying madness suddenly seemed…
right.

"Jesus," he breathed against her temple, while his
hands roamed her back and arms, seeking assurance
that she was okay. "Don't ever scare me like that again.
I swear, you took fifty years off my life."

"I'm okay, Ian," she murmured, trying to do her
own search of his body. "You're the one who's covered in blood."

"I promise I'm not hurt. Just be still…be still and let
me hold you." Closing his eyes, Ian rocked her in his
arms, his head buried in the curve of her shoulder, shuddering as the fear slowly receded, leaving a shaky, exhil-
arated feeling in his chest, as well as a sweet, unfamiliar
burn of happiness in his gut. His eyes were hot, a gruff
rumble of sound breaking from his throat, and he honestly didn't know whether he was laughing or crying or
doing both.

Molly shifted in his arms and lifted her palm to the
scratchy surface of his cheek, brushing away his tears,
while a radiant smile bloomed over her mouth.
"Ian…my God, I'm so proud of you. You did it!"

He pressed a soft kiss to her temple, his voice
hitching as he quietly said, "No, baby, it wasn't me.
Elaina…Elaina did it."

Shock had her stiffening in his arms. "Your
mother? But…how?"

"I'll explain later," he breathed in her ear, "when
we're alone."

MOLLY WANTED TO DEMAND an explanation right then
and there, but as she followed Ian's gaze, she finally

realized they weren't alone. A soft gasp fell from her lips when she spotted Kierland and Quinn, as well as a scary-looking giant of a man she'd never seen before. They stood a short distance away, their dark eyes all trained on her and Ian.

"You came," she whispered, staring at Kierland in shocked disbelief, unable to wrap her mind around the fact that he and Quinn were actually there. "I can't believe it. You broke your rules."

"We figured it was time to say to hell with the rules," the Watchman drawled, while a wry smile played at the corner of his mouth. "A certain mouthy little human informed me not too long ago that when something's important, we have to do what we know is right, even if it means breaking a rule or two. Turns out she knew what she was talking about." He sent a shadowed look over the destroyed yard, noting the scorched earth and clawed-up ground, then turned his pale green gaze back in their direction as he said, "But I'm afraid that by the time I realized it, we were too late to be of much help here. We arrived just in time to witness the explosion."

"Still, it's the thought that counts," she murmured, giving him a shaky grin. Molly could sense the slight burn of jealousy coming from Ian as she talked to the handsome Watchman, and she lovingly stroked her hand along the tensed muscles of the arm that banded her waist, silently reassuring him. "Isn't that right, Ian?"

He grunted in response, pulling her tighter to his chest in a blatantly possessive hold. "So what are you doing here?" he asked, jerking his chin toward the scary-looking stranger with shaggy black hair and a dark scowl. The man had his arms crossed over his T-shirt-covered chest, and Molly eyed the tattoos circling his left bicep, before lifting her curious gaze to an oddly familiar shade of deep blue eyes, wondering who he was...and how Ian knew him.

"We contacted him," Scott responded, pushing his hands into the front pockets of his jeans, the blue denim sporting dark splotches at the knees from where he'd knelt in the charred debris that covered the front yard. "We went to tell him what you were going up against, and ask if he wanted to come along to help his brother. But when we got to his apartment, he was already packed. Seems he'd heard from one of your neighbors that you were coming here, and had already decided to come and find out what you were up to."

"No way," Molly whispered, suddenly realizing who the stranger was. "I don't believe it. *You're* Saint Riley."

A thunderous scowl pulled tight over the man's face as he glared at Ian, muttering, "I told you to stop using that damn nickname."

Ian snickered in response. "But it suits you so well."

"Yeah, well, laugh now," Riley grunted, "but when you get home, you and I are going to have one hell of a long talk. If I'd known in time that you were planning on doing something this stupid, I swear, I'd have locked your crazy ass up in a cell and kept you there."

"And maybe that's why I didn't tell you," Ian drawled, rolling his eyes.

"Stupid jackass," Riley burst out, and Molly could see from his haggard, strained expression that he was truly shaken by the fact that his brother had been in such extreme danger. "You disappear on me, won't return my calls, and meanwhile I've got dead bodies popping up all over the place. You're lucky I don't give you the ass-kicking you deserve for not coming to me for help."

"WELL, YOU'RE going to have to hold that thought." Ian sighed, shifting his gaze back to Scott, "because there's something I need to tell you guys."

Scott raised his brows, his expression revealing his interest.

"Just before it died, I saw…something. Memories from its mind…or hell, I don't know." He took a deep breath, struggling to make sense out of the information crowding through his brain, while Molly stroked his chest in a sweet, soothing gesture. "But I know what they're after. They want the Markers."

"The Markers?" Scott muttered, shaking his head. "To destroy them?"

"Legend says they can't be destroyed," Quinn murmured, speaking up for the first time.

Ian rolled his shoulder. "All I know is that he wanted it, but I couldn't see what for."

"Whatever they want them for," Scott muttered, "it can't be good. Before we know it, we're going to have a war on our hands."

"I also saw that he wasn't the only one. More of his kind are already here, and they want the crosses, same as he did."

"Jesus," Scott hissed, scrubbing his hands down his face, before pushing them back through his hair. "How many more are we talking about?"

"I'm not sure, but I got the feeling he wasn't happy about having the competition. Whatever is happening, it's moving quicker than you thought it would," Ian told them. "Which means that Saige is vulnerable in South America with only one Watchman for protection. She needs to be brought to Colorado. Immediately."

Scott nodded. "I'll put in the call to Templeton," he rasped, and then he surprised Ian by saying, "When can we expect you and Molly back at Ravenswing?"

Ian held the Watchman's piercing stare, wondering what the hell he was talking about. "What makes you think we're going back?"

Scott crossed his arms over his chest, his expression determined, as if braced for an argument that he didn't plan to lose. "You're both a part of this now, whether you like it or not. And you're the only one who's gone against one of these bastards and won. As much as it pains me to say it," he muttered, giving him a hard smile, "we need you, Buchanan."

"He's right," Molly whispered, staring up at him with a stunning look of pride shimmering in her eyes. "You have to go back, Ian."

"You, too, Molly," Scott added with a soft rumble of laughter. "Don't think you're getting off the hook that easily."

She blinked, sending the Brit a soft look of confusion. "But...I'm only human."

"Not hardly," Ian snorted, pulling her face back toward him with the touch of his fingers upon her chin. "You're unlike anyone I've ever known. Hell, Molls, you faced down that psychotic son of a bitch and didn't even bat an eye."

She smiled at him as if he'd just paid her a profound compliment, her loving look hitting him low in the gut, and Ian decided the conversation had already gone on long enough.

"You're needed," Kierland was saying with firm conviction. "Both of you are."

"We'll talk about it tomorrow," Ian rasped, setting Molly by his side so that he could move to his feet. He took her hand, helping her up, then turned back toward the others. "Now, not to be rude, but you guys need to get lost."

Riley snickered, and Quinn shook his head, drawling, "Whatever happened to that legendary Southern hospitality you hear so much about?"

"You want hospitality?" Ian grunted. "Try a hotel."

"As subtle as always, Ian," Riley laughed, stepping closer and holding out his hand. "Here. I think this belongs to you."

Ian took the cross from his brother, amazed to see that it looked unchanged, as perfect as it did before it'd melted into his palm. But then, its power was certainly one of miracles. Despite his lingering headache and the blood that covered most of his body, his injuries were no longer there, as if the Marker had miraculously healed him. He couldn't explain it, but he wasn't going to argue his good luck.

They said a quick round of goodbyes, agreeing to meet again in the morning. Then Riley and the Watchmen headed back to the rental car they'd left parked on the far side of the house, and Ian lifted Molly into his arms, carrying her inside.

MOLLY TRIED TO TELL him she could walk on her own, but he pressed his mouth to her temple, saying, "I need to hold you, so stop complaining."

Too tired to argue, she wrapped her arms around his shoulders and accepted his soft confession, allowing him to carry her through the shadowed rooms of the house. They took a long, lingering shower together, washing away the grime of the horrifying night, touching each other with trembling hands, and then he carried her into the bedroom, laying her out over the soft, down-filled sleeping bag.

As Ian stretched his long, beautiful body out beside her, Molly sensed that there was something he wanted to say, and her heart fluttered in her chest like a trapped bird as she wondered what it would be…almost too afraid to hope for what she wanted. Which was to hear him say that he loved her again. That he'd *always* love her.

That he'd spend his life with her. Forever.

He moved over her, caging her body beneath the heat and strength of his larger frame, and stared down at her, his smoldering eyes burning with an inner fire, as if a bit of the Merrick still lingered within him. "Before I get distracted by this luscious little body of yours," he rumbled in a deep, gritty voice, "I'm wondering if you can explain what the hell you thought you were doing tonight. Do you know what *stay put* means?"

Molly frowned, thinking that was hardly the romantic declaration she'd been hoping for. "I'm not a dog, Ian. I don't take orders."

He snorted. "Trust me, I noticed."

"Listen here," she muttered, bristling at his tone. "Just because you turned into some hunky Merrick and saved the day, doesn't mean you get to go acting all cocky now, like a bloody caveman."

"Hunky?" he croaked, looking as if he was trying to fight back a smile, the corner of his mouth twitching with an endearingly adorable, boyish grin.

Molly narrowed her eyes, wondering what she was going to do with him. Luckily, she had some *really* good ideas. "Mmm," she murmured, running her hands over the hard, bulging strength of his biceps, finding him perfect…no matter which form he wore. "To be honest, I could really get used to all those muscles you were sporting."

"Typical," he drawled, his deep chest vibrating with a low, husky thread of laughter as he settled himself more deeply between her splayed thighs, his cock a hot, heavy weight against her most tender flesh. "I should have known you were only after my body."

She opened her mouth, on the verge of telling him that she was after more than that—that she wanted it all, everything he had to give—when something stopped her.

Her humor faded at the realization that she was still afraid. Not of making herself vulnerable, but of scaring him away…of making him run again, when she knew that this time it would destroy her.

As if he read the thought in her eyes, he pressed his long body more heavily against hers, the muscled slabs of his chest cushioned against her sensitive, swollen breasts. With his forearms braced either side of her shoulders, his ruggedly beautiful face hovered just above hers, eyes dark and deliciously intense as he stared down at her. Holding her gaze, Ian slowly pushed his cock into her body, forging his way in with such firm, unrelenting pressure that it stole her breath. "I'm sorry, Molly."

"For what?" she gasped, her heart pounding faster…and faster, speeding down the tracks toward an unknown future.

"You deserve so much more than what I can give you," he whispered in a deep, rough-edged voice, so close she could feel his heart beating against her own as he rolled his hips, grinding against her in a way that made her body arch, her knees lifting higher as she struggled to take more of him into her. "I know you deserve better, but I can't…I can't give you up."

"Oh, God," she breathed out, her voice trembling, and a hot wash of tears filled her eyes. She was almost afraid of the blossoming hope expanding inside of her, threatening to break her apart.

He made a harsh sound in the back of his throat, and pressed his mouth against her cheek, kissing away her tears, then moved lower, kissing the quivering column of her throat. His tongue rasped tenderly against the sensitive bite he'd made earlier that day, and her inner muscles tightened, rippling around him, making him buck.

He growled low in his throat, and then he was pulling out of her, his strong hands turning her…directing her into position. When he was done, she found herself on her hands and knees, her arms shaking as she braced herself on her bent elbows, so excited she could barely breathe.

"Is it too much like this?" he groaned, feeling even bigger at this angle as he quickly thrust back inside with a thick, desperate lunge.

Her head shook from side to side. "No…no…" she panted, and a low, devastatingly sexy burst of masculine laughter filled her ear as he curved his body over hers like a hard, beautiful shelter, pressing an open-mouthed kiss to the back of her neck, his breath hot against her skin.

"You know," he rumbled in a gritty rasp, "we really have to do something about this penchant you have for lying, Molls." His hands found hers, closing around them, while he touched his mouth to the side of her throat, his sensual lips moving against her skin as he spoke. "But don't worry, sweetheart. I'll be careful with you."

"Don't you dare!"

His low chuckle bled into a deep, visceral growl as she pushed back against him, and she could feel his control slipping away, being torn from his grasp.

"*Molly,*" he groaned against her ear, his breath jerking from his lungs in a deep, shuddering rhythm, and she had the strangest sensation that he was asking her for something. Begging. Pleading for it with the driving urgency of his body into hers, the mattress slamming into the wall from the powerful, primal force of his thrusts. And then the answer suddenly bloomed from someplace deep inside of her, flowing out in a shimmering, incandescent wave of awareness.

Molly relaxed beneath him, softening, and with a deep breath, she opened herself and invited him into the secret places of her heart, of her soul, where no other man had ever been. Intimate, emotional places that belonged to no one but Ian. She sought out his hard, powerful fist with her lips, and pressed a tender kiss to his battered knuckles, trying to tell him how she felt, struggling to get the words out over the choking lump of emotion in her throat. "*Ian…I, oh, God, I love…I love you.*"

A harsh, guttural sound tore from his chest at her words, trembling and savage and raw, and his body came down heavily over hers, shaking with a staggering, violent release, his hips shoving against her in hard, hammering lunges that powered them across the mattress. Molly screamed, thrown into that dark, raging chaos of ecstasy with him, slammed into it, until the clenching, mind-shattering waves of bliss consumed her…pulling her down into a warm, languid state of oblivion. Rich, exquisite pleasure suffused her body, pulsing in her fingers and toes, and the next thing she realized, Ian was holding her in his arms, both of them lying on their sides, his panting breath warm against her scalp as he growled, "You're mine, Molly."

She absorbed the rough, shaky words, holding on to them, locking them away in her heart like a treasure. But as they drifted off to sleep, she realized that despite her passionate declaration, he hadn't made one of his own. Though he'd told her with his body, Ian had yet to repeat the words he'd given her before walking out to face the Casus.

And Molly couldn't help but wonder if she'd ever hear them again.

EPILOGUE

Laurente Cemetery, Tuesday Afternoon

As THEY MADE THEIR WAY down the cobbled pathway, Ian clutched Molly's hand in his, pulling her closer to his side. It'd been an eventful few days, and this was their last stop before heading to the airport, where they'd take a flight back to Colorado.

After he'd held her close through the long hours of darkness on Saturday night, Molly had awakened Sunday morning to the thick, decadent pleasure of Ian's body pushing into hers. They'd spent the next hour steeped in the hot, provocative burn of insatiable desire, each time they came together somehow hotter than the last…and then they'd showered, dressed and met the others in the kitchen, where doughnuts and coffee were waiting. Kierland had finally demanded an explanation of how Molly had ended up in South Carolina with Ian, since he still didn't know that she lived in Laurente. Then the talk had centered on the things Ian had learned from the Casus, and what they should do about them. They'd also discussed Ian's contracting business, which he'd agreed to close for the time being, since both of them would now be living at the compound. As noon had approached, the men had headed back to the airport…and Ian had taken Molly back to bed.

It was then, as they'd lain in one another's arms, their slick, heated bodies replete with the lingering pulse of pleasure, that he explained to her what had happened the day he'd left Colorado. And though he still hadn't repeated his stunning confession, Molly refused to give up hope. Each time he took her beneath his body, Ian pursued her declarations of love with single-minded intensity, shredding her defenses, refusing to allow her to hold the words inside, as if he needed them to ease some new, unquenchable craving. Molly clung to the hope that one day his own defenses would crumble, and he'd open his heart to her once again.

On Monday, they'd finally made their way to her apartment and packed her clothes, then made arrangements for a moving company to deal with the rest of her things, as well as her car. It was Tuesday now, and their flight left in a little over three hours—but they'd saved the most important task for last.

As they reached the end of the path, they came to Elaina's grave, and Molly squeezed Ian's trembling hand, offering her silent encouragement. They didn't understand how Elaina had been able to tell Ian how to use the Marker against the Casus. All they knew was that she'd saved their lives, and after so many bitter, resentful years, Ian had finally made peace with his past.

Clutching the bouquet of pure white roses in his free hand, he knelt down and laid them at the base of the tombstone, staring at the simple words carved into the smooth granite. Molly sniffed, wiping the back of her wrist over her watery eyes as he reached out, tenderly touching Elaina's name with his long fingers. As he straightened, moving back to her side, a mysteriously cool breeze blew through the trees, rushing against their warm bodies. The chilly air swirled around them, ruffling their clothes, and they both went completely still, their eyes wide with awed wonder as the faint scent of honeysuckle filled the air. Then the breeze gently flowed away as quickly as it'd come, leaving them standing there beneath the sweltering summer sun.

A silent thank-you? An I love you?

Both, Molly thought, leaning up to press a tender kiss to his mouth. "I think this meant a lot to her," she whispered with a soft smile, though she was unable to control the hot flood of her tears.

"It means a lot to me, too," he told her, pulling her against him, burying his face in her hair. He held her like that for a long, endless moment, his body vibrating with a low, tender frequency of emotion, and Molly stroked his broad back, offering her comfort.

"I have no right to do this to you," he suddenly whispered, breathing the words into her hair. "But I can't fight it. I know the coming times are going to be hell, Molly. This is the start of something that's going to last for God knows how long, and you don't deserve to be trapped in the middle of a bloody war, but I can't…I can't walk away from you. After all these years, I finally know where I'm meant to be."

"And where's that?" she asked, her voice hitching as she tried to breathe her way through a dazzling, overwhelming burst of joy.

"Wherever you are. Always where you are, because I…I love you, and I can't live without you," he rasped, his deep voice harsh with emotion as he kissed her temple…the corner of her mouth, the poignant touch of his lips as powerful as it was beautiful. "I'm sorry the words don't come easy to me, Molls, but I swear that they're true."

Ian kissed her then, long and deep and hungry, stealing her breath, reducing her to a maddened, desperate state of craving that only he could ease. And when he growled low in his throat, forcing himself to break the devastating kiss, he held her tear-drenched face in his rough hands, staring deep into her eyes as he stroked his thumbs against the heat blooming beneath her skin. "I need you," he told her, the words pouring out of him in a halting, grating rush, "and if you'll give me a chance, I swear I'll never make you regret it. I'll do everything in my power to make you happy, to give you the life you deserve. I'll be your partner, your lover, your husband and the father of your children, and I'll *always* be faithful. You won't ever have to doubt me, Molls. I swear it." The corner of his mouth twitched with a rueful, endearingly crooked grin, making her melt with tenderness as he pressed his forehead to hers, saying, "I wish I could say it all pretty and poetic like, like you deserve, but you know that's not me. All I can give you is my heart, and promise that it will always be yours."

"Ian," she whispered, undone by his words, never imagining he would open himself up in such a romantic, breathtaking way. "I don't know what to say."

A tremor ran through his body, melting into hers, so that they stood together in a knot of shivering, trembling emotion. "Say you'll give me the chance," he groaned, putting the hoarse words into the sensitive curve of her shoulder as he lifted her off the ground.

"I'll give you anything." She half laughed, half hiccupped, undone by the way he clutched her against his body, his possessive hold so tight, she knew he'd never let her go. "Anything you want, Ian."

He grinned like a devil, his eyes glittering and bright, and then he took her mouth in another slow, deep, intimate kiss, before pulling away and saying, "Because you love me, Molly?"

"Because I love you," she said softly, gently. "And because I believe in you, Ian. I always have."

A rough, desperate sound of need rumbled up from his chest, and Ian began calculating how close it was to the nearest hotel. They had a plane to catch, but more important than that, he needed to find a place where he could have her. Where he could lay her down on crisp, cool sheets, take her beneath his body, and show his woman just how much he loved her.

Quickly setting her back on her feet, Ian clasped on to her hand, pulling her along behind him as he dug into his pocket and handed her his cell phone. "Do me a favor and call the airline. Tell them we're going to need a later flight."

"What? Why?" she panted, practically running to keep up with his long steps as they headed toward the car. "Ian, what's going on?"

"We have someplace we need to be," he told her, ready to offer up a silent prayer of thanks when he remembered there was a hotel only three blocks away.

In the next instant, Ian swept her into his arms, clutching her soft body against the violent pounding of his heart, so full of happiness and love, he didn't know how he carried it all inside.

With a warm, wicked smile of anticipation, he bent his head, whispering his intentions in the delicate shell of her ear, and at the husky, joyful sound of her laughter, Ian held her tighter…and began running—not from the shadows of his past, but toward a bright, breathtaking future.

* * * * *

Be sure to watch for Saige's awakening in
EDGE OF DANGER,
coming next month to HQN Books.
And now for a sneak preview of the second
romance in the PRIMAL INSTINCTS series,
be sure to turn the page.

CHAPTER ONE

Thursday Evening, The Amazon

IF THE WOMAN WAS TRYING to blend in, she wasn't very good at it. It'd taken Michael Quinn no more than five seconds to pick her out in the dim, crowded interior of O Diablo Dos Angels, a rickety roadside *barra* in the bustling market town of Coroza, Brazil. He'd been traveling for two days now, working his way through the stifling, humid depths of the Amazonian rain forest, and it showed in his haggard appearance. Two days that felt more like weeks, each passing hour grating against his nerves like a rusty nail, until he was in what could only be classified as a category five, off the Richter scale, completely uncharacteristic shitty mood.

Not that he was usually cheery. Normally Quinn just…existed. It'd been years since anything, or anyone, had managed to touch him or throw him off his firm, even keel—and now this. He couldn't explain it, but from the moment he'd been given Saige Buchanan's photograph, his cool, steady calm had begun to fade, slipping away from him like water spiraling slowly down a drain. And in its wake, he'd been left with this seething intensity…this gripping tension.

What made it even worse was the fact that Quinn hadn't even wanted the assignment—had, in fact, been adamant in his refusal. And yet, here he was, with his damp shirt sticking to his skin, the heavy scent of tobacco and sweat making his head hurt, while something piercing and uncomfortably sharp slithered through his system at the sight of his prey.

Huh. So this is little Saige, he thought, moving along the wall, away from the door, careful to avoid her line of sight as she sat at a small table on the far side of the room, a bottle of water held in one delicate hand. At her side sat a young man who couldn't have been more than nineteen, his dark skin, hair and eyes attesting to his Brazilian heritage. The boy's lips were moving, and though Quinn's hearing was far better than a human's, he couldn't make out the words over the raucous cacophony of sound coming from the crowd.

It seemed a strange setting for an American woman and her young companion, and yet, no one bothered them. Not even the drunks. Was she a regular, then? Under the owner's protection? Or was there some other reason the locals kept their distance?

Whatever the answer, it couldn't be from lack of notice. Saige Buchanan stood out among the weathered patrons like a neon sign in the midnight pitch of night, glittering and bright.

Quinn rubbed his palm against the scratchy growth of stubble that came from going several days without a shave, then slowly shook his head, already revising his analogy. No, the reportedly brilliant anthropologist wasn't brash or bold, like neon. As bright as she shone, there was a soft, almost tender aura about her, which probably made her stick out even more than that angelic face, lush body or unusual shade of hair. Neither red nor brown, it hovered somewhere in between, picking up the soft, hazy glow of light that spilled down from above, struggling against the lengthening evening shadows.

Saige Buchanan may have been *more* than an average human female, but then he was hardly an average man. He could scent that her Merrick had yet to fully awaken—and until it did, he would be able to retain the upper hand when it came to physical strength.

Later, *after* her awakening… Well, he'd never gone head-to-head with a Merrick female before, but he sure as hell hoped she wouldn't be able to kick his ass. If that ever happened, his friends back at the compound would never let him live it down.

As a member of the Watchmen, an organization of shape-shifters whose duty it was to watch over the remaining bloodlines of the original ancient clans, Quinn had been taught a little about the Merrick, once one of the most powerful nonhuman species to walk the earth. And since the crap that had recently gone down with Saige's older brother, Ian Buchanan, he now knew even more. But Saige was…different. Unlike her brother, who experienced certain physical changes when the Merrick blood in his veins rose to the surface of his body, it was believed that Merrick females, while gaining in strength and agility and heightened senses, didn't change in appearance. She wouldn't sport talons on the tips of her delicate fingers. Wouldn't bulk up with thick, massive muscles. And her nose wouldn't alter its dainty, feminine shape.

But...you're forgetting the fangs.

Ah, right. Evidently, that was one of the changes the Merrick women *did* experience, in order to feed the primitive parts of their nature. Lifting his hand, Quinn rubbed at an odd tingle on the side of his neck, as if he could already feel the pleasure-pain of Saige Buchanan sinking her pearly whites into his flesh, taking the hot wash of his blood into her mouth, at the same time she took him deep into her body.

Whoa...

Scowling, he lowered his hand, fingers curling into a tight fist, and wondered what was wrong with him. Had the heat gone to his head? Had going without sex addled his brain? Or was he truly losing his mind?

Leaning his elbow against the small counter built into the side wall of the bar, Quinn shook off the irritating thoughts and signaled a stout, middle-aged woman who roamed the room with a tray, delivering drinks while she chatted with the customers. As she stepped closer, he could read the name Inez embroidered onto her apron, and despite the friendly way she'd handled the crowd, she leveled a cold, chilling look on him. Her dark eyes were wary now, and as they slowly inspected him from his scarred boots, up over his dirt-streaked jeans and damp black T-shirt, he said, *"Una cerveza, por favor."*

"Tell me," she replied in heavily accented English, "why do you watch our Saige like you are hungry?"

Quinn locked his jaw, angry that he'd revealed the focus of his attention to those watching him.

"Well?" she pressed, the corners of her wide mouth pinched with suspicion.

"No idea what you're talking about," he countered in a low, graveled voice, returning her hard stare. When it was obvious he wasn't going to back down, she muttered under her breath and turned around, making her way back to the bar.

Mentally kicking himself in the ass, Quinn purposefully withdrew his attention from the American and looked around the *barra*. In a strange way, he felt as if he'd walked onto a movie set. It was that surreal, complete with braying donkey outside the front door, the veil of smoke from cigarettes and cigars so thick you could all but slice it with a knife. The only thing that made it bearable was Saige. Her scent wrapped around him like a soft clinging vine, enticing and warm and sweetly addictive. It was like…like a rain shower, refreshing and clean, washing away the suffocating grime. It even eased the tension he felt at being in such a crowded, noisy, closed-in space. With a conscious effort, Quinn focused on that mouthwatering scent, drawing more of it into his lungs, desperate to block out the rest of his surroundings.

Unable to help himself, his gaze slid back to Saige, greedily soaking up the visual details, hungry for the data.

It was at that moment that she turned her head, angling it to the side, revealing the vulnerable length of her throat, and hungers too-long restrained stretched to awareness within him, the animal side of his nature blinking its eyes open to a lazy, dangerous, smoldering fire. He didn't take blood in the way that a Merrick did, but he still longed to clamp his teeth onto that tender, provocative part of her, while sending himself as deep into her as he could get.

As if she'd felt the press of his stare on that pale, feminine curve of flesh, she lifted her hand to the side of her neck. Then she suddenly twisted in her chair, scanning the room, and he quickly turned toward the wall, giving her his back. His fingers clenched around the bottle, nearly shattering the glass in his grip, while desire played hell with his control.

Had he gone out of his mind? All hell was about to break loose, and here he was nursing a warm beer, with a raging case of what could only land him in trouble. He didn't have time for this crap.

Stop stalling, dammit, and get on with it.

Turning purposefully back toward the room, he watched as she said something to the boy and stood up, making her way to the bar. She was talking to the short, smiling man behind the counter as Quinn moved to her side, draining the last of his beer. The second she turned and caught him in that deep, dark blue stare, the color as fascinating as the luminous perfection of her skin, he knew he'd been marked.

Quinn set his empty beer bottle down on the counter, preparing to introduce himself, when she reached for it. He wondered what she was doing as her fingers closed around the thick green glass, her expression instantly shifting from wary unease to full-blown panic. Then, before he could even guess her intention, she suddenly hurled the bottle at his head. The glass cracked against the edge of his right eyebrow, splitting the skin, the hot wash of blood flooding his vision.

Son of a bitch.

She immediately started running, shouting something in Portuguese to the boy, who took off past Quinn, out the front door. Moving in the opposite direction, Saige hefted the backpack she'd grabbed from the table onto her shoulder and pushed her way out the back exit, disappearing into what Quinn knew was the jungle.

Swearing, he tossed a wad of bills on the counter, and set off after her, hoping to God he could catch her before the fool woman managed to get herself killed.

As he ran out of the bar, into the humid warmth of the evening, the air thick and damp against his skin, the last watery threads of sunlight began fading beneath the heavy weight of night. Quinn followed her scent, dodging the clinging vines of the jungle, his long legs making good time against her shorter strides, but she was fast.

Too fast, he realized in the next moment, as a strong, noxious odor reached his nose, coming from the same direction Saige was moving.

We're out of time, he thought, gripping his T-shirt and pulling it over his head as he allowed the change to flow over him.

Hell was already there, and she was running straight into its deadly grasp.

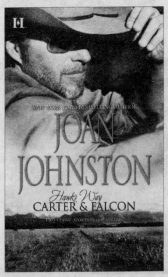

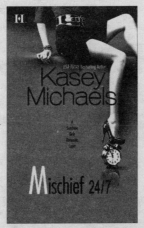

REQUEST YOUR
FREE BOOKS!

2 FREE NOVELS
FROM THE ROMANCE/SUSPENSE
COLLECTION PLUS 2 FREE GIFTS!

YES! Please send me 2 FREE novels from the Romance/Suspense Collection and my 2 FREE gifts (gifts are worth about $10). After receiving them, if I don't wish to receive any more books, I can return the shipping statement marked "cancel." If I don't cancel, I will receive 4 brand-new novels every month and be billed just $5.49 per book in the U.S. or $5.99 per book in Canada, plus 25¢ shipping and handling per book plus applicable taxes, if any*. That's a savings of at least 20% off the cover price! I understand that accepting the 2 free books and gifts places me under no obligation to buy anything. I can always return a shipment and cancel at any time. Even if I never buy another book from the Reader Service, the two free books and gifts are mine to keep forever.

185 MDN EF5Y 385 MDN EF6C

Name _____ (PLEASE PRINT)

Address _____ Apt. #

City _____ State/Prov. _____ Zip/Postal Code

Signature (if under 18, a parent or guardian must sign)

Mail to **The Reader Service:**
IN U.S.A.: P.O. Box 1867, Buffalo, NY 14240-1867
IN CANADA: P.O. Box 609, Fort Erie, Ontario L2A 5X3

Not valid to current subscribers to the Romance Collection,
the Suspense Collection or the Romance/Suspense Collection.

Want to try two free books from another line?
Call 1-800-873-8635 or visit www.morefreebooks.com.

* Terms and prices subject to change without notice. N.Y. residents add applicable sales tax. Canadian residents will be charged applicable provincial taxes and GST. Offer not valid in Quebec. This offer is limited to one order per household. All orders subject to approval. Credit or debit balances in a customer's account(s) may be offset by any other outstanding balance owed by or to the customer. Please allow 4 to 6 weeks for delivery. Offer available while quantities last.

Your Privacy: Harlequin is committed to protecting your privacy. Our Privacy Policy is available online at www.eHarlequin.com or upon request from the Reader Service. From time to time we make our lists of customers available to reputable third parties who may have a product or service of interest to you. If you would prefer we not share your name and address, please check here. ☐

BOB08R